THE *SPIRIT PHOTOGRAPHER*

THE
SPIRIT
PHOTOGRAPHER

A Novel

JON MICHAEL VARESE

OVERLOOK DUCKWORTH
NEW YORK • LONDON

The author would like to thank the following people for their contributions to this work: Thomas Banks, Serena Benedetti, Donald Booth, Manoah Bowman, Jessica Breheny, Lisa Campbell, Nicolas Campbell, Myriam J.A. Chancy, Rosana Cruz, Mary Curtis, Chelsea Cutchens, Pam del Rio, Christopher de Spoelberch, Jacques de Spoelberch, Malcolm Gaines, Joseph Geller, Rebecca Godson, Margaret Hogan, James Ivory, John Jordan, Karole Kelly, Sofie Kleppner, Emily Mather, James Maughn, Elizabeth Musser, Elizabeth Pérez, Alex Rothenberg, Jeremiah Rusconi, Thomas Uskali, and Carolyn Williams. Also thanks to Lissa Capo, Daniel Hammer, Mary Lou Eichhorn, and Jennifer Navarre at the Williams Research Center, Historic New Orleans Collection, and to Ott Howell at the Beauregard-Keyes House, New Orleans, Louisiana.

This edition first published in hardcover in the United States in 2018 by
The Overlook Press, Peter Mayer Publishers, Inc.

NEW YORK
141 Wooster Street
New York, NY 10012
www.overlookpress.com
For bulk and special sales, please contact sales@overlookny.com
or write to us at the above address.

LONDON
30 Calvin Street
London E1 6NW
info@duckworth-publishers.co.uk
www.ducknet.co.uk

Cataloging-in-Publication Data is available from the Library of Congress
A catalog record for this book is available from the British Library

Book design and type formatting by Bernard Schleifer
Manufactured in the United States of America
FIRST EDITION
1 3 5 7 9 10 8 6 4 2
ISBN 978-1-4683-1587-5 (US)
ISBN 978-0-7156-5300-5 (UK)

For Jacques de Spoelberch

AUTHOR'S NOTE

This work of fiction is inspired by events that took place during the Spiritualist movement in nineteenth-century America. While some of the story is based on the life of William Mumler (the first American spirit photographer) and other historical figures, it makes no claims to accuracy with regard to characters, places, or events.

If I do not remember thee,
let my tongue cleave to the roof of my mouth.

Psalms 137:6

BOOK I
REUNION

Banner of Light

Boston, Massachusetts
Saturday, August 5, 1865

A NEW PHASE of spiritual manifestations is exciting a great deal of attention and wonder in those who take an interest in the grand and beautiful subject of spirit communion. If this phenomenon in spiritual manifestation be genuine, it is the greatest and the best yet given to outside perception, and bears incontrovertible evidence of the truth that spiritual communications are what they claim to be, viz.: actual manifestations of the "dead" to the "living."

Mr. Edward Moody is the medium and the artist who makes photographs of spirits. His business has lately been ornamental engraving—a very profitable business, which he says has paid him upwards of nine dollars a week—but, from causes he cannot explain, he is being forced to leave it and engage in photography, which art he practiced under the employment of Mr. Matthew Brady in the years before and during the war. Mr. Moody is not a Spiritualist, nor, he says, has he ever believed in Spiritualism, but on the contrary has opposed and ridiculed it. He has many times been told by mediums that he was a very powerful and peculiar medium. This he did not believe, and only laughed at the communications.

A few Sundays since, he being alone with Mrs. Lovejoy in her photograph saloon above her silver goods store at 258 Washington Street, he produced a picture of Mrs. Lovejoy, which, to his great astonishment and wonder, revealed not just the sitter on the developed plate, but also a picture of a young woman standing by the sitter's side. While looking upon the strange phenomenon—the picture of two persons upon the plate, instead of one—the thought and the conviction flashed upon his mind, THIS IS THE PICTURE OF A SPIRIT. And in it Mrs. Lovejoy recognized the likeness of her deceased cousin, which is also said to be correct by others who have seen the picture, and who knew her.

Mr. Moody related this wonderful experience to some persons who were interested in Spiritualism, and they at once eagerly sought to have the experiment tried upon themselves, the result of which has been that some ten or more persons have now had their pictures taken, and the picture of one or more spirits has been upon the same plate. Many of them have been recognized as friends that once lived on earth. The picture of the spirit is fainter and less distinct than that of the one who sits. The pictures of the spirits are not alike, each one being extraordinary and different.

I

ON THE DAY before Senator Garrett's departure for Boston, news of impending storms had disrupted the city, and so by the time his brougham began climbing up Pinckney Street toward Louisburg Square, nearly all of the windows on Beacon Hill had already been locked and shuttered. Up ahead, on the corner of Pinckney and West Cedar, Garrett spied two lone figures, their hands firm on the brims of their hats. It was old Dovehouse conversing with the new choirmaster from King's Chapel.

The carriage approached, its wheels rattling in the street.

"Back again, old boy?"

"I am, sir," Garrett replied.

"Good to have you. Congratulations on your victories. I never doubted them for a second."

The senator returned a nod. Dovehouse never doubted anything—a characteristic that had been amusing Garrett for close to forty years. The "victories" to which old Dovehouse referred were the many Republican triumphs from the previous congressional session: the ratification of the Fifteenth Amendment, giving freedmen the right to vote; the passage of the first Enforcement Act, empowering the Federal Government to prosecute the Klan directly; and the election of Hiram Revels, a black Mississippi minister, to Jefferson Davis's old seat in the Senate chamber—a change unimaginable twenty years earlier, when Senator James B. Garrett, at the age of thirty-nine, had begun his career as a statesman.

"I suppose we can move on with things now!" Dovehouse called out as the senator's carriage continued up the street.

Garrett offered no reply. With the readmission of Georgia—the last of the outcast Confederate states—back into the Union, there were those, like Dovehouse, who had emphatically declared the country reunited. But Garrett had no intention of "moving on"—at least not until he had secured fundamental rights for all the country's citizens.

When the senator at last arrived at his house, it too was dark and motionless, except for the swirling clusters of maple leaves in front of it. The house glared at him as if it were displeased with his lateness, and its unblinking frown gave him no comfort. When the front door opened, and Garrett descended from the carriage, a sudden gust of wind scattered the leaves from his path. In the doorway stood a heavyset woman wearing a gingham dress.

"Welcome home, sir," Jenny said.

"Dear Jenny . . . is something the matter?"

"It's Mrs. Garrett—she's received a letter. She's waiting for you in the drawing room."

His Jenny. She had been with him for nearly twenty years now. He stepped inside, handing her his hat and his gloves. His face, he knew, betrayed him.

"Sir?" Jenny said.

"Thank you, Jenny," Garrett said.

The groans of the hinges welcomed Senator Garrett as he opened the great doors of the drawing room. The room's curtains were drawn, blocking out most of the day's remaining light, and outside the wind howled unmercifully.

"Elizabeth?"

In the dimness, his wife's profile emerged.

"James—" she said. "We've heard . . . we've heard from . . ."

Elizabeth's chin fell, and Garrett moved toward her. She released what was in her hands with a surprising lack of resistance. Garrett approached the curtains and held the letter near the split of light.

17 July 1870

Dear Mrs. Garrett,

I write to inform you of the miraculous news—we have received word from your son, William Jeffrey. He has made contact through a dream, and he is bathed in flowers and sunlight.

I realize that this message arrives sooner than I had predicted, but the movements of those in the spirit world can be rather sudden, and as such we must move with great speed. Please come to the gallery tomorrow at one o'clock in the afternoon, so that we may execute your photograph immediately.

Yours sincerely,

Edward Moody, Photographer
258 Washington Street, Boston

Garrett read the "news" with a mixture of uncertainty and disdain. Two weeks earlier, Elizabeth had written him in Washington to tell him that she had made a visit to Mr. Moody—the so-called "spirit photographer" who had achieved notoriety in recent years. "It appears that Mr. Moody has a gift," she had told her husband, and when he read those words he was surprised, for his wife had always been the more skeptical of the two of them. A man who could photograph spirits? It was not something one would have expected Elizabeth to believe in. He had thought that her initial letter might have described a whimsy; but when a second letter arrived, citing Colfax's highly publicized visit to Moody, he recognized that his wife had become attached to this idea.

Now she was looking over at him imploringly, which was another strange thing, because his wife usually demanded rather than implored. But he understood, for just the sight of his son's name scribbled on a folded piece of paper was enough to unbury what so much rehearsed forgetting had kept secreted away for years.

"Elizabeth—" Garrett said.

And when he said her name she knew, because she was able to read him better than he could ever read himself.

"James," she said, "I know your thoughts on this matter. I too have my reservations. But if he *is* a man of extraordinary power, as some claim, and if he could provide us with—"

She paused, no longer his supplicant, but his commander.

"Think of what it could mean."

He studied the letter again, read it from beginning to end.

"James, we must waste no time."

The senator inhaled deeply.

"Very well then," Garrett said. "We'll go tomorrow afternoon, as he says."

That night, as Elizabeth breathed quietly beside him, Garrett clenched the bed sheets and stared at the moving shapes above his head. The wind had grown even more impatient, causing a violent parade of shadows on the ceiling.

II

THERE WAS NOTHING new about the spirit photographs—they had been circulating since the end of the war—but the recent acceleration of publicity around them had won Edward Moody widespread attention. Elizabeth Garrett had paid her first visit to him after reading of a woman whose lost child had appeared standing beside her in a photograph. The article was one of hundreds of pieces that the Spiritualists had been publicizing in their papers.

Dovehouse, of course, dismissed the Spiritualists as swindlers and imposters, and since her husband held Dovehouse's opinions in such high regard, Elizabeth knew that she would need to tread carefully. In her fashionable Boston circles, there were the women who believed and those who didn't, and while the Spiritualists had managed to penetrate into every rank of society, it was still a delicate matter as far as the electorate was concerned. Elizabeth had successfully avoided ever declaring precisely where she stood. An inquiry about a portrait need signify nothing more than curiosity.

Mr. Moody worked in the central part of Boston, in the building where Elizabeth had once gone to have an addition to her bridal silver engraved. She was initially surprised by the photographer's appearance. Attractive—even handsome—but terribly unkempt.

"Mrs. Garrett," he said, "I trust you have come because you are a believer in spiritual communion?"

His voice lacked energy. That too came as a surprise.

"Mr. Moody, I—"

She paused, wondering if the famous "Moody" was the same dishevelled man who sat before her.

"Worry not, Mrs. Garrett," he said. "These wonderful concepts are often difficult to grasp at first. In your letter you mentioned your son—"

"Yes, William Jeffrey."

"How long?"

"Eighteen years. He was three. It was eighteen years ago now."

"And it was the fe—?"

"Yes—I believe he contracted it when we were in Washington. I have found it very difficult to return there ever since."

"Unfortunate."

"Yes."

His eyes were profound—beautiful and lonely. The eyes of a man who was heartbroken.

"And the senator?" Moody said. "He will be sitting for the portrait as well?"

"I have not yet told my husband of this design," Elizabeth replied.

"Mr. Colfax was here, as you probably know."

"Yes, I am acquainted with the vice president's portrait. The *Harper's* article has excited great interest in it, and I know that it has become much talked about in Washington."

"A vast majority of the community, having fought the cause for abolition, are sympathetic to much of the good senator's beliefs. If there is any hesitancy on your part due to the senator's unique position, dare I suggest that a photograph might even work to his benefit?"

Elizabeth perceived his meaning.

"Mr. Moody," she said, "I can assure you that is not the intention of this investigation. My husband's reputation is not something he would ever surrender to the charms of spiritual fanatics and—*artists*."

Her emphasis on that last word produced its intended effect. Moody failed to respond, and she observed his hands moving uncomfortably in his lap.

"Mr. Moody," she said, "I don't mean to be unkind, but you can understand my concern. Many have expressed their doubts."

Moody's face became rigid, and his eyes fixed on hers.

"Your son is everywhere around you," he said. "And soon, Mrs. Garrett, you will not doubt that!"

He was so emphatic—it was almost like an attack—and her momentary confidence was gone.

"The photographs—" he continued, softening, "They give us an opportunity to go back. They reunite us with those we've lost. We call spirits forth from their beautiful kingdoms, beckoning them to return to this hard and earthly world. We cannot determine how long they will linger . . . we can only hope for some gratification. There is such sweetness in it, when it does come."

She was silent, and now her hands betrayed her nervousness.

"Isn't that what you desire, Mrs. Garrett—more than anything?"

She stared at him.

"The gratification of seeing William Jeffrey again?" he pressed. "Reunion, in this life—and the next?"

A sharp pain gnawed inside her. She knew that it could never be the same as it once was, and yet—

"Yes, Mr. Moody," she replied. "That is what I desire."

WILLIAM GARRETT'S DEATH some eighteen years before that first encounter had marked the beginning of Elizabeth Garrett's struggle with her own beliefs. The day William's silver rattle appeared on the entry hall table, for instance, a full two years after the child's passing, had initially convinced Elizabeth of nothing more than Jenny's mischievousness. Jenny had been against purging the house of William's playthings; she warned that doing so would only result in angering the boy's spirit. "You know how Master William loved that rattle," Jenny had said, "and you know that he's going to miss it." Outraged, Elizabeth had only grown more determined, and tossed the rattle into a wooden box designated for one of the West End orphanages.

But when the rattle appeared—worse yet, when it appeared on what would have been William's fifth birthday—Jenny was nowhere to be found. The day before, she had gone to see her sister who worked in Cambridge, and did not plan on returning until later that evening. Elizabeth had passed by the entry hall at least twenty times since Jenny's departure. She had seen nothing unusual, and no one else was in the house. Yet on that morning, when she passed the front door, there was William's toy.

Elizabeth immediately jumped to conclusions—Jenny had always found subtle ways of retaliating. Elizabeth knew that when she had commanded Jenny to get rid of the rattle, Jenny had not liked it, and would remember. The negroes had their own ways of thinking about these things, and even Elizabeth had come to appreciate that. But she was the mistress of her house, and no matter how much equality her husband liked to preach, she was not going to comply with taking instructions from her own housemaid.

And so the rattle was there, two years after she was sure that she had ordered Jenny to send it away in the wooden box. But was she sure? She looked at it—its dull glow growing in the morning light. And as she moved toward it, hesitating with each step, the unevenness of the glow seemed to make the rattle pulse.

He had been holding the rattle when she lost him.

"It will be gone soon," he had said.

"What will be gone, my little darling?"

But the child never answered. The child never spoke again.

As successful as Elizabeth was at forgetting things, that was one moment she never forgot. Then she remembered—the rattle had not gone off to the orphanage with William's other things. She had plucked it from the box at the last minute. There was a part of her that realized that Jenny was right, that the rattle should have remained in the house; but there was also that part of her—the unyielding part—that never could have surrendered to Jenny. And so once the box was full, and Jenny was out of the room, Elizabeth had quickly seized the rattle and hidden it where even Jenny would be unlikely to find it.

The rattle. She had taken it! And she had found it in her pocket one day, too, long before that day when the rattle appeared on the entry hall table. The child had been dead for only a few months, and Garrett had been gone, in Washington. She had just wanted to hold the rattle for a little while, to have her moment alone with it, which was something that she had taken to doing in those months following William's death. This impulse signified what Elizabeth thought of as a weakness, but she had succumbed to it, until she heard Jenny's footsteps in the hallway. She had quickly shoved the rattle into her pocket—yes, she remembered now—she had shoved it into her pocket, wrapped tightly in her handkerchief so as to muffle the rattle's sound. Even so, when Jenny entered the room Elizabeth sensed that she suspected something. Jenny was never very careful about suppressing her suspicions.

There was some house matter or other to deal with, Jenny had said—what it was Elizabeth could not quite remember—but hours went by before Elizabeth reached into her pocket again, only to discover the rattle. It had been a narrow escape. Jenny had not found her out. Elizabeth would need to keep the rattle hidden—forever.

But on William's fifth birthday, when the rattle appeared in the entry hall, Elizabeth was forced to remember that narrow escape. She remembered the sense of panic that had overcome her on that day, when she had plunged her hand into her dress pocket to find William's rattle wrapped within her handkerchief.

It started there—with the rattle on the entry hall table, two years after William had gone. It was the first event that she could not explain. Others followed, of a less physical nature, most of them involving sounds, and at times William's voice. She was always alone when it happened, and extremely thankful for that, for the notion of Senator Garrett's wife having "Spiritualist tendencies" was not something she could have accepted in those days. After all, public outcry had forced John Edmonds to resign. The papers had excoriated him, claiming that his championing of the Spiritualists had rendered his intellect "unreliable." It was not, the papers said, "befitting of a state Supreme Court justice to be seen gadding about with people who believed in ghosts."

By the time the war came though, the influence of the Spiritualists was reaching far beyond that set, and Elizabeth was becoming more convinced that William had not entirely "moved on." When Constance Merriwhether, the wife of Garrett's former law partner, invited the Garretts to a séance at their home, Elizabeth admitted her desire to attend. Constance's brother had fallen at Gettysburg, and Constance was one of thousands who was desperate to reconnect with someone who had never returned. "I need to know that he died a good death," she told Elizabeth. "I need to hear that his death was honourable."

When Elizabeth told Garrett that the Merriwhethers were hosting a séance, his reaction was quick and predictable: "Elizabeth, can you imagine a bunch of lawyers sitting around a table with their wives, waiting for some rap-tap-tapping or the meowing of a cat? Ridiculous. Merriwhether has gone out of his mind."

But she knew that even he experienced his own doubts. When the death tolls reached him by messenger, one night in September after Antietam, he had retreated to the drawing room and asked to be alone. After three hours had passed and he had still not emerged, Elizabeth interrupted him. He was sitting before the fireplace, staring at it, motionless, and she guessed that he had been in that position for several hours. Drawing closer, she immediately noticed his expression—the emptiness, the utter despair of all hopes lost. She recognized that look as one she had never wanted to see again. William had been dead for ten years at that point.

She placed her hand on his shoulder, and still Garrett did not move.

"McClellan has lost over twelve thousand of our men," he said. "The dead will never forgive me."

It was then that she truly understood that her husband also feared his own secrets—not simply the practical kinds, the kinds that could ruin families and careers—but the deeper, intangible, recalcitrant secrets that could destroy the foundations of everything one believed in.

III

ON THE MORNING of the photograph, the sky was black and gray, and by that afternoon, when the Garretts left their house, light drops of rain had been falling for some time. As the carriage rocked, crawling down toward the Common, Garrett could not help reflecting on how much Elizabeth had changed. They had been married for over twenty years, and he still remembered how she had first captivated him. There was an absolute self-assuredness about her that had set her apart from other women. Of course she was Elizabeth Beauregard back then—a distant third cousin of the notorious Confederate general. Her family was from Philadelphia and supported the abolitionists, though they had also maintained relations with their plantation kinfolk in Louisiana.

During the first years of their marriage Elizabeth had won over the women of Boston, whose envy of her self-confidence surfaced as deference, rather than resentment. She was beautiful, intelligent, and circumspect with her opinions—progressive enough to sit comfortably with the abolitionists, yet conservative enough so as not to offend the other side. There was a great deal of mystery about her, too, which was at the heart of the draw for many. One could never quite tell exactly what she was thinking, and it made you want to know. Garrett, clearly destined for the Senate even then, had a natural ability to command rooms and crowds; but she could command people. There was such a fine distinction.

Even Dovehouse—Garrett's closest confidant since his undergraduate days at Harvard—liked her. Or at least it seemed that way. Dovehouse had originally opposed the marriage, warning Garrett that a man with an eye on politics could not risk the association with "southern skeletons." Her family's ties to the old Louisiana sugar plantations, Dovehouse said, would not be of small concern, especially to Garrett's opponents. But when Dovehouse realized that Elizabeth was nothing if not a realist, his opinion changed, and he accepted her as one of his own. This woman from Philadelphia was certainly no fool, and all the better that she was ten years Garrett's junior. Her

charms—and certainly that was what Dovehouse considered them, charms—
would help propel Garrett toward his political destiny.

When the baby arrived, Elizabeth lost little strength, and Garrett remembered how the speed of her recovery had astonished Boston society. Garrett was not yet in the Senate then, but he was already involved in the debates
over the western territories. Publicly, he spoke out in favor of abolition and
the limitation of the South's influence as the country expanded; but in more
private settings, where people aired their prejudices with less restraint, it was
Elizabeth who promoted the virtues of her husband's positions. She was, after
all, someone who had relations in the South, and she could testify to the brutality she had seen there. When Garrett was elected to the Senate, he was not
unaware of how instrumental his wife's support had been.

But the baby's death just two years after Garrett's election had left Elizabeth disconsolate and muttering in her sleep about "punishments." What
was strange, however, was the inconsistency of her sadness. In those early
years following William's death, Garrett would often find her in a stupor, un-
willing to look at him or speak; then only hours later, she would be entertain-
ing Constance Merriwhether with all of the usual gregariousness that people
had come to expect from her. He did not understand the secret thoughts his
wife harbored, and the irregularity of her behavior frightened him.

By the time the war came, many years later, the legacy of that dark period had receded. There were days, of course—there would always be days—
but new forms of darkness had pervaded the nation. Garrett's attentions
turned almost exclusively toward the advancement of the cause, and Elizabeth's mission remained that of a surveyor over Boston's drawing rooms. She
continued in her role as Garrett's domestic ambassador, but now when she
spoke, she did so with noticeable reserve. She had never been a firebrand, and
he had never expected her to be one, but there was something different, even
indifferent, about the way she communicated during the war years. She was
strong—that was one attribute of hers that had remained constant—but her
passions were a mere ember of what they had once been.

Those were the war years, when everyone's passions were uncontrolled,
and when families' differences split them apart in ways unexpected and hor-
rendous. Had the impossible occurred, and had they grown apart? Garrett
hated the idea because he knew how much he had relied on her. And sometimes he would go even further in his private thoughts, and admit that he

would have been a failure without her. Such a belief was somewhat danger-ous—a type of shameful surrender. Dovehouse would certainly have thought so, but then again Dovehouse knew that his friend had indeed surrendered, much to Garrett's own benefit. If Elizabeth were retreating, there was not much Garrett could do to stop it. There had never really been a period when she adored him. She admired him, yes, but she had never adored him.

She was withdrawing—not abandoning him, never that—just with-drawing. She would do his deeds for him, support his ideas, maintain his sta-tus—and hers. But she did withdraw. The confirmation came for him that September following the end of the war, when Johnson ordered the return of all confiscated land to the plantation owners. The president's "odious decree," as Garrett called it, was a strong blow to the radical cause, and to Garrett in particular, since he had been arguing for years that it was the gov-ernment's responsibility to redistribute the land to the freedmen. He thun-dered as much about it at home as he did in Washington, until one night Elizabeth finally said: "James, you can't give them everything." Her coolness was shocking, and in that very moment, in hearing that mere fragment of resignation, he realized that somewhere, somehow, he had lost her. He also realized that he had been losing her for over a decade, and that their connec-tion had slowly been . . . disintegrating. Of course, anyone watching from the outside would be inclined to trace her detachment back to the loss of the baby, but Garrett had come to believe—knew instinctively in his heart, rather—that it had always been more than that.

And so there they were, some years after the war, the senator and his wife, going to sit for a spirit photograph with Mr. Moody. Once partners in everything, from drawing rooms to the national stage, they had now become strangers, even as the carriage's sway pressed them intimately against each other. The drive across town to Moody's gallery was not a long one, but to Garrett, trapped in the narrow compartment, the ride seemed interminable. He did not entirely understand or remember how it had come to be like this. He only knew that he had agreed to accompany his wife more out of fear than understanding.

IV

H E HAD SENT her the letter—a summons.
It was important that she had received it as a summons. When she had entered that first time, he had not been surprised. She was aloof, aristocratic—like one of those fine ladies in the British novels.

Moody had wondered if in that first meeting he had been right to bring up her husband. In Moody's mind, a successful photograph of Senator Garrett would cause even more of a stir than the vice president's portrait. Schuyler Colfax had struck Edward Moody as a simpleton, but Senator Garrett was different: he was renowned for his acumen.

It had been a risk, but Moody had taken it. He could see that she was already questioning.

Then he had startled her—into submission almost. This woman who was steeled against even the subtlest flatteries. But it did not make a difference who Mrs. Garrett was, for she had lost something, and that would make her a believer. He did not think about this callously, or with any kind of disrespect. It was simply how it was: there were those who would believe, and those who wouldn't.

"The photographs—" Moody had offered, "They give us an opportunity to go back . . ."

He could take her back, as he had taken so many others. It was, after all, what Elizabeth Garrett desired. And why should he not give this sad woman what she longed for? He had helped many hundreds of people reunite with their loved ones, and he would do whatever it took to ensure Mrs. Garrett's gratification. There would be such sweetness in her eyes when she at last saw her child.

It was a sweetness that Moody himself had tasted, over and over again.

OF COURSE, ELIZABETH Garrett's visit to the spirit photographer had followed on the heels of a great public debate. Were the ghosts in Edward Moody's photographs real, or weren't they? Every newspaper, coffeehouse, and drawing room had been taking part in the argument for years. The "enemies of truth," as the Spiritualists called them, were of particular concern, for these were the most vocal of the doubters—different from the common prattlers—and they shouted their accusations in every place they could. But Moody did not fear them. He had providential support, and whenever the cry of these enemies grew rampant, Providence seemed to intervene to counter them.

It had happened, so easily, in the case of Samuel Fanshaw, the renowned portrait painter who had come to Moody in search of a likeness of his mother's ghost. The spirit photographer had obliged, and the next day the man was running about Boston, proclaiming the likeness "more truthful and more accurate than I myself ever painted of her in life." The *Banner of Light*, Boston's leading Spiritualist newspaper, also published Moody's response to the "miracle." Mr. Fanshaw's testimony was so valuable, Moody said, "inasmuch as it disproves what is so often stated by skeptical people—namely, that my pictures are likenesses only when persons imagine them to be so."

Moody enlarged the Fanshaw portrait and hung it prominently in the gallery.

Soon though, the challenges to Moody's art intensified, and the editorials took bolder steps in raising the question on everyone's mind: Could he, Edward Moody, the spirit photographer, produce a spiritual likeness under conditions of strict monitoring, and with another person selecting the glass for the negative? Of course he could. Edward Moody could do anything! He was not afraid of whatever silly contests they might throw his way.

Then one day the three men from New York appeared unannounced, and even Moody's faith in himself was tested.

They were a strange delegation—Moody recognized none of them—and they spoke to him with their hats on, as if they did not plan to stay. "We were entire strangers to each other," Moody would later tell the *Banner*, "this being the first time I had ever encountered any of these gentlemen. I remember *every word* that passed between us as vividly as though it happened but an hour ago, from the fact that I was confident that I should astound Mr. Gurney, who as everyone knows is one of the great masters of photography."

For yes—it was indeed Jeremiah Gurney, the most celebrated photographer in New York, if not the country, who had come to meet Edward

Moody and observe his fantastic "art." Gurney had brought with him Charles Livermore, of the banking firm of Livermore, Clews, and Company, and Charles Dana, editor of the popular *New York Sun*. It was Mr. Livermore who sought the portrait, Gurney explained, and whose idea it had been to come to Boston.

Moody did not need to hear anymore. He knew the name of Livermore, and that Livermore was a Spiritualist. Several years ago the man had lost his wife and believed that she was always with him.

"We were tenderly attached," Mr. Livermore confessed, "and that tenderness is what I feel still binds her to me from afar."

Then Mr. Dana interjected.

"Mr. Moody," he said, "do you consider it within your power to reunite Mr. Livermore with his wife as you have done for so many others—under the constant eye of Mr. Jeremiah Gurney, even allowing him to select the glass?"

No one had ever dared to ask this of Moody before.

"Gentlemen," Moody said, without hesitation, "it would be too great an honor."

Upstairs in the gallery, Livermore told Moody more of his story. He spoke of his wife with great affection—how, even in life, she had promised him that she would never leave his side. There were, of course, the fevers—many of them—and Livermore had thought that she'd be strong . . .

But none of this really mattered to Moody. He would get Mrs. Livermore's portrait.

When the sitting was finished, Moody breathed heavily and leaned upon the camera. He appeared exhausted, so much so that the visitors must have wondered if he would be able to go on.

"Are you alright, Mr. Moody?" Mr. Dana finally asked.

With barely a nod, Moody straightened himself, and motioned for the group to follow him into the darkroom.

"As promised—" he whispered, "I will now expose the rest of my process to your scrutiny."

Edward Moody, full of energy, was thrilled to have a newspaperman present. The article from this sitting would describe his greatest triumph yet.

New York Sun

New York, New York

Sunday, February 14, 1869

A FEW SUNDAYS since, we had the pleasure of visiting the Boston gallery of Mr. Edward Moody, the photographer who professes to take pictures of spirits. The sitter for this spiritual investigation was Mr. Charles Livermore, the Wall Street banker who lost his wife some years hence, and accompanying him, as an observer, Mr. Jeremiah Gurney, whose daguerrean saloon on Broadway many will remember as the first of its kind in this country.

Upon entering the gallery, which is decorated with some of the finest specimens of Mr. Moody's art, the photographer, ascertaining the reasoning behind the presence of so many persons, said, "Mr. Gurney, be thorough in your investigations." He then pointed to the camera, saying, "That is the instrument I propose to use; you are at liberty to take it to pieces." Mr. Gurney examined it, and said, "That is all right," before proceeding to select a glass plate, from a group of ten or twelve, at Mr. Moody's invitation.

Mr. Moody next permitted a full inspection of his dark room, bath, & c., and then fell to the business of coating the selected plate with collodion, and immersing it in the silver bath. When this was done, Mr. Gurney rested his hand on the edge of the bath, and looked, as though he thought to himself—"I don't lose sight of this plate from now on." Mr. Gurney then said: "Mr. Moody, in the best interests of Mr. Livermore, let me see your plate-holder; I have understood there is a false back in it." Mr. Moody obliged by handing him the holder, which he examined and declared to be "all right."

Taking the plate from the silver bath, Mr. Moody then placed it in the holder, handed the whole of it to Mr. Gurney, and led our small congregation to the skylight room. Mr. Moody sat Mr. Livermore close to a window, placed the holder in the camera, raised the slide, and removed the cloth and exposed the plate. Upon conclusion of the exposure, Mr. Moody was much exhausted, but recovered momentarily, stating that it was often thus when the spirit presence was particularly strong. Mr. Gurney, who wore an incredulous smile, remarked, "Mr. Moody, I should be willing to bet on one thing—that you have got Mr. Livermore's picture." The photographer answered, "So would I," to which Mr. Gurney replied: "And I guess that is all." Mr. Moody smiled briefly and said to the company: "Very likely. I do not get them every time."

Mr. Moody then requested that Mr. Gurney remove the holder and carry it to the dark room, which he did. On arriving there Mr. Moody handed him a bottle of developer, with the request that he would develop the negative himself. This Mr. Gurney declined to do, saying, "I would rather you develop it; I am not acquainted with the working of your chemicals, and I might spoil it." And with marked emphasis he added: "You are not smart enough to put anything on that negative without my detecting it." Mr. Moody replied that he was well aware of that fact, and then tipped the plate on the flat of his hand, and poured on the developing fluid.

Soon the likeness of Mr. Livermore appeared, and then another form became apparent, growing plainer and plainer each moment, until a woman appeared, with her arm upon Mr. Livermore's breast, while Mr. L., watching with wonder-stricken eyes exclaimed:

"MY GOD! IS IT POSSIBLE!"

Mr. Livermore then asked Mr. Moody to let him have the negative, with which request, after the process of varnishing, Mr. Moody immediately complied. Mr. Livermore, placing his hand in his pocket, asked, "How much am I to pay?" Mr. Moody told him: "Not a cent—this communion shall be yours with my utmost compliments to you—and to Mr. Gurney."

The spirit's face in the Livermore portrait was perfectly distinct. But even beyond this, there was something inexplicably singular about the likeness of Mrs. Livermore. The spirit had thrown its arm loosely about her husband's neck, so that its hand, holding a bunch of lilacs, fell gently upon the man's breast. The spirit looked down lovingly at the sitter, who stared unawares into the camera. The spirit, Moody inwardly boasted, was . . . *alive*.

Charles Livermore returned to New York both satisfied and heartstricken, so powerful was the reappearance of his wife, and so faithful the spirit image. All who saw the picture agreed that the face, un-blurred and distinct in its reproduction, belonged to Arabella Livermore. "That picture contains in itself a volume of proof of the reality and reliability of spiritual manifestations," the *Banner of Light* reported. "In *this* instance it can be nothing other than true; and if *this* is true, may not other similar pictures be *bona fide?*"

Moody was delighted with the effect of these advertisements—namely, the tremendous increase in traffic to his business. Indeed, it was in response to the article in the *New York Sun* that the vice president had determined to make his own trip to Boston. Mrs. Lovejoy's store was soon attracting hundreds of spirit-seekers, and Moody's gallery became thronged with visitors from all grades of society—the high and the low, the rich and the poor—many of whom had traveled to Washington Street out of idle curiosity. They all came to see him, whether they could afford it or not, and Moody developed into something much more than a celebrity. He was becoming a kind of spiritual leader—someone to whom the grieving could turn when their desire to continue was at its end.

The crowds gathered, rambunctious, and the first floor of Mrs. Lovejoy's filled up daily. And on occasion, Edward Moody fashioned the staircase into an impromptu pulpit.

"And what is there—" he asked the gatherers . . .

> *"What is there that is more important than the life to come? After a man has passed through middle age, he looks forward, at the best, to but a few years of earthly existence, and naturally asks, 'Is this all of life? Is there a hereafter?' And as the years roll on, seemingly but little longer than weeks in his youth, bringing him nearer to the solution of this great problem, the question becomes, to him, one of great moment. The anchor to which he has been clinging for safety begins to drag; the advance of science demonstrates that the world was not made in a brief period, but has existed for innumerable ages, and where is he drifting? Spiritualism comes to him like a beacon-light to the mariner; and thousands who were tossing wildly about upon the waves of doubt and skepticism are quietly resting under the protective shelter of this beautiful truth."*

The *Banner* printed nearly every word that Edward Moody preached in public—yet another thing that merely fueled the fanatical demand for spirit photographs. According to the *Banner*, one could hear the applause of audiences from afar whenever Moody spoke, even as the "enemies of truth" persisted in their attacks. "Necessity compels me to state," someone was once reported to have said, "that Mr. Moody, or someone connected with Mrs. Lovejoy's rooms, has been guilty of deception in palming off, as genuine spirit likenesses, pictures of a person who is now living in this city!" But it seemed that no one in the crowd that day wanted to hear this accusation, and the waiting list for spirit photographs continued to grow without end.

But there was yet more in store for Edward Moody, even after photographing spirits had become so profitable. Some months before Elizabeth Garrett's visit to Washington Street, Joseph Winter, a veteran of the 5th Massachusetts Colored Cavalry, appeared at Mrs. Lovejoy's door. He was handsomely dressed, wearing the bowler hat and checkered waistcoat so popular amongst the working class at that time.

"You do not recognize me?" Winter said, as Mrs. Lovejoy stared at him from behind her counter.

"I'm afraid I do not, sir," Mrs. Lovejoy replied. "Have we met before?"

"We have, madam," Winter said. "In this very building. Though it was not under such leisurely circumstances, you might say."

Winter eyed her knowingly, and Mrs. Lovejoy returned his gaze. Then her eyes widened, and she moved out from behind the counter to grasp the visitor's hands.

"Of course!" she said. "You came through here many years ago—long before the war. I remember. You must forgive me—there were so many poor souls back then. My dear child, how have you been?"

"I have fared well, Mrs. Lovejoy, thanks to you and the kindness of many others. And I have returned because I have a desire to remain in this city, and so I am seeking employment."

"Oh, Mister . . . ?"

"Winter, madam. Joseph Winter."

"I'm afraid I have nothing for you here, Mr. Winter, as much as it pains me to say. Perhaps one of the colored aid societies might be of some help?"

"Thank you, madam, but it is Mr. Moody whom I've come to see."

Mrs. Lovejoy was confounded.

"You mean—you desire a spirit photograph?"

"No, Mrs. Lovejoy. I am a Spiritualist, and a maker of spirit photographs myself. I would like to discuss the matter over with him."

Mrs. Lovejoy had certainly heard of the many "colored studios" that had surfaced around the country, but she had never heard of anything so revolutionary as a colored spirit photographer. The high price of spirit photographs alone, she thought, would have prevented most negroes from seeking them out.

"I am happy to introduce you to Mr. Moody," she said, "but I must warn you that he is intensely private about his art."

"I understand," Winter replied, declining to back down. "But I assure you that Mr. Moody will want to hear what I have to say."

Upstairs in the gallery, after Mrs. Lovejoy had left them, Moody eyed Joseph Winter with no little amount of suspicion. The stranger's dress and demeanor were an obvious distraction. Moody had seen these types before.

"I have something to show you that I think will be to your interest," Winter said, pulling a thin leather case from inside his jacket. The case was embossed with serpentine decorations, which had been delicately outlined in gold.

"A lovely piece of craftsmanship," Moody said. "I used to make those myself."

"The case is my own work," Winter said.

"Ah—a leather man?"

"Yes sir, but more than that."

Winter opened the case—a picture holder, Moody now saw—to reveal a spirit photograph of a black man with what was likely his deceased wife standing behind him. The expression, clarity, and positioning of the spirit was magnificent—much better than anything Moody had ever produced himself.

"This is wondrous," Moody said.

"Thank you, sir. Mr. Jones, a merchant from Charleston—and his wife."

Moody continued to examine the picture.

"It's extraordinary," he said. "You are a man of great power."

"Very likely," Winter said. "But I do not get them every time."

Moody started at the recitation of his own familiar words. So, this man was not about friendly business.

"There's more," Winter said.

He withdrew, again from his jacket pocket, another picture holder, this one made of flimsier board. Moody opened it.

"Mrs. Jones," Winter said. "As she appeared in life."

Moody compared the two pictures—the spirit photograph to the living portrait of Mrs. Jones. The faces were identical, and Moody surmised that Winter had used the portrait as the source for the "spirit." The unevenness of one eyebrow and the curve of the left earlobe were the telltale signs of the duplication.

"As a man of your training can no doubt see," Winter said, "I've been able to bring that likeness of Mrs. Jones into communion with her husband."

"Spiritual communion—" Moody said.

"There is nothing spiritual whatsoever about it," Winter replied.

"Mr. Winter, if you have come here to accuse me of fraud, you are not the first. The enemies of truth are daily at my door!"

"Please calm yourself, Mr. Moody. I have not come to accuse you of any fraud. Rather, I have come to commend you for it."

Winter went on to describe how he had obtained his spirit photograph. The addition of a previously prepared positive on glass, he said, inserted into the plate holder *in front of* the sensitized negative, allowed him to adjust his "spirit" individually, independent of the sitter's image. Preparing the positive on a glass slightly smaller than the negative allowed for further—and significantly more refined—adjustments. The success of the method of course depended on the quality of the positive, which, in the case of Mrs. Jones, had been taken from an extraordinary likeness.

"And this method—" Winter said. "Are you familiar with it, Mr. Moody?"

"This approach is useless," Moody replied, though he was indeed familiar with the method. "It takes but one look into the plate holder by a knowing eye to expose the trick for what it is."

"True," Winter said. "But my clientele, being mainly colored folk, do not understand the science enough to question it. I suspect that the majority of your sitters are equally ill-informed, though I have read about the exceptions, and the challenges to your art."

Moody re-inspected the stunning image.

"Even if some of my clientele did know enough to suspect," Winter continued, "I can't say that they would *want* to question the appearances that manifest here. Therein lies the success of the spirit photograph. Surely no one understands that better than you, Mr. Moody."

Moody sighed in order to better disaffect the nervousness that was agitating him.

"What is it that you want from me, Mr. Winter?"

"I have not come to try to extort you," Winter replied. "I have only come to suggest . . ."

"Yes?"

"A partnership, as it were."

A partnership. The man must have been out of his mind. Men like Moody—and Winter, for that matter—did not take on "partners."

"It strikes me," Winter continued, "that you might do well with an assistant—or an apprentice perhaps, if you would prefer to think of it that way. I have read of your images in the Boston and New York papers. Philadelphia and Washington are quite taken with you too. The Livermore portrait of last year—that seemed a great triumph."

Moody nodded.

"And the original?" Winter asked.

The man's confidence was bewitching. Moody wished that he possessed such confidence. How had this devil acquired such mastery . . . such *artfulness*? One needed to be seductive, that much Moody knew. But this Winter man, he was quite—

"The original?" Winter repeated.

The spirit photographer hesitated, then said:

"The original, I had on hand. Mrs. Livermore had come to see me years ago, when I was dabbling at Brady's in New York."

The men stared at each other. There was silence—then a smile.

"But they were unannounced," Winter said. "And Gurney—"

"Gurney doesn't know half as much as he thinks he knows," Moody said.

Winter held up the portrait of Mrs. Jones, which he had taken back from the spirit photographer.

"It is easier to come by such items as these than you might think," Winter said. "And it is just as easy to return them—without anyone having noticed they were gone to begin with."

Then, reaching his hand into his jacket, Winter pulled out Moody's pocket watch.

"How on earth!" Moody exclaimed.

"It is easier than you might think," Winter repeated.

And to reinforce the point, Winter tossed Moody's own silver money clip over to him.

"One question for you," Moody said. "Do you, Mr. Winter, truly believe that the dead are around us?"

"I do," the man replied.

And he locked eyes with Moody.

"And I also believe that when they finally have their day with you, they'll not be kind."

It was a brazen thing to say, even for a fellow charlatan, but it demonstrated exactly the kind of courage that Moody himself had never quite been able to muster. In that one sentence Moody perceived a threat, but also an opportunity. The man was daring, quick, confident—even ruthless. And his talent was unquestionable. And then there was this matter of stealing and returning pictures of the departed . . . something Edward Moody had never himself considered.

"And what might you expect, Mr. Winter?"

"A fair share of the profits, no more, no less," Winter said.

"You realize that there is more to this than profit," Moody said.

"Of course I do," Joseph Winter replied. "I think you will find yourself quite surprised at what I can realize."

And so the unlikely partnership was formed, so quickly and so casually, that by the time James and Elizabeth Garrett were on their way to Moody's gallery a few months later, Joseph Winter—photographer, Union army veteran, and thief—had established himself as an indispensible "assistant" to Edward Moody. Winter was helping Moody clean the camera when Mrs. Lovejoy interrupted them on that dark and blustery day, after the rain had started to fall. Near the doorway with Mrs. Lovejoy stood two figures, dressed in black. Their garments sparkled with beads of drizzle.

The Garretts had arrived for their photograph.

V

"SENATOR GARRETT, IT is an honor," Moody said, extending his hand. "And Mrs. Garrett—a great pleasure to see you again."

Garrett glanced about the gallery. It was a hollow, oblong chamber, long enough to support three skylights. The rain beat down upon the skylights and flowed in rivulets over the glass. On the walls there were portraits—too many to count—enlarged, framed, and displayed like works of art. So, these were the "spirits," with their sad companions on earth. Every face was long and unfathomable.

Garrett did not like this room, and he did not release Elizabeth's arm.

"My wife has become quite . . . taken with your art," he said.

"I assure you there is no art in it, sir," Moody replied. "I am merely the connection between this place and the spirit world. And you sir, do you believe—"

"Do I believe that hocus pocus and humbug are everywhere about us, Mr. Moody? I do. But I also believe in the inexplicable and the impossible. I believe that man is not beyond achieving the impossible."

"You yourself, sir," Moody said, "have helped achieve in your lifetime what most men said was impossible. I am a great admirer of you, sir, as are many of my Spiritualist brethren."

Garrett nodded and felt Elizabeth tense. Her attention had been drawn toward the other end of the room.

"Ah," Moody said. "May I present my assistant, Mr. Winter."

"I did not know that there would be others present," Elizabeth said.

"Mr. Winter is a Spiritualist, and an accomplished photographer himself," Moody said.

She disliked him at first sight, and knew that her slight recoiling as he approached would not go unobserved.

"Senator," Joseph said, turning toward Garrett and seizing his hand. "It is a great honor to be in your presence. I must thank you for all that you've done for us. I must thank you for all that you've done for me, sir."

Garrett loosened. It was typical. His defenses were very different from hers.

"My good man," Garrett replied, "yours is a struggle fought but not yet won. Tell me, where did you learn this trade?"

"In Cincinnati. I trained with an excellent colored photographer there, after the war."

"Cincinnati," Garrett said. "And before that?"

"I lived in Canada, sir—and Louisiana before that."

"Ah," Garrett said. "I see."

Now the scene had changed, and her husband would be more amenable. It was still surprising, Elizabeth thought, how easily his sympathies could be manipulated.

"Mr. Winter also served in the 5th Massachusetts," Moody said.

"The colored cavalry?"

"Yes sir," Joseph said. "And it was in service that I first entered into communion with my spiritual brethren. It was during a reconnoiter of Petersburg, after we had lost three men. They spoke to me that night, in a dream."

"A dream?" Elizabeth repeated.

He made it sound romantic.

At the end of the gallery, under the last skylight in the room, the spirit photographer had positioned the chairs, the backdrop, and the camera. As the Garretts took their seats, Joseph Winter disappeared behind a curtain, and returned some moments later carrying the plate holder for the camera.

"We must work with the little light that we have on this day," Moody said. "The exposure will unfortunately need to be longer than usual."

The rain splattered the skylights as the Garretts held their positions. The chairs were uncomfortable—excruciating almost—and Elizabeth fought against her impulse to flinch. She and her husband had sat for photographs before, with William Jeffrey even, during those early days of the daguerreotype. But the process had never been quite this—

"William Jeffrey is here," Moody said. "Hold! He is here! Hold your position now!"

Her hands had grown cold, yet a tidal heat was coursing through her. Everything she had been thinking about her husband all at once fell away. There was anger in the room with her now, and her heart began to beat. Was the boy angry? Did he blame her? Did he not understand that she had loved him? She sought answers, and failed. She had once been capable of loving.

She did not know for how long she sat there. It was quiet, except for her heart. During those moments she realized the torment that the eternity of stillness could bring.

Then, after some time, the photographer raised his head.

"It is finished," he said, returning the heavy cloth to the camera.

And as he moved, a great noise sounded outside the window—a kind of thud, as if something had hit the glass, and then dropped.

Elizabeth gasped.

"It is nothing," Joseph said.

The man was standing near the window. The sound had been a bird . . . or a dislodged piece of wood . . . or perhaps just a beating from the wind.

Garrett looked about the room. On his face there was no sign of the endlessness he too had felt. He knew that his wife had grown to despise him, and the despisal had never been more evident than it was during that sitting. He had waited for a flicker of . . . something. Something he had lost long ago. But what he waited for never came.

Then the spirit photographer removed the plate from the camera.

"Everyone, to the dark room!" Moody ordered. "This plate is trembling with life."

MOODY'S DARK ROOM was not a proper room, but rather a large area at the end of the gallery enshrouded by a heavy curtain. Above, he had erected a false ceiling to block out the light, and had covered the windows on the wall inside with coats of thick black paint.

Moody lit a small amber lamp as Joseph drew the curtain. Then Moody removed the glass negative from the shield, held the glass over the washbasin, and began pouring out the developer fluid. The glass, he assured himself, was the one he had prepared earlier, for even in the darkness he could see where he had marked one of the corners. The Garretts were no professionals, and there was no need to take extra precautions. They were likely to see the spirit even if he botched the whole development.

"This is simply an iron preparation," Moody said, "which brings the captured image to the surface."

As Moody poured out the developer fluid, the Garretts stood close to him, watching. On the glass, their black clothing remained ghostly and invisible, while their faces emerged like dark masks amidst the silver.

Joseph stood beside Moody, his breath heavy and regular.

"There," Joseph whispered. "There—the spirit comes."

At the center of the negative, behind and above the sitters, something—a hazy image—was fading into view. Strange, Moody thought, for he was certain that he had placed the image of the boy much closer to the glass's edge.

"Yes," Moody added. "Yes, the spirit comes."

Then the face came into sharp focus—and in an instant, there she was. Moody blinked.

"No," he muttered. "No—it is impossible."

Elizabeth was the next to notice the spirit, though she did not yet grasp its identity. All she could see was that a young woman had appeared, standing closely behind her, where William Jeffrey might have been.

"Mr. Moody," she said, bending over to look closer, "that's—"

But the crash of glass shrieked through the dark room at that moment . . . followed by the howling of wind. A dull gray light splashed into the room, coating all of them—and the negative—in a soft, luminous glow.

Moody dropped the negative into the liquid of the washbasin.

"I am sorry!" he cried.

For the thing had finally happened.

Then Joseph Winter lunged to block out the light, and forced a bundled tarp into the space of the broken pane. Though the floor was wet with rain and splintered glass, it appeared that nothing else had come in.

The room was now black again save for the flicker of the amber lamp, and a dull outline that haloed the bundled tarp.

"Mr. Moody," Elizabeth said. "The negative, if you please."

But Edward Moody was not quite hearing what Elizabeth Garrett said. The spirit had taken him back. The spirit had come back.

Moody reached into the washbasin and held the glass up to the lamp. The sudden burst of light had ruined the image. A milky white glow seeped out from one side of the negative—partially erasing Garrett, spreading over most of Elizabeth, and barely reaching the upright woman, whose face remained untouched.

Elizabeth suppressed her gasp. It was just as she had feared.

Then Garrett responded, for he too now recognized the face.

"My God in Heaven," he said. "It cannot be."

Garrett stiffened, and turned ferociously toward Moody.

"Who are you, sir?" the senator said.

"You must forgive me—" Moody began.

But Elizabeth interrupted.

"James," she said. "Not another word. Mr. Moody, we must thank you for your time."

Elizabeth took Garrett's arm and disappeared beyond the curtain, leaving Joseph and Moody in the darkness. Moody stood motionless, looking after them for some time, until Joseph pressed his hand on the photographer's shoulder. Moody held the glass to the flickering amber, scarcely able to believe the glowing shadow before him.

It was Isabelle—his lost Isabelle. She had finally returned.

VI

2 May 1852

My Dearest Edward,

You will believe me when I say that these past eight months have been some of the happiest in my life. I know then that it will not be easy for you to hear that I must leave you for a time. It is not easy for me to write it.

I can provide no explanation—I can only tell you that I must go. I must go from Boston, and from you, and from all else I hold dear.

It is not because we are different. It is something I must do.

I take my leave of you with two promises. The first is that my heart will always be yours, and the second is that I will return as soon as I can.

Yours ever,
Isabelle

THIS HAD BEEN the last from her, and Moody could still feel the same despair, even though more than eighteen years had passed since he had first read those mysterious words. Only that week before, he had ridden with her to the outskirts of the city. There were fields there, and alone, where they could sit in the sunlight without judgment, she had lowered her head when he mentioned the possibility of someday marrying her. He did not understand at that point why she had been compelled to look away. When a honeybee began crawling up a fold in her skirt, she studied it, unafraid.

He was twenty-five years old and she a few years younger. They had everything before them. And nothing.

He knew very little of her past, for the girl had been quiet from the start, as if she had been charged with protecting an entire world beyond herself. What he did know had been revealed to him a few weeks before that day in the fields. She had, for some unknown reason, begun telling him about Ohio.

"It was cold there," she had said. "The winters were cold there, but not like here. There was a heat that always followed you there, because even in the cold of winter, you weren't safe."

He asked her how old she had been in Ohio, and it was then that she told him of her mother.

"I never knew her, of course. She was owned by a horrible man—a French planter from the islands."

Her words had stopped time. That was it then, Moody thought. That was what those beautiful eyes contained—a sorrow that hid out in the open.

She went on to tell him of Louisiana. How she had been born there— but not on the plantation.

"It was a place called Bellevoix—"

"Bellevoix?" Moody intoned.

The name sounded romantic, musical.

"Yes, Bellevoix. And my mother tried to escape its cruelty, only to be captured and returned a few days later. She was carrying me when she fled, but when they caught her, I was gone. Others took me into their care, and from that moment I was blessed. Later I would learn that they recorded me as stillborn. So from the first, you see, I had to die in order to live."

What it meant was that she was free. She was free because she did not exist.

She was unclear—rather purposefully, Moody remembered thinking— about her movement from Louisiana to Ohio, and eventually to Boston. She gave details and she didn't; views from partially curtained windows.

And then she never spoke of it again.

So he invented, because even in those early days, that was one of Edward Moody's habits. He told himself that her secrets were not something to be feared, but rather something exciting to discover. Yes, it was true, he had been blinded by a sudden love for her—a type of love that had seized his imagination, and placed her in the realm of the sacred. But how her looks confirmed him . . . drew him in deeper, encouraged his devotion! He was too naïve to think that there might be something from him that she wanted.

During those first months of their meeting, the winter of 1851, she had taken a great interest in his hobby. He noticed that her eyes—for he was always watching her eyes—became spellbound whenever he showed her his experiments. The daguerreotype still reigned over photography then, but Edward Moody was toying with wet-plate collodion, a new method that produced astonishing results on glass negatives. Her fingers touched the negatives, and he could not stop looking at her fingers. She handled the negatives as delicately as one might handle a fallen leaf.

She was fascinated and he would show her. He would be her instructor. This poor girl would love him all the more if he could open her eyes to these wonders.

And so he did, for eight months. He shared with her the secrets of his own obsession: how to mix the iodides and the bromides, the ether and the alcohol, to make the sticky wet substance that would remind her of thinned syrup. When he held the plate by one corner and poured collodion over the glass, he called it "flowing the plate." She'd been seduced by that. There was little she could do to resist such beauty. On the glass there were lakes and streams, and the reflective silver of other mirrors. Her eyes told him that she would absorb everything he had to give her. She stood so close to him while he worked that he could often feel her breath upon his neck.

These were the memories that he had carried for some years—collected, changed, and refined to suit what he wanted to keep. And then later, as things happened, many of the memories fell away, because the pain that accompanied remembering her surmounted the delight of anything else. It was too difficult for Edward Moody to go on remembering her. There was too much anguish in continuing to think about what he no longer had.

There was one memory, however, that Moody had never quite been able to banish. It was one that reminded him of his early career, working at the back of Mrs. Lovejoy's as an engraver. His booth was small, sequestered from the reception room, which he liked because it gave him his privacy. Surrounding him, the latest items that awaited his attention: silver teapots, silver trays, serveware, and table cutlery. Mrs. Lovejoy was demonstrating a Geneva musical box to a customer when Moody became aware of the figure standing beside him. She was a servant woman—just a girl, really—yet she hovered over him like an apparition. She had come to order a monogram for a child's silver rattle.

• • •

FOR A DAY and a night after the Garrett's photograph, Moody remained so weak that he could not return to his own lodgings. It was as if an accumulation of his many feigned exhaustions had rushed upon him all at once, and finally taken him down.

When he did awake, the room was strange. And at his bedside was Joseph Winter.

Moody moaned.

"You are all right," Joseph said. "You took very ill after the photograph. The fumes—"

"Where—"

"We are in Mrs. Lovejoy's apartments."

Moody looked around the room.

"Of course. How long?"

"A little more than a day. We have not been able to stir you since your collapse."

Moody blinked. A pink and orange glow was stretching in from two small windows. Joseph Winter was a dark clay figure outlined in the twilight.

"My God—the negative," Moody said. "Where is the negative?"

Joseph leaned toward the floor and tapped his hand on a plate box.

"It is safe," he said. "It's here."

Moody lifted himself from the pillow. He was not quite remembering yet. There was the plate, and the storm, and the appearance of the spirit . . .

"The Garretts—" Moody said. "Have there been any inquiries?"

"None," Joseph assured him. "And Mrs. Lovejoy closed the gallery."

The gallery. What had happened? Yes . . . the Garretts had arrived at the gallery. William Jeffrey Garrett. Moody had been trying to get the boy.

She had come to him.

Then Moody remembered—Joseph had flowed the plate. Joseph had gone into the darkroom, and returned with the plate in its holder.

Ah, that was it then. A perfect explanation.

But no—

"Sir?" Joseph said.

"What kind of mischief are you playing at?"

"I don't understand."

"I prepared that glass myself," Moody said. "*With the picture of a child.*

I marked the glass in the corner, and I made sure to show you the mark. And when I developed the negative . . . the mark was there."

"I assure you," Joseph said, "I used the marked plate that you prepared. When the woman appeared, I thought that *you* had decided upon another spirit."

"I did not put that woman on the plate!" Moody said.

"Nor did I!" Joseph protested.

Surely, if anyone had wanted to play a trick on Edward Moody, Joseph Winter was the man who could have done it. But there was something so different about this picture—something so frighteningly *authentic* about the image—that to Moody it seemed beyond even Joseph's capabilities.

"Who *is* the woman?" Joseph asked. "You know who she is."

And that's when Moody saw the eagerness in Joseph's eyes, an eagerness that Joseph could not conceal. Joseph Winter was no different from any of the others. They all wanted something—wanted some piece of Edward Moody. And the most disheartening part about it was that Edward Moody remained alone.

How was it that she had come back to him?

"She was—" Moody began.

But he stopped, because for the first time he realized what he had never wanted to know: if Isabelle had truly come back to him in this photograph, it would mean that she no longer walked amongst the living.

"She was the one I loved."

There he was again, in the darkroom, where he had not been with her for more years than he could remember. He had wanted to forget that day. He wished that it had never happened. But he had done it, and the memory of it would never disappear.

She had been close to him, watching him, breathing upon him—she touched him. Her hand had touched him and his entire body had surged with irrepressible fire.

He was methodical—precise. Everything was under his control. Caressing the photographic preparations in the way that he knew she loved.

It had not been an accident. Her hands were on him.

She was sad.

"Isabelle—"

Her breast was heaving.

"Isabelle, what is the matter?"

He placed his hands upon her arms. Her body was also trembling. The amber light was very dull, and darkness was all around them.

"Edward," she whispered. "I don't know what to—"

The motion of her mouth . . . the way her lips swelled and moved. She was saying what he had been longing to hear. Her tears, the apprehension shining in her eyes, were all because of him. Because she loved him but could not say so.

His grip tightened, and he pulled her closer toward his body. And even then she did not resist him.

She barely whispered the words.

"No, Edward," she said. "Please, no . . ."

For the first time he could not resist, and surrendered to what he knew he must do. A fevered pushing, a blinding moment of release. It would not take very long for her to forgive him.

But he would never forgive himself. The years would not bring forgiveness.

"We were young, with no hope for a future," Moody said.

Joseph eyed Moody.

"And what happened to her?" Joseph asked.

"I don't know," Moody said. "She left."

Silence followed that last word, as if the word itself had sent her away.

"This woman is a powerful spirit," Joseph finally said. "But why did she leave? And where did she go?"

Moody did not answer. In that moment he hated Joseph Winter.

"Mr. Moody," Joseph said, "I swear there is no trickery here. I coated the plate as you instructed, and verified the corner mark before I began. The plate was prepared as you prepared it—no other was in the rack. My belief is that something did not go wrong; rather, something went terribly right. Even with the damage, you can see that the woman in the photograph is truly . . . of the divine."

She had become his, even after his transgression. It was a miracle that she had excused him. He had tried to erase the images—of his groping, of her slapping his face right after he had finished. But nothing about her or that day had ever really left him.

And now Joseph Winter dared to speak of the divine. Moody did not want to hear it.

"When I saw the image," Joseph said, "I was convinced that you had placed a more powerful spirit there for the Garretts. She is a powerful spirit. Mrs. Garrett could not abide the sight of her. And the senator was unsteady."

Then Moody turned toward Joseph.

"What are you saying?"

"The spirit," Joseph said. "That spirit is the one they did not want to see."

And then it became clear, what Joseph Winter was trying to say. But what Joseph Winter said was preposterous. The spirit in the photograph belonged to Moody—not the Garretts. Isabelle was Moody's spirit.

"The senator was about to say something when Mrs. Garrett pulled him out of the room," Joseph said. "She did not want him to speak, and it was evident. But the senator's face—I can still see it now. The senator was defeated by the spirit."

"I could not see anything else but the negative," Moody said.

"The Garretts recognized that woman—I am sure of it," Joseph said. "Did you not know her to be related to them in some way?"

Isabelle—related to the Garretts?

His Isabelle.

"I don't know," Moody said. "She did things . . . she was gone. I did not know what she did. She worked as a servant—in houses."

"For the Garretts?"

"Perhaps. I did not know of the Garretts then."

"Think, " Joseph said. "You must think back to the time you knew her. Is there any reason—any reason at all—why she might want to appear now with the Garretts?"

"No," Moody said. "I can only think of why she would want to appear to me."

As he admitted these words, Moody's face darkened with his own disgust—disgust at what he had believed in all these years, and what he had chosen to forget. The great Edward Moody, the spirit photographer—yes, that was who he was. But he was also someone who had loved a long time ago, and who had died from the inevitability of loving. There was nothing that could change him, nothing that could challenge him—but that one thing, lost and forgotten. And in the confusion that was rapidly dismantling everything he believed in, only this much was clear to him now: this vision of Isabelle could not have been more real had he placed her in the photograph himself.

VII

WHILE MOODY SLEPT, little more than silence pervaded the great house on Louisburg Square. The storm had passed, but a storm of a different sort was brewing quietly indoors. Few words had been spoken during the carriage ride from Moody's, but the exchange had followed Garrett home, and remained with him.

"It was her," Elizabeth had said.

"The man is a fraud," Garrett replied.

"It was her," Elizabeth repeated.

There was no point in protesting, for Elizabeth was right: it was her, as beautiful as the last time he had seen her. The servant girl, Isabelle—yes, her name had been Isabelle. She had been so tender with William Jeffrey, and the boy had loved her dearly. Other than Jenny, the Garretts had retained no other servants since Isabelle, which had made it difficult for Garrett to forget her.

They returned home after the sitting to find the house dark and still. It sat there in the rain, stony and unimpressed, its silence more admonishing than the beat of any gavel. Elizabeth felt this deeply, and had been feeling it for years. She had never regained comfort there since the time of her boy's death. The silence reminded her of the emptiness that had followed the removal of William's body. Garrett had stood there, no more emotional than a monument. She had wanted to strike him—to hurl at him anything she could reach. The good senator from Boston. She blamed him, and despised the idea of living another day with him in that house. But she knew it was not his or the house's fault. She mostly blamed herself.

Upstairs, on the third floor, Jenny was sweeping up glass. A window had broken in one of the rooms—the room in which Isabelle had briefly slept. When Elizabeth saw Jenny with the broom and the dustpan, she understood what it meant.

"A window has broken in her room," she told Garrett. "I wonder if you'll excuse that too."

"Elizabeth—" Garrett said. He would try, but fail, to comfort her. She would disappear until she was ready, and there was nothing he could do to stop that.

"Jenny, what happened?" Garrett said.

"While you and Mrs. Garrett were gone," Jenny said, "the wind was fierce, sir."

Jenny finished the sweeping and left him alone in the room. He rarely had cause to be on the third floor, as the rooms were smaller, and mainly Jenny's domain. That room . . . over the years it had become something of a storage room, where the winter rugs hibernated and the old mirrors hid their faces. It was dark, and Jenny had left the room in haste. There was still a piece of glass on the floor.

He picked it up—a single shard, cleanly cut. Near the window, the remaining intact panes permitted the storm's grayish light to seep into the room. In the glass shard Garrett could barely see his reflection. When he tilted the shard, it silvered, like a mirror.

It was unusual for him to go up to the third floor in those days too, but back then little William would scale the steps, and Garrett sometimes followed him up there. The boy loved that room. Yes, Garrett remembered now. The boy was always going up to that room because he had such an affection for Isabelle. There was that week when Elizabeth's mother had gotten sick, and Elizabeth had left suddenly for Philadelphia. She had left William behind because there had been a fever outbreak down south, and Garrett could see him now, sitting at Isabelle's side on her bed, as Garrett peeked through the crack in the door.

"Does it still hurt, my little cabbage?" she said.

She had placed her hands on his head.

The boy nodded, and Isabelle moved her fingers through his hair. She was gently consoling the child, whispering something Garrett could not hear.

"It hurts at night," William said. "But sometimes during the day too—like now."

"Don't worry," Isabelle said. "It will be gone soon. It will be gone soon."

Garrett had pressed his own head against the trim of the door. She was so beautiful—and yet, not his.

. . .

FOR A DAY and a night, Garrett and Elizabeth did not speak, and Garrett was left with the sounds of his own elusive memories. Then at breakfast, after dismissing Jenny, Elizabeth finally addressed him.

"What are you going to do about that picture?" she said.

"Do?" Garrett said.

"The picture," Elizabeth said, heating. "The picture!"

Her eyes were red; she had not slept through the night.

"There is nothing whatsoever for me to do about it," Garrett said. "I do not want to see the picture again. It was damaged, in any case. God willing it continued to spoil."

"If he publishes that picture, it could lead to our ruin."

"Ruin?" Garrett said. "Elizabeth, don't be ridiculous. Anyone with a modicum of sense knows that the man is an imposter."

She looked down into her lap, and then back up at him. He knew that she longed to be away from him.

"The wives of your colleagues—" she continued. "I've known them for over twenty years. They'll shift the debate. They'll no longer discuss the truth or falsehood of spirits—they'll instead speculate about nothing but the identity of the spirit itself."

"No one has seen that girl for years."

"They'll remember, James. And people will make . . . assumptions."

"He won't publish the picture," Garrett said. "At the very least he'll attempt to extort something from me first."

"And supposing he doesn't. You don't know what he believes, and you don't know his motives. Suppose he goes straight to the press."

"So they'll ask questions. The girl is barely recognizable."

"The girl is as clear as you sit here before me!"

She was screaming at him now.

"Elizabeth, please—"

"It's all very well, James . . . to think that your reputation will shield you from suspicion. But it won't, and if anyone resolves to learn more about that woman, we'll be living on the north side of the hill, with the rest of them."

Garrett was mortified. She had attacked him before, but now his wife was heading someplace dangerous.

"She was always determined," Elizabeth said. "And she still hasn't forgiven you."

Garrett looked at her blankly.

"Forgiven me?"

He stared into her eyes—the eyes of his once-beautiful bride. Her eyes were now full of rage and accusation.

And it was then that he realized that Elizabeth knew. Elizabeth had known all along.

"It was nearly twenty years ago," he said.

"There is no expiration on disgrace."

"Elizabeth—" Garrett could barely manage the words. "Elizabeth . . . it was a mistake."

"A mistake!" Elizabeth cried. "It was a mistake, he says! A mistake that might have cost us everything! I saw her . . . I saw her with William. When she left, she took him with her. It was she who took my child. We'd still have him. We'd still have him if—"

The sharp pain began again in Garrett's head. Elizabeth did not let things go.

"The picture must be destroyed," she said. "You can't leave it in that man's hands. Not to mention that odious coon of an assistant—"

"Elizabeth!" Garrett said, slamming his hand down on the table.

She remained quiet for a moment, but then pressed.

"There is more to this, James, and it is all coming back. The photographer is only a small piece."

"The man is a scoundrel and an imposter."

"It is not the man, James. It is *her*."

Garrett stared back at his wife. She seemed disgusted by his confusion.

"Her!" Elizabeth repeated. "And don't try to tell me that it isn't."

Garrett thought for a moment. He could not let this turn into a debate. Elizabeth was too far gone, and her own weaknesses were resurfacing. She was susceptible, especially when it came to the child. He would not let her begin talking of Isabelle and of ghosts.

"I could have taken it, Elizabeth. I could have taken it right then. You forced us out so quickly—there was no time to act."

"You were about to say something unwise," she said. "I could see that you were not of right mind."

"Not of right mind!" Garrett exclaimed. "How dare you? It is all fine and good for you to speak of right mind, Elizabeth."

"And just what do you mean?"

"Of right mind . . . of right mind . . . all this ridiculous hocus pocus. Ghosts in photographs. Voices—spirits. Isabelle coming back! It is utter nonsense, Elizabeth. I have faced worse enemies than this."

She might have been defeated by his outburst, if she hadn't heard the tremor in his voice.

"You are your own worst enemy," she said. "The people will find out, and they will judge you."

"I have not accomplished what I've accomplished by distrusting the people," he said. "The people are of sound mind."

"Yes, James," she replied, "the people are of sound mind. Until they find out you brought a nigger into our bed."

Garrett's hand raised to strike his wife—but only in his fantasies. He was not and had never been a violent man, and the thought of striking her was repugnant to him. And yet, what was most repugnant seemed at that moment most unavoidable. More than unavoidable—it was alluring. He pressed his fingers into his palm, tightening a fist that he would not lift. He would not lift that fist for anything in the world, though he would have obliterated his wife if he could have.

VIII

BENJAMIN P. DOVEHOUSE leaned much further toward the conservative side of the Republican party than his close friend James B. Garrett. He did not believe, for instance, that blacks should have been given the right to vote so soon after emancipation; nor did he subscribe to the idea that free blacks—even the most educated amongst them—were capable of governing themselves. He came from one of the old Brahmin families and was a long-standing member of the American Colonization Society, though his views on the deportation of freedmen had changed considerably since the end of the war. He lived on Mt. Vernon Street in an imposing brick mansion, which contained amongst other relics the dark old portrait of an ancestor who had served as a juror at the Salem Witch Trials.

Dovehouse held secrets—more secrets perhaps than all of the great houses of Boston combined. Decades of circulating amongst the Brahmins had honed his powers of perception to near perfection, and those who had reason to feared him. He could detect a lie in a change of breath, an indiscretion in the shift of an eye, and very few, though they smiled, approached him without caution. Because judgment ran in his veins, so too did an extreme sense of his own "moral duty." He believed in the sanctified order of things, and the role of great families in maintaining that order. He did not believe in compromise, and he did not believe in ghosts.

For these reasons, Senator Garrett kept his regular dinner appointment with Dovehouse that week—a tradition that had been continuous since they had met in the Porcellian Club some forty years earlier. To cancel on Benjamin Dovehouse, Garrett knew, was to risk the raising of his suspicions. Only Garrett's calls to Washington ever interfered with their engagements.

"Well, Garrett," Dovehouse said, "you got your amendment through. More than once you've set out to achieve the impossible, and you've done it again. Congratulations."

He was raising his brandy glass toward the uncomfortable senator, and using the other hand to gesture with his cigar.

"My opinion, though," he continued, "and you know I always give you my opinion, is that you've stirred up a real snake's nest this time. Not that you've ever minded doing that, of course. As your oldest friend, I have always been supportive of your endeavors, even when our beliefs have drastically differed. But this business with the voting, Garrett—it will simply never work."

"It has already worked," Garrett said. "The necessary states have ratified the amendment."

"Ratified the amendment!" Dovehouse said. "Only because you forced them into it! If you hadn't made ratification a condition for reentry, there's no debating where your fifteenth amendment would have gone—down the steps of the Capitol and straight into the gutter! Which is where, might I point out, many respectable Northerners think it should be."

He took another puff of his cigar, the smoke forming halos around his head. Like Garrett, Dovehouse had been a great orator and debater at Harvard. His was the kind of voice that filled the room, even when he spoke in whispers.

"You saw what they did to that Dupree man in Mississippi," he said.

"I saw," Garrett said.

"Slit his throat and disemboweled him, in the yard in front of his wife. Lawless barbarians. Lincoln should have thrown them all into prison—or better, executed them—when he had the chance. They say they fought for honor, but they have none. It's abhorrent."

"We will not return their independence—if we ever do that—until we've subjugated every last one of them. They forfeited their right to independence when they rebelled against the United States."

"There is nothing on this earth like your optimism," Dovehouse said. "For forty years it has truly astonished me."

"They will be at the mercy of our laws!" Garrett said.

He was growing impatient, which was not uncommon these days during conversations about the new order of things.

"They *will* follow the law or they *will* pay the price," he added. "I am absolutely sworn to make them follow."

Dovehouse shook his head in condescending disagreement.

"Do you think those traitors care a bit for your price? They've already lost everything they had . . . except for their land, of course, which Johnson gave right back to them. Disgraceful. But the land must still be worked, Garrett—that you can't deny. And the negroes are the ones to work it. If they somehow manage to survive down there—and mind you, I do have grave doubts about that—they will never realize the kind of equality that you and your radical friends envision. The traitors will see to that."

"I will see every last traitor lose even the notion of power—lose it by the freedmen's ballot!"

Dovehouse again shook his head.

"I take it you've read this," he said, picking up one of the papers. "Your opponents have been quite eloquent of late. 'A semi-barbarous race of men who worship fetishes and practice polygamy, intent on subjecting all white women to their hot, unbridled lust.' It's powerful stuff, old boy, and, though exaggerated, it's not without some truth. The negroes are little more than children, no matter how much you might insist on their equality. You can't expect them to grow up overnight, and you can't expect them to understand the kind of power you're trying to give them."

"Oh, Benjamin!" Garrett exclaimed, because they had reached this point before. "You speak with every prejudice of the Democrats, and it causes me great sadness."

"I speak with every prejudice of an American," Dovehouse said, "because my forefathers founded this country. Abolition was an economic— even moral—necessity. That I never disputed. But citizenship? Voting? The party's agenda has gone too far. What's next for us, old boy—mixing of the races? Mulatto children on every corner? Even the idea of it is unnatural, and threatens the reversal of our evolution. I, for one, do not wish to live to see such a thing, if that is the fate to which your new laws have condemned us."

"The people have elected me because they believe in equal rights for the negro," Garrett said.

"Might I remind you that the people do not elect their senators at all— the state legislatures do that job for them. So your 'people,' the very same who adore and empower you, are a much smaller set of sycophants than you would like to think."

Garrett and Dovehouse had been debating such matters for as long as they had known each other—Garrett taking the more radical stance in the years leading up to the war. He knew Dovehouse too well to ever attempt to sway him. In Dovehouse's Boston, most things were immovable.

"Benjamin," Garrett said, "might I raise a . . . delicate matter? I'm afraid I am in need of your assistance."

Dovehouse peered over his brandy.

"Oh my, old boy," he said. "Don't tell me there's a girl in trouble."

"No—it's nothing of that sort," Garrett said. "It's Elizabeth . . . and, well . . . there is a predicament."

Dovehouse placed his glass down on the table and took another puff of his cigar.

"She has been," Garrett continued, "she has been—suffering some difficulties of late. She has had it in her mind to get a picture of William Jeffrey. She has been investigating the possibilities of a spirit photograph."

"Dear God, Garrett, you can't be serious."

"I am. And so I accompanied her to Edward Moody's, and we sat there for a picture."

Dovehouse scowled, moving forward in his chair.

"Edward Moody? You went to see that blasphemous imposter?"

"I did, Benjamin."

"Oh, Garrett, that man should be thrown in jail—and would have been by now, if I had anything to say about it. He's worse than the Confederates, you know. At least they stand out in the open for what they believe in. But that man lurks about in the shadows, hoodwinking some of the most prominent members of society. They're the only ones who can afford his outrageous prices, the scoundrel. And he's got a negro working for him now too, I hear. The whole thing stinks of foulness."

The whole thing did stink. But Garrett would still open the door.

"And the 'predicament'?" Dovehouse said.

"There was an accident, and the photograph was spoiled. But Elizabeth is convinced that it was no accident. She is convinced that ghosts are punishing us for any wrong we may have done in the past."

"Wrong?" Dovehouse said. "According to the papers—well, the decent ones, of course—you've only done right, as far as I can tell."

"She has been unwell since the photograph."

"Well, I'm sorry for her. When was it?"

"Day before last. Elizabeth was quite upset. We left hastily after the sitting—without the negative."

"I see. And the picture? What's on it?"

"It's the negative, really—no pictures yet, as far as I know. We watched in the darkroom as he developed the negative."

"And?"

"And there are shadows on it—nothing more. The result of an accident with the chemicals."

"And you want to retrieve the negative, because you fear he may print pictures and use them to his advantage? I hear he's getting ten dollars for a dozen *cartes de visite*, sometimes more. The Spiritualists collect them, you know."

"Yes, that. And . . ." Garrett wasn't sure how to continue. "It would just be best if we were able to retrieve the negative. But I cannot risk drawing attention to myself—or Elizabeth. I was hoping you might have a . . . connection."

Dovehouse eyed his friend.

"There is something else, Garrett. Tell me."

Garrett met Dovehouse's gaze, but held it for only a moment.

"It is Elizabeth. She has become possessed with the idea of obtaining the negative."

"I don't really see the predicament," Dovehouse said. "Why don't you just go and ask him for it? He's nothing but a mercenary. At worst, you'll have to pay him something."

"There is something about him I do not trust. My feeling is that he won't surrender the negative—not willingly."

"Something you don't trust? Well, I should think so!"

Rarely had Dovehouse beheld his friend the senator so distressed. Usually Garrett reserved such emotions for politics—or worse, the negroes. There was something more to this situation, something more to Elizabeth's concerns. Could his friend of forty years have finally succumbed to some secret weakness? Was it possible that he believed in ghosts?

"You know, Garrett," Dovehouse said after some time, "Bolles has been building a case against him."

"Bolles?"

"Yes, Bolles—the same whose appointment you helped secure not so long ago. They have apparently been after Moody for some time, waiting to seize on some sort of tangible evidence, but so far they have been unable to procure any. I hear, though, that other developments, so to speak, have been in the works."

"What's your meaning?" Garrett said.

"I think a visit to the young inspector might prove to be of some benefit."

New York Daily Tribune
New York, New York
Sunday, July 17, 1870

IN RESPONSE TO your letter of last week from the esteemed Mr. Hinckley of the American Institute, Photographic Section, denouncing the scientific impossibility of spirit photography based on the assumption that what the eye cannot see cannot be photographed, we would like to draw attention to the following:

A few months since an article was printed in Scientific American *quoting Prof. C. F. Varley, of London, the celebrated electrician, who recounted how he had made experiments by passing a current of electricity through a vacuum tube, the results of which were indicated by strong or faint touches of light about the poles: "In one instance, although the experiment was carried out in a very dark room, the light was so feeble that it could not be seen, and the operators doubted if the current were passing. But at the same time photography was at work, and in thirty minutes a very good picture was produced of what had taken place. This is a remarkable fact—indeed, it borders on the wonderful, that a phenomenon INVISIBLE to the human eye should have been, so to speak, seen by the photographic lens, and a record thereof kept by chemical agency."*

What is electricity? We know it is a force; it passes silently and invisibly over the wire and performs its work; therefore we know it exists. But can this same electricity be made visible? Mr. Varley says yes, by employing a MEDIUM, in the shape of a vacuum tube, when by connecting it with the battery, a stream of invisible electricity is made visible to the human eye. Mediums stand in the same relation to spirits as vacuum tubes do to electricity: they supply the necessary elements by which spirits are enabled to be seen; whether those elements be aura, magnetism, or anything else, they are, in our belief, essential to all spiritual manifestations.

Luther Colby
Editor, Banner of Light
Boston, Massachusetts

IX

T HE "SPIRITUALIST BOSH," as Marshall Hinckley called it, was influencing the minds of unsuspecting people to tragic ends, and posing dangerous challenges to the reputation of legitimate science itself. In a meeting with other members of the American Institute for the Encouragement of Science and Invention, Hinckley denounced the comparison between spirits and electricity as "utter nonsense." A fuzzy image here, a somewhat representative image there—all of it, he said, relied on luck and technical cunning. Of course, the Spiritualists would say that the living could not control spiritual energy in the same way as electricity, since spirits had once been of free mind on earth, and would be of equally free mind in the other world. But this was just another part of the Spiritualists' game, and for respectability's sake—not to mention for the sake of science's reputation in general—that game needed to be stopped.

It was not the Spiritualists' use of technical instruments like cameras that disturbed the members of the Institute; nor was it that the Spiritualists had concocted chemical formulas and methods to help them play their tricks. But the fact that the Spiritualists had dared to begin claiming science as *their own*—had begun to insist, even, that spirit photography was no less scientific than the study of electrical currents—this had enraged Marshall Hinckley and the other members of the American Institute immeasurably. One Spiritualist had gone so far as to write that spirit photographs would soon become as common and popular as the electric telegraph, or the sewing machine. "At no distant day," this blasphemer wrote, "the world at large—and the investigating minds of the world, in particular—will be perusing a *scientific* work upon the whole subject, which will dispel the darkness that yet broods over this grandest revelation of God's mysterious providence." These criminals were duping the public in order to realize their own mischievous ends—whatever those were. Using the good name of science to do so was the height of arrogance and wickedness.

Worse still, word had recently reached the Institute of other spirit photographers beginning to practice these artful tricks—one in Poughkeepsie, another in Philadelphia, and there was rumor that spirit pictures were even popping up in London. The members of the Institute feared an epidemic, which furthered the urgency to eliminate the impending plague. And since no one had been a greater carrier for the Spiritualist cause than Edward Moody, it was his fraudulence that the Institute sought most to expose. The papers of Boston and other cities were aflame with reports of this imposter's "talents." In Moody, Hinckley and his colleagues saw an opportunity to quash the Spiritualists once and for all: take the founding card down, and the whole house would crumble.

"He must be made an example of," Marshall Hinckley told Inspector Bolles. "It is the only way they are going to stop practicing these outrages against unsuspecting people."

"It will be difficult to prove that he is breaking the law," Bolles said.

"There are higher laws at stake here, Inspector," Hinckley replied. "The laws of science are sacred. We can help you find a way."

For some months Inspector Montgomery Bolles had been looking into the matter—he himself being of the mind that Moody's spirits were likely a sham. He had turned his attention toward the newspapers, where one could hardly flip a page without reading something of spirit photography. How did Edward Moody photograph "ghosts" with such fidelity? And in the cases where he didn't "get" the spirits perfectly, how was it that people still left his gallery comforted by what they saw? According to the most recent accounts, face after distinct face had lately been emerging on Moody's negatives—a phenomenon that had transformed the city of Boston into a cacophony of ecstatic widows and widowers.

"Many of my earlier tests were not entirely successful," Moody told one reporter, "but the beauty and truthfulness of these images demonstrate what no man has the right to deny."

He knew how to promote himself—that much was plain. It was an interesting turn for a man who had started out as a humble engraver. He had first experimented with photography during his early days at Mrs. Lovejoy's. "But so many were experimenting with photography then," Moody said. "It was many years before the war, and I had not yet seen the dead in the fields. I was young and my eyes were still closed."

The war. So, Moody had indeed gone off to the war. But a few years before that, he had left Boston for New York.

"I went to New York to apprentice with Matthew Brady. And then the war came. I was not looking for the opportunity."

Brady had sent Edward Moody into the field, and the young photographer took pictures of the worst of the carnage at Antietam. "It was, for me, transformative," Moody told another reporter, "because Mr. Brady's project was, for the first time in our history, laying bodies at our very doorsteps. But when it was finished I gave up. I had to give up. Because the ghastliness of capturing those images made photography disgusting to me. I did not want to be a part of something that could depict reality so mercilessly."

So he found his way back to Boston, determined to abandon photography and return to his original trade. It was only at the entreating of his employer, Mrs. Lovejoy, that Moody agreed to mix his chemicals once again.

"Mrs. Lovejoy's picture was indeed a very strange-looking one," Moody later told the *Banner*, "and, considering that it was taken when no one else but Mrs. Lovejoy was in the room, the indistinct and shadowy outline of the young girl who appeared in the picture was, to me, unaccountable. I immediately submitted the negative to Mrs. Lovejoy—an accomplished photographer herself—for inspection, and her opinion was that the glass had been used previously for a similar photograph. An insufficient cleaning, she said, likely resulted in residue remaining on the glass, and when a second negative was imposed upon it, the latent form, so to speak, was re-developed."

Moody confessed that Mrs. Lovejoy's theory was quite acceptable to him at the time—that is, he did not suspect the presence of a spirit on the negative. "The picture was, to say the least, a novelty. I had one printed for my own amusement, and propped it up in my work area."

The matter might have ended there, were it not for Dr. Asaph Child, a well-known Spiritualist and author of many books about Spiritualism. When Dr. Child, by chance, visited Mrs. Lovejoy's store and spied the photograph, he stopped and stared in amazement, forcing the engraver to look up from his work.

"Do you know what you have there, sir?" the doctor said.

Moody replied that he did know what he had—a picture of Mrs. Lovejoy, taken by himself, when no other visible person was in the room.

"Admittedly," Moody said, "I was toying with the doctor. For I was young and stupid, and I did not yet understand."

Doctor Child left the store and returned the next day with an investigatory committee of four gentlemen, all of whom wanted to learn more about the "extraordinary picture." They conducted a thorough examination of the photograph, and after little consultation, declared the work a "miracle." Then each one of them requested spirit photographs on the spot, offering to pay the engraver ten dollars *a picture*.

"It was a very great deal of money, even for an artist as gifted as Mr. Moody," Mrs. Lovejoy said. For she too had appeared quite a bit in the *Banner of Light*, and the *Spiritualist Magazine*, and a host of other publications concerned with this craze. It was by one of her accounts that Inspector Bolles learned how easily Edward Moody had come into his spiritual inheritance. "These gentlemen were very insistent on having their pictures taken," Mrs. Lovejoy said . . .

> " . . . *and Mr. Moody was resistant to the idea because he had given up the art. But unable to avoid yielding under the relentless weight of their entreaties, he finally agreed to sit them for a picture. Of the first gentlemen—Dr. Child, I believe—an excellent spirit photograph was taken. Two of the other gentlemen also received good spirits, and the other two were not successful. The following Sunday the article in the* Banner *appeared, and the very next day, by the time Mr. Moody arrived at the store, there were no less than fifty persons awaiting him in my reception room. I was behind the counter, and when he entered the store I made the announcement, 'Here comes Mr. Moody!' The people had grown so impatient during the wait that I began fearing a riot in the store."*

The mob surrounded Moody as he entered. Then, from the mass of admirers, two distinguished gentlemen pressed forward, "very desirous of having Mr. Moody take their pictures at that very moment." The photographer declined, saying that he was no longer dedicated to photography; but the gentlemen persisted, and less than thirty minutes later, they were descending the gallery steps, declaring that Mr. Moody had "photographed yet more spirits!" Mrs. Lovejoy recalled that there was also a scientist from Cambridge present, who had claimed to be thoroughly acquainted with the art of photography. When someone suggested that one might introduce a second image into a photograph by using an imperfectly cleaned glass, he had replied that such an "earthly" explanation was much more difficult to accept than the spiritual. "While it might be possible, and even probable, in daguerreotyping," he said, "it is nearly impossible to accomplish when taking a photograph on glass."

It went on, and it grew—this obsession with Edward Moody and his photographs—until it had succeeded in touching nearly every level of society. Those who could not afford their own sitting with Moody could purchase *carte de visite* copies of others' "miracles." And then there were those at the very top of the ladder who had converted to Spiritualism after only one visit. "Like a young robin," said Walter Barnes, the wealthy banker from Beacon Hill, "I hold my mouth open to the heavenly world for its truths to feed my soul. I swallowed Spiritualism, but not before I opened my mouth, in earnest faith, to receive it."

Edward Moody was a problem, and not one that could go un-dealt with. So Inspector Bolles, and Hinckley, and Senator Garrett had gathered at Dove-house's to discuss what to do.

"It's preposterous," Dovehouse said to the inspector, "the way these Spiritualists are going about hoodwinking the public. For the working class, I can understand the novelty—even at the prices they're charging for their *cartes de visite*. But intelligent men of society, like Barnes? And the Merriwhethers holding séances in their dining room? It's setting a horrible example."

"I don't care a fig about society," Marshall Hinckley said. "If your cronies are stupid enough to hand over their money to that charlatan, that's their business. It's the assault against science that I want the police to address—and address it they can, by proving the man a fraud."

Inspector Bolles considered the two gentlemen, and then glanced toward Senator Garrett.

"As you know," Bolles said, "we have been building the case against him with the help of certain members from the Institute's Photographic Section. We know that a spirit photograph can be produced by taking a picture on a glass that contains the residue of a previous image. We also know that one can use a positive image on glass, in front of the negative in the plate holder, to achieve a similar effect. One member of the Institute has also suggested a third method—the actual printing of a photograph from two separate negatives. But this latter method Moody could only achieve alone, and in privacy. It does not account for the countless instances during which he has produced spirit photographs under close scrutiny."

"Close scrutiny!" Marshall Hinckley howled. "I say that if he has achieved the effect under scrutiny, there was not scrutiny enough."

"But the case, Inspector Bolles," Dovehouse said. "What is the basis of the case itself?"

"Our own spirit photographs," Hinckley interrupted. "We've made a bunch of them ourselves, and detailed the exact methods for the authorities. We've even gotten Barnum to pose for one—with the 'spirit' of President Grant."

"A spirit of a living person—ingenious," Dovehouse said.

"Ingenious, yes," Bolles replied. "But it does not necessarily guarantee a conviction."

"I will settle for nothing less than a conviction," Hinckley said.

"The conviction—" Bolles continued. "The conviction can only come through physical evidence. So far we have no real evidence that Moody is fabricating his spirits. It is all speculation on our part."

"I have seen the man at work," Garrett said, "and I am convinced that his only talent rests in preying upon the desperate and the grieving."

Garrett touched his neck, for his collar had grown tight around it.

"Which brings us to the matter at hand," Dovehouse said. "We have come to the conclusion that it might be time to, shall we say, speed things up a little?"

"Appleton is fully prepared to prosecute the case," Bolles replied. "But as I said, we do not yet have the guarantee."

Dovehouse narrowed his eyes.

"You can obtain the guarantee by searching the gallery and seizing his instruments—can you not?"

"Perhaps," Bolles said. "Even likely. But again, there is no guarantee of what we will find."

"To the devil with guarantees," Hinckley said. "We have enough. Our fabricated spirit photographs are every bit as good as his are—even better in some cases. The jury will have no problem seeing the fraud."

"Mr. Bolles," Dovehouse said, addressing him as a gentleman, "there are some necessities that sometimes take precedent over technicalities like guarantees."

"Sir?" the inspector said.

"There is a negative in that gallery," Dovehouse continued, "a negative that must never be exposed to the public. I trust I have your confidence in saying that its ultimate fate is of great *personal* interest to us."

"I'm not sure I understand you," Bolles said.

Garrett stiffened and leaned forward.

"What Mr. Dovehouse is saying, Mr. Bolles, is that there is a spirit photograph of me and my wife somewhere in that gallery."

Garrett paused.

"And that we would like to . . . how shall I put this—"

He looked toward his friend Dovehouse, and then stared straight back at Bolles.

"Obtain it."

"You have gone for a spirit photograph, sir?" Bolles said.

The senator nodded.

"Garrett," Hinckley exclaimed. "Good God!"

"It is of no great concern," Dovehouse said, "a mere whim of Mrs. Garrett's, and it appears that there is nothing remarkable on the negative, but the release of such a photograph would undermine the cause of the case— and the Institute—irreparably. It's why we must act with such speed, before Moody has the chance to profit from this work."

"But if there is nothing remarkable on the negative," Bolles asked, "how can the man stand to profit by it?"

"Nothing is beyond that man," Hinckley interjected. "He could turn a puff of smoke into the face of my dead mother, and find a way to make a profit."

Bolles turned toward the senator, whose bottom lip had frowned.

"Senator," he said. "You have done so much for me—"

"Your father was a great man—one of the dearest friends I had."

"And you know," Bolles continued, "that there is almost nothing I would ever refuse you. But it seems that you and Mr. Dovehouse are suggesting the—"

He paused uncomfortably.

"—confiscation of important evidence."

Garrett did not reply.

"We prefer the word *obtain*," Dovehouse said. "And yes, it is a delicate matter. The last thing we wish to do is compromise you, my good man. We only ask that you consider the seriousness of the senator's situation."

Then Garrett spoke up. He was careful to measure his words.

"I agreed to accompany my wife to a sitting with Mr. Moody, not realizing how much I would regret my actions when the deed was over."

"Everything you've been building—" Dovehouse continued. "It will all be further compromised if the Spiritualists get their hands on that photograph. The man has the image. You saw how much press he got from Colfax. Imagine what he could do with the image of a man whom the people adore ten times as much."

"I agree," Hinckley interjected. "The time to move is now. The last thing we need in the press is the spirit photograph of another illustrious figure. Next thing you know, he'll be finding some way to get Grant to come in for one."

"Senator Garrett?" Bolles said.

Garrett looked into the eyes of the inspector. He had known him since he was a boy.

"It would be . . ." Garrett said with some difficulty. "It would be a great favor to me."

Inspector Bolles and Marshall Hinckley left Dovehouse's not long after this exchange. It was agreed that Dovehouse and Garrett would be permitted to "inspect" Moody's gallery during the seizure of evidence. Of course, the negative could be anywhere—locked away in any number of cupboards, or even somewhere downstairs in Mrs. Lovejoy's store—but this was the chance that Garrett was willing to take, and after Moody's removal from the building, he and Dovehouse would have their time.

X

HE HAD LOOKED for her, of course, though not right away. When she said that she would come back to him, he had believed her. But then when no letter or word from her arrived, Moody's worry began to take hold. Where had she gone? How was she living? And what could have been so horrible that it was keeping her away? And then . . . after more than half a year had passed, he was overcome with despair, and the realization that there was nothing he could do. He didn't even know how to start looking for her—he knew none of her acquaintances, and certainly, she had no family. All he possessed were those few small scraps about her past: the plantation, her mother, her freedom.

One day he had gone to the colored section of Boston and asked questions of anyone who would talk to him. He spoke with an old woman who ran a boardinghouse on Russell Street.

"Oh yes," the woman said. "She was here—about two years I guess. Pretty girl. She came and went. Kept mostly to herself. Except for the children."

"Children?" Moody asked.

"Yes," the old woman replied. "The children in the neighborhood flocked to her. She was always bringing them little treats. Sweet cakes and things, little pieces of yarn. A nice girl. But, well—"

"Did she give any reason for leaving, or tell you where she was going?"

"Ha!" the woman said, suggestively. "They never do. Suspect she went to her relatives somewhere. If they would even take her."

"And her employers?" Moody asked. "Do you know?"

"She worked for people," the woman said. "In houses."

Isabelle had said that her heart belonged to him, and that too he had desperately believed. He had needed to believe it, because after his misdeed, the idea of her forgiveness was the only thing that mattered. He had held no delusions about what a woman like her might have seen; but when she listened to him, and gazed back into his eyes, there was a goodness there that no indecency could have touched. No—she had loved him, he was sure of it. He had never been so sure of anything in his whole life.

He had photographed her—only once. It had been afterward. She had been resistant, but she had let him. She understood that he needed to do it.

It had all been so long ago. There was so much he did not remember.

And then the thought struck him—had she returned to chastise him? Had she grown so displeased with what he was doing that it had somehow forced her out of the grave? He studied the negative, for he had still not made a print of it. Her eyes returned strange emotion. No, that could not be it— she would not have come back to admonish him. She would, in an odd way, have approved of what he was doing—the healing he was responsible for in returning people to their loved ones. Was she reaching out to him for some other reason then? To let him know that she had never left him?

"But the Garretts," Moody thought. "What has she to do with the Garretts?"

He stared at her, waiting—even begging—for an answer, but of course, no answer ever came. The longer he peered at her, the more unyielding she grew, standing upright behind the Garretts with a kind of quiet defiance. And yet, even in the rigidity of her unreadable stance, she remained so slight, so impalpable, and so luminously transparent that she appeared more like a mirrored reflection of herself than anything real or alive. He was desperate to know what she wanted to say to him, and it rent his heart to look at her.

As for Joseph—Moody noticed that he too seemed heartbroken whenever he studied the negative. It was plain that Isabelle's spirit had captured him as well, despite Joseph's attempts to disguise this. And yet, Moody thought, the man stank of fraud. What could his motivation have been if he had indeed played such a trick?

"This is a powerful spirit," Joseph said. "And as I told you before, she may be carrying many messages."

They had returned to the second-floor gallery, where the clamor of carriages rose up from the street.

"Such messages can be difficult to untangle," Joseph added.

Moody looked at the image. It was her . . . and yet it wasn't. He wanted nothing more than to believe that it was Isabelle.

"If it is truly her," Moody said, "why would she appear now? And why in *this* picture?"

"It may have nothing to do with you," Joseph replied. "There is more here than we understand. The Garretts reacted, and we must discover the connection. There *is* a connection, I assure you."

Moody did not like Joseph's insistence that Isabelle somehow "belonged" to the Garretts. If Isabelle's spirit had returned, she would have surely returned for him.

Then Joseph reached into his pocket and pulled out an object—some sort of silver box, or a case.

"If you will indulge me, Mr. Moody," Joseph said. "I would like to try to make you remember."

Joseph then asked the spirit photographer to lift his eyes and focus.

So . . . Joseph Winter was a mesmerist too?

"You wish to put me into a trance," Moody said.

There seemed to be no end to the absurdity.

"I wish you to remember more than you think you are able to remember," Joseph said. "The trance can, as you know . . . take you back to certain places. There is a connection between Isabelle and the Garretts, I am certain. The clues may be somewhere in your memory."

"I would think that I would be able to remember such details," Moody said. "She was with me—right here in the gallery!"

"You yourself have said—" Joseph urged.

"Yes, I know what I have said!" Moody shouted.

It was not that he did not believe in mesmerism, for he had seen convincing displays of it before. But the appearance of Joseph, and now Isabelle, and the emergence of other things . . . these were all part of a journey Moody had not prepared himself to take.

"Your method," Moody said. "Just how . . . ?"

"During the war," Joseph said, "there was an old surgeon who practiced it on patients—to relieve pain, and even to operate in some cases. He had studied mesmerism in England, and I asked him to teach me. Sometimes there was not enough ether or chloroform for colored troops."

Joseph looked away.

"I learned how to use it," he concluded. "To great benefit."

Then Joseph turned back toward Moody, who neither acquiesced nor resisted, as Joseph raised the silver object close to Moody again. Moody, exhaling, carefully set down the negative, and focused on the shiny thing in

Joseph's hand. Sun streamed in from the windows, causing an almost blinding reflection from the silver. From somewhere in the room, the clock's ticks struck and faded.

Joseph pivoted his wrist, though the movement was barely perceptible. The object in Joseph's hand was bursting—a sun-drenched mirror.

Seconds melted into minutes. Moody's eyelids fluttered—and closed.

"Can you hear me, Mr. Moody?"

Moody remained still, then nodded.

"I want you to see Isabelle," Joseph said. "I want you to see her for the very first time."

Moody's eyes had closed, and the ticking of the clock continued.

"Yes," Moody said, "I see her."

"What does she look like?" Joseph quietly asked. "What is Isabelle wearing?"

"She is beautiful," Moody said. "She is wearing a gray wool coat, because it is cold. It is winter. The coat is unbuttoned, and beneath she is wearing a thick cotton dress—blue and white. She has walked through the store and come to see me at my stall. We are alone together at the back of the store."

"And what then, Mr. Moody? What does she say?"

"At first, she says nothing. I am working and I do not notice her. I am engraving a silver amulet, and I am fixated on my work. But then I feel her presence. She almost frightens me—like a ghost. I look up to see her standing there. Her face is delicate, and she does not smile."

"Continue," Joseph said. "Does she speak to you?"

"She does. The light is bouncing off a shiny object in her hands. Her voice is beautiful . . . so beautiful. I hear the request—I hear her words. But I am blinded by her face, and the bright light shining in her hands. She reaches out toward me. She is holding a light, and she offers it to me."

Moody gasped—as if he were trying to catch his breath.

"Then . . . then . . . she hands it to me. I take the light in my hands. It is a rattle—a child's rattle—crafted of the finest silver. She asks me to engrave it for her, and I say that I will do it. The rattle is for a boy very dear to her heart, a boy she fears may not be long for this world. I ask if the rattle is for her own boy, and she tells me no—the boy is one she cares for."

"The boy," Joseph said. "Who is the boy?"

"I do not know. I do not ask her anything else. I am only anxious to oblige her request and I offer to engrave the rattle right away. Her request is a simple one, merely three letters. I perform the engraving on the spot."

"Engrave it for me, Mr. Moody, if you please."

Joseph placed a fountain pen in the spirit photographer's hand, and laid Moody's other hand upon a clean sheet of paper. Moody gripped the pen as if it were his old engraving tool. Then he carefully "carved" three letters into the blank sheet before him.

WJG

Joseph studied the three letters.

"W-J-G," he mumbled. "W-J-G . . ."

The hypnotist snapped his fingers, and the spirit photographer awakened. Moody held keys to locks. It was simply a matter of finding those keys.

"These letters," Joseph said. "What do these letters mean to you?"

Moody inspected the paper. He had never seen it before. And yet, it was as familiar to him as anything else he might have written.

"They're initials of some sort," Moody said. "They could be—"

"She came to you with a rattle," Joseph said. "Isabelle. This is what you engraved for her—W-J-G—on a rattle."

"Yes, I remember the rattle," Moody said, "and I do remember the lettering, now. But I never asked whom the rattle was for. I never presumed to ask her questions."

Then he eyed the paper again.

"W-J-G."

Moody looked at Joseph.

"The boy," Moody said. "She—"

"William Jeffrey Garrett!"

"The boy's nurse," Moody said.

"She must have come on an errand for the Garretts! As the boy's nurse, she may have even lived in the house with them. No doubt she knew things, saw things . . ."

And then, the strangest feeling overcame Edward Moody—an inexplicable weakening. The negative's return.

"What happened to her?" Moody said.

He held his heart. He was breathing heavily. Once again she was pulling him back.

"The Garretts are terrified of this photograph," Joseph said. "She had a power over them then, as she has a power over them now. They will want this photograph destroyed."

"Destroyed!"

"Yes—destroyed. The photograph unearthed something for them—something they had no intention of admitting."

Moody again picked up the negative. Isabelle's stare was dark and mournful. No sleight of hand could ever have recreated such an expression. It did not matter who Joseph Winter was at this point. Other things needed to be done.

"We must go to Fanny Van Wyck," Moody said. "We must have her examine this negative."

But before Joseph could respond, a loud commotion outside distracted them. Downstairs, in the street, two carriages had pulled up in front of the store.

"Wait here," Joseph said.

And he fled from the gallery as Moody moved closer to the window. Outside, two plainclothes men were stepping out from a hansom cab, and two uniformed police officers from another. Across the street sat a third carriage—a brougham—its windows shadowed by the buildings.

So, they'd come for him after all.

Moody wrapped the negative in brown paper and slipped it into a small leather-bound case. He could not allow anyone to capture it. He had loved her too much to give her up again.

Joseph returned and locked the gallery door behind him.

"We have very little time," he said.

"They have come to arrest me."

"Yes," Joseph said. "Mrs. Lovejoy did what she could, but they are on their way up to the gallery."

"Garrett is parked across the street."

Joseph nodded.

"It is certain, then," he said. "They have come here to seize much more than you."

Joseph had not yet finished his words when the heavy thud of boots sounded on the staircase.

Then, a pounding on the door.

"This is the Boston Police."

The boots stopped, and for a brief moment there was silence.

"Mr. Moody," Joseph whispered. "You have the negative there?"

Moody clutched the negative to his chest.

"They must never get their hands on this."

Then the walls of the gallery shook as someone again struck the door.

"I COMMAND YOU TO OPEN THIS DOOR."

Moody looked about the room. The police would tear apart the gallery. There was no safe place for the negative. And there was no other way out of the room.

"Mr. Moody—quickly. This way!"

And there, at the far end of the gallery, was Joseph Winter, standing near one of the wall panels. He was prying at it, as if trying to strip the panel from the wall, but in a moment had released the panel, which swung out toward him on hidden hinges.

"Mrs. Lovejoy," a voice said outside in the stairwell. "If you please, open this door."

There was the jangle of Mrs. Lovejoy's keys, and there was Joseph's urging near the opened panel.

"Quickly!" Joseph repeated.

It was an impossible thing—a trick of Moody's troubled vision. Could such a convenience ever have been true?

Moody ran toward Joseph, and Joseph shoved him into the passage. For that was indeed what was waiting for him: a passage within the walls of the gallery. Then Joseph himself jumped through the wall's opening and pulled the panel shut behind him.

"Go . . ." Joseph whispered. "Go forward, quickly now."

Moody hurried across the passage's rickety floorboards—a secret set of floorboards that had been living there all this time. The passage was dark and narrow, illuminated here and there by stray bands of light that seeped in through cracks in the plaster. Soon Moody arrived at the top of a set of stairs, where the passage widened slightly. Joseph moved around in front of him.

"We'll go down," Joseph said. "They should not be able to hear us. We are now deep inside the walls of the next room, but still we must take care."

Joseph then began inching his way down the steps—a crooked pathway descending into the cold and the must. The wood was brittle and Moody tried to step down . . .

But then he stopped.

"Mr. Moody," Joseph said. "Mr. Moody, you must come!"

Moody's legs had grown heavy—he tried to lift them, but couldn't. A coldness rushed into his lungs—so forcefully that his next breath caught in his throat. His legs had become chained to the top step of the staircase. It was not possible for him to continue.

Joseph struck a match, and the smell of sulfur suffused with the must.

"Mr. Moody!" Joseph said.

But still Moody did not move.

"Edward!"

Joseph was already farther down the staircase, his free hand stretching up toward the spirit photographer. Moody extended his arm—he could not quite reach Joseph Winter.

Then at last their fingers touched, and Joseph's hand inched forward.

"Joseph—" Moody said, his feet unfreezing. "How . . . how did you know?"

The match's light cast a menacing glow over Joseph's face.

"This is not my first escape," Joseph replied. "And this is not my first time running from the law."

XI

I T HAD BEEN eighteen long years since his seclusion in the passage, but for Joseph the memory was as clear as if it had all happened the day before. For three days Joseph had remained in that dark, narrow passage, while the advertisements for his reward ran in the faraway southern papers. "Very dark, with a surprisingly narrow nose," one of them had read, "and of remarkable intelligence for a negro."

Three days in absolute darkness, save for a few thin cracks of light. Mrs. Lovejoy had brought him food, and a bucket, and a small canteen of water, which he drank from sparingly. For the most part, he remained still—crouched and hugging his knees on the steps, or lying flat on the floorboards where the passage led to the secret panel on the second floor. Sometimes though, the restlessness had surmounted him, and at night, when he was sure that all people had gone from the store, he would pace the pathway of the passage. Up the steps and down the steps, along the interior floorboards of the second floor and the basement . . . up and down and back and forth, like a bewildered animal trapped within the walls. It was not until the third day, after sparing replenishments from Mrs. Lovejoy, that another woman came to lead him from the place. Not only did the light of the lantern blind him when she opened the passage, but she herself was a vision—a flaming angel from Holy Scripture. She was incandescently beautiful, and she held his hand as he crept out from his hole. Her touch gave him the strength that he needed to continue, and yet he never learned her name.

To his surprise, the woman revealed yet another passage connected to the one he had been in—a tunnel, hidden by another false door that led underground, into blackness. He had never expected to be in this tunnel again— to smell its dampness, feel its walls, hear the echoes he had fled from. But now, here he was, this time with Edward Moody, on an escape that was not so different.

Once underground, the tunnel widened considerably, though it was so dark that Joseph and Moody could only sense this by feeling. The walls and ceiling of the tunnel were formed from hard, packed earth, as was the dirt floor beneath them. Carriage wheels creaked and horse hooves clapped above their heads. The sounds were muffled yet distinct.

"We are beneath Washington Street," Moody said.

"Indeed," Joseph replied. "We are crossing it."

Joseph and Moody soon emerged in the dusty basement of Smith's Apothecary—the building across from Mrs. Lovejoy's that had been vacant since the end of the war. Upstairs, on the first floor, the grimy windows of the building's storefront provided a camouflaged screen from which the two fugitives could look out. One or two of the panes were broken, letting in the noise of the street.

Garrett's shiny black brougham, with its burnished brass trim, was parked directly in front of them.

"I told you," Moody said, "It is Garrett. He has come to witness my arrest."

Joseph continued to peer through the windows.

"There's something more to it than that," he said.

The police carriages remained parked across the street at Mrs. Lovejoy's, and inside Garrett's carriage there were two silhouettes. Neither of the figures showed any sign of motion until a plainclothes man, rather young and with a moustache, came out from Mrs. Lovejoy's and crossed the street.

The man circled around the rear of Garrett's carriage and—

Looked straight at Joseph Winter.

Or, rather, the dirty window.

Had they been discovered? The man's gaze lingered. He could not have been looking at his own reflection.

Then the man turned his back, and addressed the other men inside the carriage.

"Senator Garrett—" he said, "I'm afraid there is a complication."

Garrett's companion leaned forward.

"What sort of complication?" he asked.

"Well," the young man answered, "Mr. Moody seems to have—"

He paused, and Garrett's companion bent closer toward him.

"Yes?" the other man said. "Moody seems to have . . . ?"

"Vanished."

"Vanished? Bolles, what on earth are you talking about?"

"The man has vanished. He was scheduled to see a Mr. Bronson for a picture—we confirmed the time with Mr. Bronson himself. Moody was in the gallery. The proprietress led us up the stairs. The door was locked from the inside, and . . ."

"And?"

"And he vanished."

"Of all the nonsense!" the man in the carriage exclaimed. "We've not let our eyes off the front of that store since you entered. Are there no back stairwells? Alleyways? Windows, for heavens sake?"

"None, sir. And all of the gallery windows were locked from within."

"Have you scoured the room for closets? Loose floorboards? The scoundrel may still be hiding."

"We have, sir, and I am sorry. Mr. Moody is simply . . . gone."

The gentleman opposite Garrett struck his cane hard on the floor of the carriage.

"So you don't have the man," Garrett said, "but you do have access to the gallery."

"We do."

"Unlimited?"

The man nodded.

"Then Mr. Dovehouse and I can still make our inspection."

"You can, sir. My men have not yet begun the search for evidence, and are awaiting my orders outside the gallery."

The young man opened the carriage door for the senator, and all three men crossed the street.

"So," Joseph said, "Senator Garrett has made his own private arrangements with the police."

"Search as they will," Moody responded. "They will not find the negative."

And he held his hand to the breast of his coat, where Isabelle's likeness was hidden.

"Were it not for you," Moody said, "I'd have been forced to surrender."

But to Joseph it seemed Edward Moody had already surrendered. Not to him or to the police or to any other man, but to the power of the negative and all that the negative represented.

"Darkness is at work here," Joseph said. "It is my duty to counter it."

The two men waited in the gloom—the filth of the place was staggering. A rat scurried by, followed by two others. Eventually the carriages and their men would depart.

"We must remain here until nightfall," Moody said. "I've had a round or two with them before. There are conspiracies against me, and these men have been persistent. There's no telling when they will go, but when they do we'll ride out to see Fanny Van Wyck. She has had qualms with me in the past, but—"

"Qualms?" Joseph asked.

"Yes, qualms. It will not take you long to understand that Fanny has little tolerance for . . . our kind."

The sun was not long in setting, for Inspector Bolles had come to make his arrest late in the day. Moody and Joseph watched from the windows until the carriages departed. Then, as the last line of sunlight disappeared, they heard something sounding in the basement. Footsteps—soft footsteps—were coming up the steps. The room had grown dark. It was difficult to see—

"Ah," Mrs. Lovejoy said. "Thank heavens you are safe."

She offered them two of her strongest horses, which she kept in the stables behind the Old South Meeting House. She'd take them there later, when it would be much safer to leave the city—on horseback, she said, as the police would be watching every hackney cab and public vehicle.

THAT EVENING THERE was a great white moon in the sky, lighting Mrs. Lovejoy's way as she returned to her store. By the time she finished retracing her steps from the stables, Joseph and Moody would be out of the central district, nearing the outskirts of the city. The night was warm, yet Mrs. Lovejoy shivered. It had been many years since she had aided in an escape, and her own ghosts seemed to have come back.

Inside the store, the glow of silver bestowed strange greetings—the mouths of vases, cups, and teapots stretching and groaning in the blue light of the moon. Mrs. Lovejoy might have gone to her nearby apartments straightaway, but she would secure the store once more before retiring.

No lamps were necessary, as the moon provided sufficient light, and besides, she wouldn't stay in the store too much longer. A quick check to ensure that the lids of the music boxes were closed, and that the fine cutlery was lined up and on proper display for the morning. There was no pressing need for her to return upstairs that night—it would require days, rather than hours, to make the gallery presentable again. The police had spared no effort in turning Mr. Moody's workplace upside down, and Mrs. Lovejoy would decide how to deal with it in the morning.

But then there was the noise.

It was a muffled thud above her head—not unusual, since the building was old, and had a character of its own. But then the sound came again, and Mrs. Lovejoy held her breath. Perhaps Mr. Moody and Mr. Winter had returned . . .

Unlikely, she thought. She had loaned them the horses, and plenty of money, and they had been anxious to get on their way. Still, she knew there was this business about the negative, and maybe they had returned, for some reason, through the tunnel.

The building remained quiet as Mrs. Lovejoy ascended the steps.

"Mr. Moody—Mr. Winter. Is that you?"

The gallery door was unlocked, as Mrs. Lovejoy had left it earlier, and moonlight streamed in upon the cheerless sitters in their picture frames. One of Mr. Moody's finest pieces, the portrait of Mrs. Bobbin with her deceased husband, glowed with pronounced sadness—the face of a widowed bride. The spirits kept close watch over that room. The police had left it in such disarray.

Then the smell hit her, and she recognized it immediately—a hideous odor that rose from a faraway place within her memory. It was the smell of moist tobacco, almost vinegary in its wetness, reeking with traces of whiskey and other things sour on the breath.

A ghastly face flashed inside her head.

It did not take her eyes long to fully adjust to the darkness, and in the dull moonlight the spirits' faces grimaced. He had heard her approaching, and so he was already standing near the door—his enormous, hulking figure towering over her like a demon.

"Still moving out niggers, after all these years," he said.

And he spit a stream of tobacco on the floor.

Mrs. Lovejoy's mouth tightened as her face retracted from his breath.

"Leave my building this instant," she demanded.

But the brute arm rose above her, and the hand struck her hard in the face. The old woman reached out to steady herself, but then fell to the ground, unconscious.

XII

FANNY VAN WYCK lived in an old farmhouse near Concord, and was renowned as the medium for the *Banner of Light*'s "Message Department"— a popular section of the paper devoted to publishing spirit-messages from the dead. Since the start of the *Banner* nearly twenty years earlier, she had been presiding over large gatherings in the paper's ample offices. "The many invisible guests of these 'Spirit Circles,'" one journalist noted, "throng the *Banner*'s rooms, which the editors of the paper open free to public crowds."

The idea for the Spirit Circles had come from Fanny herself, who suggested that the *Banner*'s editors provide a venue for her spiritual pronouncements. "And there, as opportunity permits," another journalist wrote, "the spirits pour forth, through the entranced organism of Miss Van Wyck: the tales of their earthly lives, their vices and errors, their bitter lamentation for time misspent, and messages of love and consolation to absent friends." Fanny was known for performing all of this with such great voice, tone, and gesture, that witnesses "readily persuaded themselves that they were in the actual presence of the various characters."

While the *Banner*'s Spirit Circles were free and open to the public, subscriptions to the *Banner* were three dollars per year, and so those who had a financial stake in the life of the paper regarded Fanny and her Circles as instrumental. During the war, Fanny's republished messages from dead soldiers had become so prolific that the *Banner* couldn't print enough copies to meet the demand—proof that the Circles exercised not only great influence over the *Banner's* readership, but over the economic sustainability of the paper itself.

It was a sorry day for the *Banner* when an infirmity of the legs—something that Fanny had suffered with since childhood—finally prevented the famous medium from traveling into Boston. After the war, she began holding much smaller séances in her home—a change that forced Luther Colby, the *Banner*'s editor-in-chief, to dispatch reporters to cover these more intimate "circles." In its apology for the suspension of the Spirit Circles in Boston, the *Banner* had assured its readers that the community had not lost its most vital medium: "Rarely can any mortal say more truthfully than she," the *Banner* wrote, "that their burden is greater than they can bear."

> *Seemingly her spirit is held to the body mostly by the sympathy and aid of other spirits—on the two sides of the separating veil. Thus frail, burdened, and saddened is the instrument for clear, strong, forcible, and correct enunciations. Who wields the instrument? Frail Miss Van Wyck alone? Let common sense make the answer.*

Fanny's house lay in a great meadow of lush, lilting grass—a field so vast that the house's windows appeared as mere stars to nighttime visitors. On the north side, the house was protected by fine, old-growth timber, and on the south side the blue grass swayed and stood guard over the main approach. Restless loons and wood ducks sung the only lullaby of this place, sometimes aided by the lone cow that freely roamed the flat fields of Fanny's property. The small apple orchard not far from the house hadn't produced fruit for two generations—it was, as Fanny's grandmother used to say, "disobedient."

Fanny lived alone in the house, save for an old farmhand named Eli. Fanny's father had taken him in years ago because people used to say that he was "queer." The farm itself being dead, Eli had in recent decades become the only escort to Fanny's guests, guiding them from the house's large, spare entryway to Fanny's more intimate parlor.

When Joseph and Moody arrived, it was indeed Eli who answered the door. They stated their business, and he disappeared for some time before returning to let them in. He said not a word as he led them down a hall toward the part of the house where Fanny's parlor was situated. The taper he carried illuminated pictures on the walls—faded seascapes, etchings of birds, and silhouettes of Fanny's ancestors.

Then at last the group arrived at a closed door. Eli knocked, and a voice within called "Enter."

Joseph was initially surprised at Fanny's appearance. There she was, in all her petite splendor, seated at a table with a dressing gown wrapped around her. Having read her "voice" in the "Message Department" for years, he had expected a large woman, with a powerful body and a thick neck from which would flow stentorian commands. But sitting there, with her two small hands upon the massive table, Fanny was much more finch than hawk—an elf with black eyes and a beak.

"So, Moody," she said as the photographer took his seat before her, "still up to your old games I see. What do you mean bothering me at this hour?"

From behind Fanny, a taxidermy squirrel interrogated the visitors, its eyes as black and glassy as the medium's.

"It has been many years, Fanny," Moody replied. "Our spirit friends have taken good care of me."

"They have done nothing of the sort!" Fanny said. "I can hardly go a week without someone bringing me one of those spirit pictures. You are doing unkind things, Moody . . . unkind things."

No skin cracked around Fanny's mouth as she spoke, for her face was as porcelain-like as a doll's. That was one of the strangest things about Fanny Van Wyck—in the dark she seemed no more than a child, while in the light one might have mistaken her for an old woman.

"But I must confess," she continued quietly, "that every now and then, one of them—"

And she paused, looking about the room.

"That now and then, one of them . . . cries out to me. I once told you that you possess some powers as a medium."

Moody nodded.

"So I will take this opportunity to chastise you once again for abusing your most precious gift."

"The spirits," Moody said. "You know as well as I that we cannot control when or to whom they choose to appear."

"And you know as well as I," Fanny glared, "that spirit appearances are sacred, and no earthly being should be tampering with them!"

Moody bowed his head. He had never formally "confessed" to Fanny, but the mood between them had always seemed to be one of complete disclosure.

"And you—" Fanny said, turning abruptly toward Joseph. "I see you've come here for the same reasons. You don't own the answers—yours are the same as his."

Joseph remained silent. He did not want to provoke the medium.

"Fanny," Moody said, "I am in need of your assistance."

Fanny raised a thin eyebrow and spread her claw-like fingers on the table. The air was close about Joseph and Moody, and the portraits of Fanny's ancestors scowled down on them.

"I need you to tell me . . ."

"Hand me the photograph," she said.

"Yes," Moody said, removing the negative from his coat. "As I'm sure you've already gathered, my questions have to do with—the woman."

Fanny took the case from Moody, removed the negative, and held it up to the lamp. Then, with no trace of a ripple in her voice, she said:

"Ah, Edward Moody—you've finally met your match."

Fanny studied the negative, tilting it back and forth so as to scrutinize it in varying shades of light.

"Your people," she said, glancing at Joseph, "their cries are amongst the most pitiful coming from the spirit world. I have heard them, over and over again. They cry, for there are no great reasons for them to stop."

There was sadness in Fanny's voice. Perhaps it was a genuine sign of her sympathy.

"This woman is crying out," Fanny said. "Crying out for justice. There is great sorrow here—anger too—and her cries are loud."

"Crying!" Moody exclaimed.

Then, collecting himself, he asked calmly:

"What happened to her? Where did she go?"

But Fanny did not answer him. She stood up, holding the negative.

"Give me a moment," she said.

And she moved out from behind the table.

"But—"

"Please, Moody!"

Her shout silenced the spirit photographer—a wicked mother scolding a child. Was she moving toward the door? Would she leave with the negative? Moody was about to stand up.

Then Joseph set his hand firmly on Moody's arm.

"Edward," Joseph whispered, "she will not leave the room."

"How can you be certain?"

"I am certain."

Indeed, Fanny was not making for the door, but rather walking ever so slowly toward the other side of the room. As she retreated from the table, the walls of the parlor stretched, and the two men had the sense that Fanny was traveling a great distance. The ticks of the grandfather clock resounded steadily, though the swing of the pendulum remained hidden behind its case. There was something wrong about the clock—while the hour was correct, the moon dial above its face displayed a tall ship in the sunlight.

"She is—" Moody said.

"Yes, she is trying to reach the spirit."

"It's not right," Moody returned. "It is unusual for her to leave the table."

Fanny appeared far away to them now, and shuddered with barely perceptible tremors. The clock hands descended, but the hour's progress remained slow. Fanny lingered beyond their reach as time's passage seemed to fail.

Then the sound of papers fluttering sang throughout the room, though none of the windows were open, and there were no papers anywhere to be seen. The medium turned and faced them.

"It's as I have always told you," she said, "but you refuse to listen."

Her eyes were bright black gems, and soon she was back at the table.

"You refuse to listen, even when they speak. Your tricks, Edward Moody—your tricks! This woman . . . the spirits. You have stirred up great anger. There is great anger coming from this spirit—and pain. The pain is . . ."

Fanny released the negative onto the table, and leaned forward as if losing her balance. Before falling, however, she inched back into her chair. Then Joseph and Moody heard a sound unlike any they had ever heard before. It was guttural—something between a low growl and a moan—and it vibrated uncomfortably in their ears.

The strange groan came from Fanny, as her lips quivered in the flickering light.

"The spirit—" she rasped. "The spirit—"

Then she moaned again, louder this time, before collapsing deeper in her chair.

"I see now—she cannot tell you," Fanny said. "She . . . she cannot speak!"

Fanny's hands pressed the table.

"She wants to say that she is not here. No, she is not here. She is . . . she cannot speak."

"Who cannot speak?" Moody demanded. "Who?"

"It is the girl," Fanny said. "It is the girl who cannot speak."

"Isabelle!" Moody gasped. "Isabelle, is it you to whom we speak?"

Fanny began weeping.

"Isabelle!" Moody repeated.

But Fanny's mouth remained closed, her lips curled inward as her tiny body shook with muffled cries.

Beside Fanny, not far from the lamp, was a black slate and a white piece of chalk. Joseph extended his arm across the table and pushed the chalk and the slate toward her.

"Where are you?" Moody said. "Why did you leave?"

Fanny stopped shivering, and took the chalk in her hand. She was no longer whimpering, but sitting erect, the front of her body now close to the table.

The chalk made painful screeches as Fanny scrawled on the slate.

NO

"No?" Moody said. "Are you not here?"

And then he added:

"Have you not returned to me—my love?"

Again, Fanny scrawled the two terrible letters.

NO

"The pain," Fanny whispered. "It is the pain of your silence. Your suffering—your sacrifice. Tell him. You must tell him what he wants to know."

Then Fanny's hand moved to the center of the slate. Again she wrote the two letters, but this time with something more.

NO—I HAV RETURND.

"You have returned," Moody said. "You have returned."

And again, the words were dry within his throat:

"You have returned."

Silver lines of tears moistened the base of Moody's eyes, while Joseph felt his own muscles tighten.

"No," Joseph said. "This is not right."

An owl-like shriek blared from the squirrel behind Fanny. Outside, the wind combed through the meadow's pliant grass; the cow moaned once . . . a tree branch snapped and fell.

Then the swirl of the room came to a stop, as Fanny opened her eyes, and looked at them.

"*Find her.*"

Moody, Joseph, and Fanny remained quiet, until Moody finally mumbled: "Find her—find her where?"

But Fanny did not reply.

"I am weak—" she said, rising. "And now I must retire."

Moody nodded, and as if by summons, Eli appeared in the parlor.

"You are welcome to stay the night," Fanny said, "but I will not consent to that photograph remaining in this house. Eli will show you to the barn, where there are comfortable-enough beds of straw, and room for both your horses."

HOURS LATER, JOSEPH Winter finds himself standing before a great field of sugarcane, the tall green blades waving back and forth in strange unison. As they bend, the blades rub against one another, gently, like saws. The air is heavy; the smell of the earth strong and humid. Joseph's body grows hot, for there is no doubt about where he is.

But there is no one else here this time—no fellow workers, no overseer. No one at the edge of the long field behind him, poised near the trees with a gun. There are not even any buildings nearby to remind him of others. There is just the sugarcane swaying languidly in the wind, bending away from him as if it were crying.

He is not too close to the cane, maybe a hundred feet away, and so the entire breadth of that tall, green ocean spreads its waves out before him. The cane rolls, stopping abruptly in front of him where the flat ground meets its borders.

He sees her the moment she appears.

She is dressed in gauzy material—white—not the working clothes of a laborer. And her head is uncovered, her black hair loose and rippling over her shoulders, as undulous as the cane fronds themselves.

It is her—he is sure of it. The face more beautiful than he remembers.

She raises an arm and he walks toward her. Then she turns her back to him and disappears. The cane has swallowed her. She is lost to the billowing green folds.

There is a swath cut away from the edge of the cane, right at the place where she had been standing, and upon reaching it he can now see that it narrows into a kind of path. He steps into it and walks along, the cane forming dense green walls on either side of him. Then he spots her again—ahead of him in the cane, her dark eyes beckoning him to follow.

It had not been like this the last time.

The feeling of her closeness—the closeness of freedom—is so great, that he almost whispers her name aloud.

But he does not know her name. He never learned her name.

At points the surrounding cane stalks are so thick that their leaves arch together above him and form an interlaced canopy. Even in the darkness of this impenetrable jungle, he can still see her ahead of him—always ahead of him, never close enough to approach.

He continues through the sugarcane, curling his shoulders inward to avoid the sharp branches and blades. He walks for what seems like miles, the air growing ever hotter as he moves on.

Up ahead, there is a shock of light where the path through the sugarcane ends. He runs toward this opening, which at last leaves him standing in front of a long stretch of land. The land fans out in all directions before him, extending toward the banks of a mighty river. The crystalline reflections off the water almost blind him, and amidst those diamond-like flashes, she stands.

Now he will go to her. She will save him.

He tries to lift one foot, then the other, but neither moves. They are rooted in place as if the mud has sucked his boots to the ground. He struggles to lift his legs, but remains anchored in place. He looks down: heavy chains are binding his ankles.

Why is she so far away?

Then he hears the hounds, and the thunder of a horse's gallop. The crashing of stalks, and the beat of heavy footsteps. An unbearable blast of heat washes over him. He gasps for air. And in the heat, a terrible pair of hands grabs his shoulders.

The horses are whinnying all around him, their black hooves scraping the earth.

He cries out, and thrashes his arms, but the hands are firm upon him. He cannot move his feet, and he cannot escape the hands.

"Joseph!" a voice yells.

And again—"Joseph!"

He cannot shake off these hands of fire—the hands are determined to keep him.

Then a third time: "Joseph!"

JOSEPH OPENED HIS eyes to see Edward Moody. All four sides of the barn were ablaze with fire, and the horses were screaming in their stalls.

"Someone has bolted us in!" Moody yelled.

So—it had not been her after all.

Still dazed, Joseph jumped to his feet, and grabbed the beam that was securing the doors of the stalls. Moody seized the beam's other end, and hugged it close to his side. *Could such a thing even penetrate these walls?* The smoke was thick and gathering all around them.

Moody motioned his head toward the farther end of the barn. He was sweating, and clenching his teeth.

"Over there, I think—" he said, struggling to move the beam. There was no telling how long Moody had been awake.

Then the stall doors swung and crashed, and one of the horses broke free. The horse circled furiously in the center of the barn.

"He is blocking the way!" Moody hollered. "I cannot—"

And again he was cut short, this time by something—impossible. The horse had let out a terrified scream and charged through one of the burning walls.

Now there was an opening in the blaze . . . vaguely discernible through the smoke.

The other horse, as deranged as the first, stood inexplicably still in its stall. It brayed and heaved as the smoke continued to gather, its muscles rippling beneath its sweat-soaked coat.

Joseph dropped the beam and dashed to secure the stall door.

"Take the horse," Joseph said. "He will charge through the opening as soon as I release him."

Moody hesitated.

"I cannot leave you."

But there was no time.

"Go!" Joseph shouted. "I will meet you on the other side."

Moody entered the stall and climbed upon the animal. Then Joseph yanked open the unsecured door, and the horse leapt for the gap in the fire.

Moody tugged the reins. The horse screamed and wrenched its neck.

"I will not leave you!" Moody shouted.

Joseph grabbed ahold of the saddle and lifted himself up onto the horse. The smoke had become so dense that they could barely see their escape. They hurtled through the opening—beams and boards crackling all around them—crossing over into something that washed over them like a dream. A burst of cool air . . . a star-studded sky. The drooping grass had collected its dew.

They had not even cleared the heat of the fire when they saw him. He was mounted atop an enormous black horse. The fire's glow was absorbing a circle of the darkness, but he sat just beyond the edge of it, waiting. He was one with the horse, tall and unmoving—a misshapen monster, gathered up in the gloom.

The rider's horse snorted, then began a slow trot toward them.

"Go," Joseph whispered.

Moody gave a kick, and they galloped toward the road. The rider followed, his horse panting as it increased to a steady charge.

"Go!" Joseph repeated, louder this time.

He was holding onto Moody, but also fumbling with his sleeve.

"Who is the man?" Moody said.

But Joseph did not answer. He now held a derringer in his hand.

Behind them, the rider's steed was heaving and blowing, its breath growing louder as it gained ground with great speed. Moody urged their horse on—it was all that he could do—as Joseph gripped the handle of his gun.

The barrel gleamed in the moonlight. Joseph turned and prepared to shoot.

And then—

Silence. A shadow. Or no shadow left at all.

Perhaps it was a trick of the nighttime . . . one of those late summer illusions that belonged to another realm. More distant now, the barn burned in Joseph's vision, and the dark pursuer had gone.

"Is he gaining?" Moody asked.

Joseph looked through the gloom into the trees.

"Is he gaining?"

The meadow's edges would not reveal the man. The trees kept secret what they had seen.

"He's disappeared," Joseph said. "But for the life of me—do not stop!"

Moody kicked again . . . and away they dashed through the endless, enveloping countryside. They spoke little as the moonlight guided their way. Moody wondered about Fanny—had the rider gone to ravage the house first? Unless . . . Fanny. Could she ever have betrayed him like that?

They traveled at full tilt for nearly an hour, stopping only when they had gone as far as Westborough. There, the old inn leaned—still asleep and quiet—offering its porch as a place to dismount and rest.

"It is not safe to stay here," Joseph said. "The sun will be up soon, and we now know that we're being hunted."

"But how—" Moody said.

"These men, they have their ways. I know them—they hunt. That was no man of the law. It's now clear that they are not trying to detain you. They will not stop until you—and that negative—have been destroyed."

"Garrett—" Moody said.

"Again, as I told you . . . the spirit's power over him is great. For him to go to such lengths to destroy the negative—"

"If Garrett harmed her," Moody sputtered, "if he had anything to do with her—"

"Calm yourself, Edward," Joseph replied. "You have no power here—and we must go. We are in danger as long as we are within Garrett's reach."

Moody considered Joseph. There was a strange knowingness to everything he said.

"Joseph . . . I am the fugitive here. You should not put your own freedom at risk."

Joseph's expression darkened, and he glared at Moody with an almost malevolent eye.

"I am not doing it for you," Joseph said. "You are not the only man who loved her."

Moody blinked, bewildered, as if everything he had ever believed in turned untrue.

"You—" he gasped. "Joseph, you—"

"Yes, Edward. I knew Isabelle . . . and I loved her too. And now I finally know, after many years of searching, where I can find her again."

**Newsletter of the American Institute for
the Encouragement of Science and Invention**
New York, New York
Wednesday, July 27, 1870

*THE MEMBERS OF the Institute's Photographic Section, Boston
Branch, have sent word regarding the "spirit photographs" that have for
some years been making appearances in that city. Last week, Marshall
Hinckley, our esteemed colleague in Boston who is known for his photographic lectures to the New York and Washington branches, reported
that the police have at last moved forward with their case against Edward
Moody, the photographer whose name many will recognize as the Spiritualist behind these charades. Mr. Hinckley informed us that the police
have formally charged Mr. Moody with multiple counts of fraud and larceny, crimes for which he will stand before a jury of his peers. This is a
great victory for all men of science, with only one problem remaining:
Moody is nowhere to be found. Moody, whose gallery resides above Mrs.
Lovejoy's Silver Emporium at 258 Washington Street, Boston, was al-
legedly present in the gallery when Inspector Montgomery Bolles, of the
Boston Police Department, and his officers arrived to arrest him, but
upon entering the rooms where this imposter makes his photographs, the
police found that he had "vanished into thin air." It has been suggested
that Mr. Moody was not, in fact, on the premises when the police arrived,
but already somewhere else altogether, having been forewarned by one
of hundreds in the loathsome network of Spiritualists whose eyes are
on constant watch. Moody is believed to have fled the city with his ac-
complice, a negro who goes by the name of Joseph Winter. The search
for Moody continues in the environs of Boston, and the Federal authorities have also been informed, in the event that he has left the state.*

BOOK II
VISION

Banner of Light

Boston, Massachusetts

Saturday, July 23, 1870

From "THE MESSAGE DEPARTMENT"

Through the instrumentality of Miss Fanny Van Wyck

LITTLE VICTORIA

MA'AM, IF YOU please, I'd like to send some word to my old massa, George Burgess. He's in Louisiana—Orville. [Can you spell the name of the place?] Ma'am, I can't. I wants him to know that twelve of us are here in the spirit-land—twelve that once belonged to him. We are happy and free—twelve of us are here. I wants him to know, ma'am, when he comes here we'll meet him, and old missus too. [You mean twelve of you once in bondage are now all free together?] Yes, ma'am, that's what I mean.

Massa George's brother Edward is in the spirit-land too, and he says tell Massa George he wants to speak; tell Massa George he was shot at Pillow and that's why he never come back. [Fort Pillow?] Yes, ma'am, that's what it was.

[Say all you wish to say.] I've got heaps to say, ma'am, but I . . . He knows about this, ma'am. He knows. [What does he know?] Who I am and who I belong to. He knows. [What was your name?] Vic—. Little Victoria. [How old were you?] Don't know; I reckon I was ten. He knows about this—he knows.

[Say anything you think will make him remember you.] He will remember me—he will.

XIII

"WELL, SHE'S COME back to haunt him. It's obvious, isn't it?" Hearing this, Elizabeth blinked out of her reverie and glanced at the faces that surrounded her. She had somehow forgotten about the three other women in her drawing room—forgotten that they had all just dined together, and that she was, in that moment, their hostess. The dinner had been interminable, with a guest list larger than usual: John and Constance Merriwhether; Senators Cragin and Patterson, both of New Hampshire, with their wives; and Dovehouse—who had steadfastly remained at Garrett's side since a day or two after the photograph.

Playing hostess at a time like this, she thought. Isabelle had come back. It was all coming back. But Garrett would not hear of canceling the engagement. And so there she found herself, a prisoner in her own house, stationed before a small tribunal of women after dinner.

But which one of them had said it? Which one of them had dared mention what had so purposefully come back?

Then her friend Constance Merriwhether continued:

"The negroes have been making all kinds of noise lately—from the other side, I mean."

Ah, it was Constance. Of course it had been Constance, who had probably been talking about spirits for the past several minutes. Elizabeth's mind had wandered far out of the room by then, as it had during most of their dinner.

"Oh, yes," Constance continued, "they've become a great deal noisier—more vocal, you might say. And rightly so, I suppose. It's as if their freedom has given them a new kind of voice. They've come back to communicate with their old masters, perhaps even to chastise them for their wrongdoings."

"Perhaps?" Elena Cragin responded. " I think you're being much too kind. The negro spirits—or at the very least, these mediums who claim to conduct them—seem more interested in reckoning. The messages are retributive."

"Retributive?" Constance questioned.

"Yes, retributive," Lucretia Patterson emphasized. For both Lucretia Patterson and Elena Cragin were married to Republicans who were every bit as radical as Garrett.

"The negro spirits are angry," Lucretia continued. "They are angry with the way that the aftermath of the war has unfolded. They are speaking out in order to hold their old masters accountable. These ghosts—if such they be— are the ghosts of moral retribution."

"It's more than mere chastisement, dear Constance," Elena added. "The spirits are *exposing* their old masters for the vile hypocrites they've always been. These southerners—their immorality has gone unpunished for nearly two centuries. There's vengeance in the cries of these spirits—not just for themselves but for the poor souls who are still alive."

Constance's face revealed some discomfort. She never would have taken it that far. Even the most vociferous and admonishing of the spirits had always seemed peaceable and forgiving.

"Do you have any idea what's going on down there?" Lucretia said.

And then, not waiting for Constance's answer, she whispered:

"They are defiling black women throughout the South every day. Whipping and murdering their husbands. Beating their children. Chasing whole families into the woods and burning their houses to the ground."

"The reports from Louisiana are particularly horrific," Elena said. "I've seen them on Aaron's desk. He doesn't know I've seen them, but I have. The ones that they've decided not to make public. Surely, Elizabeth, you've seen some of these too."

"No," Elizabeth returned. "James rarely leaves his work unattended."

"And the women," Lucretia went on, "they can't rightly dissuade their husbands from going to the polls and voting the Republican ticket, as they have every right to do. But they know—as do their husbands—that retaliation from the Klan is certain. Every night, mothers face the possibility of being dragged from their beds, and—"

Lucretia leaned in further toward the center of their circle.

"—*violated in front of their own children.*"

Constance gasped and drew herself back in her seat.

"Animals," Elena said. "And it does not stop with wives and mothers. Some of the reports indicate that the marauders have gone after the children too."

"This I had not heard," Elizabeth offered.

"Yes," Elena said bitterly. "The children."

Constance Merriwhether, even in the luxury of her Beacon Hill home, had not remained wholly ignorant of the recent surge in Ku Klux Klan atrocities—especially throughout the parts of the South where black voters turned out in the greatest numbers. But of such horrific crimes against women and children, Constance had certainly never heard. Elizabeth watched as her friend's cheeks flushed red. Constance had always been a bit naïve. It was difficult for even Elizabeth not to pity her.

"But Little Victoria . . ." Constance protested. "That sweet little spirit! She talked of being free and happy . . . of welcoming her old master in the spirit world."

Unexpectedly, Elizabeth's pity changed to anger.

"She talked of the unholy crime between her old master and her ruined mother," she said, "of which she was the unfortunate offspring!"

Constance Merriwhether, Elena Cragin, and Lucretia Patterson, all turned toward Elizabeth. She was herself surprised that she had voiced such a thing, and with such intemperate force. She had never—at least publicly—been guilty of an outburst, and up until that moment she had barely participated in the conversation. It was Constance—stupid Constance—who had been sold on the Spiritualists from the beginning. Constance understood so little of what went on beyond the borders of New England.

"I'm sorry," Elizabeth apologized. "But I find the negro messages rather distressing."

The women looked at her.

"I mean, insofar as they *are* messages."

Elizabeth paused there and retreated, for she had already said too much. These women, who all seemed to adore her on the surface, had been, in her mind, amongst her fiercest judges over the years. All of them had children, and had time and again prattled on about their little darlings while Elizabeth sat silent, as they knew she would be forced to do. No one had ever directly criticized her for her "condition," but listening to the maternal joys of others was a kind of indictment all the same. Through time she had grown to occupy a place of self-condemnation when coming face-to-face with these women. She had even troubled herself wondering if Elena Cragin, the proud mother of four, had ever considered her unworthy of being Senator Garrett's wife.

But what did they know—these Washington chatterboxes, with their husbands who devoted more time to their mistresses than they did to their own families. Elizabeth may have been childless, yes, but she understood the larger world, and had witnessed things that these women could never have imagined. What right, for example, had they to describe the sufferings of the negroes when their knowledge of life in the southern states extended no further than the pages of *Harper's*? That very week, in the *Banner of Light*, she had read of another negro spirit, speaking from the beyond. "How I hated the brute that had purchased me," the spirit said, "and how I strove to revenge myself! He inhabits a much darker sphere than I, and ages will elapse before he will see the light." There was a darkness to what the North had fought so valiantly against during the war; but it was a darkness so evil and so omnipotent that any attempt to surmount it had proven pure folly. These women could talk, and pretend to understand federal policy all they liked, but they would never be able to perceive what they were incapable of seeing.

Elizabeth had seen.

Of all the trips, that first trip down to the Beauregard plantation, when she was seven or eight years old, had left the most indelible impression upon her. Elizabeth's father was still doing business with his southern cousins back then, and he had taken the family down to Louisiana at the start of the sugar harvest. Of course, this was many years before the political crises of the 1850s, when the Whigs began dividing along sectional lines. The radical abolitionists had only started to murmur in those days, and her parents had yet to join their ranks.

The plantation house was smaller than one might have imagined for such a vast expanse of cane fields and oak trees. It was one of the old three-room Creole houses that an elder Beauregard had raised to include a brick-walled, aboveground basement. A magnificent veranda, which ran the full length of the front of the building, overlooked an inland road that traversed the land the French used to call "Terre-aux-Boeufs." But cane, rather than cattle, grazed freely over the land now, and from the veranda one could gaze out over the untamed marshes of St. Bernard. On this careless, open-aired porch the women fanned themselves in the shade, while the men remained out of sight, running the harvest and the business of sugar. Here, too, in the hazy gray shadows of the overhang, the women spent whole afternoons conversing in private.

One day, what looked like a little white boy ran by in front of the house, and his appearance immediately inspired an unsubtle exchange of knowing glances. His skin was fair—freckled even—and at first he seemed no different from any other boy of Elizabeth's age and station. But the young Elizabeth Beauregard had not yet learned that particular southern art of looking deeper—the same art that revealed certain irrefutable signs once you had learned *how* to look. You needed to study the planes of the face mostly, the women had said . . . the way the skin sloped away from the cheekbones, and how the eyelids fell just so. There was also the shape and the color of the eyes themselves, the waxy pallor of the skin, and the giveaway shade of the fingernails. In the North, there was no question that this little boy would have been white. In the South he was quite something else.

That's what these women sitting and talking on the porch knew . . . what they had come to pride themselves on knowing over the course of their lives. They had developed, out of a kind of social necessity, the uncanny ability to detect negro blood. That, and the ability to sniff out pregnancies before their announcements, and the exact length of gestations, which were also of great concern. Elizabeth remembered being curious as to how her mother had slipped into these discussions so effortlessly, adding to the observations of her southern cousins-in-law as if she herself were from the South. There was something mysterious she must have shared with these women, though Elizabeth did not know what it was. And so Elizabeth listened, her young ears attuned to the private rhythms of the veranda, following the lips of these genteel speakers and learning to see what they saw.

Of course, the hatred of these women for those of mixed race was extreme, and so whenever one was publicly whipped, and the whole population of the plantation was called out to witness it, there was a noticeable absence of the remorse and recoiling that a little girl might have expected from others. This was particularly true during Elizabeth's first visit to the plantation, when one of the victims—a light-skinned field worker whom the overseer had deemed "too slow"—was brought to an open area at the back of the house and forced to lie on the ground. It was the pretty one—the same one who had been smiling at little Elizabeth from around the porch corners all week— and she could not have been more than sixteen or seventeen years old. The overseer had forced her down and pulled her dress up to her neck, revealing the shocking nakedness of the young woman's amber stomach and thighs.

"Serves her right," Elizabeth heard one of the cousins remark. "Always nosing about instead of working, as she should be."

Elizabeth hid behind her father while it happened, though she could not help but peek around his coattails as the girl screamed in agony. How quickly the pretty face on the ground transformed . . . how monstrous and ghastly the distortion that Elizabeth would forever see. But as the whip lurched and cracked, and welts began to form on the girl's thighs, Elizabeth experienced a kind of unfamiliar pleasure, which even as an adult she would never quite fathom. It was not pleasure at the poor girl's suffering, but at the idea that *someone else* was experiencing the suffering. That someone else's body—not hers—had become the recipient of so much degradation. One might have described this as pure relief, but no, there was a misplaced sense of pleasure in it—the kind of pleasure a small child feels when a brother or sister receives a punishment instead. That girl on the ground might well have been someone else's sister, or Elizabeth's cousin, for all Elizabeth knew. Amongst the children who ran about and played on the plantation, there was no real awareness of who was related and who wasn't.

Elizabeth never forgot what she saw that day, nor her father's question to his cousin when the whipping was over:

"Was it necessary to punish this young woman so severely?"

"Oh yes," came the reply. "If I hadn't she would have done the same thing again tomorrow, and half the people on the plantation would have followed her example. The niggers would never do any work at all if they weren't afraid of being whipped."

Later that afternoon, before the mosquitoes had started their buzzing, the women refrained from referring to the incident—at least directly. There was more talk of the harvest, and of the younger Beauregards, who had gone off to school in New York. And there was even the requisite acknowledgement of "the insubordination of the niggers," which seemed to bring an edge of hostility to nearly every woman present. Only later, when she was older and had acquired more education, would Elizabeth realize that overt hatred of the "mulattoes" was something that southern gentility did not quite condone. Rather, her cousins and all of their kind would need to work out their despisal in a complexity of behaviors and verbal codes. Elizabeth's mother had certainly taken this truth back to Philadelphia, and had all but announced it to Elizabeth's father on the way home. "Their men seem to think themselves models of husbands and fathers," she had said. "But in reality, they live all in one house with their wives and their concubines."

And so for Elizabeth to listen to Elena Cragin or Lucretia Patterson speak of politics or ghosts, even in their justified passion, always seemed something of an exercise in patience. For she understood, in ways much deeper than they, that former peddlers of human flesh had so much more to fear should their unknown offspring decide to reveal themselves to the world. If those ghosts chose to shatter the comfort and silence of the grave, what avenue of denial would remain available for the guilty?

"I've heard, too," Elena Cragin said, "that the negroes have started appearing in the spirit photographs."

"And there will be more, you can be sure," Constance said, still somewhat discomfited, "if what you're telling me about the goings-on down south continues unabated and unpunished."

Elizabeth grew even more anxious than she had been all evening. The conversation was taking an unwelcome turn, and she could not wait to get these people out of her house.

"James has said time and again," she offered, "that nothing will really change down there unless the entire society is destroyed. We've done that militarily, but the cultural vestiges are alive as ever."

"They must *embrace* their wrongs," Lucretia Patterson declared. "It's as Mr. Dovehouse was saying earlier. They've not been held accountable by the government, and so the violence continues to erupt."

"If what you say is true though," Constance said, "it's a wonder to me that the women of the South can abide such barbarism."

Constance's comment seemed to encapsulate all that had gone wrong after the war.

"And just who do you think is sewing the hoods?" Elizabeth said.

The women all fell silent at this.

XIV

IN THE DINING room, the men sipped their brandy.

"It seemed a reasonable investment," John Merriwhether was proclaiming. "Indeed, one I couldn't in good conscience refuse."

"And you were right not to refuse it," Dovehouse added in support. "I think your investment in Mississippi land entirely wise. What the South needs most right now is northern capital—not negro voters and legislators."

"We have given them a voice!" Senator Cragin erupted.

"No," Dovehouse replied, "what you've given them is the hopeless *idea* of a voice that those damned rebels are determined to suppress—at any cost."

With the women out of the room, Dovehouse's restraint had died away. The five men faced one another like reluctant leaders at a negotiating table: Merriwhether and Dovehouse on one side, Senators Patterson and Cragin on the other, and Garrett in the chair at the head of the table, though his position was far from the middle.

"It is true," Senator Patterson said, "that northern capital is of the utmost importance in the South, but mainly insofar as it is *in support* of the negro, and not at his *expense*."

Garrett tensed, for he knew the storm that was about to follow.

"Pshaw!" Dovehouse said. "Policies of outright land grants for the negroes would be at the expense of no one but legitimate property owners. Mind you, I do not apologize for the rebels, and would have seen them all hung if anything else, but I tell you—the property rights of citizens in this country *must be respected*."

And he three times struck the surface of the table, emphasizing the importance of his last words.

"White citizens," Senator Cragin added testily.

"*Propertied* citizens," Dovehouse corrected. "If the negroes do not own property—yet—there is precious little the federal government should be doing about that. I am a citizen of this country and I am a man of property. The idea of giving free land to the negroes or anyone else insults the very principles upon which this nation was founded!"

During the past week or so, the intensity of the Moody situation had all but muted discussions of politics between Garrett and his old friend. But here was the same debate rearing its ugly head again—one of many that had put a strain on Garrett's friendship with Dovehouse in recent years. Yes, the negroes were free, Dovehouse liked to say, and needed a dependable means to earn their living. But let them work to earn that means, and learn the good habits of working men.

"It is certainly true," John Merriwhether continued in his own defense, "that no race of men has ever acquired a right to the soil with more vigorous exertion than the southern negroes. But I agree with Dovehouse—to allow them to receive land so easily would only encourage them in their idleness and unthrifty habits. For their own good, the intervention of northern investment will help them to learn that, like everyone else, they must pay for what they get."

"And I suppose you will be amenable to reselling this wonderful land to the negroes?" Cragin said. "At the appropriate time, eh? And at a price they can afford?"

"As long as the price is a fair one," Merriwhether said.

"Which is as it should be," Dovehouse added.

Senator Cragin slammed the table.

"But the freedmen have no capital! And never will, without what you insist on calling 'favors.' We've released four million persons from bondage, and have yet to settle on a practical plan for their welfare. How can you expect the freedmen to establish true independence when we give them nothing to start with?"

"Did our forefathers 'start with' something when they came here?" Dovehouse responded. "Were there patrons waiting for them on the shores of Massachusetts and Virginia, with gifts of land and money aplenty? No, I tell you—no! There were red-skinned savages and wild beasts—a wilderness of nothing out of which they eventually formed a civilization. And so it is the same for us all. Good men like Merriwhether here are investing in the South, helping to rebuild its economy, which in turn will help *rebuild this nation.* And when you get down to it, Cragin, we need to keep the cotton flowing. There is simply no getting around that."

"True," Senator Cragin admitted, "but there are more equitable ways of ensuring the cotton supply."

"But the negroes don't want to grow it!" Dovehouse fumed. "They prefer sowing corn and potatoes, and anything else that's *not* cotton. The idea! Turn the land over to the negroes, my friend, and the riches of the most fertile soil in the country will be squandered away before our very eyes."

At this, Senator Patterson leaned forward into the argument. Like Garrett, he was a man of carefully measured words.

"You say that free negro labor under good management can be made a source of profit for the employer. That is all well and good, and yes—the cotton is not to be overlooked. But by God, Dovehouse—they are hiring former overseers to supervise the blacks on their former plantations! They care nothing for how much flesh they work off the negro provided that it's converted into a good cash crop!"

"The old systems must be eradicated," Cragin said. "If they aren't, our cause—and the entire war—will have been for nothing."

"I have *always* been of the firm belief," Dovehouse said, "that abolition, and in turn the conversion of the South into a land of free enterprise, was of the utmost necessity with regard to the destiny of this nation. But what I cannot—nay, what I *will not*—ever condone, is the privileging of one group of citizens over another."

Dovehouse looked at Garrett. He would never insult his friend directly.

"It was madness for the party to try to legislate free land for the negroes."

"That is much more than we have ever done for white men," Merriwether added.

"White men have never been in chains," Garrett said.

They were the first words that Garrett had spoken since dinner, and his deep voice resounded like the groan of an iron bell. Like Elizabeth, he had allowed other preoccupations to claim his thoughts that evening, but the conversation, he could now tell, was on the verge of spinning out of control. He had heard these arguments time and time again. "Bringing *loyal Northern men* into harmonious terms with the *owners* of the soil," so the party line went, "would create perfect partnerships through which the application of negro labor would guarantee the peaceful pursuit of agriculture." The ingredients necessary for the economic recovery of the South—and the nation—were already within reach. Men of industry simply needed to make sure that the freedmen continued to work the land.

The room was quiet, the walls and guests awaiting Garrett's next words.

"Property," Garrett finally said. "The interests of sacred property . . . are combining, both openly and secretly, to keep the negro in a practical state of bondage. These interests—of which Merriwhether here has recently joined the ranks—pay the negro reluctantly, break his labor contracts, attempt to govern him by pistol and whip, hinder his education, destroy his schoolhouses, and in several states kill him and his representatives, leaving many others maimed for the rest of their lives. Do you know that they wanted to imprison a man for five years for stealing a pig? Yes, gentlemen—five years. Starve the man to death, and make sure that his family remains starving, and then imprison him for five years when he tries to steal his supper. Imprison him so that hundreds more already on the chain gang stand ready to welcome him . . . and all because he refuses to lie down like a dog and grow your cotton!"

And here Garrett paused to survey his audience—these gentlemen who had come to dine in his home.

"These landless, indigent negroes are being imprisoned, murdered, and mutilated by the thousands. And nothing—*nothing*—can reach and protect them but the vigorous, united arm of the government."

A moment of silence followed the senator's oration. Ah, Senators Cragin and Patterson thought . . . *that* was the James B. Garrett they knew, the Garrett who had come to power in the early fifties, and who had grown famous for condemning the South's attempts to block freedom in the territories. That Garrett—the vicious, unrelenting, abolitionist Garrett—had, in a way, been born during the crisis in Kansas. It was then that his speeches had brought him to the center of the national stage, and had earned him the respect of even the most radical abolitionists. "The House of Bondage stands erect," the young senator had declared, "clanking its chains on the open land of this free territory. Not in any common lust for power has this uncommon tragedy had its origin. The crime against Kansas is the *rape* of a virgin Territory . . . compelling the South into the hateful embrace of its harlot!"

No one could phrase it like Garrett—not even Thaddeus Stevens in the House. It wasn't for nothing that Longfellow, hearing him in those early days, had described him as "a cannoneer, ramming down cartridges." Senators Cragin and Patterson, along with the rest of the radical leadership, had been admiring Senator Garrett for close to twenty years. As they sat there in his dining room, seduced by his poignant treatise, they understood that the old codger had no intentions of slowing down.

But Garrett's triumphs—political and otherwise—had not been without their costs. Dovehouse for one had grown increasingly suspicious of his friend's reason, privately, and sometimes even publicly, observing that Garrett had "simply gone too far." Abolition and the progress of free labor were one thing; civil rights for the blacks quite another. And so when Johnson, in his State of the Union Address a few years earlier, had professed that the negroes "had shown a constant tendency to relapse into barbarism whenever left to their own devices," Dovehouse, almost in retaliation for his friend's fanaticism, had openly praised the president's speech. It was growing more and more useless, Dovehouse thought, to continue this conversation with the radicals, for Garrett and his cronies had become incurably biased against investors from the North. Of course, Dovehouse could have transformed the entire conversation that evening, being the only one at the table who remembered Garrett's political ghosts. But now was not the time to resurrect such things, so Dovehouse refrained from mentioning them.

THE HOUSE QUIETLY groaned, relieved that the guests had gone, as Elizabeth lay still beneath her bedclothes, and Garrett huffed and tossed at her side.

"The audacity," Garrett said. "Men like Merriwhether should know better. It is all for the damned profit. Dovehouse I understand, but Merriwhether . . ."

She did not even hear the end of his sentence. She could not stand the sound of his voice.

Elizabeth studied the contours of the ceiling—the many smiles and frowns in the plaster. She half listened to her husband as he raged on beside her. His passion would eventually subside.

"I have given over my entire life to this cause," he was saying, "and Merriwhether knows that—knows better than almost anyone else! Of course, he's not trying to work against me directly, but his participation in the scheme undermines everything I'm trying to do. The more profit they make, the less anyone will ever entertain the idea of giving *any* land to the negroes."

He was distracted. It was typical. He wasn't even thinking about her.

"Yes, James," Elizabeth said tiredly, "I know."

"A damned hypocrite," Garrett said. "Says he's for one thing, and does the other. The hypocrisy of it is what riles me most, Elizabeth. We need willing, honest men behind the effort, not opportunists who will change course for an extra dime. North as well as South are conspiring against the negro. The North is infected with hypocrisy."

She turned her gaze from the ceiling and considered her husband. There was his angry profile silhouetted against the windowpanes. Her disgust with him in that moment erased the renowned handsomeness observed by others. He of all people . . . talking of hypocrisy in their bed.

"The people's belief in you remains firm," she said. "No one will ever be able to accuse you of anything less than devotion."

XV

THE FADING MOON showered Joseph and Moody as they fled through the countryside, the night itself having become a ceaseless observer. Was the assassin still tracking them quietly from somewhere in the darkness, or had he abandoned his quarry for now? All around Joseph and Moody, a suspicious silence lurked, as if the trees were conspiring to hide something.

At Westborough, Joseph had picked a simple lock, and they had stolen a second horse from the stables at the inn. They would follow some of the horse trails, or even the train tracks where they could, taking care at all times to remain in the shadows. For Joseph the flight from Concord signaled another kind of journey—a journey that forced him to reevaluate everything he had ever believed in. He had spent years putting aside memories of the roots of the movement—the beginnings of the struggle that had torn the country apart. Now, being drawn back, he remembered how Senator Garrett had become the stuff of legend, and how the "Rape of Kansas" speech had placed Garrett at the center of the movement. That controversial path had continued, uninterrupted, through the first days of the war, when Garrett's advocacy of enlisting colored troops had made him unpopular. After the war ended, he had continued to press forward, inspiring leaders like Frederick Douglass to praise him as "one of our people's oldest and truest friends."

Yet here was Joseph's hero—the man whose very words had encouraged him to join the Union army—on a crazed path, trying to destroy him.

How could this be? Joseph still couldn't reconcile it—how a man of Garrett's significance could stoop to the level of a common criminal. Could Joseph and so many thousands of others have been wrong about him all these years? Could the unimpeachable Senator James B. Garrett be someone who had cloaked an eviler spirit in the gallant rhetoric of equality?

No—it could not be. To think of Senator Garrett as an imposter was to admit the bleakest defeat.

And yet, all signs pointed undeniably toward the senator's guilt. From the instant that Joseph had observed Garrett's reaction to the photograph, Joseph knew that there was much more to Garrett than his public image disclosed. Garrett was a man who was terrified of something—terrified of what the image of Isabelle represented to him. And so for Joseph the question around Garrett immediately became, what would the truth about Garrett's relationship with Isabelle reveal? Joseph wondered what could be at the heart of Garrett's fear . . . what secrets the senator must have had, what he needed to protect. But Joseph also held an intimate understanding of the nature of secrets, and so it was not very long before he had drawn his own conclusions.

These thoughts consumed Joseph as he and Moody sped through Connecticut, inching closer toward New Haven, where, outside the reach of the Boston Police, they would leave the horses behind and board a train. But there was yet another problem, and that problem was Edward Moody, who would expect nothing less than a full explanation. Joseph had been rash to reveal himself so soon after their flight, but he could not risk Moody disappearing. Joseph needed Moody as much as Moody needed him, and Joseph's love for Isabelle—unlike Moody's—did not blind him to that reality.

The train from New Haven pulled out of the station, its wheels beginning to churn with taunting irregularity. Joseph and Moody had secured a private compartment, which for the time being would provide them some safety.

Moody spoke in a low voice, his anger quite palpable.

"You will explain yourself."

"Yes . . ." Joseph said. "It is only fair that I do. Forgive me, Edward. I am not the man I said I was."

Moody's face displayed no surprise, for his mind had been turning too. He was the old suspicious Moody now, not the partner whom Joseph had saved from arrest. Joseph would need to tread carefully upon this ground. He would need to seduce Edward Moody all over again.

"You knew Isabelle—*my* Isabelle," Moody said. "I knew there was something ugly about this from the beginning."

Joseph raised a hand.

"It's true that I have been dishonest," he said. "But I see that you are a friend to me now. I did not know that when we met. I had marked you as my enemy, and I was determined to—"

He paused, for he would finally tell Moody the truth.

"I was determined to expose you."

But there were forces at work against them now . . . the same forces that had harmed Isabelle. Joseph and Moody needed to remain united against them; Moody needed to understand that.

"We must work together," Joseph said.

"Together!" Moody fumed. "What had she ever to do with a scoundrel like you?"

"I have been a scoundrel—yes. I have been a scoundrel with *you*. But I swear—Isabelle meant as much to me as she ever meant to you. The very idea of her kept me alive when I thought I might not go on."

Moody frowned, his face twisting with disgust. He would not sympathize with Joseph's truth . . . at least not yet.

"Listen to me," Joseph said. "This is no time to succumb to petty jealousies."

Moody glared at him.

"How dare you?" he said. "I could have you thrown out of this car."

"And I could have you thrown in jail," Joseph said.

There was silence, and Moody turned to look out the window. Was he turning over thoughts about how Joseph had been fooling him, from the start? The silliness of this partnership—a partnership between two confidence men! How could he have let himself believe that such a thing could ever work?

And what about the negative? What did Moody really believe about the negative?

The train had reached its full speed now, its great iron wheels grinding with a heavy steadiness beneath them. As they passed beyond New Haven, heading southwest toward Manhattan, a blanket of morning mists lifted itself from the procession of moving trees.

"Where are we going?" Moody finally said.

Joseph's voice was quiet.

"From New York we can board the Pittsburgh-Cincinnati line. Then we'll go on to St. Louis."

"St. Louis!" Moody exclaimed.

"The Cincinnati line provides a less conspicuous route to our destination."

"I did not know we had one," Moody said.

Moody would never be able to trust Joseph again, and none of this had been part of Joseph's plan. But there was still a chance. Joseph could still secure Moody's faith—if Edward Moody had any faith left.

"The man who tried to kill us . . ." Joseph said. "I knew him too."

"You . . ." Moody staggered. "You knew him?"

And then:

"To the devil with you."

"Listen to me, Edward—just listen. Yes, I did know him. But to him I was just another fugitive he could return for profit. I was running for my life, and that man was hunting me. Others hunted me too, but his drive was something . . . different. His name is Wilcox—or at least that's the name he went by then. He once sliced off the ear of a free negro. We all knew him."

Moody leaned forward.

"You knew this . . . this . . ."

"Demon," Joseph said. "He came very near to finding me once, when I was in hiding at Mrs. Lovejoy's."

And so Joseph began to recount the story of his escape: about his journey from New Orleans to St. Louis by steamboat, and eventually on to Boston, as a stowaway on a train.

"There were many who helped me along the way . . . a young priest in New Orleans . . . the conductors in St. Louis. But Boston was a mistake—my route was never supposed to take me there."

Joseph spoke of that night when his conductors had hidden him in the back of a wagon. They were transporting him to a safe house—farther north, outside St. Louis—but upon nearing the train depot, they had been forced to stop.

"The sheriff and some others had set up a blockade," Joseph said. "They were tearing apart the wagons in search of another family."

Joseph's conductors could not communicate with him; to do so would have meant instant discovery. So Joseph slipped out of the wagon. And then—

"At the very moment I crept from the wagon, another cart was rounding the bend. The driver was racing to meet one of the departing trains, and did not see the blockade in time to stop. He was transporting sugar, and when he veered from the road, the weight of the barrels caused the wagon to overturn. Some of the barrels cracked, and sugar spilled into the road. In the commotion that followed, I was able to crawl away."

It had been a miracle. Something one could only attribute to angels.

Joseph found safety in a nearby freight car that had been packed to capacity with cotton bales. Moments after Joseph had leapt through the open door, someone slid the door closed, and the train began to move.

"A day or two passed. The train slowed and sped up many times, and then finally came to a stop. When the doors opened I realized that it had reached its destination, but I did not move from my hiding place."

Eventually, Joseph jumped from the car and crawled beneath the train. There he remained hidden until he saw the second miracle . . . a white woman, finely dressed in silks and gloves, supervising the loading of a covered wagon. She oversaw two men who were carrying oblong, wooden boxes, and as the men stacked the boxes, the lady looked about. Hers were not movements that anyone would notice, but once the phantoms appeared, Joseph understood. There, in the darkness, the forms of two others just like him floated from one of the freight cars and into the woman's wagon.

Could this woman have been a friend to him? Joseph knew that she would be. And so he crawled along the train tracks until he had arrived near her feet. He whispered to her, and she gestured with her hand—a signal for him to stay. The two men continued loading the wagon with boxes, but soon the woman motioned again. It was the call, and Joseph leapt. She secured the drape once he was in.

During the ride to Mrs. Lovejoy's, Joseph stared at the other passengers. They gazed back at him too, through the spaces between the boxes. The man and the woman were a bit older than he was—not yet thirty perhaps—with immovable faces. All three of them remained still as the wagon moved through Boston, each of them protecting their own fate with their silence.

At Washington Street, the wagon pulled up alongside Mrs. Lovejoy's, and the woman herself stepped down from the driver's seat. She supervised the operation again, this time in reverse, as her men emptied the wagon of all but one of the wooden boxes. The runaways now had a full view of one another—all three of them exchanging glances, no one daring to speak.

Then one of the men returned with a large iron crow, and pried off the lid of the single box that remained.

What Joseph saw at that point was a vision of sheer wonder.

The child sat up, wearily rising from its forced slumber. The child had been locked inside the box for nearly two days.

How the whispers of a destitute mother must have fed that helpless child . . . for only a mother's words of comfort could have kept such a captive quiet.

The mother rushed over to the child, and scooped the child into her arms, nearly swallowing the small body with her embrace. The child vanished into the mother's bosom as the mother's body shivered—her face the fixed expression of her heavy, silent cries.

Then a hand grabbed Joseph's arm. It was the hand of Mrs. Lovejoy.

"Come away, my son," she said. "You must follow me this very moment."

She placed a large satchel in his arms, to give him the appearance of a worker. He followed her into the store, and the wagon—with its secreted cargo—drove away.

FOR THREE DAYS Joseph remained inside the wall at Mrs. Lovejoy's—pacing the interior staircase by night, and doing his best to stay in place by day.

"It was then that I first saw you," he admitted to Moody. "That's when I first saw you with *her*."

There had been a small crack in the wall plaster of one of the developing rooms, and from here Joseph had been able to observe Moody and Isabelle when they were alone. He had seen Moody teaching Isabelle how to coat glass and mix chemicals. He had seen the tenderness between them when they handled the negatives. But Joseph had also seen other things.

"I was convinced that you were trying to ruin her," Joseph said. "And so later—much later—when I learned that she had left Boston, I knew in my heart that you must have been to blame."

Moody sat back in his seat. So—Joseph was aware of what had gone on . . . how Moody and Isabelle had touched each other in the dark. Joseph had seen Isabelle kiss Edward Moody. He had seen her hand run up the inside of Moody's sleeve.

"You watched," Moody breathed. "You watched us."

Joseph looked down into his lap.

"I did," he replied. "Can you blame me for what I felt?"

Joseph worried that Moody would despise him for invading his memories. The way she looked at him, breathed upon him, caressed his cheeks and hands. Moody had taken her into the dark room and shut out the light. And now Moody would believe that Joseph had come back to steal from him.

It was disgusting. Edward Moody would think him disgusting. No words moved between them. The trees outside were a blur.

"I would have done anything for her," Moody finally said.

There was nothing in his voice—no anger, no passion. Just deadness. Was it possible to lose so much, and then lose even more?

Some moments passed before Joseph continued with his story, for he had been robbed too, and understood the shame that comes with robbery. For three days Mrs. Lovejoy had tended to him inside that wall. She had treated him with dignity, and her kindness had been almost too much.

On Joseph's third day in hiding, the man named Wilcox entered the store.

"There was a nigger came into this store carrying a sack a few days ago," he said. "Where is he? He work for you?"

"A hired hand from the train depot," Mrs. Lovejoy replied. "I hire a lot of them—they're cheaper than the Irish."

Wilcox spat on the floor. The smell of wet tobacco polluted the room.

"If you please, sir!"

"Now you wouldn't be lyin' to me—would you?"

Mrs. Lovejoy said nothing.

"Supposin' you tell me how it is that a nigger come through that door one day, and never come back out?"

"Are you suggesting that I'm harboring fugitives?" Mrs. Lovejoy said.

"I ain't suggesting nothin'—just asking you a question you ain't answered."

"I will see you to the *back* door of this establishment, sir. And I will kindly ask you to leave by that door, as your kind should."

A twitch of the cheek showed that Wilcox hadn't liked that, but for the moment, he bore the insult without reply. And as Mrs. Lovejoy escorted the intruder through her aisles, Wilcox stopped and sniffed along the walls. He tapped one of the panels, but the panel was solid, and Mrs. Lovejoy moved him along.

"The spirits were with me," Joseph said. "It is the only explanation."

And all of it had been happening right beneath Moody's nose. That would be the hardest part for a man like Moody to absorb.

"Of course she was working for the railroad," Moody said. "If only I had known. I may have been able to—"

"It wouldn't have been any different," Joseph interrupted. "She kept her secrets to protect you."

To Joseph, Isabelle had been, in a word—feisty. But this was not something that Joseph was about to add to his story. Moody's vision, Joseph knew, had been frozen in time—and the spirit photographer had taken great care in stylizing it. No, no . . . Edward Moody would not want to hear of the wild, tempestuous Isabelle, the Isabelle who had come to claim Joseph from Mrs. Lovejoy's. And besides, even if Edward Moody were willing to listen, there was that part of Isabelle that Joseph was determined to keep for himself.

"It is no longer safe for you to be here," she had said to him. "You must follow me. We are going to take you to the other side of the hill."

She had been radiant—a vision. He had never seen another woman like her. Yes, he had had his share of does on the plantations, but Isabelle was another creature entirely. Her eyes possessed a depth and power that captivated him immediately. Her skin glowed, no matter whether the light was dull or bright.

She provided no name, no introduction, no pleasantry. But the sound of her voice still worked over him like a spell.

They moved him, and for six days she cared for him: brought him food and water, fresh clothes and blankets, emptied his bucket. She told him that very soon, he would be back on the road to freedom. Of course the new laws had forced all of those roads to lead to Canada. She would put him on that road, she told him. This was the promise she would fulfill.

And that's when he had fallen in love with her. This living saint, this heroine . . . this *angel*. Two days before his departure, before either of them knew where or when he would be moved, he told her that he wanted to marry her, and demanded that she come with him.

She stared him straight in the face, as if he had insulted her. She had never even told this runaway her name.

"What is your name? Won't you tell me?" he had said to her.

"It's better if you don't know," she replied.

He insisted that he meant what he had said, and that in Canada they could be married. In Canada he could work to give her a good life. In Canada they could both be free.

Again she stared back at him, half in pity, half in fury. It was not the first time a stupid man had professed his love to her.

"Every year," she said, "a hundred thousand newborn babes are brought upon the auction blocks of Richmond, Charleston, and New Orleans. Every year, tens of thousands of lives are sacrificed to the lash in the South."

Her eyes were burning into him. She was turning into fire.

"These sights should send a thrill of horror through the nerves of every citizen, and impel the heart of humanity to do good. And so they might, if men had not found out the fearful alchemy by which they can turn this blood into gold. Instead of listening to the cries of agony, they only listen to the ring of dollars!"

She was ferocious, angry. His proposal, it had been—

"And you ask me to leave here?" she went on. "To abandon my work and come with you to Canada? You, who understand so little? There is no freedom for me there while even one of my brothers or sisters remains in chains. You would do well to remember that once you are lucky enough to reach freedom."

And so Joseph had never mentioned the prospect of her coming with him again. The woman who had saved him—the woman whose name he did not even know—had made quite clear what he could say, and what he couldn't.

There was no need, Joseph thought, to reveal this other Isabelle to Edward Moody, for what would be the point in claiming ownership over someone who had never belonged to either of them? For now, it was enough to inform Moody that Isabelle had been his savior, and that from the moment he left Boston, he had forever sworn to repay her.

"In Canada, every day," he told Moody, "I vowed that I would return to pay her whatever thanks I could. I would educate myself, become an honest man, and do as much good as I could in this world . . . not so that she would have me, but so that I could honor what she had done for me. I would repay her in doing that at least, if I could not repay her directly."

Then the war had come, and Joseph had gone off to fight, and when the war was over he learned that she was gone.

"She seemed to have vanished," Joseph said, "and try as I might I could not find out what had happened to her. I knew how much she wanted to stay in Boston, and that there was only one thing that would have forced her to leave."

"And you determined that I had wronged her," Moody said.

"That is exactly what I determined. And so I went to Cincinnati to study photography, resolving to come back to Boston, and work my way into your good graces. To find out exactly what chicanery you were up to, and if possible, get to the bottom of what happened to Isabelle."

"And the photographs?" Moody said.

"Yes, I would do my own thing with the photographs . . . if it would lead to getting the information that I wanted."

Moody rested a clenched fist over the negative in his coat pocket.

"No," Joseph said. "I never took my hand to that."

The train coursed over the uneven Connecticut landscape, exhaling gray coughs of smoke from its engines. Joseph's deviousness was undeniable, but it was a deviousness that stemmed from history. Edward Moody could never pretend to understand the scars that Joseph bore.

"My jealousy blinded me to your character," Joseph said. "I'm sorry that I misjudged you."

Moody looked out the window. There was no telling what he was seeing. But one thing was certain—Edward Moody would hate him. Moody would hate Joseph because he had dared to love Isabelle too, but all the more so because Joseph could do what he did without shame. For Moody, there was shame in it, and fear of discovery, and though that is partly what had fueled him, it had been his very destruction as well. Yes, Edward Moody would truly hate Joseph Winter, but at the same time Moody would be forced to find Joseph irresistible. Joseph represented a connection that Moody never could have had, and so now it was also certain that Moody would never let Joseph go.

"You have still not told me what we'll find in St. Louis," Moody said.

"There is nothing for us there but a boat," Joseph replied. "St. Louis is merely a connection."

"And then?"

Joseph reached into his coat pocket, producing a pencil and a scrap of paper. He laid the paper flat upon his knee and re-inscribed the familiar words:

NO—I HAV RETURND.

"Fanny's message," Moody said.

"*Isabelle's* message," Joseph corrected.

And when he said this, the train windows shuddered.

"The message leaves all questions unanswered," Joseph said. "You can be sure there is more to this message than what it seems to say."

Joseph then drew the pencil close to the paper again, and underlined the last three words.

"I have returned," Moody murmured.

"Yes, she has returned, but where?"

Moody whispered the words again, slower this time. The words beat with a life of their own.

"If she has returned, Edward, she has returned to the place she's come from."

Moody thought for a moment. Isabelle had told him so little about her past.

"And this is one of the few things you *do* know about her," Joseph said. "You know from where she came."

Then the lost detail rushed upon Moody.

"Bellevoix—" Moody said.

"Precisely," Joseph replied.

"But that's no more than the name of an old plantation—the place from which her mother escaped. Isabelle never told me where it was, and to this day I have no idea. All I know is that the mother was recaptured, and that Isabelle was recorded as stillborn."

"Ah," Joseph said, "but I do know where it was—and perhaps still is. There is no man—black or white—who could have lived in Louisiana in those days and not known of Bellevoix. It was amongst the greatest of the down-river sugar plantations, owned by the cruelest of masters."

"So you have known this all along!" Moody exclaimed.

"It's true," Joseph said, "that I hid this knowledge from you too. But I didn't understand its importance until Fanny delivered the message. I don't know what we will find there, but I am certain Bellevoix can tell us something."

Joseph once again glanced down at the piece of paper, and now underlined the first part of the phrase.

"No," Moody said.

Joseph underlined the phrase again.

And Moody repeated the word: "No."

"Remember," Joseph said, "how much your existing knowledge has guided your thinking. During the delivery of this message, you were concerned with answering your own questions. But the spirits' messages—

especially written ones—are often tangled. Incomplete and obstructed."

Moody continued staring at the piece of paper on Joseph's knee.

"She was not telling you 'NO,' Edward. She was giving you a location. She was letting us know that if we want to find her again, we must return to the place from where she came."

"Bellevoix . . ." Moody whispered. "But where is this place?"

Joseph underlined the first two letters on the paper one last time.

"New Orleans," Joseph said. "Isabelle has returned to New Orleans."

XVI

JOSEPH HAD ANSWERS—answers to questions Moody had never dreamed of asking—and Joseph's history had helped Moody fill more cracks in the broken windows. To hear of Isabelle's secret role as a conductor on the Underground Railroad, of the dangerous work she had done, and of the vital part she had played . . . all of this added more detail to the portrait of Isabelle that Moody had years ago locked away. Now, at last uncovered, that same image had been enhanced—like the rouged cheeks and gold buttons on one of his old hand-colored daguerreotypes.

But it wasn't all beautiful, as he had tried to forget. He was ashamed of his thoughts—of undressing her when he was alone. Of imagining his hands running over her body . . . of the way her lips and eyelids tasted. She was a real thing to him then, and the idea of losing her was not something that had crossed his mind. She came to the gallery. He saw her. He loved and desired her more every day.

But what was he to her? He thought that he knew.

And then he had done it—forced himself upon her, no better than one of the others. Until she slapped him, he hadn't realized what he had done. "No, Edward," she had said. "Please, no . . ." But he hadn't listened. He had disgraced himself, and she'd never trust him again.

Had he driven her away? Had he been the one to do it? No . . . of course not. She had forgiven him! Even as he blubbered before her like a fool. He did not understand how well she understood him. He was too selfish, too patronizing, to realize how deeply she could see.

"The photograph captures the fleeting moments of life," he had once told her . . . that same day in the meadow, before the honeybee had crawled up her skirt. "And it preserves what the mind sometimes cannot," she had responded. "It is the reminder of what we may forget." The logic had surprised him. It was—unromantic. He was the scientist, the teacher, the man of knowledge, the pioneer, but from the first she had demonstrated a kind of inexplicable authority. Now he was remembering. When she had listened to him talk about chemicals or lighting, he had sometimes felt as if he were telling her things she already knew. Yes, she had listened to him attentively, devouring all he had to say, but it had often been with the earnestness of a mother listening to a small child.

And so, when he wrote to her during those horrible days after Antietam, he knew that she would be listening—though from where, he did not know. At that point she had been silent for close to ten years, yet he had never stopped talking to her, never stopped telling her things. The letters, which he wrote and kept in that same box with her goodbye letter, were like little talismans that preserved their feeble connection. He did not think of the ugly moments. The dreams of her return were much, much greater.

But after Antietam, he could no longer believe.

Not after he had seen the scores of men being brought back to the encampment, their arms and legs missing, snapped from their bodies like twigs, their lives abandoning them as they cried. Not after he had seen what could happen to a man's body . . . how easily guns and cannons could turn a person into something monstrous. There was a boy, a dead drummer boy. Someone had wheeled him back to the encampment. The delicate form could not have been more than seventeen years old. His flaxen hair and porcelain skin would have singled him out as an angel, were it not for the missing arm, and the filthy, shredded skin beneath his shoulder. People would tell his mother that his rewards in the next life would be plentiful. But how could there be anything—in this world or the next—that would welcome such horror and mutilation?

After the gunfire had stopped, and Brady sent him out to take photographs, Moody found the slopes of the hills playing host to piles of dead men. The bodies were at rest now—fallen and lifeless—but the stench of their decay still fought against the perfume of crushed corn stalks. The horse carcasses rose from the ground like mountains. Everywhere, men's blood had drenched the fallen corn . . . the grass, the ragweed, and the clover.

A young private lay on the ground, his body mangled and twisted, his fingers still gripping a framed picture of his loved one. She had been with him in that final moment, when the last river of blood had trickled from his mouth. "How beautiful," one of the papers might later say, "that even in the ultimate throes of his life, his darling could be with him." But it sickened Moody to think of how powerless—how *useless*—that picture had been. What did it matter? The imagined comfort of a loved one? What could it possibly have meant amongst so much carnage and senseless death?

Isabelle would have had something to say. But she was gone, and now he had nothing.

20 September 1862

My Dearest Isabelle,

We have just returned from photographing the battlefield, Mr. Brady being intent on having us capture the scene before it alters. I have never in my life been so repulsed by what I saw, and my deepest regret about today is that I surrendered myself to an effort to make permanent all the ghastly horrors of this battle. What awfulness it was to look through the camera and try to maintain focus on the strange spell that dwells in dead men's eyes! It seems iniquitous that the sun looking down on those slain, blistered faces should be the very same sun that caught their features upon the glass. It seems a crime that the sun blotting out all semblance of humanity from their bodies is that same sun that now gives them perpetuity forever. But so it is.

My subjects today did not make appointments for their sittings. They were photographed as they fell, their hands clutching the grass around them, or reaching out for help that never came. The red light of battle is faded from their eyes, but their lips are still set with that last fierce charge which loosed their souls from their bodies. The ground upon which they lie is torn by shot and shell, and the grass trampled down by the tread of hot, hurrying feet. Little rivulets that can scarcely be of water are still trickling along the earth like tears over a mother's face. It is a bleak, barren plain, and above it bends an ashen sky; there is no friendly shade or shelter from the noonday sun or the midnight dews.

I cannot shake from my thoughts the one side of these pictures that the sun did not catch . . . the one phase that has escaped our photographic skill. It is the background of widows and orphans . . . mothers, sons, daughters . . . torn from their natural protectors by the remorseless hand of battle. This war has made thousands of homes desolate, and has forever quenched the light of life in thousands of hearts. *Imagination must be the one to paint all this desolation, for I cannot—broken hearts cannot be photographed.*

Nor mine. When you did not come back, I thought I would perish from grief, but I found ways to keep you alive, and the photographs did more than the letters. Every photograph I took led me to wonder what you would think of it, for I know how you loved them, and would have wanted to see them all. From somewhere you must have been listening when Mr. Brady told me I had an almost unnatural talent, and that he would entrust me with the most important of his projects, and that they would turn me into a man of means. You loved this, I felt it, because I loved it too. We were together in the photographs—every one.

But this—this atrocity—I do not want you to see. I do not ever want you to see this, and would give anything if I could wipe it from the slate of my own memory. I cannot look through the lens of the camera again. I can never make another picture without seeing the eyes of a dead man. And so now I tell you what you already know, which is that I will forsake photography forever. I will do the remaining work I have to do for Mr. Brady, but after this . . . after this war, I am finished. I cannot bear the agony of the photograph. It has become something repulsive to me.

You will not resent me for this, for you have already said your goodbyes. I must say my goodbyes now too. It is what was deemed to be.

Edward

That was the last letter he wrote to her in an effort to banish her from his memory. After all that time had passed, what Moody really needed to do was to forget. The next evening, he went to see the black whore who lived on the outskirts of Sharpsburg. The soldiers all knew about her, and told their stories about her around the fires, and Moody had always listened, ashamed. But now his shame was gone, because everything was gone, and Edward Moody had nothing left to lose. He was wretched—so wretched that the woman pushed him away. But that angered him, and he slapped her, and took her.

In the days following Antietam, the woodcuts began appearing in the papers—reproductions of the photographs that Moody and Brady's other men had taken on the battlefield. The illustrations duplicated those that Moody had captured, but without the singular horror that the original images revealed. Here and there the newspaper artists had added their own touches— bending a knee slightly higher to make the pose appear more lifelike, or turning a face so as to expose more of its features. The effect was a kind of washing over of the original images—a tidying up of the inhumanity, a rinsing away of some of the blood. While appalled, Moody could take only so much offense at this, for he and the others had also been guilty of adjusting the bodies where they lay.

"This one is most affective," Brady said some days after Moody had returned. "The grass almost seems to be cradling him."

"Yes, well—we placed him like that," one of the photographers replied. "The angle of the body accentuates the gentle slope of the ditch."

"Trench," Brady corrected. "We might call this one a trench. Ditch has a hardness that is somewhat off-putting."

He studied the small image for a little while longer and then said:

"Mr. Moody, what do you think?"

It was only a tiny thing . . . a *carte de visite* of a fallen soldier, so precious that it could fit into the palm of your hand. It would be sold, with hundreds of others like it, as a souvenir at Brady's exhibit.

"It's a ravine," Moody said.

And the great Brady lit up.

"Ah, yes—a ravine! You are a true poet, Mr. Moody."

Moody did his best to suppress his discomfort. He was, to his own dismay, remaining a conspirator to the end.

Then the other photographer chimed in.

"Call it a 'little ravine,' Mr. Brady. That would provide some relief from the gruesomeness of the image."

Again Brady was impressed, for the words needed to be perfect. Printed on the back sides of the souvenirs, the captions would mean the difference between mournfulness and horror.

"Yes . . . yes!" Brady enthused. "A 'little ravine'! A Confederate soldier, dragging himself to a little ravine, before his death. There's something quite lyrical about it."

The description of that particular photograph underwent many more revisions during the next hour, though Moody refrained from contributing to them. He had grown too disgusted at the idea of profiteering from the dead to help stamp Brady's products any further. The widows and orphans who haunted him as much as dead soldiers would see no more of his participation when they read the reverse sides of their souvenirs.

BRADY'S ALBUM GALLERY.
No. 554.

CONFEDERATE SOLDIER,

Who, after being wounded, had dragged himself to a little ravine on the hill-side, where he died.

☞ The Photographs of this series were taken directly from nature, at considerable cost. Warning is therefore given that legal proceedings will be at once instituted against any party infringing the copyright.

The exhibit opened in New York to great acclaim, as no one had ever seen anything of its kind before. "Mr. Brady has done something to bring home to us the terrible reality and earnestness of war," the *Times* reported. "If he has not brought bodies and laid them in our dooryards and along the streets, he has done something very like it." The article described the little placard outside Brady's Broadway gallery, inviting passers-by to come upstairs and view "The Dead of Antietam." Inside, throngs of people examined the battle photographs—some with handheld magnifying glasses, perhaps searching for someone they knew. "Of all objects of horror one would think that the battlefield should stand preeminently repulsive. But on the contrary, there is a terrible fascination about it that draws us near these pictures, and makes us loath to leave them." Those with more intense fixations could take the Dead of Antietam home with them, for Brady was offering *carte de visite* souvenirs, "priced attractively at 25 cents each."

Years later, the irony of Moody profiting from spirit photographs was surprisingly lost on him. By then the ability to soothe the brokenhearted was a lure so powerful that he was unable to resist it. Never did it occur to him that he had become another kind of Brady. He considered himself unique—in possession of a "gift" even. "Yes, of course, it has been very much about the money," he once admitted, "but to witness the subdued joy on the face of the mother who finds her lost daughter . . . the tranquility that befalls the father who sees his beloved son again . . . *this* . . . this raising of the dead from their graves is what we need in order to endure our most fragile days. Though my enemies will never believe me, I will go to my own grave insisting it: everything I have done since the first spirit photograph, I have done out of compassion, and out of love."

XVII

THEY WERE EVERYWHERE now. On the walls and in the window-panes. On the pavement outside the doorstep, and in the seats of passing carriages. These shades—these *phantoms*—had a way of insisting upon themselves, and Garrett could not shake them, no matter how often he shut his eyes. Even Jenny had turned into one. His sweet and faithful Jenny, whom he had purchased from bondage with his own honest money. Jenny had remained the one stable comfort to him over the years, especially during the more recent years of his increasing estrangement from Elizabeth. He and Jenny were not equals—could never be equals—and yet Jenny seemed to have an understanding of him that others would have considered improper. No words could describe such a relationship, or the gratitude that radiated from both sides.

But for over twenty years there were things he had turned away from. He knew what her scars looked like, and he did not want to see them. He had washed all of that away for her long ago . . . washed away her pain and her blood—or so he thought. The devils were roaming the streets back then, hunting down people and collecting their rewards. But this one called Jenny would not need to go back. Even Elizabeth had agreed: it was the righteous thing to do.

That smell was coming back to him now . . . the smell of that *devil* who had spit tobacco on his doorstep. He was a sinister man, a malevolent brute, and his eyes had burned something infernal.

The man had threatened Garrett . . . had called him *senator* repeatedly, with emphasis. For he knew that the young member of Congress needed to guard his reputation. While it might have been acceptable to the whole of Boston to harbor fugitives, in the end it was still a violation of the law.

"And what would the papers like to make of that?" the man had said.

He was repulsive, that shiny brown wetness on his lips.

That's when Elizabeth stepped forward. The idea had been hers. The man was looking for money, she said, otherwise he would have been there with marshals. He would return with marshals the next morning if Garrett didn't offer him something. But paying off this mercenary was not going to be enough. That solution was not going to resolve the larger problem.

And so *she* was the one who arranged it . . . the one who reviewed the documents, and dealt with the devil. Jenny's freedom came at a cost of four hundred and fifty dollars. It would have been double that amount had Jenny been young enough to bear any more children.

Some papers signed in the dining room, some money exchanged, and all would go away.

"You've got a fine place here, Mrs. Garrett," the man had said. "A very fine place, if I do say so."

"We thank you for your time, Mr. Wilcox," she had responded. "And now I must ask you to leave."

Garrett felt ashamed. To let a man like this into his house. To subject his wife to a man like this. He stank of the taverns he frequented, and the dust of his filthy trade. Elizabeth was a saint for consenting to the whole thing. Elizabeth bore everything with dignity.

The house kept the secret for them—never discussed the four hundred and fifty dollars, nor the extra two hundred dollars paid to the unwelcome negotiator. Of course some, like Dovehouse, would know what had transpired, for even a house as stolid as Garrett's could not hide what was really transpiring during those years. But to most "the Garretts' Jenny" soon became just another domestic servant . . . one of the faceless masses who had no origin, and whose footsteps rarely moved beyond those walls.

"Sir?" Jenny said, waking Garrett from his stupor.

He looked at her. He could still see the younger Jenny . . . the desperate woman he had saved.

"Sir," she repeated, "the inspector's come to see you, and he's alone. Do you want me to show him in?"

"Thank you, Jenny," Garrett said.

And Jenny floated back out of the room. Everything in front of him was floating these days.

When the young Bolles came in, he seemed a ghost too, for he looked much like his father, whom Garrett dearly missed. It had not been two years since Monty Bolles had died a martyr in Louisiana—tortured before being shot for daring to teach the freedmen how to read.

"Senator," the young Bolles said, "are you . . . unwell?"

"I am fine, my boy," Garrett replied. "Thank you for asking. A late night with a few immoderate guests."

"Mr. Dovehouse?" the inspector asked. "He mentioned to me this morning that he had dined with you last night."

"Ah, you saw him?"

"Yes, I did sir, which is why I've come to see you. I wanted to ask you . . . do you believe Mr. Dovehouse is acting in your best interests?"

"Entirely," Garrett said.

Bolles appeared dissatisfied with Garrett's swift assertion.

"It's just that Mr. Dovehouse seems to have been a bit *pressing* of late."

"Pressing?"

"Yes, sir. Pressing. He has twice now visited me independently inquiring about the Moody case. And while I am under no obligation to reveal information to him, he acts as if I am. Furthermore, he takes his leave by reminding me that I must 'come to him straightaway' in the event that my men recover the photograph."

"Really?"

"Yes," the inspector answered. "And while I know that you and he are old friends, something about the intensity of his interest seems—"

And he turned his head to the side before saying:

"Not quite right."

The boy was as intuitive as his father. It was the reason that Garrett had taken so much care to help the young Montgomery Bolles throughout the course of his life.

"May I ask again, sir, now that we're alone together . . . what exactly is the nature of the photograph?"

"Negative," Garrett corrected. "It's merely the glass negative."

Then in an unpredictable outburst he said:

"God help me if the man has made photographs!"

Bolles stared back at him.

"You must forgive me," Garrett said, "but as you know, the issue is sensitive."

"I have received that impression," Bolles said, "and so I ask you if there is something more."

Garrett returned the question with silence. He was unsure of what to say.

"Is there something more about the negative that I need to know?"

Bolles continued. "If I knew precisely what we were dealing with I might be in a better position to help you."

And then, almost as if the shade of Dovehouse had appeared, Garrett's defenses returned, and he raised a clenched fist in anger.

"We are dealing with the basest of criminals," he said. "Someone who preys on the weak and the helpless, and who shows no remorse for his wickedness. He is a parasite who cares for nothing but his own advancement, while he tramples over the grieving, and steals money from open palms."

This was Garrett, the senator, coming to life once again—the Garrett who had presided over the moral tides of the country for the past twenty years.

"You are a great man, Senator."

But Garrett did not answer.

"It is my hope—for all our sakes—that your greatness remains undiminished."

It was exactly the kind of thing the boy's father would have said, for Monty Bolles had been the exemplar of tact. There were very few men like Monty Bolles anymore—men who were willing to step aside for the triumph of the greater good.

"And the case?" Garrett asked.

"Well there is news," Bolles said.

"Yes?"

"Two men matching their descriptions were seen boarding the Pittsburgh-Cincinnati line at New York. The information came from one of the station attendants, however, and the train had already departed, so no one could question the men. Do you know of any reason why Moody and Winter would be traveling west?"

"You said the Cincinnati line?" Garrett asked.

"Yes, the line terminates at St. Louis."

"Cincinnati," Garrett said. "Winter is from Cincinnati."

"I thought he was from Canada."

"He is, but after the war he spent time in Cincinnati. It's where he trained as a photographer. It was a fleeting detail, but one I remember from the conversation that took place when we met."

"So his connections there are deep, and it is a place where he might find shelter amongst allies?"

"Likely," Garrett said. "Very likely."

"Very well then. We have nothing much else to go on but this. I will telegraph Cincinnati and alert our agents there."

Garrett nodded.

"And Mr. Dovehouse . . . I take it he already knows of this news?"

"Yes," Bolles replied, "I informed him earlier this morning."

Garrett gave another nod. Dovehouse was becoming a problem.

"The main issue is with the crowds," Bolles went on. "For if Moody and Winter don't exit the train together, it will be that much more difficult to identify them. The sketches only do so much, as you know, and Moody may have shaved, and—"

"I have the utmost confidence in your abilities, my dear boy. It is sometimes hard to catch a rat, but he with the greater resources always wins."

His reply had the tone of a paternal—almost prosaic—lesson, for Garrett's defensiveness had somewhat softened again. The young Inspector Bolles had become like another son to him. Old Monty would have been exceedingly proud. This young man had devoted his life to the pursuit of justice, and yet he realized that doing the right thing sometimes required bending the law. Garrett would make sure that Montgomery was taken care of, whether or not the inspector managed to take care of him.

The house had condoned Elizabeth's putting her ears to the doors. Garrett, she thought, had handled the visit well. Yes, her husband had been guilty of his outbursts, but like her he knew when to recant. Much remained unsaid, and of course the inspector would know that, but all who entered the house could not help becoming complicit with its ways. The place for truthfulness did not exist anywhere out in the open, but in crevices and dark corners, with the rest of the house's secrets.

XVIII

THE TRAIN SHOOK the man as it escaped the spidery railways of Manhattan—this southwest-bound train, whose route would cut a diagonal through the southern states. The train was filthy and fast, much like the man himself. The piece of paper in his hands did not matter; the destination was all that mattered.

Wilcox reread the letter:

> They have left Boston and are on their way to Cincinnati. Winter has his connections there, as you probably know. Perhaps they intend to wait there for some time, or perhaps they will immediately move on.
>
> You told me years ago that you had taken the girl to a place from where she would never return. You did not tell me the place then, and I do not want to know it now. But I am sure that that is where they are going.

It was true—he *had* taken the girl to a place from where she would never return. A place so far south that any hope of return was impossible. That's what you did in those days. That's how you handled it.

They were going due west to St. Louis. They were breaking up the route. But he'd stop them before they could get to where they needed to go. He had boarded the Knoxville-Mobile line—that would put him there before them. The steamboat would take them at least three days, maybe four.

In New Orleans, he would be waiting.

XIX

**Newsletter of the American Institute for
the Encouragement of Science and Invention**
New York, New York
Wednesday, August 3, 1870

*THE INTEREST IN the Moody case continues. Last week, we reported
that Marshall Hinckley, our esteemed colleague from Boston, had sent
word regarding the escape of the "spirit photographer" from the authorities. Our readers will recall that Edward Moody has been charged with
fraud and larceny—crimes befitting this swindler and enemy of science.*

*It appears that there is now another wrinkle in the story. Moody
was believed to have been traveling to Cincinnati by rail with his negro
assistant, but upon arrival of the identified train, the police seem to have
apprehended the wrong pair, and by the time the error was discovered
the suspects were again nowhere to be found.*

*The Institute will continue to monitor the case, and report back
to its readers accordingly.*

"THE DAMNED SCOUNDREL!" Marshall Hinckley exclaimed when
Bolles delivered the news. "What kind of witchery is that man
working?"

It was a fitting question to ask, as they sat beneath the portrait of Dovehouse's ancestor. Garrett, Dovehouse, Hinckley, and Bolles had all assembled
to discuss the debacle.

"Do you mean to tell me," Dovehouse added, "that there were *two* sets
of white men with negro companions on that train? And that the police, upon
seeing one of them, just happened to chase the wrong pair?"

"I don't know if there were two, or four, or any other number," Bolles
replied, "but Moody and Winter are not the only black and white men traveling together. The mistake, in my estimation, was an honest one."

"Of all the nonsense," Dovehouse said.

And it did sound like nonsense, but as Bolles recounted what had happened, one had to understand the error, too. When the train pulled into the station at Cincinnati, Bolles told them, the police had been standing by, ready to examine the disembarking passengers. Soon, an officer identified two travelers—a bearded white man with a black companion—and made to approach the suspects. The two men were snaking through the crowd with great purpose—a behavior that only increased the pursuing officer's suspicions. When the officer increased his pace, the men hurried their steps as well, suggesting that they might have had good reason to flee.

"Confidence men," Bolles said, "just another set of swindlers making the rounds. Selling worthless plots of land for outrageous prices, and passing off empty swamps for 'Eden.' The negro apparently drew in negro investors who could afford it. These men had every reason to run."

"But were there not other officers?" Hinckley asked. "Examining the whole line of the crowd?"

"There were," Bolles replied, "but once the main officer blew his whistle, all attention followed the con men."

"Right out of the train station," Hinckley concluded.

Bolles nodded.

"It wasn't until a good hour later that the officers apprehended them, but by that time the crowd had dispersed, and the train had left the station. There was no point in resuming the search."

"They could be anywhere now," Hinckley said, "anywhere in the whole of Cincinnati!"

"Or Columbus or Louisville," Dovehouse said. "Who says they even got off the train? If they were on that train, they may have decided to continue on after seeing the commotion. What is the train's final destination?"

"St. Louis," Bolles said.

Dovehouse sat back in his chair.

"Garrett," he said. "Anything for them in St. Louis?"

Garrett slowly turned.

"Not to my knowledge," he replied. "But then again what is there for them anywhere? These are men on the run. They are running from something, not to something."

It was such an abstract observation, Dovehouse thought, and not at all like anything Garrett would normally say. But then again, Garrett had been acting so strangely since this whole Moody business had started.

"We'll keep going," Dovehouse said. "Keep the efforts focused in Cincinnati. Seek out his negro connections and the photography studios. Someone must know something there."

"Very well, Mr. Dovehouse," Bolles said, glancing at Senator Garrett.

But Garrett was not looking at the inspector, or anyone else. His eyes were—surprisingly—closed.

XX

HAD IT BEEN luck? Again and again, the question confronted Edward Moody, as if it were a dissatisfied patron doubting the manifestation of one of his spirits. The train had pulled into Cincinnati and the authorities had been waiting—Joseph had pointed that out even before the train had come to a stop. But as Moody watched Joseph turning over other ideas in his head, the most extraordinary thing had happened: the police had run away.

"They've gone after the wrong men," Joseph had said, "but it won't be long before they realize that."

Joseph and Moody simply remained on the train. Something more than luck had followed them.

It was not that Edward Moody had suddenly come to "believe"—for he had been believing, and not believing, and then believing again for many years. But Isabelle had returned in some way—through the negative, through Joseph—and he was experiencing the mounting traces of her presence like one feels the increasing warmth of a fire. For the first time Moody was undergoing the same transformation he had affected in others—the changeover from despair to hope, from darkness into light.

Part of what had mesmerized him so much about Joseph's story was the idea that for Joseph, Isabelle had never died. Joseph had memorialized her as an angel even when she was living, and so there was little difference between the woman Joseph had loved and the one who had gone away. It was profound—what such a flame of devotion could do. Joseph might have been a blackguard, but at least he had kept Isabelle alive.

The train moved on, and they disembarked at St. Louis. There were no policemen there to greet them—just a throng of men and women, all exiting the doors of the station. The people moved in great masses into the city or toward the levee, and anyone could have been in the crowd. Joseph spotted two police officers—likely on routine patrol, he said—but still, he did not want to take chances. He and Moody lost themselves in the immense density of moving bodies, weaving in and out of the people as they made their way down to the levee.

The plan had been discussed. They would purchase their tickets as individual travelers—Moody as a stateroom passenger, and Joseph traveling on deck. It made sense because most of the steamship companies segregated their crowds, and any attempt to travel together would have attracted attention. The great disadvantage was of course the danger of their separation, for if any trouble were to arise they would be without each other.

But there was a bit more to it than that. Moody wanted to be alone with the negative.

The levee at St. Louis gradually sloped down into the river, leaving the commercial avenues and buildings of the waterfront on slightly higher ground behind it. In the water, which gave the false impression that it had come to rest in a shallow bowl, sat the endless hordes of steamboats, pressed into the levee's edges. The north-south curve of the miles-long levee meant that one could not see where the line of stationed boats began or ended. The line was infinite—a row of smoke-stacked monsters, their fat bodies sucking at the edges of the land.

Moody was no stranger to boats or busy waterfronts; but this place was something entirely different from the jumble of wharves and tall ships of Boston. The width of the levee was astonishing, and though it had been constructed to battle the volatility of the river, the people of St. Louis took every advantage of its wide expanse. Here, for the first time, Moody saw the "business" of the revived southern economy, which, by anyone's assessment, did not look all that different from before the war. The levee was suffocating under the burden of its bounty—great mounds of cotton bales, stacked barrels of sugar, and ten-foot high piles of fresh timber—all being weighed, measured, loaded, and unloaded by armies of freedmen. There were overseers here too, brandishing long wooden billets, and beating the workers who did not load or unload the goods fast enough.

Moody asked a drayman for the location of the nearest ticket office, and soon he and Joseph were moving toward one of the waterfront buildings. The buildings faced the steamboats, and stared out at them across the levee, their visages quite superior to the rest of the neighborhood's chaos.

Moody purchased the tickets, and returned, and handed one to Joseph.

"And now," Moody said, "it is time."

Joseph nodded uneasily. He did not want to separate. And he did not want to leave Moody with the negative.

"Remember," Joseph said, "should we fail to find each other in New Orleans, we must meet at L'Archevêché—the Archbishop's residence. There we will find a friend—a man who helped me once."

Joseph searched Moody's face for consolation. There was nothing. The cold eyes stared back him—steely and gray. Did those eyes despise him, want to seek revenge?

Then a cloud shaded the levee, and Moody touched Joseph's arm.

"I will not be far away," Moody said.

The crowd divided them, and great swells of people carried Moody toward the boat—a massive three-tiered side-wheeler whose name was the *Sotto Voce*. The landing stages had been lowered, creating two paths for passengers on either side of the bow, and the crowd trampled over them, overrunning the front of the steamer. Moody ascended the central staircase, but not before noticing where the deck passengers were stationed. There on the main deck, mingled amongst the cotton bales and the lumber, a swarm of tattered travelers was assembling with chickens and bedclothes and dogs.

"Careful," a man said to Moody on the staircase. "You stare at those mutts too long and they might bite ya!"

Inside the main saloon, which ran nearly the entire length of the upper deck, an ornamental gilt ceiling and a series of chandeliers glittered with reflections from the skylights. It was not, Moody thought, unlike the lobby of a great hotel, with travelers carousing everywhere, and negro servants making fast progress. A corps of waiters was setting a long row of tables, the dinnerware and silver jingling unapologetically amongst the voices. Toward the end of the saloon, around the bar and captain's office, clusters of passengers had gathered to talk and drink. A thick blue cloud of smoke was rising from this crowd—the effect of so many pipes and cigars.

"Edward Moody!" a loud voice rumbled.

Moody spun around to see a fat man with his arm extended out toward him. The man was chewing on a cigar, his cheeks already rouged with too much drink.

"I'm sorry," Moody said, "do we—"

"Pemberton!" the man exclaimed. "Pemberton—from Boston!"

Moody studied the swollen face, but he could not remember where he had seen it.

"Ah, Mr. Moody," Mr. Pemberton said, "I don't expect a great man like you to remember an old fellow like me. But you helped me once. It was a great thing that you did for me. I carry it with me always—see?"

And the man reached into his breast pocket and pulled out a spirit photograph.

"My Anabelle . . . my Anabelle," Pemberton said, almost tearing. "She is always with me now. You gave me that gift, Mr. Moody."

"Of course," Moody said.

And the spirit photographer smiled at him—the best sort of smile he could manage.

"Oh, Mr. Moody . . ." Pemberton went on, "after I lost her, I had a terrible time. A terrible time, as you know. And so right after the war, not long after I came to see you, I left Boston, looking for opportunity in the South. You see, Mr. Moody, after I received this message, and once I learned that she was with me, I knew I could go anywhere—do anything."

Moody nodded with feigned interest. This fool could be a problem.

"Anything!" Pemberton said, grabbing a tight hold of Moody's arm. "Anything, Mr. Moody. Do you hear me?"

Moody looked at the man's hand, and then looked at Pemberton.

"My apologies, Mr. Moody," Pemberton said, releasing and then smoothing Moody's sleeve. "I am sorry—I do still get in a passion about it."

"No offense, my good man."

"It's just that I know she is so happy with what I am doing now. I am doing *good* for the country, Mr. Moody. Good for myself, yes, but good for the country as well."

Pemberton had obviously not been reading any of the northern papers.

"And where do you do your business now?" Moody asked. "Have you left Boston entirely behind?"

"Oh no, Mr. Moody . . . I still maintain my close ties with Boston. My connections there are many, and my daughters—do you have children, Mr. Moody?"

"I do not."

"No matter. But my connections there are many, and I am—well, I am in cotton now!"

"How grand for you," Moody said.

"Yes, cotton. It is the substance of reunification!"

And he brought his face closer to Moody's.

"The substance of everything we fought for, if you ask me."

Moody turned his head. The alcohol on the man's breath was staggering. Moody would need to listen to him for awhile. He would need to treat him like every other client.

"Oh, but the negroes down here," Pemberton whispered, "they are shamefully abused, Mr. Moody. Shamefully abused. They've been promised that if they'll remain and work the plantations, they'll have a share of the crops. But come harvest, the planters give them nothing, and so the darkies have caught on. They have no confidence in southern men anymore, and will not hire out to them. But—"

And here Pemberton paused to raise a distended finger.

"They are eager to engage with northern men."

The crowd was growing thicker and louder all around them, and it dawned upon Moody that Pemberton might not be the only one. This buffoon—

"This is how it goes with them, Mr. Moody, let me tell you . . . I have hired out a plantation at Natchez from a man by the name of Taylor. Now this Taylor has four hundred sheep, seventy milch cows, fifteen horses, ten mules, and forty hogs, all of them saved when our armies raided the country, by one of his old negroes who ran them off across a swamp. Now would you believe that this Taylor never gave that negro five cents? Another one, who once belonged to him, had a cow of his own, and from that cow he raised a fine pair of oxen. Taylor laid claim to those oxen and sold them. It goes this way, round and round . . . Taylor promising his negroes a share of the crops, but then selling the cotton himself, and never giving one of them a dollar. He says this is how the northerners treat their laborers, isn't it? So why shouldn't he do the same?"

Moody looked around. More passengers were flooding the cabin. Pemberton took a large draw on his cigar, and exhaled smoke toward one of the chandeliers.

"You see, Taylor has two plantations," Pemberton continued, "and rents one of them out to me. He told me at the start that he would take all his negroes from my plantation, but when I came to take possession of the land, I was astonished to find all of them there. 'How's this?' I says to him. 'I thought these people were going with you?' He said that he couldn't induce even one of them to work for him, and that he had about given up on the idea. He had offered them twenty-five dollars a month, plus board and medical attendance, but the negroes wouldn't even engage with him for that. So I went to those negroes, who knew me to be a northern man, and said, 'Mr. Taylor offers you twenty-five dollars a month, but that is more than I can afford to pay.' I offered them ten a month, and I tell you, faces never lit up so. They said they'd rather work for ten dollars and be sure of their pay, than for twenty-five dollars and be cheated out of it."

"Ain't no cheating a nigger," someone added, "if you believe niggers is for workin' the land, as they ought to be."

Pemberton at last stopped speaking, and Moody turned to see a man dressed in drab linen—one of the many southern planters in the saloon.

"You see, gentlemen," the man said, "we may have lost the old ways, but there is still something to be made out of a nigger. My niggers here won't work for me no more, so I've got to go down to Vicksburg to get me some new ones."

And the man turned a dark eye toward Pemberton, who was chewing on the wet tip of his cigar.

"Gentlemen," Moody said, "I'm afraid I must—"

"I can tell you're a northern traveler," the planter interrupted, "and I've been listening to this fellow here explain the 'situation.'"

"This man is no simple traveler!" Pemberton said excitedly. "This is—"

"Please, Mr. Pemberton," Moody said.

"I'd be lying if I said that Mr. Pemberton here hadn't described the situation *somewhat* accurately," the planter said. "But the niggers won't work. None of you Yankees seem to understand that. And here's a bunch of you coming down here and trying to make sure they can vote."

"If the negroes won't work, as you say, Mr.—?"

"Loftus—Samuel Loftus," the man said, shaking Pemberton's hand.

"If the negroes won't work," Pemberton continued, "then why are you going down to Vicksburg to try to contract with them?"

"Well everyone's just crazy 'bout niggers right now. Have been since the end of the war. And if everybody else is going in for hiring 'em, and if there's anything to be made, I don't want to be left out in the cold."

And then this planter leaned in closer toward Moody and Pemberton, his face twisted into something hideous.

"If everybody else would have refused to hire 'em anyhow, that would have suited me just fine. I'd have been willing to let my plantation go to the devil for a year, just to see the free niggers starve."

The mighty whistle of the steamboat released its deep and prolonged cry.

"Ah," Pemberton said, "we go!"

The crowd, with great energy and spirit, began to roll out of the saloon. The planter disappeared, and Pemberton moved toward one of the doors.

"You'll join me on deck," he said, "won't you, Mr. Moody?"

"I will, in a moment," Moody said, "but if I might ask you . . . I am traveling south on some delicate business, and I'm wondering if I could entreat you to—"

"Say no more, Mr. Moody, say no more. A great man like you runs a confidential business. I will exercise the utmost discretion on this journey."

"I thank you," Moody said, shaking Pemberton's hand.

In truth Moody realized that Pemberton's "discretion" would last as long as his resistance to the next drink. If at any point the man were to receive news from Boston, Moody and Joseph would need to reconsider their course.

IN THE PRIVACY of his stateroom, Moody could at last be alone with the negative. He felt weary—not simply from the relentlessness of the journey, but from the drain of so much remembering, and the inundation of so much uncertainty.

Moody lit the lamp and sat upon the narrow bed. The room's tiny windows emitted only meager rays of light.

The negative. It had been three days since he had seen it . . . though he did not need to see it to understand that it had claimed him. He removed it from its leather case and held it beneath the lamplight. *Isabelle.* There she was again. Her face clear on the shimmering glass.

Or was it?

He looked closer. Something was different about the face. Something was in fact different about the entire stretch of her body.

What was it? Moody rose and moved closer toward the window, holding the negative just beneath the column of graying light.

"No," he whispered.

And then again: "No."

It happened sometimes—when the silver did not take. He stared into her eyes. She was fading.

Joseph had assured him that he had varnished the negative, and the sheen on top of the portrait confirmed that that was so. And the Garretts—Moody scrutinized every bit of what remained of them. Even with the blackened damage, their figures were crisp and distinct.

It was her, only her. Isabelle's image was—

How had he come to be in this place? On a boat down to New Orleans, on the run from the law? He remembered the days just after the war, when he had returned to Mrs. Lovejoy's with no more ambitions beyond engraving. She had given him the stall at the back of the store. He had wanted nothing more. He had never wanted any of it.

But then he had gone on to become Edward Moody, the spirit photographer. He had done such great things. Why, even that imbecile had just told him so. He had never meant to hurt anyone; he had only wanted to help people . . . help people to escape from the hopelessness of their own sorrow. The sleepless nights, the heavy hearts, the horrors of the unknown. Yes, he had now and then laughed at the success of his own duplicity, but this was nothing compared to the transformed lives that departed from his gallery. He had given people something to *believe in*. No person deserved to live with the pain he had carried. People were not meant to survive that kind of pain.

He had saved people from despair.

He looked closely at the image again. An untrained eye would not have been able to tell. But it was clear to him that she had faded.

"What do you want from me?" he said. "Tell me what you want!"

Her face was firm, her cold eyes fixed in judgment.

"I'll tell you," she said. "If it will quiet your ravings. I want you to stop trying to forget what happened."

He bowed his head. He could not face his own shame.

"I cannot—" he said. "It is . . . too much."

She would not excuse him. She would not let him go.

"Something is lost when you forget," she said. "Stolen."

Moody grew hot. He could not endure more accusation. He could not endure the accusation from *her*.

"I am no thief!" he cried. "It is I who have been robbed! What more do you want me to do?"

But her lips were tight—thin silver lines of unfeeling.

That was all.

The voice was gone.

XXI

A VOICE . . . A rattle . . . the sounds commingled in Elizabeth's head. Was she hearing both of them again, or was the voice coming from somewhere else?

The rattle was in her hands. She had needed to hold the rattle.

It had been calling to her during these past few days—calling out like a neglected child. "Mama," she heard the little voice say—that quiet voice, not yet trained or formal. It was the voice she preferred, the voice that touched her in the tenderest places. It was a much easier voice to accept than the final voice, the dying voice—the one that had said it would be gone soon.

She hadn't understood what he had meant. What would be gone? If only she had understood.

The rattle gleamed in her palm. She was cupping it as if it were wounded. She ran her fingers over its face . . . the side that held the engraving. There was a roughness there. She had never liked the feeling of those three elaborate letters.

It itched. She wanted to scratch away the roughness of the engraving. But something was different about the letters. A slight difference only—something almost imperceptible. What was wrong with it? The rattle now felt more like a worn-out spoon.

She raised her hand and finally inspected it.

No, she was not seeing clearly.

She pressed her fingers into her eyes, and then examined the letters again.

$$\mathcal{VJG}$$

V-J-G. Those were not William's initials. Someone had been in her bedroom. Someone had exchanged the rattle.

Or had someone simply altered it? The rattle was almost twenty years old. Who could have found the same kind of rattle, and used it to replace her William's?

She looked at it once more. The rattle glistened back at her. Had someone scratched out one of the W's lines? Where were the signs of the crime? The silver was smooth. The silver was perfect.

Could the girl have come back into the house?

No, Elizabeth thought. It was that impudent Jenny. This time she had gone too far.

Elizabeth screamed and Jenny rushed into the bedroom. It was the first time that Jenny would see the rattle out in the open.

"Ma'am!" Jenny exclaimed. "No . . . no!"

Elizabeth was pacing now, the rattle in her hand. Her eyes were reddened, and she glared at Jenny. She could not restrain her hatred.

"You wicked creature," she said. "After all that we've done for you. After all that James has done for you. How could you be so cruel?"

"Ma'am, no . . ." Jenny fumbled, approaching her mistress with caution.

"Explain this to me right now, you wicked, wicked creature!"

And she thrust the rattle before Jenny's eyes.

"Master William," Jenny whispered.

"Yes, that's right," Elizabeth said.

And then she cried out: "William!"

Jenny touched the shaking hand, her coarse fingers brushing Elizabeth's sleeve.

"Explain it," Elizabeth said. "I demand that you tell me what this means. Tell me what you mean by meddling with my William's rattle, or I swear, Jenny . . . I swear by God—"

"Ma'am . . . Master William's rattle . . . you ordered it out of the house all those years ago. I took those things out of the house myself."

"The letters, you brazen woman. Look at these letters!"

And she forced the thing into Jenny's hands.

Jenny studied it.

"I'm not sure what it is you want me to see," Jenny said.

Now she was really playing tricks. This thankless woman whom they had saved. She was old and growing more useless. And in recent years her sight had begun to go. In the old days, she wouldn't have fetched two hundred dollars.

Elizabeth snatched the rattle from Jenny, and collapsed upon the bedroom floor. She wanted to continue this fight—to slap Jenny as she had once before—but the floor had pulled her down, and she could no longer wage this battle. The rattle had sounded when she fell . . . a tiny tinkling that mocked her muffled cries. She could not see anything beyond the rattle now. The rattle was only a light.

Jenny kneeled down next to Elizabeth, and took the shining object from her hands.

Jenny understood. She knew what it meant to lose.

"It's alright, ma'am," she said. "Everything will be alright."

XXII

WHEN JOSEPH AWOKE on deck the next morning, the boat was approaching that twisted place in the river that joined the deformed fingers of three separate states. Even there the river was wide—about a half a mile in breadth—and because of the many bends the boat faced great challenges. On one side of the river, green forests covered elevated banks, and on the other, yellow sand shelves extended out into the water. Sometimes the sand was on the right, and sometimes on the left—always stretching out from one side, but never from both sides at once. The river had stolen from Kentucky what it gave to Missouri, then robbed Missouri to pay back Kentucky for what it had taken. Year after year it had been forming and destroying plantations . . . tearing away, without remorse, the land that it had so suddenly built up.

The boat pressed on through that second day, nearing Memphis by sundown that evening. At every stop along the way, no wharves greeted the steamer, but the empty riverbanks alone, which demanded skilled maneuvering. Near Memphis, the plantations practically stooped down to touch the river, their landings little more than tree clearings where groups of freedmen and mules stood waiting. Planters exited the boat at nearly every makeshift landing, and though a few continued to board, the crowd thinned considerably after Tennessee. The same held true for the deck passengers, who carried away their life's possessions as they made their way off the boat. Bedding and washbasins, cold chests and spinning wheels, hen-coops and kettles were all part of the parade. North of Vicksburg, a group of sixty workers took leave of the steamer in unison, their destination one of the many plantations still in ruins on the banks of the river.

It was not until late in the evening of that second night that Joseph spied Moody again, creeping down one of the staircases.

Joseph leapt up, and stepped over a sleeping body.

"Edward," he whispered. "Are you out of your mind?"

And he moved forward, grabbing ahold of Moody's arm, and forcing him into the shadows.

"I told you that you can't be seen down here. We still have nearly two days—"

"We may be in even more danger," Moody insisted. "Something has happened. Something—"

Moody spoke deliberately, but with a slight tremble.

"What is it?" Joseph said.

"It's the negative," Moody answered. "Something is happening to her."

The small leather case was in his hands now, and he was opening it, and removing the negative.

"You must see the thing with your own eyes," Moody said.

And he looked at it, but did not offer it to Joseph.

Joseph reached for the glass, but Moody held it firm. Moody was not letting go of the negative.

"I cannot see," Joseph said, tugging.

But Moody tightened his own grip.

"Edward—" Joseph said.

And Moody at last released the glass.

Joseph tilted the negative and the varnish shined silver. In the moonlight, the negative became a mirror. On the surface there was Isabelle, in all her stunning beauty—and there, too, the Garretts, half-occluded by their stains.

Then he noticed it.

Was it—? No, it couldn't be. He had varnished the negative immediately— right after he had led Moody out of the dark room.

Joseph peered into the negative, tilting it again in the moonlight.

"I see it," Joseph said.

"And you are *certain* you varnished the negative?" Moody said.

"The varnish is plainly there."

The two men looked at each other in the darkness. Was she leaving them again? Were they both driving her away?

"What does it mean?" Moody demanded.

But Joseph did not answer. He could not bring himself to admit what he was seeing. There were of course chemical reactions—mistakes—that could cause such things, but he had been so careful during every step of the preparation.

"I don't know what it means. It's strange—that this would happen as we draw—"

And then it hit him all at once, like a downpour.

He looked at her. He could see but her silver remnants in the shadows. She was receding as they drew closer. Joseph now understood what she wanted.

"We are on the right path to finding her," Joseph said. "She has returned so that we might find her. And when we find her—"

He paused, calmly handing the negative back to Moody.

There was no need to explain. When they found her she would be gone.

XXIII

FOR TWO MORE days the *Sotto Voce* sailed through rising mists, as the riverbanks continued to crumble. The river had made a practice of breaching the neglected levees, and in many places had swept them entirely away. It had flooded whole plantations, and carried boats and rafts inland. Where it had generously retreated, roads of debris marked its path.

While the ruin was constant, the landscape began to change just north of Louisiana. Moody watched from the promenade deck as the trees grew their beards—"Spanish moss," one passenger explained. The clumps of hairy strands, which became ever more widespread as the boat traveled south, accentuated the riverbank's already somber and dismal character. In New England, memories were locked behind brick walls and heavy doors. Here, the trees seemed to weep with them.

At Natchez, Mr. Pemberton at last disembarked.

"It has been a great pleasure, Mr. Moody, a great pleasure," he said. "If only we had been able to dine together more often. Do you eat, Mr. Moody? I must say, I tried my best to find you at dinner, but never with success. And as you can see, I'm a man who doesn't wait to do his eating."

"I have been—" Moody began, but then thought the better of it. "I have been overcome with spiritual messages on this journey, and have needed to keep to my room."

Pemberton nodded ferociously.

"Of course, Mr. Moody, of course. A great man like you—"

But Moody held up his hand.

"Good day to you, Mr. Pemberton."

"Good day to you, Mr. Moody."

And then bending forward, as if to whisper a secret, he said:

"And worry you not, sir. I've told no one of your passage. There was a gentleman at dinner one night who had never heard of the spirit photographs. I told him my story—of my Anabelle—referencing the empty chair that I had saved for you. This man was astonished—man by the name of Wells,

Mr. Moody, in case you should ever need to know—this man was astonished, and talked of going to Boston to meet you. And I said to him, I says, 'You never know where the spirit photographer is likely to appear,' and I give a nod to your chair as if you might be expected. But I said not a word more than that, Mr. Moody, and the gentlemen present were none the wiser."

"I thank you for your discretion," Moody said.

"I am only at your service."

And with that, Pemberton joined the mass of planters and freedmen who were pouring out onto the land.

THE BOAT SAILED, and on the final day of its journey, the landscape changed once again. The dense forests that lined the river, and the surviving cotton fields that competed with them, gave way to acres of sugarcane in that last coiled stretch after Baton Rouge. The cypress trees still towered from their strongholds in the water, but the cane fields dominated the flat open spaces that lay beyond the river's edges. The sugarcane swayed, its sharp tips pricking the sky. An endless green ocean bound the river's muddy waters.

This was the land that Joseph had left behind—the plants and soil that he still smelled in his dreams. The last time he had seen these fields he had been traveling with the man who had saved him. Together they had stood on the deck of a steamship, watching the land go by. The sun had been setting on that day, too . . . setting over the sugarcane fields and tree-lined edges of the horizon.

The boat rammed into the levee at New Orleans a bit farther upriver than the central landing at Jackson Square. Here, as in St. Louis, the packed earth sloped down toward the water, and small cities of cotton bales awaited departure, by river or by land. The levee was a fury of activity—mules, horses, carriages, and working men all moving in opposite directions. From a distance the cathedral's steeple seemed to be glowering down at all the commotion, but its opinion—and certainly its dignity—was overshadowed by the countless feathered smoke stacks of the steamboats.

Even as the light was fading, the commerce of the levee showed little signs of slowing. And this was fortunate for Joseph and Moody, who reunited and then blended into the crowd. They made their way through the mules and the cotton bales to Levee Street, the thoroughfare that rimmed the old

French Quarter. Crossing over it, they entered into a city ablaze with life . . . a place of so much color that no picture could ever have captured it.

Joseph had returned, and the smell was much the same—hot brick and dry dust and pipe smoke and horse urine. But the balconies and concealed gardens of those houses closest to the river released the aromas of their tropical inhabitants, in defiance of the city's ranker smells. There was the fragrance of sweet olive, the scent of oleander and jasmine, the damp smell of banana trees, their six-foot leaves drooping toward the ground. Oranges protruded from decorative iron railings, and white roses climbed upon trellises and verandas. Where the old Spanish buildings had left room for larger things to grow, moss-draped oaks shaded the courtyards and the streets.

Because a number of steamboats had released passengers at once, the crowds piling into the streets of New Orleans were unusually dense. In that crowd, Joseph noticed, every class and color of person was represented—white planters, black workers, white workers, and well-dressed freedmen. Creole mistresses, Creole servants, and mulattoes, old and young. The shop windows displayed signs in French and English. Everywhere around him, there was the clattering of both tongues.

Joseph bumped into an old dark-skinned woman, dressed in vibrant silks.

"*Faites attention!*" she scolded.

"*Excusez-moi, madame,*" Joseph said.

And the woman moved on.

"You know the language," Moody said.

"I—" Joseph offered. "Well—it has been many years."

The two men continued moving with the steady stream of people, but once they had crossed over Chartres Street, Joseph slowed his pace.

"Joseph?" Moody said.

But Joseph did not respond. He was staring at an enormous building whose elaborate façade shadowed the street. He was inside of it again now—the old St. Louis Hotel—with its massive, echoing rotunda. He would be part of one of the sales, because old man Winter had gone and died. The sales took place here every afternoon—from twelve to three.

From the oculus in the ceiling, the sun cast circular sprays of light, illuminating the alcoves where the auctioneers announced their goods. In one bay a man sold paintings; in another, goats and mules. Still other auction blocks sold deeds to estates . . . bales of surplus cotton, and barrels of spirits.

The beauty of the room had been commented upon by all of the visiting journalists back then, for the Creoles had spared no expense in the building of this modern palace. Strangely, they had chosen to decorate it with depictions of eminent Americans—busts and frescoes of Washington and Jefferson, and other revolutionary heroes who had led the cause for freedom.

Two men approached the auction block where Joseph and the others sat waiting. One eyed Joseph, and said something to the auctioneer. After more conversation, they led him behind a screen.

"You speak English, boy?" one of them said.

Joseph nodded.

They then ordered him to remove his shirt.

"A few marks," one of them said. "Not ideal, but a very good sign."

The men then exchanged some words with the auctioneer. Joseph understood what was next. One of the men tapped his riding crop below Joseph's navel. Joseph released his waist string, letting his pants fall to the floor.

And then, the most unimaginable thing happened. They did not examine his thigh muscles. Nor did they inspect his calves. They did not feel his naked hips for robustness, nor move around in back of him to assess the rear flanks and the buttocks.

The men stood before Joseph, looking down at his body.

And then they laughed.

"A lot of good in this one," the auctioneer said.

"He'll do," one of the men said. "Do you know the age?"

"Twenty-two or twenty-three," the auctioneer replied. "Certainly no older than twenty-five."

Back out in the rotunda, one of the fancy girls stood upon the block. She had been dressed for sale in luxurious greens and golds. Gold earrings had been attached to her ears.

"Now gentlemen," the auctioneer boomed, "who will show interest in this lovely *light beauty*. As you can see she is smooth of skin, supple of form . . . and marvelously full-chested. A young, light-skinned beauty . . ."

There was a row of women waiting. It would be some time before the auctioneer came around to Joseph.

The men had laughed, and Joseph had not known what it had meant. Laughter was not usually part of this scene. There had been no laughter for him since the death of Mr. Winter . . . kind old Winter, whose daughter had sent Joseph away. She had always been afraid of him, since the day he had arrived. He had never given her any reason to fear him. She had feared him for the sake of being afraid.

And here he was now. His turn was coming up. The men had laughed at him, and he did not understand.

The woman on the auction block was holding back her cries. A young assistant, ebony-skinned, held up one of her arms for better viewing.

Then a crash sounded from somewhere within the rotunda. A dropped mirror? One of the windows? The splintering echoed throughout the chamber.

But Joseph was in the street again now. He was back in the street with—

Moody was grasping his arm. The levee crowd's steady progression had degenerated into disorder. In front of the hotel, all traffic had stopped. A small wagon full of windowpanes had hit a curb and toppled over.

"We must move," Moody said, trying to pull Joseph aside.

But Joseph remained transfixed on the building. The hotel had taken its hold.

All around Joseph the crowd swayed and roared, for the accident had caused a great disturbance. The wagon was blocking St. Louis Street as well as the entrance to the hotel. Boots and shoes were trampling through the debris. On one corner, an old black woman was selling paper-wrapped pralines, and laughing.

Moody moved Joseph away from the commotion—into an alleyway, across from the hotel. It was an airless, narrow passage, barely wide enough for a carriage. Many of its storefronts had been abandoned, and dirty rags hung in its windows. Joseph knew this place too—it was the old *Passage de la Bourse*, where merchants had exchanged all manner of property in the old days.

They had marched him through that alley that same morning, before the auction. There were others there—for sale. The bidding took place out in the open.

Joseph stopped. The air in the alleyway was stifling.

"It has been such a long time . . ." Joseph said. "Such a long time. I—"

But Moody understood. It was as if he himself had been there before. The commerce of the old days had sprung back to life. In the end, there was no getting away from it.

"I know," Moody said. "I see it."

It was everywhere, especially in the dirt that coated the bricks. The walls held unrelenting knowledge in that dirt. The mortar looked soft, as if you could dip your finger into it. This place was wet and luxurious—a place that never let things go.

"We must leave," Moody said, "before—"

But the words stopped short. There was a stunning blow . . . it had come from somewhere amongst the shadows.

Joseph lost his balance, for he too had been struck. He landed against a wall . . . his head throbbing, his sight blackening. From St. Louis Street, the gas lamps spat pathetic bits of light into the alley. And not far from Joseph, Moody lay on the ground.

The figure stood above him.

Then it happened. The man was down upon Moody. The knife went up and the hand plunged down—straight toward Edward Moody's heart.

"No!" Joseph cried.

He had abandoned Edward Moody. He had followed his own path back into the darkness.

The giant rose to his feet, his eyes meeting Joseph's. He was gripping the bloodstained knife at his side.

The crowd moved in ripples in the open channel of St. Louis Street, while the flickering of the gas lamps sent shadows down the alley. Joseph glared back at him. The shadows were distorting his face. Beneath the shadows, in the gaslight, the face was leering and misshapen.

The man stepped toward him.

"I know you," Joseph said.

But the assassin did not respond. There was a glaze over his eyes, and he was staring straight through Joseph. Joseph's back was against the wall—something was holding him in place.

Then another figure was beside him—a tall form cloaked in black.

"Devil!" the voice said. "You have no business here."

The figure wore robes that enveloped him like armor. He was holding a long hand up toward the murderer.

The assassin studied the intruder, then returned his eyes to Joseph. More glass crashed—some last bits falling out in the street—and as if by summons, the assassin began to retreat. At the farther end of the alley, other gas flames cast their reflections. Joseph did not see exactly how or when the man disappeared.

The stranger stepped forward, a large gold cross gleaming on his breast.

"Father!" Joseph cried.

"You've returned," the priest responded.

And both men rushed over toward Moody, whose clothes were drenched in his own blood.

XXIV

"ARE YOU ALRIGHT, madam?" the inspector said, almost wincing at Mrs. Lovejoy's bruises.

"Ah, well . . ." Mrs. Lovejoy replied. "It looks much worse than it feels, inspector. Thank you for asking. The truth is I'm getting clumsier and clumsier. I should know not to be meddling around in the dark."

The inspector couldn't help but examine Mrs. Lovejoy's injuries. Such marks were not simply the effects of a casual fall. The day after Moody's escape, she had mysteriously disappeared from the store. Now, a week later, he could see the reason for her absence.

"Is there anything I can—" he continued.

"Oh no," Mrs. Lovejoy said. "It's quite alright, I assure you."

And then, moving down the counter, slightly away from him, she said: "And how can I help you?"

Bolles hesitated another moment before pursuing his questions. Mrs. Lovejoy looked as if she were still in great pain.

"Mrs. Lovejoy, I must ask. This injury . . . has it anything to do with—"

Mrs. Lovejoy raised an eyebrow.

"With Mr. Moody," Bolles said.

"I'm not certain what you mean," Mrs. Lovejoy said.

"Mr. Moody . . . was he in any way related to, or perhaps even the cause of this injury?"

"Mr. Moody!" the woman exclaimed. "The cause of an injury! Why there couldn't be anything more preposterous. Mr. Moody may be many things, but he is not a violent man."

Bolles studied her face. She had not been abused by Moody.

"As I said, inspector," Mrs. Lovejoy said, "I'm just getting clumsier, and, well—"

And she began fiddling with some salt cellars, realigning them unnecessarily.

"You do understand why we're pursuing him," Bolles said.

"Yes, I understand that you are bringing charges for fraud against one of the greatest artists and Spiritualist mediums of our time. Yes, I understand that, Inspector Bolles."

"You are yourself a Spiritualist then, madam?"

"I am," Mrs. Lovejoy replied, "and a believer that all things come to justice, in the end."

"The charges against Mr. Moody are very serious, and if found guilty of these crimes he could go to prison for some time."

"I am aware of that, inspector."

"And you are aware that you are obligated, by law, to assist in the prosecution of this case, or you yourself could be held accountable for aiding criminal activity."

"Listen to me, inspector. I will say this to you one time. I have committed more 'crimes' in my lifetime than you have seen in the entirety of your green years. As many of the residents in this city know, I was perhaps one of the greatest 'criminals' in Boston, before the war, when it was legal for a man to own another man as property. So I am not afraid of being a criminal, inspector, if being a criminal is the right thing to be. But I swear on my honor, I know nothing of Mr. Moody's whereabouts, or his intentions, or his guilt or innocence, or anything else it is you want to know. I only know that Mr. Moody has gifts beyond anything that you or I could ever hope to understand, and that to jail him would be unjust. You yourself would be committing the crime."

Mrs. Lovejoy was one of the most respected women in Boston, and Bolles could see how she had earned that place.

Then she softened.

"Your father was a wonderful man, inspector."

"Ah, you knew him then," Bolles said.

"Yes, of course I knew him. He was a great, great supporter of the cause. It is atrocious what they did to him, when he went down there after the war. If only he had had better protection. So many of our brave souls were defenseless. And still are. But you must never dwell on that, my dear boy. What he did . . . most men will never be able to claim such honor. He died in service to his country. He died in service to *humanity*."

Inspector Bolles did not receive these words with any amount of surprise, for his father, Montgomery Bolles Sr., had been lauded by radicals and conservatives alike. He had been a man of unimpeachable character, they said, whose judgment had always fallen on the side of "decency."

"You have what he had," Mrs. Lovejoy said.

Bolles looked at her inquisitively.

"The ability to see," she said.

"See?"

"Yes, see. Which is why I don't understand all this nonsense about pursuing Mr. Moody. Surely someone with your character and insight can understand all the good that man has done for people, whether or not you believe in spirits yourself."

"I have no personal investment in this matter," the inspector replied. "The community at large is demanding the investigation. My duty is to respond to the community."

"The community!" Mrs. Lovejoy exclaimed. "Yes, I know all about that community. They are displeased because a photographer is producing things they can't explain . . . offering interpretations to the world that they cannot comprehend! You are acquainted with Senator Garrett, I believe?"

"I am, madam."

"To be sure the senator is a great man—perhaps one of the greatest this country has ever seen—but I know his business in this. I saw him when he came here—both times. And I saw him when he left. If he is at all representing this 'community' that you speak of, I am very sorry for it. Very sorry for it indeed."

"May I ask, Mrs. Lovejoy, what is your knowledge around the connection?"

"What connection?"

"The connection between Mr. Moody and Senator Garrett."

Mrs. Lovejoy looked away from him.

"Is there one?" she said.

"I don't know," Bolles replied. "That's why I'm asking you. You have known both of them for a very long time."

"And Mrs. Garrett," Mrs. Lovejoy added. "An honorable, and much respected woman. We engraved some pieces of her wedding silver for her. But Mr. Moody was not here then."

"Yes, I know," the inspector said. "He first came here in the mid-fifties, I believe?"

"Earlier," Mrs. Lovejoy said. "It was probably fifty-one or fifty-two.

I remember, because the railroad was afire with activity then . . . because of the new fugitive laws. Those disgusting—"

And she turned her head aside, visibly appalled by what she did not say.

"Was Mr. Moody ever involved in your railroad activity?" the inspector asked.

"Mr. Moody? Oh no-no-no. The poor lamb. No, he was never involved, or knew anything for that matter. Of course, it was a bit strange, given that—"

And she paused, bringing her hand up to touch one of her bruises.

"Yes?" the inspector said.

"Well, Mr. Moody . . ." she said. "You see . . . Mr. Moody suffered a kind of . . . incident."

The inspector encouraged her to go on.

"It was the girl, you see. He is the way he is today—because of the girl. He loved her. And she left. I'm afraid the man never fully recovered."

All of the newspaper accounts had concentrated on Moody's evolution and career as a spirit photographer. No one had ever said anything about a romance. Indeed, the papers had made him out to be above the realm of earthly affections.

"I never saw anything like it," Mrs. Lovejoy continued. "He became inconsolable—quite hopeless—after she disappeared. Which is why when he went off to study with Brady in New York, it was a truly wonderful thing for him. Mr. Moody is . . . well, Mr. Moody is easily consumed."

"And this woman," the inspector said. "Who was she?"

"She was called Isabelle," Mrs. Lovejoy replied. "She was a free woman of color. She lived here in Boston. And she was—"

And again Mrs. Lovejoy paused, measuring her words before she spoke.

"She was one of those helping with the railroad."

Bolles returned a respectful nod. Even now, five years after the war, he understood that there remained a kind of sacred reticence amongst those who had hidden fugitives.

"Of course, everything was kept very quiet in those days," Mrs. Lovejoy said. "There was a great deal at stake—for everyone involved. Back then, your neighbor could have been hiding runaways right under your nose and you'd never have known it. She was a sweet girl—a beautiful girl. She was here much more than necessary, which is how I knew. And after a short time, there simply was no hiding it. Mr. Moody was quite the different man back then."

"But she was a negro, you say. That—"

"Made it impossible? Yes. But what great love isn't impossible in some way, inspector. Tell me that."

It was disconcerting for Bolles to hear Moody talked about in this way. This was not the Edward Moody he was investigating.

"She was quite taken with him," Mrs. Lovejoy went on. "You could see that plainly, when she came in. It's a mystery though—"

And she stopped, looking off.

"Yes?" Bolles said.

"Well, it's a mystery as to what happened to her. One day she simply vanished. But those were strange times, Inspector, and strange things happened to everybody. And of course . . . there were other delicate matters one has to consider. But I cannot be the one to judge."

"Do you mean that she might have been with—"

"It could have been the reason," Mrs. Lovejoy interrupted. "I cannot say, and hate to think it. Perhaps Mr. Moody knew absolutely nothing about it. Or perhaps he knew everything. He may have even had cause for *wanting* her to go away. But one thing I can tell you . . . he was never the same man after that day. After Isabelle left, it was simply as if a part of him had—died."

"When was the last time you saw this woman?" the inspector asked.

"She came here. She left a letter for him—just slipped it under the door without coming in."

"And then?"

"And then, she walked away from the store and I never saw her again. She may not have even been a free woman, for all I know. She may have needed to go to Canada. Those were dangerous times, Inspector. There were forgeries, kidnappings . . . all sorts of evilness about."

The inspector was not ignorant of the things Mrs. Lovejoy described. He had been aware of such crimes and abuses, ever since he was a child. In his household, the talk of the necessity of abolition had been constant. His father had not been a man who was afraid to speak.

"I must thank you for your time, Mrs. Lovejoy," Bolles said. "But if I may ask you one last question—do you know if Mr. Moody has any connection to New Orleans?"

"New Orleans . . ." Mrs. Lovejoy said. "No, I don't think so. Why do you ask?"

"A report has come in," Bolles said, "from a passenger on one of the steamboats, who claims to have traveled with Mr. Moody from St. Louis as far as Natchez, Mississippi. The passenger took leave of the boat at that point, but the final destination was New Orleans. And that boat should be reaching that city sometime this evening, assuming it has remained on schedule."

"How odd," Mrs. Lovejoy said, "that we should be talking about the girl."

"And why is that?" Bolles asked.

"Because I do believe that's where she was from."

"New Orleans?"

Mrs. Lovejoy again touched her bruise.

"Why, yes—she came from New Orleans. I am quite sure of it now."

XXV

THIS WAS MOODY'S vision:

A young woman on a small boat, making her way through a swamp. She pushes the boat with a pole. The pole makes little noise in the water.

And this:

The woman's face—tired and hurt. The face is worn with suffering. It cannot keep the secret of who she is.

And this:

The glow of lamps, far off in the distance. Bits of flames flickering between thick columns of cypress.

She is escaping.

She is resolved.

He is nowhere in her vision.

He is awake and yet he isn't. The feeling in his heart is heavy. There is a weight there, pressing, for this is where he has been carrying her. The weight is suffocating his heart.

He can hear his heart beating. It is begging to be set free.

"Edward," a voice says. "Edward . . . can you hear me?"

It is not her voice. It is a man's voice. He opens his eyes. It is Joseph's voice.

He struggles, but Joseph holds his body down. Joseph has tricked him again. He will take her—hide her. She will no longer be his.

"Where is she?" Moody says. "You devil—tell me where she is!"

"She's safe," Joseph says. "All is safe, and you must rest."

Joseph has that look of truth—an angel in the mist.

"Know this," Joseph whispers. "She has spoken. She has saved you."

XXVI

THE ROOM WAS plain. On one side, a bureau, with a statue of the Virgin Mary atop an embroidered cloth. Across from the bed, a fireplace, and above that a wooden crucifix. The walls were white—painted plaster. The room was close, and smelled of clean linen.

Joseph sat beside Moody. The photographer was sleeping. There was a bandage wrapped around his head.

For two days Moody had wavered in and out of sleep, awakening now and then, his eyes fixed in desperation. He was having visions. He had lunged out more than once. Perhaps in his weakened state, he had mistaken Joseph for the demon.

At other times Moody had spoken, but the words had been muddled. Conversations . . . confessions . . . imagined exchanges. Moody seemed to be communicating in some other distant world. Sometimes the mumbling was loud—sometimes nothing more than a whisper.

The priest entered the room.

"Has he awakened since I left you?" he asked.

"No," Joseph answered. "But his murmuring continues. I have made out the name . . . many times now. It is her name—always her name."

Joseph gazed down at Moody. The negative had saved him. The murderer's knife had struck the negative's case, then slid down Moody's side, and cut him. Had the negative not been in Moody's breast pocket, the knife would have plunged through his chest and into his heart.

Isabelle had saved him. It was proof that she was guiding him. Moody was the one she loved.

Joseph had been foolish for thinking that Isabelle ever would have fled with him to Canada. And she had scolded him—*scolded* him as if he were nothing more than a child. He hadn't understood back then, hadn't fathomed how dedicated someone could be to a cause. He had been so consumed by his own survival that it had blinded him to the trials of others.

But that wasn't true. He was a good man—an honest man. He had taught others to read, once he had learned himself, in Canada. He had helped build a house for a family of fugitives . . . sowed potatoes with them in their yard, skinned a rabbit for them and roasted it. He had only been well-intentioned. Even the photographs—

He had been selfish.

He had been selfish and he could no longer hide it from her. There was nothing she could not see. There was nowhere for him to hide.

And here he was again in this room—the room that had briefly concealed him. And once again, as if captured from a dream, he saw himself running away.

L'Archevêché. It was the place some still called "the convent," since the Ursuline nuns had originally built it and later given it over to the archdiocese. First the bishops, and eventually the archbishops, gladly occupied the stately property, which stood out like a countryside mansion amongst the cramped townhouses of the old French Quarter. Those first bishops roamed its cool, tiled hallways, in those dark days before the war. And so too roamed the servants—the many well-dressed and well-cared-for servants—all of whom were nevertheless still the property of the archdiocese.

They were baptized—saved souls. And yet the bishops sold them to pay debts.

One of them had helped Joseph. She was the first, after Father Thomas. The first of many on that path up the river to St. Louis, and then on to—

Her name was Tilly, and she was a kitchen maid. She was the one who had caught Father Thomas sneaking Joseph into the residence. It had been dark, and Father Thomas did not have a plan. Only later did the priest reveal how terrified he had been.

Father Thomas O'Shaughnessy, the man who had appeared like a vision: a tall, black-clad, unearthly vision that stood before Joseph in the street. Joseph was fleeing from the levee after a great explosion. The steamship that was to transport him upriver had exploded.

Such accidents were common in those days—the boilers exploding—and survival oftentimes depended on one's distance from the boiler room. Of course, as with any accident, survival also depended on luck. The trader in charge of Joseph's coffle had been unlucky.

Joseph was chained to five others—there were six of them total—all held together by a long string of iron. The padlock at one end secured the entire group together. Strangely, it was their captivity—their immobility—that had saved them. Had they been coming down the staircase, they too would have been killed. In an instant the explosion had devoured a number of moving men.

The trader had the key, and he now lay on the splintered deck. Blood covered his clothes, and the broken banister pierced his neck.

Joseph and his chained companions pulled themselves toward the dead man. The key was somewhere inside the bloodied waistcoat—they had all seen the man place it there. Joseph fumbled through the pockets and felt nothing at first. And then at last, the key was in his fingers.

It was a fine key—silver—much finer than the keys he was used to seeing. Similarly, the lock it would open was not the kind of thing normally used for the coffles. This lock and this key . . . they did not belong on a chain. Rather, one might have expected to find them guarding the trunks on a fancy carriage. In Joseph's rough hand the key looked an odd specimen, its surface bashfully mirroring the bright flames from the explosion.

Beyond the flames and the smoke and the eviscerated boat, the levee was a chaotic scene of panic and confusion. For the towers of cotton bales still waiting to board the steamers had been drenched in a shower of the explosion's fiery debris. When Joseph jumped from the boat, a metropolis of cotton bales greeted him . . . its lanes and tunnels afire, but beckoning. Offering him places to hide.

But there was no time to hide . . . there was only time to move. And Joseph moved, burrowing through the bales, like some blind but determined creature. He jumped from one group of bales to the next, inching himself away from the steamboats. There were gunshots—measured gunshots. Someone was firing. But that endless maze of cotton bales was his path to freedom.

At Levee Street, the horses and mules had grown frantic, and everywhere people rushed to and from the waterfront. In the confusion, Joseph was able to travel a short distance up another street, hugging the walls of the buildings, trying to make himself one with the shadows.

And that was when he saw him—when the vision of Father Thomas first appeared.

Their eyes locked, and Joseph could see that he had been discovered. Father Thomas knew at once what Joseph was—and what he had done.

But luck was with Joseph, for on that street, in the darkness, he had come across one of the few white men in New Orleans whose conscience was conflicted. One block to the left, or even half a block to the right, Joseph surely would have encountered a planter—or worse, a trader. But on that walled, empty street, not two blocks from the levee, a sympathetic spirit had miraculously come into being.

The priest eyed the runaway. He had only a moment to decide.

"In here, quickly," he said.

And he opened a narrow gate. That gate was there, in the wall, hiding like a sly observer.

That was how it all began—Joseph's journey toward freedom. An accident, some luck, and the appearance of fortuitous spirits. When Tilly, the kitchen maid, caught Father Thomas smuggling Joseph in through the refectory, her knowing glare paralyzed the guilty priest in his place. Father Thomas was not a man who had done anything like this before, and the look of terror in his eyes revealed his inexperience. But Tilly was no stranger to the wrong turns made by hapless runaways. The girl had seen it all before, and knew what needed to be done.

She had rushed Joseph into a storage room, then a sick room, and finally into the room once used as the orphans' dormitory. With Tilly's help, Father Thomas had been able to keep Joseph out of sight for two days. Then the day came for Father Thomas to travel upriver, and he boarded the steamboat with a manservant. Joseph's new clothes had been plucked from the laundry, which Tilly also oversaw.

It wasn't until they had reached the boat that Joseph realized he had failed to thank her. She had opened the gate, shoved him out, and then shut it. There had been no time for thank yous or goodbyes.

"Tilly," Joseph said, for the name had seized upon him. "After the war . . . do you know what became of her?"

"Sadly, I do not," the priest replied. "The bishop sold her after the epidemic—not long after you left here. The fever brought great losses."

"Tilly," Joseph repeated. "One of the many souls who saved me."

"And me," Father Thomas said. "She could have shouted—given us both up. I've never been so afraid. But God was with us in that moment,

Joseph. God was guiding us both through that darkness."

It was the first time they had spoken of Joseph's escape since that night, for the letters to and from Canada had remained purposefully innocent of the past. Before the war, the policies of the archdiocese had aligned with those of the southern states, and anyone involved in abolitionist activity would have been branded a criminal. The archbishop would have excommunicated Father Thomas for what he had done. Even after the war had ended, neither Joseph nor Father Thomas dared refer to their experience in writing.

"I am sorry, Joseph," Father Thomas said. "I am sorry that I could not go farther with you. It might have—"

"You have nothing to apologize for," Joseph replied. "You took me as far as St. Louis. Had you accompanied me any farther, you would have put yourself in even more peril. The railroad took me in then, and you see . . ."

The priest nodded. But something in his face said that the guilt was still there.

"I advanced in those years—after you were gone. First chaplain to the Ursulines. Then Diocesan Chancellor. And finally, the Vicar General you see before you now. But through all that time, though I never spoke or wrote of it, I could not suppress the memory of that journey we took together. How every moment of that journey was a step toward cleansing my soul. When I returned from St. Louis, I was forever a changed man. It took everything in my power to keep my beliefs a secret."

"Those were dangerous times," Joseph said. "For all of us."

"But the others," the priest said, "the thousands and thousands of others—"

"Millions," Joseph said. "There was no way for you to save them."

The priest lowered his head.

"And we will forever be atoning for that sin."

Moody stirred. The groan was loud . . . louder than any sound Moody had made that day. Joseph moved closer to the bed, and placed his hand on Moody's arm.

"Edward," he whispered. "You're safe."

Then Father Thomas stepped forward, and touched the top of Moody's head.

"*In nomine Patris, et Filii, et Spiritus*—" he began.

But the gentle words seemed to have a sudden effect, for Moody opened his eyes, threw off the bedclothes, and leapt to his feet. He stood there before them, his arms outstretched, as if he had gained the strength of a thousand men.

"I know what I must do!" he cried. "I have seen everything, and I know!"

"Edward!" Joseph exclaimed. "You are badly hurt. You must not—"

"Curse the wound, Joseph!" Moody said. "Here it is, and what of it? I am no madman—I remember everything. I looked into his eyes . . . looked into those eyes of evil, before the fist thrust out to strike me. I know what it is that we face, and I am not afraid of it. In that darkness, I received the most beautiful gift. I saw everything, Joseph, and there is only one thing left for me to do—"

"Edward, you must do nothing right now. You must—"

But Father Thomas touched Joseph to quiet him.

"I've seen everything," Moody said. "She was hidden away, where no one could find her . . . where no one would ever be able to know her for what she was."

"Isabelle—" Joseph whispered.

"She has been guiding me," Moody said, "just as you have always suspected. How long have I been here? There is no time to waste. We must go. I must bring her back!"

Moody was pacing, his cheeks colored bright red. His life had returned to him, and he had reawakened with a mission. He understood that the priest had saved him, and that Joseph, too, had been guarding his soul, but there was one thing that had become undeniable in the face of so much doubt:

Only he, Edward Moody, the spirit photographer, had the power to raise the dead.

XXVII

"AND YOU SAY you do not know where he's gone off to?" Dovehouse asked her.

"I do not," Elizabeth replied. "Perhaps he is down at the coffeehouse."

Dovehouse looked inquisitive. He was sitting in her drawing room. He had begged for but a moment of her time, and now she sat before him, his prisoner.

"James has been spending many hours down there of late," she added.

Dovehouse smiled slightly, taking in her explanation. Had she not been in the front hall when he rang, she never would have answered the door.

"Since we have this moment," Dovehouse said, "I was wondering if I might—"

"Yes?" she said.

She knew what he was up to. It was important to preempt him.

"It seems . . ." Dovehouse said, "that my friend has been—"

And he paused, searching her face for stray hints of anticipation.

"Not quite himself these past ten days."

"No . . ." Elizabeth said.

"Ah, you take my meaning then?"

"It has been a difficult time," she said.

"But it all seems to have been brought on by this damned business with the photograph."

He was watching her closely. He wanted the word to upset her.

"The photograph has thrown him out of sorts," Dovehouse said.

For more than twenty years, Benjamin Dovehouse had been observing her—through her courtship with Garrett, through the early days of her marriage, through the death of her child, and through the worst days of the war. He had been collecting notes on her reactions and behaviors for two decades, and filing them away in his repository of knowledge.

But she knew him too, and she would not give him what he wanted.

"These changes have been somewhat disconcerting to me," Dovehouse went on. "Surely they've been troubling to you as well?"

Elizabeth did not offer him a response.

"Aren't you concerned?" Dovehouse said.

"Concerned?" she repeated.

"Yes, about your *husband*."

And he enunciated the word, as if trying to communicate with an idiot.

"I am concerned with a great many things," Elizabeth said. "James does carry the weight of the nation on his shoulders."

"You know that's not what I'm talking about," Dovehouse said.

Elizabeth winced—an understandable break in her resolve. It was that tone—the same tone he used whenever he believed someone was trying to deceive him. For the most part he had respected her over the years, but she had also seen what his brutality could do to people.

"The photograph," Dovehouse continued. "There is much more to this photograph than—"

"Forgive me," Elizabeth said, "but would you mind telling me . . . how is it that you've come to be involved with our photograph?"

"My understanding is that it is *your* photograph," Dovehouse said.

And at once Elizabeth realized the error of her inquiry.

"Again, I must apologize," Dovehouse said. "I know that the matter is delicate. It takes all of us back . . . back to that time . . ."

"You were here," Elizabeth said. "You know how it tore James apart."

"And you," Dovehouse said. "Let's not forget *you*, my dear."

That voice. Even when low and whispering, that voice resounded like iron.

"It is true," she said. "The spirit photography has . . . revived things. I know you think such matters silly, but there are—"

"Say nothing of what I think is silly, and what is not," Dovehouse said. "I am many things, but I cannot claim to be all-knowing."

It sounded ridiculous—disingenuous—coming from the likes of that man. Then Dovehouse fixed upon her.

"He told me that the photograph was your idea."

Of course it *had* been her idea, but what had Garrett told him? Was Garrett now the one who needed her protection?

"It was," she said. "It was entirely my idea."

"Entirely?" Dovehouse asked.

"Yes, entirely," she said. "In fact, I went through a great deal of trouble—to convince him to sit for the photograph."

"And he agreed for your sake?"

"I suppose," Elizabeth said.

"You suppose? You do not know?"

"No, I'm sorry. I do not know what James may or may not believe with regard to these things. He is very quiet about such matters. You better than anyone must understand the sensitivity around the subject, given who he is, and what he represents."

"I understand exactly what he represents," Dovehouse said. "But . . . what do *you* believe, Mrs. Garrett?"

This was an old trick of Dovehouse's—the pointed question to which there could be no correct answer.

"I believe that there are many things we cannot explain," Elizabeth said.

Dovehouse grinned.

"This is true," he said. "But I am curious . . . if the photograph was your idea, why did James need to be involved with it at all? I've seen plenty of these—"

And he paused again.

"—*photographs*," he said. "Of widows alone with husbands, of mothers with their dead children . . ."

He was trying to wear her down.

"*I* am curious," Elizabeth responded, "as to why you are not discussing the photograph with James yourself?"

"Ah, my dear," Dovehouse said. "My apologies, my apologies. I do not mean to be so intrusive. But James has been somewhat reticent on the matter, as you might expect. Our good senator has many enemies, waiting for him around every corner. My concern is primarily for his—and your—well-being."

"To be sure," Elizabeth replied. "Your concern is greatly appreciated."

And she smoothed her skirt, hoping to bring an end to the conversation.

"But what is it?" Dovehouse pressed.

"What is what?" Elizabeth said.

"The photograph—what is it about the photograph?"

"I'm not sure I understand you."

Dovehouse was growing impatient.

"The photograph!" he exclaimed. "I know my friend. I have watched him these past ten days. I have never seen him so distraught over something in all his life!"

The outburst was so unmeasured, but Elizabeth was careful not to reveal her surprise.

"It is important that he retrieve the photograph," she said. "The photograph could ruin him."

"But it confuses me," Dovehouse said. "We have dealt with nonsense worse than this before. He has been saying things—doing things. He has been so unlike himself."

"James carries great burdens—always. You know that."

"I am not talking about his burdens," Dovehouse intoned. "I am talking about *this* burden."

His voice was calm but his face was terrible. She had seen Dovehouse restraining his frustration in the past, but never had it defied him quite like this.

Then a strange, milky pall descended over his eyes. He grew quiet, his face motionless.

"I may be able to help," he said.

"You have always been a great help to James," she replied.

And she smiled at him. He could not win.

Then his anger returned, like the sharp strike of a match. But his voice remained low and steady.

"I know you," he said. "And I have known you from the first."

His insolence was astonishing. Elizabeth stared back at him calmly.

"Thank you for inquiring after James," she said, "but I'm afraid I must ask you to leave."

Dovehouse rose from his chair and stepped hurriedly out of the room. He had challenged her, and she had gone beyond standing her ground. She remained seated until she heard the front door close. Now there was no turning back.

XXVIII

SENATOR GARRETT SAT in the window of his neighborhood coffee-house, watching the lines of people pass by. Outside, a light drizzle was falling upon Charles Street, and the stone curbs were beginning to shine. Garrett gazed through the window, the crowd oblivious to his company. His own reflection was little more than a faded face amongst the many.

The day had seized him—or rather, something else had seized him—and he had felt compelled to escape from the house. The house was full of whispers. Remembrances, visions. And he felt bound there, and unable to breathe. Yes—since the negative, his breathing had been changing; barely noticeable at first, but requiring more effort in the last few days. The breaths were slower now—heavier—as if a great weight lay upon his chest. And Jenny's concerned looks told him that his difficulties were not invisible.

During that past week, the coffeehouse had offered him something like a refuge—from Elizabeth, from Dovehouse, and from all other pressures. But it was an escape in name only, for his troubles followed him there. A short walk down Pinckney Street to Charles, and then left toward the Commons. He could escape from the house's shadow, but not from what it knew.

But why had these specters pursued him? Why so viciously? And why now? He needed to run from them . . . deny them the places they demanded. They could not chase him forever, even if they did know his secret.

His secret.

That was what stood at the center of it all. The secret that he had been laboring to suppress for an eternity. It was the secret that no one else but Elizabeth knew. It was the secret that would one day condemn him.

How had it come about? Had there been another way out for him? And would anyone ever have forgiven him for such a failing?

There were no answers, but if there had been, they might have been found on that night, that sweltering night back in August of 1850. The night before the momentous vote. He had been the senator from Massachusetts for only one month, having replaced Daniel Webster, who had become Secretary of State. Back then Webster, with Henry Clay, all but commanded the direction of the Whigs—the party that was becoming increasingly divided along sectional lines. Garrett was thirty-nine years old—handsome, newly married, and with a new baby at home in Boston. During those days of mounting polarization, people considered Garrett a moderate—though that too was fated to change.

The young senator had been reading by candlelight in his Washington boardinghouse when the quiet knock sounded upon the door.

"Mr. Webster!" Garrett exclaimed. "To what do I owe this honor?"

For it was indeed the old statesman himself, come to see Garrett in his quarters.

"My apologies for disturbing you at this hour," Webster replied, "but we beg your audience for a matter of urgent business."

Webster stepped into the room, joined by two other elder delegates—Senator Underwood from Kentucky and Congressman Phoenix from New York. The three men shook hands with the young James Garrett, their faces all lined with severity.

"It is urgent business, and it is unpleasant business," Webster said, "and I am afraid we have run out of time."

The old Whigs seated themselves around Garrett's table. Their presence brought a heaviness to the room.

"Tomorrow, as you know," Webster said, "is the vote on the Fugitive Bill."

Garrett nodded.

"And we have come to ask you—no, we have come to *entreat* you—to refrain from casting your vote."

Garrett was confused.

"Refrain from casting my vote?" he said.

"The Democrats have failed to secure Wisconsin," Senator Underwood said. "Both Walker and Dodge will be voting against the bill."

"And we do not yet know," Congressman Phoenix added, "which way Indiana will go."

"The bill must pass," Webster said.

"The bill must pass," Underwood repeated.

And all three of them glowered at Garrett.

The Fugitive Bill—perhaps the most controversial component of the recent compromises to save the Union. It would oblige federal officials—even in northern states—to capture and return runaways to their former masters in the South. It would legalize the conscription of northern citizens in an attempt to fulfill "the prompt and efficient execution of this law." The people of the North would be forced to betray runaways, or face outrageous fines and imprisonment.

"Secretary Webster—" Garrett began.

"I know it is no small thing to ask," Webster said. "But California depends on it, and you know this."

"California must be admitted as a free state," Garrett said. "The issue is non-negotiable."

"We are all in agreement about that," Underwood said. "But the South is loath to permit it. They would much prefer two states—one north, one south—and some of them are *still* arguing for that. The only way to secure all of California as a free state is to give them the Fugitive Bill. They will find a way to block us, if we don't."

The Senate had approved California as a free state only ten days before, and the bill would now go before the House of Representatives. The vote had been 34 to 18, with nearly every southern Democrat opposing.

"We cannot lose California," Webster said. "We've simply come too far."

"But we have won it," Garrett said. "The bill is certain to pass the House. The southern representatives do not have the numbers to defeat the bill."

"But if for any reason we should upset the *northern* Democrats," Webster replied, "there is no telling how the votes may go."

The old statesman's brow sagged remorselessly over his eyes.

"And they are expecting us to deliver the bill," he said.

It was an awful and complicated situation that had been forced upon the Congress. Neither Whigs nor Democrats—northerners nor southerners—could achieve what they wanted without help from the other side.

"The balance is precarious," Phoenix said. "And we need you to abstain. If you don't, and the Fugitive Bill is defeated, the consequences could be dire."

"Consequences!" Garrett exclaimed. "And what of the consequences for the northern people? Am I to stand by as this country adopts a law that would compel any citizen of Boston—or Philadelphia, or New York, or any other city for that matter—to aid in the capture of runaways, and return them to bondage? Is the South to trample over our liberties so easily?"

It was an impassioned reaction—one of his first amongst colleagues.

"Seward will be abstaining," Phoenix said.

"And Phelps."

"And there are others."

Garrett looked from one old face to the next. The eyes were dark, sunk deep into their sockets.

Then Webster spoke:

"If you are worried about ramifications, we can assure you that there will be no retaliation from within the party as a result of your action."

"Inaction," Garrett corrected.

The old man nodded his head.

"The members of the party would consider it a great service."

"But the people—" Garrett protested.

"The people do not elect you," Webster said. "You are appointed by the state legislature. And should you do as we are asking, your associates would be—most grateful."

"We are not asking you to cast an 'aye,'" Underwood said, "only to abstain. It is likely something people will forget."

The men left Garrett's room that night with little ceremony, as if all were trying to forget the meeting before it had even concluded. California had been admitted as a free state by the Senate, and an overwhelming northern majority in the House assured the California bill's success there too.

But did it?

The balance had to be kept, and the Whigs needed Garrett—so much so that they had sent Webster himself to ask the favor. But would the young senator follow his conscience, and vote for what the people of Massachusetts believed in? Or would he curse himself to remember his first term in Congress as one of betrayal and pyrrhic victory?

The next day, when the Fugitive Bill arrived for a vote on the Senate floor, the young senator from Massachusetts was nowhere to be found.

IT WAS NOT until years later—six to be exact—that Senator Garrett felt that he had atoned for his sin. The Republicans had formed as a party in the wake of the Kansas-Nebraska Act, and Garrett had gone over to them, and wholeheartedly embraced their principles. It was also around that time when the northern papers were reprinting his "Rape of Kansas" speech, as if his diatribe against the South were the only thing anyone wanted to read.

But it was not his speech. And that was Garrett's secret.

"The damned planters," Garrett had said to Elizabeth. "They are flooding into the territory from Missouri. The fate of Kansas will be determined by its people, and those vile invaders are trying to steal the vote."

"Yes, James," Elizabeth replied, "I have read of the crimes. The South is determined to block the entry of Kansas as a free state . . . at any cost, it seems."

"It is an outrage," Garrett thundered. "An outrage! They crawl like locusts over this free land, bringing with them their negroes. It is an outrage against God. It is an outrage against the people of this nation. I will not stand by and watch it. These criminals must be cast out!"

Elizabeth watched her husband pace about the room. His alignment with the abolitionists had steadily grown over the past few years.

"The violence," Elizabeth said. "I fear for every poor soul who lives there."

"But there are holy souls there, and unholy souls," Garrett said. "The damned southerners are the instruments of the devil."

There he stood—the young senator, but somewhat older now—his stiff white collar and thick cravat forming a pedestal for his handsome face. Strangely, Garrett became even more captivating when he was enraged. He was already not the same man she had married.

"James," she said, "there is something to consider—"

But Garrett was too angry.

"There is nothing to consider but their expulsion from the territory! I will write a speech *at once* that exposes them for the criminals they are. By God, I will not see their fraudulent votes recognized. Free labor will triumph in Kansas, or the soul of this country will be lost."

He left her then, and disappeared for the rest of the evening. He would take the Senate floor and denounce the southern parasites. "Against this territory, thus fortunate in position and population," he wrote, "an *invasion* has been launched which is without example in the past. Not in the plundered provinces of old, or in the cruelties of selfish rulers, will you find a parallel to the outrage that has been committed against Kansas. The South and its minions have openly polluted a free territory, with the desire of turning the state into another one of its hideous offspring." It was powerful rhetoric that would rouse even the most moderate of his colleagues . . . the voice the abolitionists would praise from Iowa to Maine.

At the heart of the speech was the idea of invasion—the theme that unified it in its relentless condemnation of the South. But when Elizabeth read Garrett's draft, early the next morning, she saw something entirely different. She saw a missed opportunity—a chance to excoriate the South for what it really was—as well as the prospect of creating an even greater alliance between her husband and the abolitionists. Oh yes . . . the truth was already there, hiding in Garrett's scribbles. It just needed to be acknowledged and brought up to the surface.

"James," she said. "You must go another way. You must make the attack personal, and call out the crime for what it is."

Garrett appeared disappointed.

"I have called out the crime, Elizabeth."

"No," Elizabeth responded. "I don't mean the crime that is taking place in Kansas. I mean the crime that is at the core of their entire society."

She took up a pencil and began marking the papers. For nearly an hour he watched, frozen, as she edited his words. She had of course done similar revisions for him in the past, but never with such conviction. Garrett was not worried about the number of changes she would suggest—it was the *degree* of the changes that worried him.

When she was finished, she set the pencil down upon the table. Her face was an image of sorrow. It was an image that still appeared, though less and less frequently. William Jeffrey had been dead for four years.

Garrett lifted the papers, and read over the new words. She had done it. She had transformed his speech about territory and sectional conflict into a condemnation of the South's most hideous "secret." Everywhere now, his references to violating the Kansas Territory took on double meanings that would inflame his southern colleagues and make virtuous women blush.

"Elizabeth—" he said.

But Elizabeth raised her hand.

"It is not an invasion of Kansas," she said.

She stared at him.

"It is a rape."

XXIX

GARRETT WAS STILL gazing through his reflection in the window when Dovehouse entered the coffeehouse.

"Looking for something, old boy?" Dovehouse said.

Garrett, startled, turned from the window. He had not seen his old friend come in.

Dovehouse sat down in an empty chair at Garrett's table.

"I have just come from the house," he said. "Elizabeth said I might find you here. We had a charming conversation."

Garrett returned his attention to his reflection.

"James," Dovehouse said. "I am worried about you."

Garrett blinked and looked at him.

"Yes," he said.

"Yes what?" Dovehouse said. "You are not yourself these days. Your mind is distracted—somewhere else. And I have noticed your shortness of breath."

"I know, Benjamin," Garrett said. "I know."

Dovehouse raised his hand and snapped a finger in front of Garrett.

"What is it with you, man? Where is your mind wondering off to?"

Garrett remained silent, and neither of them spoke for some time. Then Dovehouse said:

"It's the photograph, isn't it?"

The photograph, Garrett thought. He could see the image in front of him.

"It is indeed the photograph," Garrett replied. "It is everything. The photograph has resurrected everything."

Dovehouse respectfully bowed his head.

"It was long ago, James . . . it was a long time ago."

"I thought I would be able to forget," Garrett said.

In that moment Garrett considered revealing the truth—about what was on the negative, and about what he had been remembering. Dovehouse, after all, had been his friend for forty years. He had been there throughout everything . . . through the first days of Garrett's career, through the difficult debates of the fifties, through William Jeffrey's passing, even through—

"I am remembering—" Garrett said.

Dovehouse leaned in closer.

"I am remembering my first days in Congress. That impossible time . . . and how I failed."

"For God's sake, Garrett!" Dovehouse stormed. "Not the California bill again! I know that it is your chief regret, but really, it was twenty years ago."

"I failed," Garrett said. "I failed her."

"Failed who?" Dovehouse said. "Elizabeth?"

"She was the only one who would have stood by my decision."

"And seen California lost?" Dovehouse said. "I find that hard to believe."

"It was all lost," Garrett said. "Everything was lost."

Dovehouse shifted in his seat. He was becoming impatient again.

"Garrett, look at me," he said. "This will not do. Everything is said and done, and the prosperity of the future lies before us. Your melancholy is quite uncalled for. It is time for you to forget, and move on."

But now Dovehouse was asking for something more horrible. He wanted Garrett to commit an even greater sin.

"I will never forget!" Garrett said, striking the table.

"Old boy," Dovehouse said, "there are some things you'd do better to forget. Sometimes the greater the injustice, the greater the need to bury it."

Garrett bit down hard.

"I will not bury it," he said. "We have been committing crimes against the people of this country for over two centuries. It is time that we take responsibility for our sins."

"The people of this country?" Dovehouse said. "Sins? Against the negroes? By God, Garrett, when are you going to stop being such a damned fool? We may have majorities in Congress right now, and you may be able to push your laws through . . . but for heaven's sake, you above all people must realize that this is a moment in time, and things will turn again."

"We must see that that does not happen."

"It will happen!" Dovehouse fumed. "It is only natural that it should happen!"

Yes, the old ghosts. Dovehouse would never let them speak.

"You've accomplished your task," Dovehouse said. "The war is over—

and free labor is the law of the land. But it's a different world entirely down there, and they are determined to destroy anything you try to accomplish. You ask too much. It has always been your greatest strength, but also your greatest weakness."

"Damn you," Garrett said. "Damn all of you."

Dovehouse's cheek twitched before the calm came over his face.

"There will never be racial equality in this country. The sooner you and the rest of your radical cronies realize that, the sooner we can all move on."

How had it come to this? How had a forty-year friendship, full of grand and healthy debate, reached such an impasse, so late in its life? How had Garrett and the man who knew nearly everything about him grown so far apart in such a short time? Perhaps it had not been such a short time at all, but a long time—like his marriage. While Garrett had spent the past decades advancing his career, the things most personal to him had been slowly disintegrating before his eyes.

A moment of silence followed Dovehouse's remark, and both men glared at each other without moving. Then Dovehouse pushed his chair out and stood up like a marble soldier.

"Good day, old boy," he said, and left.

XXX

FATHER THOMAS HAD informed Moody and Joseph that the house still stood—just southeast of Chalmette, before the river made its great bend. The Yankees had spared the house, Father Thomas told them, not because of its greatness, but because of its strategic position on the water. That fantastical estate—a legend especially amongst those who had never seen it—had been the grandest and the most profitable of all the downriver plantations. Now though, its silence only served as a reminder of all that had been despised, and everything that had been lost.

Bellevoix, Moody thought, *she has been calling me from Bellevoix.*

Of course there was no way for Moody to know if this were true, but he had been feeling something—feeling Isabelle's presence deeply. The image that was guiding him was no image of his own making. Was she calling him back? He still did not know. But in believing, there was at least the chance of finding her again.

He struggled, for he had never been a believer . . . or rather, he had never admitted to himself that he could be one. But he was no different from anyone else trying to recover what they had lost—no different from the hundreds of people who had paraded through his gallery. While Isabelle's figure had never emerged in other photographs, she was, in a sense, in every picture he ever took. He had not seen her in those first pictures that he had snapped for the Spiritualists, nor in the many others that had helped make his reputation. But those photographs, he now knew, had been doing another kind of work for him: they had been allowing him to escape his past, while at the same time propelling him toward it.

There would never be enough. No . . . there could never be enough.

When Moody and Joseph approached Bellevoix, during the last moments of an orange dusk, it seemed that the whole place might have understood this. For Joseph, too, craved more than was possible. The house was waiting for them—as the cicadas, and the oaks, and the waterfalls of moss had been waiting—and all around them the air pressed, as if to imply that it possessed secret knowledge. They were at last entering the lost world from which Isabelle's mother had briefly escaped, and where the inventories had once recorded the woman's child as "stillborn." Where had that woman gone? Where had any of them gone? Bellevoix was a magnificent place of lost answers.

Some said that old Mrs. Toussaint—Alexandre Toussaint's embittered widow—still roamed the halls of the mansion. But nobody knew for sure. At the end of the war she had shuttered up the house and had not been seen by anyone since.

The negative weighed heavily on Moody's breast as he and Joseph stared out from the dying trees. Yes, at Bellevoix, the ancient oaks had begun to pass away because no one had maintained the levees, and the water had been crawling through the plantation since the war. This time, as in the past, the water seeped in from all directions—from the unrelenting river on one side, and the cypress swamps on the other. Even the sugar fields, which could stand some flooding, were now but graveyards of decomposing leaves and mud.

Alexandre Toussaint had had the good sense to build the house on a slightly raised spot, which acted as a nice deterrent against the greedy water and its inhabitants. Back then Bellevoix was the lively and sparkling center for many gatherings, but now the house slumped there—immense and gloomy, and barely white. Its dark, weather-beaten roof pressed its walls down into the mud, giving the house the appearance of a wheelless wagon that someone had left behind.

Moody and Joseph passed through a dense cluster of dwarf palmetto that edged one side of the plantation. Closer to the house, the cadavers of once-purple ironweed drooped toward the dampened earth. If Isabelle had "returned," it could only have meant the return to one place. Joseph was convinced that if they could solve the mystery of her birth, they could also possibly uncover the answers behind her disappearance. She was leading them to those answers. Of that much, Joseph was certain.

"It is as awful as they always said," Joseph whispered once they reached the front steps of the house. For there were many who had not been so enraptured with all of the romance that once surrounded Bellevoix.

"An awful place, truly," Moody said.

There was pain there.

And as if to scold him for thinking that unspoken truth, a crow cried out and flew away from its sanctuary above the door.

The door opened, and a pack of sparrows fled from another corner of the porch.

"What you be doin' here?" the voice said. "What's your business?"

He was a tall man—old and black. The last remaining servant of the house.

Joseph stepped forward.

"Archibald," he said, "I'm Joseph Winter."

The man in the doorway expressed no sign of friendliness or recognition. His face was as heavy as the air itself.

"We are looking for the stillborn child," Joseph went on.

And he waited a moment before adding:

"Isabelle."

The walls of such houses were impenetrable, especially after the war, and Joseph was relying on strong bonds from the past to gain him entry. He was gambling: was this old man in the doorway indeed the fabled Archibald, who had remained with Mrs. Toussaint after everyone else had left? And would the man even recognize the name of Joseph Winter—a name that resounded with hope in certain circles, and infamy in others?

The man looked at Joseph without moving, and then came out to the top of the steps.

"Winter," he said. "You don't mean Fifty-Two Winter."

"The same," Joseph replied.

"From the boat?"

"Yes. From the explosion—in fifty-two."

The old man inspected Joseph.

"You was the only one missing," he said. "They counted. And boy was there some trouble."

"I was lucky," Joseph said. "It was only by the grace of others that I made it out."

"Huh! Made it out," Archibald said. "And don't you talk fancy? Lots of folks assumed you was just dead somewhere, in the swamps. Or at least that's what they kept tellin' themselves. They didn't like when that count kept comin' up short. Anyone else find you?"

"No," Joseph said. "They tried. But I made it all the way."

"Canada?"

Joseph nodded.

"Well, good for you," Archibald said. "Probably be dead now, if they had."

Then Archibald's eyes centered on Moody.

"This is my employer," Joseph said. "Edward Moody."

Archibald's frown deepened.

"He is a photographer," Joseph added. "We take photographs. We've come from Boston."

"Ain't nothin' to photograph here," Archibald said. "Things around here don't like to be photographed."

"We have not come to take a photograph," Joseph said. "We've come looking for the dead child."

Archibald's face remained immovable, but his body leaned back slightly when Joseph said this.

"Lots of dead children around this place," Archibald said.

Moody had been silent up until this point, but a burst of impatience now overcame him.

"She was alive," Moody said. "The girl did not die."

Archibald looked at Joseph, as if Joseph himself had made the claim.

"Everybody know that," Archibald said. "Everybody except . . . some folks."

"But the books recorded her as stillborn," Moody said. "At least that's what she told me."

This last bit seized Archibald's attention, and he couldn't help but twist toward Moody.

"*She told you?*"

"Yes, she told him," Joseph said. "She was in Boston. She worked the railroad in Boston. She is the reason I am standing here."

Archibald raised his hand to his cheek and scratched. Then he stared down at his shoes.

"I see," he said quietly. "Never saw her myself, of course. Only heard about her, born out there in the swamp, during the escape. There was a child used to run through the cane fields at night, making all kinds of racket. None of us ever bothered her. Never knew what she was."

Everyone from the plantation had fled after the war, but Archibald had stayed behind—he and Mrs. Toussaint. People said that it had something to do with a strange indebtedness he felt toward her. She had once convinced her husband to spare him from the lash—and there had been murmurings of other things, too.

"We would like to inspect the books," Moody said, "if such a thing is even possible."

Again, Archibald addressed Joseph.

"She belong to him?" he asked.

"In a way," Joseph answered.

Archibald looked at Moody with an interrogating, paternal air.

"You know that girl?"

"Yes, I knew her," Moody said.

"And?"

"And what?"

"And . . . ?"

Archibald was eyeing him severely.

"And she was remarkable," Moody said. "And she was wronged. Somehow, she was wronged."

"Wronged by *you?*"

Moody hesitated.

"No . . . not by me."

"This place has something to tell us," Joseph said. "And the books might be of some help. Another name, another—"

But Archibald was gently laughing.

"Those books can't tell you nothing," he said. "They all ashes now."

At once Moody felt a pain in his chest—near the place where the knife had sliced him. He had become convinced, along with Joseph, that the records would reveal what Isabelle wanted him to see.

"And what the books going to tell you about a ghost anyway?" Archibald said. "If she'd come here—dead or alive—I would know."

"Did she?" Moody said. "Did she come here?"

Archibald shook his head.

"What year she leave you?"

"Fifty-two," Moody said. "The same year as Joseph—"

Archibald shook his head again.

"Lot of trade back then. Lots and lots of trade. The white folks was getting more and more anxious every day. And Justine—because that's who we talkin' about here, Justine was the mother of that child—he went and locked her up in the hothouse for what she done, but—"

Moody and Joseph both watched his mouth in anticipation.

"Well, he was trying to make an example," Archibald said. "He made an example alright."

The agony of it hit Joseph—for it touched that part of him that had never escaped.

"He was mighty upset about losing her," Archibald went on, "but wasn't nothin' they could do about it. Just wanted to forget it after that. Not often a soul run off from a place this far south anyways. Farther up north, maybe, but not down here. There was a reason for that."

"Mrs. Toussaint," Moody said. "Might Mrs. Toussaint know more about the girl?"

Archibald thrust his hands into his pockets.

"She won't see nobody," he said.

There was silence between the three of them that lasted for some time. It was dusk, and the cicadas were deafening.

"She won't see nobody," Archibald repeated.

"This is not to satisfy an idle curiosity," Joseph said. "We are trying to make things right."

Archibald was motionless. He would want to make things right too. Years earlier, the others had called him a fool for staying behind, but there was no denying the palpable sense of gravity that surrounded him. He was, after all, the man who had done things that others could not. It was even storied that in the old days he had sent the *feux follets* back into the swamps.

"I can't ask her to see you," Archibald finally said. "If I ask her, she'll say no. So I have to take you up without asking."

Then, turning, and dragging his feet toward the front door, he said:

"Come along—you might as well follow me."

The boards of the porch steps creaked and splintered as Moody and Joseph ascended them. The front door was open, and inside everything was darkness.

Archibald turned around.

"Now you listen, and you listen good," he said. "Sometimes she no good. She not been the same since the war. She wasn't all that great even before that, but the war—it done her in. So you listen to me. If she start cryin' or carryin' on or anything of the sort, and I tell you to go, *you go.* Understand?"

Joseph and Moody nodded. A porch sparrow returned to its nest.

The three men stepped through the front door of the house, and Archibald lit a large candelabra. The flames of the candles cast a soft glow over the entryway as the last remains of sunset peeked in through the shutter slats.

"She's upstairs," Archibald said. "She don't hardly ever come down no more."

At the center of the entryway was a grand, angular staircase that rose halfway to the second floor before splitting off in two directions. On the wall of the landing, a strange scene had been painted: a canal of beribboned gondolas on one side that commingled with a field of young shepherds on the other. There were willows near the shepherds, which seemed peculiar since there was no water. And in the flickering light of the candles, one could see that the mural's colors had once been brilliant.

When they reached the second floor, Archibald turned around to look at Joseph and Moody again.

"One more thing," he said, gravely. "It'd be best if you let *him* do most of the talking."

He had jerked his head toward Moody, though he had addressed the words to Joseph.

"She was once the mistress of a great house, and in her mind that's who she still is. You can't be expectin' her to answer a bunch of questions from some well-dressed negro."

The three men continued along the corridor until they arrived at a closed wooden door. Archibald knocked, and a voice from within called "Enter!" And Moody and Joseph followed Archibald into the room.

It was a dark room—dark like the rest of the house—with silk wallpaper that was fraying at the seams. Those walls had once been beautiful, but their now lackluster color hinted at the sorrow that had deadened them. A massive, four-poster canopy bed dominated one side of the room. And on the other side, next to a hollow, unlit fireplace, two shabby chairs stood on unsteady legs, their seat bottoms sagging toward the floorboards.

In one of these chairs, the old woman sat, skeletal in an emerald green evening gown from the finer days before the war. The neckline was unforgiving against her bony, colorless shoulders.

The woman looked up from her lap as Archibald stepped toward her.

"Someone's come to see you, ma'am. This is Mr. Moody—and Mr. Winter."

At first the woman looked confused, as if she were waking from a dream. Then her eyes set on Moody, and brightened.

"We receive guests so infrequently these days," she said, extending her hand. "I suppose you've come to see about some previous debt of my husband's?"

Moody took the woman's hand. It was a collection of bundled bones.

"No madam," he said. "I've come for nothing but the pleasure of your company. And perhaps . . . to talk of times past."

He was feeling the heaviness of Bellevoix, even hearing the voices, but the old Moody was there with him too.

"And what a fine gown you've chosen for this evening," he said.

"Why thank you," Mrs. Toussaint replied. "I'm sorry, Mr.—?"

"Moody, madam."

"Moody. Not from around here, certainly. Where do you come from, Mr. Moody?"

"A place quite far away, madam. Where the winters are long and difficult."

"It's all difficult now," she said. "Winter, summer—doesn't matter which."

She turned her head toward one of the windows, and her eyes caught the dying sunlight. She had been a beautiful woman—that much was evident.

"That your negro?" she asked.

"Yes madam," Moody said. "My manservant."

"Manservant," she huffed. "That what you call them where you're from?"

And she extended her hand back toward Archibald, who was standing with Joseph some distance from the chairs.

"My Archibald," she said. "Ever my sweet, sweet child."

Her lip quivered.

"The only soul in my life who has never abandoned me."

Emotion swept over her face but directly receded—as if she had remembered something, and then lost it.

"Archibald," she said, "please fetch Mr. Moody some tea. It's still early enough, I think. And bring some fresh mint too."

"Yes ma'am," Archibald called, "I'll do that right away."

But Archibald did not leave the room. He remained with Joseph in the shadows, listening.

"I do so love mint, Mr. Moody. But it takes over the whole yard. Senseless plant with no respect for borders. But oh my . . ."

Her voice trailed off, and she sat back in the chair. There was a faraway smile on her face.

Then she leaned forward again and locked eyes with her guest.

"Now, Mr. Moody," she said. "You must tell me a little something about yourself."

"Well, madam," Moody replied, "I was hoping we might talk about—"

And he paused, for even in his infinite experience, he was not quite sure how to make the approach.

"Yes?" Mrs. Toussaint asked.

"The business," Moody said.

"The business?"

"Yes, the business . . . and the account books from before the war."

Mrs. Toussaint squinted, as if trying to think of an impossible answer.

"The books . . ." she whispered, bringing her fingers to her lips.

Then, like a burst of sunshine upon the room's dead light, she exclaimed:

"Ah, Mr. Moody—I used to have a splendid hand!"

And she raised her fingers, and inspected them. The fine jewelry was now but a memory.

"It was me that kept the books, you know," she said. "My husband adored my hand."

Moody's heart raced—a breakthrough was within reach. Her mind was clearly lost, but perhaps it was something he could help her recover.

"Yes, it was all under my hand," she said. "The sugar, the boilers, the negroes—everything. Things used to run so beautifully around here. That's what they never understood."

"I don't doubt the superiority of your hand," Moody said.

Mrs. Toussaint smiled again.

"Do you have any of the old books?" Moody asked.

"Books?"

"Yes, madam—the ledgers. I would love nothing more than to see this excellent hand myself."

Mrs. Toussaint let out a delicate laugh that transformed her into a modest girl.

"Oh, I wish it were so, Mr. Moody," she said. "But we had to burn all of that. Not out of spite, mind you. It was just that those winters during the war were harsh, and sometimes we had nothing else for kindling. We didn't need them anymore anyhow, by the end. There was nothing left to keep track of."

"But up until then," Moody said, "you did keep track of everything with—your fine hand?"

"Oh yes," Mrs. Toussaint replied. "Our books were always very well in order. Down to the last dime."

She was so charming and hospitable—like the woman she had once been.

"Can I ask you then, madam?" Moody said. "Do you remember the one called Justine?"

Mrs. Toussaint's smile froze.

"Justine—" she said.

Then a blank look bled into her eyes—a strange prelude that altered her face. Sadness appeared first, then confusion, and finally resolve.

"Justine," she repeated. "Now that's a name I haven't heard in a long time."

Her eyes darkened, and for the first time her voice became sinister.

"Mr. Moody, I thought you were *polite*."

And she emphasized the word with a terrible look, and a weird smile that had a kind of boast in it.

"Madam?" Moody said.

"Do you think I don't know what you're about?" she said. "You've come to taunt me—like all the others. Taunt me with the memory of how he disgraced me!"

"No," Moody protested, "I assure you—"

But that quickly, Mrs. Toussaint had turned.

"Go ahead," she said. "You might as well go right on and say it. Say what everyone knew, and would never say . . . what they would only say to me with their sly eyes and simpering glances. That she was his favorite. That that whore was his favorite. Well she got what was coming to her, and she didn't come out of it so well now, did she?"

"But the child," Moody said, "there was a child . . ."

"Certainly was when she left," Mrs. Toussaint said, "but not when they brought her back. Oh yes . . . she was crying—*pleading*—for Alexandre to let her go back out there and get her baby. Crying like a senseless thing, as if it ever mattered. And my damned fool of a husband was going to go out there and look for it. But I stopped him. I told him there'd be fury if he dared to go. I wasn't about to have another one of his nigger bastards running around this house."

She glared at Moody, and then glared at something else.

"No, no. That baby was dead before it came into this world—if I had anything to say about it."

Moody had done his best to remain composed throughout the exchange, but this last bit caused him to tremble from somewhere within. As he sat there, searching for an apologetic response, a spark of quick delight flashed over Mrs. Toussaint's face. She was, Moody could plainly see, elated to have caused his discomfort.

"Go on away from here now," she said in a deep, uncaring voice. "And take your nigger with you. You're not welcome here anymore."

Archibald had moved forward. The interview was over. And Mrs. Toussaint was staring at the empty fireplace.

Outside, the sun had almost disappeared, and a group of vultures had come to roost atop one of the *pigeonniers*.

"Thank you, Archibald," Joseph said. "We have solved one mystery, but uncovered another."

"It was Mrs. Toussaint who killed her," Moody said. "Or at least condemned her to death back then."

"The question now remains," Joseph said, "how did the girl survive?"

Archibald looked out upon the dead plantation before speaking.

"That girl," he finally said, "she was lively. Like I said—runnin' through the cane fields during all hours of the night, makin' trouble that only we could hear. We never bothered her none. Couldn't. When you don't know what it is, you leave well enough alone. Some said she was dead, some said she wasn't. But when you don't know for sure, sometimes it's best to just leave it. Lasted five or six years, then it stopped. We just figured she moved on."

Joseph and Moody took all of this in with an odd mixture of interest and sorrow. They had somehow begun rearticulating Isabelle's life, yet the bones of their discoveries were only leading to more confusion. They had come to Bellevoix. They had tried, and they had failed. Where was she? Where was she hiding?

"Of course," Archibald said, "there were tales."

Archibald let out a heavy breath, and wiped his head with his hand. The first stars of evening were twinkling behind him.

"If that girl was alive, and livin' out there in the swamps, only one person who could have brought her back from the dead."

Archibald stared at Joseph.

"And I think you know who I mean."

It had been a long time, and Joseph did not know. Until, of course, the name was spoken.

"Yellow Henry," Archibald said.

Joseph's breath caught in his throat. The name had traveled through time to find him.

"Yes, you know," Archibald continued. "She the only one who can make sense of this mess for you now. If you want to find out what really happened to your girl, you gonna have to go ask Yellow Henry."

XXXI

HER NAME WAS Henriette La Jaune, but the Americans called her "Yellow Henry" because of the fever. As a girl she had fled Saint-Domingue with her father—or at least the light-skinned man who claimed to have been her father. Her own skin was dark, and so the rumors abounded. Had he simply stolen her when he left the island, with the intention of raising her to be his mistress? Others said no . . . that she really had come from a union, the most romantic of the gossipers believing her to be the child of an obeah woman from Jamaica.

By the time Henriette approached full womanhood—around 1819—the Yellow Fever epidemic had all but married her to that color. That year, the fever raged unmercifully through the city, leaving no handkerchief untouched, no water jug unspoiled. Its stench flowed from the gutters of St. Ann down to the Spanish Mercado, and indeed the Spanish, who still lived in New Orleans in great numbers, saw it as a curse upon the French—that is until the fever demonstrated that it loved no one more or less, and embraced anyone whom it could find, regardless of country or belief.

But there was Henriette—the tavern keeper's daughter—who had walked boldly amongst the fever's victims, and who had never shown signs of the disease herself. Word of her "condition" quickly spread throughout the region. Some of the Catholics said that she must have been "blessed"—that the Lord had placed a miracle in the center of the city's plague. But others leaned toward darker explanations: "There's no holy water protecting that girl," some said. "It's all blood and chicken feathers. And God only knows what else."

The father succumbed, and the tavern became hers. And the sad truth was that he was one of the very few she could not save—or wouldn't. For in addition to her immunity, she had become famous for her "cures." In certain circles people had knowledge of the private room at the back of the tavern, where, as it was said, young Henriette had saved victims of the plague. For her Spanish customers she recommended a preparation of juice made from fresh oysters; for the French, a hot drink, immediately followed by a cold one.

Some understood this and some didn't—that Henriette had her "own ways"—but in the end it made no difference. She had saved hundreds of lives. When the plague finally did recede, having taken thousands of helpless souls with it, no one could say exactly how Henriette had done what she had done. The Voodoo women from Saint-Domingue denied that Henriette was one of them—"a conjure woman . . . *peut-être*," they said, though even that seemed to be giving her too much. Only one thing remained unambiguous in people's minds: Yellow Henry could control the fever.

And so they sought her out—the wealthy and the impoverished, the free and the not free, the people of every color and religion. For nearly twenty years, the fever's death tolls remained low, until the next epidemic began devouring lives again. But by that time the tavern was empty, its windows blackened with neglect. The people came, but no one was there. Henriette had disappeared.

"Well, not disappeared exactly," Archibald said. "Left is more like it. She just up and left."

All of this history Joseph knew well, for there was not a person—black or white—who had lived through the pre-war plagues and who had not heard of Henriette La Jaune. When the epidemic of '47 struck New Orleans and Henriette was nowhere to be found, those whose faith she had confirmed over the years simply gave in to their fates. Joseph had witnessed the despair firsthand . . . mothers trying to concoct useless potions of their own, before tossing it all aside and exclaiming, "*C'est sans espoir, sans Henriette!*"

But as had always been the case with Henriette, there were rumors. She was living in a shuttered house, two blocks away from the tavern, and only maintained contact with a servant boy who did her errands.

Or—

She had purchased a steamboat, and was living in one of its cabins, aided by a crew that was terrified of her.

Or, for the more fanciful—

She had developed a serum that could turn her into a raven, and was living amongst the birds, whom she found kinder than human beings.

But none of these rumors were true, as Archibald knew, for he had been guiding people to Henriette since the beginning.

"They can talk all they want," he told Joseph and Moody. "She thinks it's funny. But she likes it this way—only people who find her is ones she *wants* to find her. And that's plenty. She ain't no hermit, like everyone say."

He had agreed to take them there the next morning—or at least set them on the right course, since nowadays Archibald would only travel so far into the swamps. He would send them into the bayous—deep into the area north of Bellevoix, where the shifting shores of Lake Pontchartrain showed little compassion for the land.

It was morning, and the pirogue glided swiftly through the tranquil waters. A soft line of ripples moved away from the bow as Archibald pushed the boat forward.

"Straight ahead, we going into Bayou Bienvenue," Archibald said. "Beyond that, Bayou Sauvage. We not going in quite that far though—best to stay out of that place."

Archibald told them that they would find Yellow Henry somewhere in the watery labyrinth between the two swamps.

"Thing is," he said. "She lives on an island. And that island kind of moves, depending on how she feels."

Even Joseph, who had spent time cutting timber in the swamps, had never seen land quite like this . . . if one could even call it land, this lacework of water and well-soaked ground that curled and curved upon itself as if someone had gouged it with a knife. Though the land here had been reduced to a fraying string of broken cobwebs, the trees and mounds of soil expressed little animosity. In the stillness one could only feel that battles had been won and lost—that the lingering silence was merely the resignation of two indecisive foes.

The water parted for the boat, but rarely for anything else—an alligator perhaps, a water moccasin, a frog. In this place, the serenity was not gentle. Even in the brightness of morning, a heavy gloom hung upon the trees, and the arms of the giant cypress, dripping with delicate curtains of moss, reached out wide to shut out the light.

At many points, several feet from the swollen bases of the trees, crooked objects—the "knees" of the cypress—jutted out and broke the water's surface. These pointed heads—sentinels ready to rise up and block the way—followed the intruders as they passed. This place was enveloping them. It was a voracious kind of place. An egret extended its neck, while some other bird screamed in the distance.

Time stopped in this wilderness, for the sun had abandoned them, and the swamp had become so impenetrable that Moody and Joseph had lost all track of their progress. At last, in what might have been hours after their departure, a vision of something unusual interrupted the somber regularity of the swamp. Ahead of them appeared a shack built on stilts above the water. Aside the shack . . . a sagging dock, and a wooden beam strung with stretched muskrat hides.

Archibald slowly moved the boat toward the dock.

"Now, this—" he began, but stopped short, as a man emerged from the shack and tossed a thick line of rope toward the boat.

Archibald and the man considered each other—they were neither enemies, nor friends. They were brothers on that continuum of relationships that had held people together before the war.

Then the man examined Joseph before setting his eyes firmly upon Moody. *"A la traiteuse?"* the man said.

Archibald nodded gravely.

"To the healer," Joseph whispered. "Archibald will go no farther."

As if to confirm this understanding, the man on the dock extended his hand. Moody gripped it, and allowed the boatman to hoist him up. Joseph grasped Moody's arm, and followed his partner onto the dock. The man on the dock said nothing.

"This fella here gonna take you the rest of the way," Archibald said.

The water swirled noiselessly as Archibald backed up the boat. In a moment he was gone—Moody and Joseph's only link back to the land.

THE SLANTING LINES of light that cut in through the trees made the darkness seem that much heavier. A glint of dew on a leaf . . . a flash reflecting off the wet bark . . . these were the random sparks that lit Joseph and Moody's way. Without a word, Henriette's boatman had taken them deeper into the swamp—into a place that moaned with shadows, where even the dead would have been afraid.

There were no banks at all now, as the water had completely triumphed here, its marks from earlier conquests ringing the fat bellies of the cypress.

Sometimes a waxier curtain of green cascaded down from a lower limb, offering another kind of light in the form of a single orange flower. Where the flowers bloomed in small clusters, their petals raged like wildfires. A few blossoms fell upon the water now and then—they never sank, but floated idly in place.

The boat passed a fallen cypress, caught and hanging amongst its brethren. The stillness was everywhere around them now, and here others played freely, without judgment.

Moody had the premonition that he might never return from this journey, for something seemed to be killing him, even as a violent force drove him on. What was it? It was something different from the exhaustion he had feigned for the clients—something much stronger than the "pull" of a random spirit. He thought of her, and pressed his hand against his coat pocket. The outline of the negative scored a rectangle around his heart.

The pirogue moved on. No words were exchanged. And frogs croaked deep ballads of welcome.

Finally, after a numberless series of twists and turns, a clearing opened up amongst the trees. At the far end of the clearing was what looked like an island, but as the boatman brought them closer, the island transformed into something else . . .

A boat—a giant houseboat—had been well-disguised as a land mass, its roof covered with twigs and vines, its deck strewn with dirt and branches. There were windows, and a door, and from within dull lights flickered. The size of the boat was staggering, like a monster sleeping in the water.

Then she appeared in the doorway, an old woman with cat-like eyes. She placed her hands on her hips and waited. There was nothing that could have moved her.

Joseph saw the signs right away—the baubles dangling from her neck, the little sacks strung from her waist, and the hundreds of leather bracelets that concealed her wrists and forearms. He did not know what so many bracelets meant, but everything signified something with these women.

The boatman tied the pirogue to a wooden post, and the old woman stepped back inside.

"*Allez*—" the boatman said, motioning his hand toward the door. "*Elle vous attend.*"

They were the first words he had spoken to them—and the last.

The deck of the houseboat was surprisingly stable, and the boat did not rock when Moody and Joseph stepped onto it. How it was anchored, and how it might have moved, remained a matter of mystery.

"Edward," Joseph said, "I'm . . . frightened."

The two men stepped into the spacious cabin, which was dim but lit with oil lamps. That was one of the things that struck Joseph immediately—the oil lamps, in a place where fuel must have been hard to come by.

The other surprise was that the old woman was not alone, for inside the cabin there were three other men. They sat at a bar that flanked one side of the boat, and stopped their conversation when the travelers came in.

"*Bienvenue*," the old woman said.

She was behind the bar now, filling two tumblers with ale.

Joseph and Moody approached the bar, and stationed themselves at one end of it. Henriette came down to them and glanced from one to the other, until her eyes finally fixed upon Joseph.

"*Il est malade*," she said.

Joseph nodded.

"*Très malade*," she added.

The old woman's face contained an irrepressible ferocity. Time had not weakened her in the least.

"He understands," Joseph said. "He is here to—"

But Henriette raised her hand.

"Drink," she said to Moody.

And then again:

"Drink!"

Moody picked up the tumbler, took one sip, then another. Henriette continued watching him until, with some reluctance, he had finished.

"You are sick, " Henriette said. "And you have been sick for a long time."

The spirit photographer did not protest this.

"*Comment vous appelez-vous?*"

"Edward Moody," Joseph said. "And I am Joseph Winter."

"Moody," Henriette said, "Moody . . ."

Her face was stern and unpredictable. She might have frowned—or laughed.

"There is something you guard that has made you sick," she said. "The pain of it has made you sick, and you are dying."

Moody bowed his head, for this was not entirely a revelation.

"You have been trying to thread the needle," Henriette said, "but your life has been more hole than thread."

Moody's hand moved over his heart.

"I am sorry for you," she said.

The spirit photographer tapped his chest—more out of reflex than with purpose. She was here with him—Isabelle was here with him now. The walls were weeping with the memory of her.

Moody reached into his coat pocket and pulled out the precious negative.

"You must look at this," Moody said. "And you must tell me what you see."

Then he removed the glass from its case, and held it toward Henriette. The negative's contrast against the bar made the glass a sheet of black.

Henriette reached for the glass, but Moody held it firm. There was no letting go of it. He would not let her go . . .

"Monsieur Moody—" Henriette said.

As he locked eyes with the woman, the photographer realized that his grip on the negative confirmed something he'd long denied . . . that there was only one thing he had wanted since his return from the war, and the beginning of his illustrious career. It wasn't wealth or fame, or the notoriety that had accompanied his "greatness." It wasn't even the validation he had sought from the doubtful men of science. No, no—those things had moved him along, but nothing had ever satisfied him. He wanted her back. He wanted Isabelle back. And his wanting had made everything else irrelevant.

Then, it was as if the thread had snapped. Henriette's pull had been so gentle.

She held the negative now, up to the lampshade. Her hands framed the glass, and she squinted at what she saw.

Moody turned toward Joseph—there were tears in Joseph's eyes. But Henriette was unmoved. Her own eyes were cold—and fierce.

"Who are you, Monsieur Moody?" she said. "Who are you? And where have you come from?"

Then her face changed, and she looked down at the negative. It was sorrow—real sorrow—that compelled her to return it to Moody.

"I see now," Henriette said. "The waiting—I see. You are sick with waiting. Sick with questions. And yet, there is more that you must wait for."

Now Moody's eyes were the ones that brimmed with tears. But these tears were not the conventional tears of sadness. Rather, they were the tears that had built up through the ages. The tears of everything he had had—and known.

"Where is she?" Moody whispered.

And then again:

"Where is she?"

A laugh came from Henriette, from somewhere deep within her belly.

"You are in agony," she said. "But there is more agony for you. You must be cleansed of your guilt before you can see her again. This is no easy lock to pick—photographer."

"I can't wait any longer," Moody said. "I will do whatever you say."

Henriette laughed again—but the room could barely hear it.

"Your agony is . . . *spécial*," Henriette said. "It is the agony of waiting—*l'agonie du néant*."

Only Joseph understood this last bit—it was the agony of "nothingness." Henriette was a friend—a restorer of souls—and yet her words sounded more like a curse.

"Heal him," Joseph said. "Take pity on him. Heal him."

"Don't you mean *you*?" Henriette said. "Don't think I'm fool enough not to see."

Joseph moved his mouth. His discomfort was immense.

"I lost her too," he said.

But Henriette took no notice. All along, she had been exhibiting a strange kind of favoritism toward Moody.

"You two go over there now," Henriette said. "I have customers, and there is plenty of time."

There was no hesitancy in her voice. Her every word was definitive.

"Later," she said. "We can begin."

XXXII

IN BOSTON, INSPECTOR Bolles studied the telegram from New Orleans.

> *The crowds were larger than normal, as there were three boats that arrived around the same time that day. A man matching the sketch you sent was spotted, with a negro, but when we pursued him past Levee Street, he mysteriously disappeared. We will continue to monitor the French Quarter closely, as we suspect he may have absconded into one of the buildings there.*

None of this was helpful, as it left Bolles with nothing new. It was as if Edward Moody and his assistant had somehow figured out how to remain two steps ahead. Why had Moody and Winter gone all the way to New Orleans? Were they planning to leave the country, via the Gulf?

There were so many oddities about this case, the fugitives' strange and purposeful route being only one of them. There was also the intensity of Mr. Dovehouse's involvement, which in the inspector's opinion seemed entirely uncalled for. The case was doing things to people . . . consuming them, changing them. Garrett, Dovehouse, even the men at the American Institute—all had taken an interest in the case that bordered on obsession.

And all of it over a photograph.

A photograph?

Bolles stared down at the telegram again.

What did the photograph show?

That was the question at the heart of this matter. The answer to that question would explain everything.

Bolles returned to Washington Street to speak with Mrs. Lovejoy. Of all the players in this game, she had been the most valuable.

"I'm sorry, Inspector," she told him. "But I never set eyes on that negative. Mr. Winter was taking care of everything in the gallery after Mr.

Moody's collapse. And really, it was no business of mine. At least not at the time."

"But that day," Bolles said, "the day the photograph was taken—you were not up in the gallery at all?"

"No, I'm sorry. I was down here in the store. Mr. Winter, well—"

She paused, and began straightening the cigar cases on the counter.

"Yes?" Bolles asked.

"Well, Mr. Winter was a bit . . . you might say, possessive—about the gallery. He didn't want anything touched until Mr. Moody had recovered. I do like Mr. Winter. I think he is a very respectable man."

"Do you mean that he prohibited you from entering the gallery?"

"No, I wouldn't go that far. But while Mr. Moody was recovering in my apartments, Mr. Winter kept the gallery. I don't know what he was doing in there, but you see . . . there had been a great disturbance. Nothing like this had ever happened before."

"What exactly do you mean?" Bolles asked.

"The Garretts," Mrs. Lovejoy said. "Nothing had ever happened—like the Garretts."

"This is a bit of a riddle," Bolles said.

"What I mean is that in his entire career as a spirit photographer—a career which I have witnessed from the very beginning—Mr. Moody has always arrived at one of two places. Either he brings forth the spirit, or he doesn't. When he brings forth the spirit, there is usually great joy. When he can't, great sadness often follows. I know because I see the faces of every customer who comes down those steps. I am always the first person, other than Mr. Moody, to see the results of the sittings."

"And the Garretts . . . when they came down that day?"

"That was what was different. That was how I knew that something different—even something terrible—had happened."

Bolles urged her on.

"It was Garrett. He looked—"

"Unwell?" Bolles asked.

"Worse than unwell. I would say—"

She paused again, searching the air for the right description.

"I would say—devastated. Mrs. Garrett was bringing him down—like an angry mother dragging away an inconsolable child. She looked enraged—

at what I cannot say. And that was unusual too, you see, because the women are usually the ones who come down discomposed, not the men. It was . . . a reversal, of sorts."

Bolles thought for a moment. Something had happened to Garrett. He had seen something, heard something—*felt something*—in that gallery. Bolles remembered their conversation, how the senator had deflected his direct questioning about the negative. Now Bolles was certain that there was something Senator Garrett was refusing to admit.

"I'm sorry I can't be of more help to you," Mrs. Lovejoy went on, "but I can only tell you what I remember seeing that day—the senator, appearing as if he were taking his last breaths, and Mrs. Garrett, as if she were the one leading him to his grave."

"Thank you, Mrs. Lovejoy," Inspector Bolles returned. "You've been of more help than you realize."

THE GREAT HOUSE on Louisburg Square had grown much sadder since Inspector Bolles's childhood. He remembered, as a young boy, coming to that house when the new baby had been born, and the great joy that had filled the entire neighborhood. "Now mind, Montgomery," the senator had said to him, "since you have no brothers or sisters, William Jeffrey here will be your brother. You will help me watch over him, as you are older than he is, and will always know more than he does." The young Montgomery Bolles had been thrilled with the new charge. Senator Garrett had always treated Montgomery like a son.

Which is why when Garrett's own son died, the young Bolles felt not for himself, but for the senator. By then he had grown used to the senator's firm yet benevolent ways . . . but the death of William Jeffrey had brought about a different senator. While Bolles's own father had expressed great sorrow over the loss, the senator himself had transformed into someone else. The senator's eyes had grown vacant.

And then there was Mrs. Garrett—dressed from head to toe in black. Emaciated and quivering, she walked about the somber, unlit house. Overnight the whole place had become unkind and unwelcoming.

Of course he had been to the house many times since then, but that house—the funereal house—was the house that never left him.

"Master Bolles!" Jenny said, when she opened the front door. "We don't see you enough. Come in, come in!"

Jenny took his hat from him. She had forever been kind and caring.

"You're looking well, Jenny. Life is treating you—well?"

Jenny gave him a smile, but beneath it there was something else.

"Yes—I know, Jenny," Bolles said. "There have been . . . tensions."

Jenny nodded.

"You remember—" Jenny said in a very low voice. "You remember the way it once was in this house, after . . ."

Her voice trailed, and Bolles laid a hand on her arm.

"It's like that again, Master Bolles. Different though. I always said the boy would—"

"Montgomery!"

The call was bright and cheerful. Elizabeth was descending the steps.

"To what do we owe this pleasure?" she said.

"Ah, Mrs. Garrett," Bolles said. "I was hoping to have a few words with you."

Elizabeth gave Jenny a nod and dismissed her. Then she led Bolles to the drawing room.

"Please, sit. Can we get you anything?"

"No ma'am. Thank you. I am sorry to hear you've been unwell."

"Unwell?"

"Yes, ma'am. The senator has told me that you've been feeling some-what upset—since the photograph."

"Did he?"

"Yes."

Elizabeth looked off to the side for a moment.

"Yes, well," she said. "It was a troubling event."

"Forgive me," Bolles said, "but this case has taken so many strange turns, and I'm wondering if you might help me."

Elizabeth again shifted her eyes in another direction.

"You see," Bolles went on, "I am curious as to why the negative itself is so important. Is not Mr. Moody the real object of our pursuit?"

She stared at him now

"The man is a criminal," she said.

"Yes, I know, but—"

"And he must be prosecuted, and stopped from perpetrating these crimes. What he has done, it's absolutely unspeakable. And the senator's reputation is at stake."

"But according to the senator," Bolles said, "there is no spirit on the negative."

"Between us, Montgomery," Elizabeth said, "the senator does not always see what other people see."

"Mrs. Garrett, do you mean to tell me that there *is* a spirit on the negative?"

"That is not what I said."

"Then what do you mean?"

"What I mean is that people will see what they want to see. The presence or absence of a spirit on the negative is immaterial. The fact that there *is* a negative—that is what matters."

"I see," Bolles said.

He paused for a moment, looking at her.

"What *is* on the negative?" he pressed.

Elizabeth met his gaze. How he knew that vacant look. It was the look that, as a boy, he had wanted so desperately to understand.

"Ma'am?" he said.

"I'm sorry," she replied.

"What is on the negative?" he repeated.

And still she did not answer.

"Is William Jeffrey on the negative?"

It was bold of him to ask so directly. Perhaps it was too bold.

Elizabeth shook her head.

"William Jeffrey is not on the negative," she said.

And that's when he realized what she was seeing. She was seeing William Jeffrey—again.

"William Jeffrey is not on the negative," she repeated.

"I believe you," Bolles replied.

She was falling away from him, but he was determined to press forward.

"Mrs. Garrett," he said quietly, bending closer toward her. "Who or what is on that negative?"

She opened her mouth to answer. Her eyes had grown wet and red. She had never, in all the years he had known her, appeared so unprotected and honest.

Then he heard the front door open, and the slam of the door as it shut.

"Good afternoon, Senator," Jenny said out in the entryway. "You're home a bit earlier today."

That quickly, Elizabeth resumed her composure. There would be no more discussion that day.

XXXIII

IT WAS A strange kind of sleep . . . neither a vision nor a dream. He was waking from it now, trying to remember how it had started. When had he first lost sight of Joseph . . . Henriette . . . the cabin? The men had been whispering with Henriette at the bar, and Joseph's whole figure had changed colors in the lamplight. Then there were footsteps . . . the closing of a door . . . and a light that faded into black.

He had drunk the ale too fast.

But there had also been Henriette.

They had been waiting for her to finish up her business at the bar. She had the answers, and this Moody intimately understood. It was an unspoken knowledge he shared with Joseph. But his partner was different now—he was no longer so brave. The place had changed Joseph, too.

She had approached them with some sort of hollowed-out gourd. Or shell, or wooden bowl—it was difficult to tell what it was. Joseph was beside him, close to him, and motionless. Joseph could not save him this time.

It was not true that he could not move, for he raised his hand to his head . . . could have stood up and left the boat if that was what he wanted to do. But the heaviness that had overcome him was like nothing he had ever felt. It was a chastising, almost painful heaviness, and he wanted nothing but to close his eyes.

"Cleansed," Henriette intoned. "You must be cleansed of your transgressions."

Joseph was undressing him—removing his coat—yet Moody clutched the negative to his chest. He felt the throb of it, at one with his heart as it had been on this journey, but Henriette nodded and then the negative was in her hands. The negative had gone to her . . . a child running back. Moody had not been able to hold onto it any longer.

Henriette removed the negative from its case and propped it on a table. There was nothing ceremonious about what she had done. It might have been any old picture . . .

The negative stared at him. Isabelle stared at him . . . though he could only catch glimpses of her in the uneven shades of the lamplight now. She had faded even more—receded farther into the blackness. His obsession had been for nothing. The protection, the pursuit . . . in the end, it would all come to nothing.

She was leaving him again. He was a fool to believe anything else. She had never really belonged to him. She had always belonged to them.

All of his clothes were now in a pile at his feet. He was exposed, and yet he was enshrouded by what surrounded him. Joseph gently took his arm and led him across the room. Henriette was waiting for him there.

"And now," Henriette said, "we go."

She held out her hands toward him.

"We go back—to get rid of this junk."

Moody touched the old hands. They were smooth, as if dusted with chalk. Her bracelets surrounded her wrists like dead ribbons on an old tree.

And then he was in it—in the water. He could not remember stepping into the tub. It was as if Henriette's hands had transported him there. Time and space no longer held any reason.

The wooden panels of the cabin smelled of an age-old must.

What were they trying to tell him? What was it that they knew?

Moody stood in the washtub, his body free in its nakedness, as Henriette held the gourd, and began dousing his shoulders with water. There was a scent to the water—something unusual, something herbal. Henriette had collected this water and suffused it with summer herbs.

Purge me with hyssop, and I shall be clean:
Wash me, and I shall be whiter than snow.

The words had come from somewhere. The words had come from Joseph.

"He knows what to do," Henriette told Moody. "He is smarter than you think. He has led you the right way. You should count yourself lucky, photographer."

Moody looked at her, unresponsive. She was pouring the water over his head.

"Do as he does," Henriette whispered.

Then, as if angered:

"Moody, say the words!"

Moody repeated the strange verse that Joseph had been chanting. He felt foolish reciting it, even in his altered state. These were not his words. These kinds of words belonged to others.

"Nothing belongs to anyone, anymore," Henriette said. "It's all been lost, and that's what you must know."

Then a kind of peacefulness overcame him, in the water. The scent of the herbs pricked his nose, but soothed him just the same. All went dark . . .

And then the visions came.

She was there—there! Isabelle was alive . . . on Washington Street, in Boston, wearing one of the calico dresses he remembered. In her hand she held a letter, and slipped it under the door. She had not bothered to enter the store. She was not going to wait for him.

The sun splashed the storefront window and the silverware exploded. The plates and the urns and the saltshakers were everywhere, but their brilliance was nothing compared to the vision of Isabelle.

The street was busy. There were carriages—and noise. She hurried away, but a man approached her on the street. The man began to talk to her, and rudely held her arm. Moody could not hear what they were saying.

Isabelle's face darkened at whatever the man was telling her. Then in a minute, she was gone.

No . . . Moody thought. No . . . I cannot lose her again. I have lost her too many times.

But he was stuck—his feet held in place.

That terror on her face—it was etched there, unremovable. In his mind, it was as if he were reading her terror on a piece of paper.

The paper moved. The page turned. And here was another, come to tell him.

SHE IS WRITING the letter to him now, the letter she has just delivered. The room is small, and there is a suitcase, and she is packing to go away. Here she writes the letter—her last words to her beloved. She is going to deliver the letter herself. She knows where she must leave it.

But her insistence in the goodbye has condemned her. Her dedication to him has condemned her. She has no understanding—no conception of this—as she is putting her words to paper.

Now she is in the back of a covered wagon, and very different. There is a dirty rag around her mouth, and her hands are bound with rope. She is terrified, and the picture in front of Moody is something hideous. Even the paper that holds the picture is caked with the filth of this crime.

She is going to a place from where she will never return. It is clear that she is traveling to her death.

The papers are full of sketches. They are better than anything he has ever done. The pages turn, and the visions sharpen with the clarity of photographs.

STRUGGLING . . . SHE IS struggling. She is on a farm somewhere—with men. And now, at last, the pictures begin to speak.

"You knew she'd be a problem. This one isn't easy."

"Wasn't easy last night either. Fought back like a calf."

There is laughter.

"Educated too—an educated nigger."

"How 'bout that."

"Pretty."

"We seen enough pretty for now."

The men exchange glances.

"Can't keep the bit on her forever," one finally says. "Won't be no good that way."

"He warned you. Said we'd have a lot of trouble with her."

"No use putting it off any longer then. If she won't keep quiet, just cut it out."

Her eyes widen, and she begins to thrash, but two men are holding her down. There are ropes binding her wrists and ankles, but it takes the men to hold her, too. A hot blade comes forward, and one of the men removes the bit from her mouth. Her head is shaking wildly, but one man steadies it with his hands.

They take prongs to her tongue, and pull it out, beyond her lips.

Isabelle tries to scream.

On the plantation, everything is as serene as one could ever hope it to be. The oaks stretch out their arms in muscular patterns against the fading sun. Three women in white dresses sit fanning themselves on the porch.

The scream swells before the silence. A window from the big house falls hard within its frame. Glass shatters, and rains over the freshly painted porch boards.

"My God in Heaven," one of the women says. "If I've told Jeremiah once to fix that window, I've told him a hundred times."

"Now look at that," another one of them says.

"Niggers always costing us double, if you ask me."

THE SUN HAS set now, and Isabelle is in a bed. The cabin is dark—lit by a candle or two—but Moody can see the rag in her mouth. The rag is damp with her blood. But this rag does not silence her.

There is another woman in the cabin—an old black woman whose bare feet are at peace with the dirty floor. She is dipping a cloth into a bucket of water, and applying the compress to Isabelle's head.

"Will she live?" Moody asks.

The old woman stares up at him. She is not a woman he has ever seen, but she is a woman he will always see.

The woman does not answer. She returns herself to Isabelle.

"Will she live?" Moody demands.

The woman does not turn to look at him.

"She shouldn't have been writin' you no letter," the woman says. "Shouldn't have been anywhere near you in the first place. She should've just been on her way—gone like all the others. Just trouble, and now look where she is."

Then the woman turns her head and glares at the spirit photographer.

"She'll live," the woman says.

And then she adds:

"So will you."

She watches Moody's eyes until the tear she's been waiting for arrives.

"Now that's what I need," she says, jumping up from the bedside. "That's exactly what I need."

She brings her old finger to his cheek.

"We're done now," she says. "Go on and get yourself out of here."

. . .

THAT WAS NOT the last of the visions, for in waking there were more to come. Moody was dressed, no longer in the tub, but his hair still smelled of herbal water. Strangely, his first waking thoughts went to the war. The bloodshed he had witnessed, and the despair it had condemned him to, piled up in his head—all those bodies he had shut out. He had written to her then . . . swore that he would never take another photograph. He had broken that oath. And for what?

But the war had also been the catalyst of his goodbye to her—the event that had pushed him to run . . . free.

Free? As if there were such a thing. He had fooled himself. He had never been free of her at all. She had loved photographs, and he had locked himself away with her, because he did not want to exist in the world without her.

He was on some sort of divan, and Henriette was sitting beside him.

"You poisoned me," he said. "But I can't deny what you've shown me."

Henriette laughed . . . that same rancorous laugh that came from somewhere deep within in her.

"I, Monsieur Moody?" she said. "What I have shown you? You've seen nothing that you didn't always have the power to see. You've ignored your power all these years. It's the cause of your greatest shame—and it is at the heart of all your guilt."

Her look was vicious—spiteful. Moody could not challenge her.

In her hands there were the papers, large sheets full of colorless scribbling.

He looked down at them.

"My drawings?" he asked. "Are these the drawings of what I've seen?"

"Ha!" Henriette said. "There is no end to your arrogance. You were never an artist. You've never been brave enough to draw such things."

Moody stared down at the papers. The drawings held him captive.

Henriette held one of them up—the sketch of a woman writing a letter. Then another—a crude drawing of a man and woman in the street. A plantation . . . a woman brutalized . . . shattered glass from a broken window. These were the representations of what he most feared—and yet, what he most wanted to see.

"If these are not my drawings," he said, "then—"

"They are your drawings now," Henriette said. "They are just as much your drawings as they are everyone else's. For what happened to her happened to all of us."

Then Henriette slowly turned her head toward the bar.

"Over there, Moody . . . over there is the artist. She is the one who can tell you everything—and nothing, at the same time."

Henriette stood and slowly moved away from Moody, and the photographer's gaze followed her as she crossed to the other side of the cabin. In a moment she reached Joseph, who was sitting at the bar with a young woman. Joseph held the woman's hands and appeared to be shivering—shivering with the suppressed sobs of a hardened man. The two of them evoked the scene of a father and his daughter.

The girl turned her head and locked eyes with Edward Moody.

It was Isabelle's face, and he wept.

XXXIV

OF COURSE THE moment that Joseph had stepped onto solid ground in New Orleans, he realized that Isabelle must be dead, for the life force that was reaching out to him at that point was not coming from the land of the living. And yet, like Moody, he too did not want to believe it . . . did not want to believe what must have been true. What the photograph was ultimately telling them.

But it was not until they reached Yellow Henry's place of refuge that Joseph realized all that the photograph had been trying to say. Isabelle had been guiding them there—that much was simple. But guiding them toward what? The answer was now plain.

It was her daughter—Isabelle's daughter. She was the ghost of what remained.

How could decades of mystery have been unlocked so easily? It was one of those puzzles that, once put together, laid bare the grains of its own simplicity.

Isabelle had planned to leave Boston because she had been carrying a child. And yet the pictures revealed a different story.

"That girl came here," Henriette had told Joseph. "Found her way here through the swamps, even after what they had done to her. Those devils . . . what they did to her. But mind you I've seen worse. Maybe she was lucky to get out alive."

Henriette told Joseph of Isabelle's escape, how she had found her way to Henriette's because she herself had grown up there, in the swamps. When she arrived, she could not speak, or even explain in writing what had happened. And in any case, words on paper would not have signified anything to Yellow Henry.

"I raised Isabelle from a child," Henriette said. "Found her as a baby tucked inside a tree. She was a gift from the alligators and the cottonmouths. Later, when she was mostly grown, I sent her off with the traders—north. To some place better. I never heard from her again, but I knew that she would work. And then when it happened . . . I also knew."

Henriette was never surprised.

"She did not need to explain to me what happened—*je savais*. Just as she knew that she would die when she had the child. And that was something I knew too. So she scribbled her words on this paper, and I've kept it all these years."

Henriette held a folded paper in her hand—it was yellowed and soiled.

"For the photographer," she said.

Moody was across the room, still in the throes of his visions.

"I named the girl Vivienne," she said. "For her sake, I erased the memory of her mother. And, for that matter, the mother before that—Justine. For you see, they had all come to me."

There was a perfect symmetry to what she was saying—the flight of Isabelle's mother, and years later the flight of Isabelle—both leading to the same place. The same hopeless salvation.

"But I did not fully understand," Henriette said, "because of course my Isabelle could no longer speak. And as Vivi grew, she could not speak either, because, you see, the girl was born without a voice. But she had something much more powerful than the gift of speech. She had the gift of sight, and her visions flowed out through her fingers."

Over the years, Henriette said, the girl had begun to draw. She had learned to navigate the swamps, to do business with the fur traders . . . had learned all of the cruder things that her mother before her had learned. But through that she drew, and her drawings became more precise. Child's sketches at first, surely, but as she grew into a young woman, her drawings developed a realness that could stop one's blood.

"That was her gift," Henriette said. "Isabelle's memories were her gift."

They were horrors—the papers. For Joseph they were horrors. Henriette could see it, and she admonished him.

"Shame on you," she said. "Shame on you of all people. You are one who has always embraced what you see, and yet this—*this*—you do not want to see."

She jerked her head toward the recumbent Moody.

"Sometimes you are no better than *him*. Maybe you need a bath too."

Henriette was right. Joseph did feel ashamed—ashamed that he had come to Boston looking for Isabelle with such confidence and arrogance. He was going to track her down, the way people had once tracked him down—and failed. He would not fail. He was Joseph Winter—"Fifty-two Winter"—a legend amongst the fugitives. A man of great importance.

And yet he did not save her. There was nothing he did to try to save her. He had saved himself, while she went on saving others.

"Yes . . ." Henriette said, "I see it. I see that she held you too, and I'd like to tell you that she left you something, but she didn't. You weren't special. She belonged to everyone—to all of us. Her voice was the voice of all of us."

Henriette looked as if she were about to spit.

"And they took it."

Joseph turned to Vivi, who had been sitting there silently since entering the room. Her appearance had not been dramatic. Strangely, it had been something expected.

"She knows the life of this swamp," Henriette said, "like her mother, and her grandmother before that. And with that comes responsibility—*Joseph Winter*."

And it was as if in saying his name, she were pronouncing him alive for the first time.

"You see who she is and you see what she is capable of. She is a woman whose drawings give you the world."

"But—" Joseph urged.

"She has no words," Henriette said. "Only visions. *Nos rêves et nos visions* . . . dreams and visions of what is to come. She forces us to see. And I am sorry for you."

Joseph held Vivi's hands. He could not stop himself from weeping. Over on the divan, Edward Moody began to stir.

"The photographer will wake," Henriette said. "And when he does it will be his turn to see."

She brandished Vivi's drawings as Moody let out a soft cry. Then she turned from the pair and began making her way across the cabin. Moody shifted and grunted, and Henriette paused, looking back toward the bar with that wry smile on her face.

"Yes," she said. "He has been sick for a long time, but even I am surprised by his strength."

. . .

HE WAS WEAK, and everything in his vision was a blur. Could what he was now seeing be real? There was a woman standing before him—a beautiful young woman he instantly knew. Not a ghost, and not Isabelle, and yet these two things she seemed to be. He had lost all sense of time, and could not tell how long he had been gazing at her. The drawings had depicted Isabelle's fate— the fate he had never wanted to see.

But she had been waiting for him. All of this time she had been waiting! He had been right to hold onto her. He had been right not to let go. She had called to him, summoned him. Down here to this wretched swamp. He had only wanted her back, and now she had come back him.

But it was not her.

He stared at her, examined her. Joseph Winter was holding her hands. The old Moody returned—the Moody who wanted to tear her away from everyone else. Even now he grew hot at the mere thought of Joseph holding her. Such thoughts could only remind him of his own failings, and his own shame.

But it was not her.

Yes, the face was hers . . . the shoulders, the neck, and the breasts. All hers. The way she breathed was her, and that shape of the mouth was hers. But as Moody's vision cleared, he could see that it was not her.

And he could see that she was not his.

At last, Moody rose unsteadily from the divan, and walked across the cabin toward the trio at the bar. He stood before them for a moment, uncertain what to do or say. The young woman shifted her gaze toward him, and stared at him with familiar eyes.

Yellow Henry took one of the woman's hands and offered it to Moody. The woman's other hand remained in Joseph Winter's.

"This is Vivienne, photographer."

Moody took Vivi's hand.

"I am sorry," he said.

There was everything to apologize for. There would always be the record of what he had done.

The young woman smiled—a remarkable smile. She possessed the easy grace of her mother.

"Now you see, photographer," Henriette said. "Now you finally see the real picture."

The three of them remained there—Joseph, Moody, Vivi—their hands chaining them together, for some time. From the table, the negative shined toward them like a coated mirror. Isabelle was all but invisible.

Henriette held up the folded piece of paper—the one that had captured Joseph's attention from the start.

"There is still the matter of this," she said, looking at Moody. "I have always known that this was for you, even though she never told me."

Moody did not let go of Vivi, but instead took the letter with his other hand. The sight of Isabelle's words again redoubled his sense of gratitude.

He whispered the words, aloud. They were too powerful to remain silent:

> *You are a great man. You will do great things for people.*
> *You will open their eyes. You will teach them how to <u>see</u>.*
> *She is all that is left of me now. She is yours. Keep her,*
> *guard her. She needs you. Everyone needs you. I left so that*
> *everyone could have you.*
> *Please forgive me.*

Her selflessness overcame him like a tide from which he could not escape. She had wanted to be gone so that *he* could be saved—so that his dishonest, ambitious self could be saved. Somehow, she had known that his fortune needed protecting.

Moody released Vivi's hand, and folded the piece of paper. He had an unshakeable sense of what he needed to do. Vivi had been waiting for him, here in these swamps. And it was Isabelle who had led him here, and left her to his care.

He moved toward the table and returned the negative to its case. The negative had brought him back to Isabelle—and now to Vivi. The letter was perhaps the last thing that Isabelle had ever touched, though a tear on Vivi's cheek might have been so, too. The letter . . . her words . . . her *voice*. It was hers. He tucked the letter into the negative's case, alongside the backside of the glass. The words needed to be near what remained of her.

"There is one more thing for you to do," Henriette said. "We need to dump that water out over your shoulder . . . go to the crossroads, and get rid of it. Even if the devil is there waiting for you, it is the last thing you must do."

She was nodding—and grinning—as if she relished the very idea of danger.

"Yes—" she said, "the water does contain one of your tears. But that doesn't fix everything. The devil gets you for your crimes."

XXXV

THERE WERE CRIMINALS and there were criminals. What ultimately made one guilty? Was it the treachery itself, or was it merely the intention, which came from a secret place in the heart?

Elizabeth leaned back in her chair, and looked about the drawing room. It was silent, and would not speak to her. For many years she had entertained the men and women of Boston in this drawing room. They had enjoyed its lush upholsteries, its luxurious curtains, the warmth of its hearth. The room had welcomed everyone from governors to masonry men. But none of them had ever really understood.

In her hand, the piece of paper—more "evidence," as it were.

As a girl she had known the land down there, had almost grown to love it, even though it wasn't hers—and never would be. At first she had been charmed by it, like any child in a fairyland would have been. But then the horrors came, and the sharp tones of her mother, and each journey back to Philadelphia became a political return to righteousness.

The first time Elizabeth had seen Isabelle, she knew—knew what the girl was about, and from where she had come. And the story that Elizabeth mapped onto Isabelle, strangely, had caused Elizabeth to momentarily put aside the girl's beauty. It was astonishing, really, since Elizabeth rarely put aside anything, but for Elizabeth there was something else beyond that first dazzling effect. In the most discomfiting way, Isabelle somehow represented every poor girl that Elizabeth had ever seen.

Which is why, after all that Elizabeth had done for her, it had been such a crime when Isabelle had at last betrayed her.

Elizabeth remembered those southern women—how they had talked on the porch about their husbands. How wives and mothers learned to spot the signs, and then decide what to do about the "situation." But Elizabeth had traveled far away from that world by then, and she lived in Boston, where such things did not happen. Or if they did happen, they happened so discretely that any knowledge of them remained buried in the bricks and mortar of people's houses.

It was Jenny who, unsurprisingly, brought her back one day.

"That girl's been eating an awful lot around here," Jenny had said.

Elizabeth looked at her inquisitively, because there was always more to what Jenny said.

"Enough for more than herself, if you ask me."

It was not a surprise, because Elizabeth had known. It was, in a way, impossible for Elizabeth not to know. Isabelle's dresses had grown a bit tighter in the waist. Her breasts had grown fuller. Her face was aglow. And of course it made sense that Jenny would lash out in this fashion—surreptitiously, subtly, even maliciously. Jenny had always resented Isabelle for who she was.

But Jenny's petty jealousies did not concern Elizabeth. The important question was . . . when had it happened?

Elizabeth's mind began to work.

Five months, six months at the most, she predicted . . . for during that length of time, Isabelle could still reasonably conceal what had happened. Elizabeth traced the months backwards, and the murky road resisted her. What would those months tell her? What would that dirty path reveal?

That was late November, early December, of the previous year—when she had gone down to see her mother, and left William Jeffrey behind. There had been an outbreak of the fever in Philadelphia, and Elizabeth had not wanted to take him down with her. Isabelle and Jenny would see to his care.

And Garrett was home. Yes, conveniently, Garrett was still home. The next session would not start until the first of December.

She returned to Boston exactly one day before his departure, and when she came into the house, all was silent and empty. It felt as if someone had been waiting there to tell her something, but that person had gone, and taken all that was left along with them.

"Jenny?" Elizabeth called.

But no answer came. And no little footsteps of William Jeffrey sounded down the steps to greet her.

"James?"

But still no answer. She was alone in the grip of the house. Its knowledgeable walls and barren rooms refusing to give her anything.

• • •

LATER THAT AFTERNOON, when they returned from the Commons, Elizabeth grew even more suspicious. Senator Garrett, Jenny said, had gone back to Washington a day early. He sent his most sincere apologies.

"Apologies?" Elizabeth said.

But then she clamped her mouth shut, because she was not about to invite Jenny into the privacy of her marriage.

Garrett had disappeared—gone back to Washington for a good reason. It was enough to suppress her suspicions yet again. Because that's what she had been doing for a few years now—suppressing suspicions. She did not want to believe that the young girl she was saving could ever have been a threat to her family.

Isabelle was pure. Isabelle was grace embodied. To see her with William Jeffrey . . . she was angelic. The boy loved her, and Elizabeth loved her as well for it. The scars of what Isabelle had suffered were evident in the strange beauty that lived in her eyes. She would have been favored where she had come from, and Elizabeth hated to imagine what Isabelle must have endured.

"That girl's been eating an awful lot around here," Jenny had said. "Enough for more than herself, if you ask me."

And that's when it all came together—Garrett's departure, his inexplicable coldness upon his return, and the girl's sudden sheepishness and prolonged absences. When Garrett was home, he now avoided the girl, or grew uneasy in her presence. It was something that Elizabeth hoped she would never see; but in the end she could not help but see it.

There was everything to think about. They would lose everything. She could lose everything. The *nation* could lose everything.

Her decision at that point became irreversible.

She had seen him in the streets a number of times since his visit to the house, when he had come to claim Jenny. The new fugitive laws had brought many of his kind to Boston, and these men had been crawling through taverns and alleyways for some time. She had never acknowledged him when she saw him, but he had seen her, and had taken measures to ensure that she knew that he had seen her. Once he had tipped his hat and offered a despicable grin. She had inadvertently met his eyes, but then looked down and moved along.

It had been surprisingly easy to find him. One or two inquiries regarding a few of the reward posters around town, and there he was, at her service.

They met at a tavern in the North End, far from the places she frequented. She wore a cloak and a hood that night, and did not remove it when they sat down.

"You're looking—"

And he spat a stream of tobacco before he went on.

"—well, Mrs. Garrett. I do say this is quite the honor."

She was not afraid. She had rehearsed the conversation in the days before. This was not the first time she had seen a man like this, and she knew how one needed to talk to them.

"The proposition I have for you," she said, "is one that will . . . *benefit* you greatly, Mr. Wilcox—if you can execute this delicate matter with the utmost discretion."

"Call me Will," the man said. "That's what the ladies call me around here. And as far as discretion . . . Mrs. Garrett, you got both my attention and my discretion."

She recoiled at the very notion of continuing the conversation, but he was a man who could get things done, and there was something remarkably appealing about that. She would be his now—perhaps for the rest of her life—because they would share a secret that no two other people shared.

She subdued that thought as she outlined the plan . . . what she needed him to do, and how it had to happen.

"And there are ways," she said, "I know there are ways—"

He was grinning.

"And I do not need to know them," she said.

He was filthy, and smelled of all sorts of things, but he was about the same age as she was, and in another time and place the exchange might have been different. His eyes darted to different parts of her body as she talked. It was as if the man could see right into her.

She did not provide the reason behind why she wanted to do it. But still, she felt that he knew.

"Shouldn't be any trouble at all," Wilcox said. "Any family I need to worry about?"

"None that I know of," Elizabeth replied.

"Now you do know, Mrs. Garrett," the man went on, "that this matter being so 'delicate,' as you say, requires quite a bit more . . . effort."

"You will be compensated handsomely," Elizabeth said.

"My, my," he said. "Ain't you polite?"

It revolted her to think of herself engaging with such a person. The association could ruin everything—but she knew that it wouldn't. These things were done, and if done the right way, never amounted to anything.

And that was all. On the day before the thing was to happen, she unlocked the pantry and gathered her wedding silver together. She hired a hansom cab to take her across town to the awful boardinghouse where he was residing. There were drunken men in the stairwell, and women with babies that would not be quiet.

She handed him the sack and he dumped the silver out on the table.

"Mighty fine," he said.

The rattling had scraped her insides.

He ran his dirty fingers over the pile . . . separated the pieces, like candy. The handles of the forks and knives poked into one another. Some were upturned, and revealed the engraving.

"*Mighty* fine," he repeated.

And he shot her a lascivious grin.

Elizabeth unwittingly clutched the front folds of her cloak.

"This will do then?" she said, steadying her voice.

"This will do . . . *just fine*," Wilcox said.

She herself looked over the silver. He had already begun to separate out the pieces from one another. And that's when she noticed it—or thought that she noticed it. Her son's silver teaspoon was missing.

"Mrs. Garrett?" Wilcox said, for he did not miss a breath.

"It's nothing," she said. "I must go."

That night when the rest of the house was asleep, she crept back into the pantry to see if she had dropped William's teaspoon. She had, and there it was, like a coin hiding under one of the shelves.

She could not help but think at that moment that the spoon had cursed her. It had remained in the house as a reminder of what she had done. But Elizabeth was strong then . . . stronger than Garrett had ever realized. Her sacrifice would ensure that nothing would tarnish his legacy. And really, there was nothing more important than that.

Now, all these years later, Elizabeth sat again in her drawing room, with yet another piece of paper in her hand that might have easily led to her ruin. It was not the only piece of paper that had been exchanged between them, for there had been many others over the years—sometimes frequently and sometimes years apart. Garrett of course never knew anything about the relationship. It was best that Senator Garrett not know anything at all.

There had been fires, a robbery or two, and other random acts of mayhem. Anything that might be required when Garrett's political "situation" was in need of that last bit of help. She never knew the details of the things the man did, and for her own good they had kept it that way.

"Mighty nice way to do business," he had once said to her. "Your husband doesn't know how lucky he is."

But now, the one act that had started it all eighteen years ago had somehow resurfaced. It had never been put to rest.

"Finish this," she said to him. "Finish this once and for all."

And he had nodded, and told her he'd take care of it.

She looked down at his note—the hideous writing she had come to recognize.

I know where ther at.
Tomorra its all finished.

She lit a match and threw the burning letter into the fireplace. For a moment, she saw a face there, with an open mouth ready to scream. The face startled her, but disappeared almost as soon as it had come, and the letter she had tossed quickly melted into flames.

XXXVI

VIVI WAS AN artist, and her pictures told many stories—not simply the story of Isabelle's kidnapping, but also the stories of other people whose spirits had lived on through Vivi's hands. There were pictures of farmers, and storekeepers, and mothers; of people working the land and people in great cities. Henriette had collected a large portfolio of Vivi's sketches over the years, though she seemed cautious about revealing it, when she exposed it to Joseph and Moody.

"Not everyone can see what this girl sees," Henriette said. "Not everyone has the courage to see."

Henriette had sheltered her, and yet, even in her silence, Vivi seemed to know much of the world. She was the child of the swamp, and yet the child of something else, and there was a sense that she was a young woman of motion. At one point she draped a gauze over her head and abruptly made to leave—as if beckoned by a call, somewhere beyond the walls of Henriette's cabin.

Henriette took no notice, and simply waited for Vivi to go. Once Vivi had departed, Henriette began to talk about their time.

"For that is how I see it," Henriette said. "Just time—which was never mine. I knew that you would come some day, and that we would need to decide what to do. She was drawing these things when she was just a little child, before she even knew what they were."

Then Henriette leafed through the portfolio and pulled out a picture that had been hiding amongst the others. It was a sketch of a young man—a handsome man, with a beard. The man bore a rough resemblance to Moody.

Henriette handed Moody the sketch. The pencil strokes were bold—almost violent.

"The girl knows," she said. "It is remarkable, what this girl knows."

That was what Moody had seen in Vivi's eyes . . . not just sorrow, but knowledge. Isabelle's knowledge, and the knowledge of the many hundreds—thousands—who had come before her.

Moody stared at the sketch—was it him, or someone else? Was he seeing what Isabelle's daughter had seen, or what he himself wanted to see?

But the swamp would only condone so many revelations, for soon the door creaked, and admitted one of Henriette's men.

There was no urgency on his face as he approached Henriette, and she looked down at the floor as he whispered into her ear. These men who surrounded her were hardened and unkind. Henriette remained unmoved by what he said.

At last the man finished and was gone as quickly as he had come.

"So," Henriette said, her eyes fixed on Moody, "you went ahead and brought the devil along with you, eh?"

Moody at once knew what Henriette meant.

"I am sorry," he said. "We should go then—right away."

"Too late—but not to worry," Henriette replied. "We've dealt with men like him before. Important thing is, we must get to the crossroads and get rid of that water. Then you can be on your way. We don't have much time . . . *you* don't have much time."

It was not yet evening, and they piled into a boat—Joseph, Moody, Henriette. Henriette pushed them away from the dock.

"And Vivi?" Moody asked.

"She has things to do," Henriette said. "But she will be there to greet us. That girl is rarely where she doesn't need to be."

Henriette navigated the boat with surprising skill, her body strong, upright, and unwavering. In the water, the eyes of alligators sparkled like pairs of misplaced coins.

No birds called—only insects screeched. It was a dreadful kind of symphony.

The lights of Henriette's cabin were barely discernable far off behind them, when the boat brought the group to an unusual bump of land, covered with thick brush. Dense walls of cypresses surrounded this piece of terrain, but a series of canals had cut through the walls too, forming ambiguous paths through the giant trees.

"The crossroads," Henriette said.

There was a figure—beyond the shore.

However it had come to stand there, it had come forward with the darkness. It was draped in the weeds of the swamp . . . but also in other things.

There was moss upon it, and rags, and a skirt that might have billowed. Who could have owned such a terrible scarecrow? Had Henriette placed it there, as a warning?

"I told you that she is rarely where she doesn't need to be," Henriette said.

And as the boat touched the shore, Moody watched the figure transform into Vivi.

Moody's breath retracted, so sudden was the transformation. The uneven shadows of the swamp had both hidden her and revealed her. Then Moody stepped out of the boat, followed by Henriette and Joseph. He wanted to run to Vivi, and seize her, and remove her from this horrible place. She seemed impalpable though . . . camouflaged beneath the murky greens and grays of the swamp. He moved forward—a small step—but then felt the pressure on his arm.

"Careful, photographer," Henriette said. "There's the water to deal with first, and we are running out of time."

Moody was confused. He looked at Joseph for an explanation. Did Joseph not understand these things, almost better than anyone else? But that quickly Joseph had jerked his head away from Moody and Henriette. He was staring at something amorphous that had risen up out of the brush.

There, behind Vivi, loomed the devil's outline itself, bearing down upon her, with a knife.

XXXVII

WHAT WAS IT that had paralyzed Joseph? For all his experience and instinct, one would have expected something more from him than fear. But at the sight of the assassin engulfing this shadow of the woman he loved, Joseph had found himself unable to move.

Everything he had ever run from was in front of him. Joseph's bravery all of those years, and what he had endured . . . the hard floorboards of freight trains, sleepless nights in old barns, and the monotony of crouching silently in tunnels. He had been running from himself—his own shameful place in the world. And today he had been found, in those swamps.

There was Vivi. He saw Vivi. The murderer held her in his grip. He had her head in his hand, the blade of his knife to her throat.

"She yours?" the man said. "Don't think I don't know who you are, Fifty Two."

Joseph could make no reply.

And then Moody stepped up.

"It's me you want," Moody shouted. "Me—not her."

Wilcox glanced from Joseph to Moody.

"I want the nigger too," he said. "I want to watch you kill your nigger."

His grip tightened on Vivi's hair, which now he pulled back to expose more of her throat.

"Have him throw you his gun," Wilcox said. "I know he's got it on him."

Joseph looked at Moody, but Moody had locked eyes with the murderer. Wilcox pressed the knife harder against Vivi's throat, and the skin beneath the blade began to pucker.

Wilcox remained fixed on Moody.

"Tell him to throw it," he repeated.

Beside Joseph, Yellow Henry released a slow, heavy breath. He searched for counsel in her eyes, but she too was staring at Vivi and Wilcox.

Then Wilcox twisted his wrist, and the edge of the blade went into Vivi. She remained silent, her eyes gazing out toward the trees, as a tiny dribble of blood emerged beneath the steel at her throat.

"No!" Joseph shouted.

And at last the murderer averted his glance. The horrible black eyes revealed only vacancy—and evil.

Joseph fumbled to release the small pistol from his sleeve.

"That's a good nigger," Wilcox said. "Now throw it. I won't ask you again."

Joseph tossed the gun to Moody, and Moody caught it between his hands. Moody looked at the pistol, and gripped it, but he would not raise his eyes.

"Now!" Wilcox shouted.

Then Moody looked up at Joseph. Joseph could see a different kind of vacancy in those eyes too.

Joseph nodded.

No words were exchanged between them, but the conversation that sounded was so powerful that one could almost hear it amongst the cacophony of the insects. Moody held the pistol firmly, but his pleading glance at Joseph said that he could never kill this man.

And then there was Joseph, who, in his resignation, was somehow confirming that there was nothing wrong with this ending.

Again, Joseph nodded—the most imperceptible tilt of the head. Vivi was far from him now, yet the eyes of glass were close.

Moody raised his arm, cocked the pistol, and paused.

A stifling cloud of malevolence had suffused with the island's moisture—a kind of humidity that defied all borders, like fingers creeping closed around a throat. Everything Joseph had fought for, everything he had suffered, would all come to nothing in this wilderness.

Or would it? She was there, before him—*Vivi*. They had found her, and when he was gone, someone would still be there, to bring her out. Joseph trusted in the righteousness of these things, even though men like Wilcox often won their battles. But there was something else here . . . a journey that had been too important and too wonderful to simply come to this. When Joseph was gone, a long-sought rectitude would follow him, and his spirit would finally be free.

And then it happened—a mysterious thing. The impossible flew in with the shadows. How, or exactly when it happened, Joseph could not tell. But now, in the awful arms of Wilcox, something else was slumping: instead of Vivi, a life-sized rag doll, without the slightest sign of life in its floppy limbs. The doll's eyes were black buttons, its mouth a zigzagged line of stitches. This was what Vivi had been.

Yellow Henry let out a "Ha!" and Joseph turned to see Vivi at her side. On the shore, they stood fearless, like soldiers. Yellow Henry held the bucket, for that's what mattered to her most, while Vivi held out a dusty pile of something in her hand.

Then a sharp burst of air—the bullet of someone's breath—and a cloud of powder that made its way toward the assassin. The cloud traveled a distance, never lingering in place but always swirling toward its target, like an unmoored galaxy in search of a place to land.

Wilcox stumbled backwards, his face now covered with the fine, pale dust. His eyes were shut, and he was forced to scratch at them.

Vivi's palm was outstretched . . . her lips still puckered from the dusty blow.

Then Wilcox thrashed and released a horrible scream, before the brush grabbed him, and returned him to hiding.

Through all of this Edward Moody had watched with the same astonishment as Joseph. But what in the past he might have dismissed with disbelief suddenly made sense to him. She was gone, and yet so much of her was still there. He could not deny that she was everywhere—everywhere around him now. The words came back to him: *She is yours. Keep her, guard her.* The voice embraced him, soothed him, even as the leaves began to melt, and a familiar lightness blurred his vision.

He touched his lips—they were chalky. Some stray flecks of powder had also reached him.

Vivi—again Vivi! Moss mingled with her hair, like lace. She was standing with Henriette, and hadn't realized how close he had been. There was only so much the swamp would permit, and the powder . . .

Perhaps he would die. Perhaps Edward Moody would finally die. Perhaps in saving him, Vivi would kill him.

But no sooner had these thoughts taken hold in Moody's mind when the water came, and drenched his whole body. Henriette had hinted at it time again: the water would save him after all.

"We are done here, photographer."

The empty bucket was in Henriette's hands.

"Time to go—he will be back. A boat will be waiting for you—beyond."

Vivi was already in the pirogue, making ready for the separation, and Moody climbed in after her. The swamp had calmed into a lullaby for the moment, but there was an uneasiness about the island, and there were those who had not recovered.

"And you—*Joseph Winter*—" Henriette added. "You must go too. This is no time to fail."

She fingered one of her bracelets.

"But first . . . I think this is for you."

She twisted her fingers around a knot, and unfastened the bracelet. It hung for a moment, like limp grass, between her fingers. Then she took Joseph's hand and clasped the leather strap upon his wrist. The countless others who stayed behind would never miss this one little piece.

"Do you know who this is?" Henriette said, her fingers still knotting the band.

Joseph felt the coolness and the smoothness of the leather . . . felt the brush of Henriette's fingers as she joined this emblem to his wrist. And then, at that moment, Joseph perceived the whole meaning . . . or *who* the bracelets represented, as monuments on the old woman's arms. Henriette had been carrying all of them. For decades, she had carried them all.

"She will go with you," Henriette said. "You came here looking for her, didn't you?"

Joseph gazed into Henriette's eyes. The mud and the cypress trees were her stage. Henriette's eyes were of so many mothers and daughters. The eyes of wives, and of children . . . of the dead and the living.

Then the eyes hardened.

"Now go," she finally said.

Henriette reached into her pocket and pulled out her own pistol. She flashed it in the air with pride. Then her face was distorted by one of her odd, smiling frowns—a kind of mysterious revelation of all the tempered pleasures she had ever felt. She parted her lips, and seemed about to laugh, but no sound came from her mouth. Then swiftly, she moved away from them, toward the torn curtains of the island's brush after Wilcox, and without another word she was gone.

Vivi pushed the boat away from the island. They were moving again in the direction of Henriette's cabin, where the little eyes of light had been puncturing the darkness all along.

They had gone out into the water some distance from the island, when Joseph, who had been silent, began to stir.

"No," he finally said.

Vivi and Moody looked at him.

"No—I must go back."

There was something on the island still waiting for him, but Moody could never have understood this.

"This is no time for heroics," Moody said flatly. "There is nothing for you here anymore."

"But there is—" Joseph said. "And there always will be."

And with that he quietly escaped over the boat's edge.

"Joseph!" Moody shouted.

But there was no pulling this man back.

"I will find you," Joseph said, as he began swimming in the other direction. "You must go ahead, Edward . . . I will find you. You must take her away."

"No, Joseph! This—"

Joseph was far off in the water, having already become one with the swamp. Like Vivi, he was a student of its habits and secrets, and there was nothing that Edward Moody could do.

"Joseph! Joseph!" Moody cried one last time.

But he was calling out for something that had already disappeared.

Vivi resumed the journey and Moody sat at the head of the boat. The place, Moody knew, was leaving him. Joseph's bold move did not alter their course, and in no time they were a good distance from both the island and Yellow Henry's.

It was quiet.

There were croaks, and strange splashes, but still there was quiet. Until the gunshots split the encroaching night's peace.

Gunshots—two gunshots. One right after another.

The horrible sounds had come from the darkness—from the crossroads, now far behind them.

XXXVIII

THROUGH THE SWAMP, the pirogue glided—an amphibious arrow that parted the water. The frogs eyed Moody with intrepid suspicion. He had never belonged there, and it was time for him to go.

With Vivi.

Who was she?

There was something in the eye, something in the face, that made Vivi more than who she seemed. Moody wanted to believe nothing more than a fantasy . . . that Vivi had somehow magically emerged from Isabelle, right at the moment of her mother's death. Vivi was a vessel that had sprung up to carry a spirit. A nymph made from Isabelle, and water.

But that could not have been so. Moody knew that it was not so. There were things that were true, and things that were not. The things Moody believed, no matter how much he wanted to believe them, would not necessarily be true.

Who was she?

It may have been hours before the pirogue reached a clearing, for the cypresses and their knees remained dense for a very long time. There had been constant darkness in the swamp because of the dense canopy of the trees, but when the boat passed through its last grove, a fading sky revealed the day. How far into the day they were, Moody could not exactly tell, but the sun could not have dipped beyond the horizon more than moments ago. It was gone now—the sun—tucked away somewhere in the distance, happy to give way to the whispers that accompanied the approaching dusk.

In the marshlands, the last cypresses lingered with Moody and Vivi for some time . . . in groups of twos and threes, but sometimes in straight lines. The trees lined edges of bayous as Vivi steered the boat through the water—the water that would eventually kill these trees, as it mixed with the salt coming in. At last, in an open expanse of rippling water, they passed one old sentinel, still standing—alone and isolated. The salt had done its work upon him long ago, and his leaves had long left him, and his branches had dropped away. All that remained of him was a thick trunk and two arms, with frail wisps of moss held against the trunk by the wind.

From a dark hump near the tree, a bird inspected the travelers. It seemed about to ask them something, when it stretched its wings, and flew away.

The water grew misty as the sky turned pink. There were islands now . . . or clusters of trees crowding clumps of land. The islands floated like clouds upon the water, limned with gray vapors that obscured where the shores began. There were reflections in the water—the sky, the small islands, the mirror of the mist itself—and in this perfect gateway of pink and black and gray, a silence pronounced the end of time.

They continued, and more land began to appear, though it never became greater than the water. Something like a coastline now and then came into view, before being swallowed up again by the mighty thing that ruled there. At one point they saw movement as they passed a higher strip of land—a lone farmer bleeding a pine tree for turpentine.

Then there was the boat, just as Henriette had said. It was there in the water—ahead.

Vivi guided the pirogue toward the boat—a small craft that held two masts. It was sitting there in front of them, as still as one of the islands, its whiteness almost garish in the serenity of this open space.

"Do you know who is there?" Moody said.

Vivi nodded.

They were close enough now so that Moody could see the men. There was a crew—mostly negroes—and standing in front of them, Father Thomas.

The look on Father Thomas's face was strained.

"Joseph . . ." he said, as Vivi brought the pirogue in closer.

But Moody's hard expression revealed the answer to that unasked question.

Some of the crew helped rope the pirogue to the boat as Moody and Vivi disembarked. Father Thomas embraced both of them, which was an odd thing for Moody, now part of this family.

Moody explained that Joseph had returned to Henriette . . . after Vivi had saved them from the assassin.

"We must send someone in to look for him," Father Thomas said.

And he turned, and spoke a muffled order to the crew.

"Henriette's network is vast within these swamps," he said. "We will bring him back. God willing, we will bring him back . . ."

The boat began to move, slowly at first, but then with more speed. They would go as far as Mobile, Father Thomas told them, and from there they could make their escape.

"To Boston," Moody said.

"Boston?" the priest replied. "You would return there? Is it safe for you to return?"

Moody looked at Vivi. Her eyes were bright as stars.

"Boston," Moody said, with an almost contemptuous tone, "is indeed the only place where I can keep this child safe."

XXXIX

IN GARRETT'S MIND, it had all happened years ago now, even though only three weeks had passed. Garrett was losing time—or his sense of it at least. The photograph . . . the search . . . his periodic discussions with the police. All of this had been commingling within him.

Then a day came when the commingling reached its pitch. It was not something he could have ever foreseen.

Elizabeth had insisted that he accompany her to Washington Street—on errands. They had not been downtown together since the photograph.

"Why?" he had returned.

Her reasoning had been shrewd.

"People are starting to talk," she had said to him. "I'm hearing it, and I don't like what I'm hearing. They need to see that you're in good health. That *we* are in good health. The way you've been going about town, in and out of coffeehouses . . . you can't expect people not to talk."

She was cold. When had she become so harsh and cold? But then, for one moment, she broke.

"I think they are afraid," she said.

And then she added:

"I'm afraid."

It was true . . . for the past three weeks Garrett had not felt or behaved like himself. Something had been happening to him—something he could not explain. There was a weakness in his heart that was having its effect over his every thought and movement. He didn't know if he needed to give in to that weakness, or if it was something he should continue to fight.

And he certainly couldn't ask Elizabeth.

"Very well," he had said. "I will go."

The traffic on Washington Street that day was particularly hectic, since the construction of a new hotel on Tremont was redirecting carriages and omnibuses to alternative channels. The people on the street seemed more numerous too, it being a pleasant day—an ideal one for spending.

He would not remember the stores, or the people, or what they said. The vision would be all that he remembered.

They were walking.

Men in bowlers, boys with boxes, and young professionals rushed past. Women with closed parasols casually sauntered by store windows. A horse whinnied, and then grunted—it had had enough of the tugs to its reins.

Elizabeth held his arm and walked closely beside him. They had not been this close since—

He remembered the spark flashing. Or did he ever remember? Perhaps he would never remember anything at all.

The sun had hit the window at the moment of their passing—the window across the street, filled with silver.

The flash blinded him, and he stumbled . . . not enough to cause alarm. It was more of a pause, which held him and Elizabeth for a moment, locked in their footsteps and staring across the street.

The door opened, and then the two familiar figures emerged on the doorstep. One of them was the scoundrel, and the other stared Garrett in the face.

Isabelle.

Isabelle?

Had that been her name after all? He had forgotten her name at some point during the years—hidden it, suppressed it. Murdered it even.

Yes. The woman was Isabelle.

The pairs of eyes on one side of the street fixated on the others opposite: Garrett and Elizabeth . . . Moody and the young woman. Each one of them frozen, like a picture.

There was one thing he remembered—that when she left, he had been relieved. It came back to him now, that immense sense of relief that had soothed his troubled thoughts when he learned that she had run off. Of course he would miss her, because over those months his care had grown for her, even though what had happened had, in his mind, not been real.

She looked at him. She knew. Her eyes told the truth. But there was also something else: there was that mist of himself on her face.

Elizabeth had gone down to see her mother, in Philadelphia, and he had stayed behind with the child. The child loved Isabelle—more, Garrett often thought, than anyone else. She had a way with William Jeffrey that was magical, and Garrett adored that.

She had crossed his path an impossible number of times. He could not deny what he felt.

"Watch yourself, old boy," Dovehouse had once said. "There are transgressions and there are transgressions. I've never taken you for a fool."

He had been careful . . . so very careful. He was a young senator, with everything to lose—or win. There was so much greatness in store for him. It was a greatness that he himself would create.

But on that one night, the world conspired against his winning. Elizabeth, his family, his career, the voice of society—none of it had seemed to matter in that moment.

"You do . . . feel something for me then?" he had finally managed to ask Isabelle.

The slight movement of her head had at least suggested the answer that, for years, he had been longing to hear.

When he approached her, she did not resist him. There were spirits on his breath. Still she barely resisted him, even when he pulled her close.

Then her body tensed. He was holding her in his arms.

"No, Senator," she said. "No!"

He did not listen. He did not hear her. He simply did what he wanted. But he would never be able to forgive himself. The years would not bring forgiveness.

The eyes that now stared into his face from across the street understood everything that had happened. For they had been there—watched it. Recorded it. Remembered it. In these eyes was the story he never told.

Elizabeth would see it. She had probably already seen it. There was no denying that Elizabeth would immediately see to whom this girl belonged. And she would chastise him for wanting to take this girl under his care. It would have been tantamount to a full confession, and Elizabeth would never stand for it.

And then, it was as if a shard of glass had pierced his heart. Garrett grabbed at his chest, lost his balance, and fell away from the street. The wall of a storefront caught him, and held him as he continued to stumble. Elizabeth was far away from him now, standing firm—and focused on the others across the street.

"Officer, arrest that man!" she shouted.

What happened next, no one could rightly say, for many accounts eventually grew out of the incident. But the young woman disappeared, "kidnapped by a black man," some said, while Moody marched forward and into the center of the street. He had made no attempt to run, as the nearby officer moved toward him. It was the traffic, and not the spirit photographer, that had made the arrest so difficult.

Many people had observed this, and many disagreed on how things happened. But there was one observer on the street that day who was unquestionably sure of what he saw—a devilish observer who glanced at the four faces, from Moody and the girl, to Garrett and Elizabeth, and then back at all four of them again.

Their expressions confirmed everything that Dovehouse believed but didn't know, as if the truth had been revealed to him from the torn pages of a stolen book.

BOOK III
UNION

Boston Daily Journal
Boston, Massachusetts
Tuesday, August 16, 1870

SPIRITUALISM IN COURT

IN ALL THE annals of criminal jurisprudence—and they comprise an array of crimes of almost every description—there has seldom, if ever, been recorded a case analogous to that now before Justice Downing, in the Superior Court, Suffolk County, in which the people are the prosecutors, and Edward Moody is the defendant. The specific charge brought against Moody is that by means of what he termed "spiritual photographs" he has swindled many credulous persons, his representations leading the victims to believe that by communicating with the spirit land, it was possible not only to bring back the departed spirit, but to photograph their immaterial forms. How many have been induced to speculate on the features of departed relatives and friends it is hard to say, but the prosperity of Mr. Moody's establishment seems to have proven beyond controversy that the number was large.

The opening of the trial drew together a large and miscellaneous audience, including a number of the most distinguished of the believers in, and propagators of, the doctrines of Spiritualism. There were also many legal gentlemen, curious to note the points of law which might arise during the trial, and a sprinkling of middle-aged ladies (believers evidently). The examination was held in the Special Sessions Court Room; members of the bar, distinguished Spiritualists (among them Judge Edmonds and Mr. A. J. Davis), and the ladies, being accommodated with seats inside the railing.

The defendant, Mr. Moody, a man of about 43 or 44 years of age, with dark hair, beard, and eyes, and whitish complexion, was seated next to a grand army of hired counsel (all Spiritualists, the principals of which are Messrs. Townsend and Day), and appeared perfectly calm and self-possessed during the first day's proceedings. Moody's face is one of the few from which one fails to gather any trace of definite character.

It is calm and fathomless, and although quite prepossessing, it is yet a face which one would scarcely be able to believe in at first sight.

The people were represented by Mr. Eldridge Appleton, whose first witness, Mr. Marshall Hinckley, a highly regarded member of the American Institute for the Encouragement of Science and Invention, first brought the notice of the spiritual photography business to the authorities. Mr. Hinckley deposed that the Institute's investigation into the "hoax" of spirit photography began many months ago, when he sent members, under false names, to have their pictures taken by Mr. Moody. The negatives from these sittings, which Mr. Moody produced right before his clients' eyes, contained dim, indistinct, outlines of ghostly faces, staring out from various corners. Mr. Moody claimed that these faces were (in Mr. Hinckley's words) the manifestations of "dead fathers-in-law, or mothers, or wives, or any other jumble of nonsense." None of the sitters, however, recognized any of the alleged spirits, and emphatically declared that the faces resembled none that they had ever known in life. These agents for the Institute, three in total, took the stand following Mr. Hinckley, and confirmed everything that that gentleman had previously told the court.

Mr. Moody is charged with multiple counts of fraud and three counts of larceny—crimes for which he could find himself sentenced to the House of Corrections for many years to come.

XL

"I THOUGHT THAT it went very well," Eldridge Appleton said. "Considering—"

"Considering what?" Marshall Hinckley responded. "Considering the Spiritualists did everything but summon the ghosts from their graves to whisper sweet nothings into the ears of the jurors?"

"No," Appleton said. "Considering the strength of the Defense's cross-examination, and how well you and your men answered the questions."

"There were snickers," Hinckley said. "Those damned Spiritualists were laughing at us."

"But they shall not have the last laugh," Appleton said.

Inspector Bolles looked at Marshall Hinckley, who would not be satisfied until Edward Moody was in prison.

"The Spiritualists have hired a great deal of counsel," Bolles said. "But the people will decide in your favor."

Bolles was making an attempt at conciliation. After only one day, it had become evident that more than a trial was taking place in that courtroom.

"It's preposterous," Hinckley said. "This gaggle of witch doctors surrounding him."

"I thought your men made him appear very foolish," Appleton said. "Ten dollars per sitting, because 'the spirits do not like the throng, and want to exclude the vulgar multitude with high prices.' It makes him out to be the money-grubbing predator that he is. I think the jury will see that."

"*Unless*," Hinckley emphasized, "those damned Spiritualists paint a picture that even one member of the jury wants to see. There is no shortage of Spiritualists in that courtroom, and even in the jury box there may be a hankering for 'beautiful communion.'"

Eldridge Appleton had done his duty that day, calling witnesses to the stand and beginning the prosecution's side of the story. There had been Hinckley's three decoys—all three of them members of the Institute—who had gone separately to visit Moody, and requested pictures with departed relatives. The negatives, upon development, had indeed revealed spectral figures behind the sitters; but the figures, according to all three of the witnesses, "bore not a ghost of a resemblance to the deceased." Appleton encouraged Hinckley's men to share the details of how Moody had attempted to coerce them into seeing something that wasn't there. "He was trying to produce a train of thought," one witness said, "that would eventually lead me to confound the picture's shadowy background with the features of my dear departed mother." Another witness insisted that the likeness of his own face on the negative was "a passable one," but that the spirit of his dead father-in-law was "a most dismal failure."

By the time Inspector Bolles took the stand later in the day to describe Moody's "escape" from Boston, the courtroom had been treated to numerous accounts of how Edward Moody had seduced many of his visitors into seeing things that were not there. It seemed a wonderful and sensible coup for the prosecution—but that was what had Marshall Hinckley so enraged. Moody's case, and the fate of photography in general, was about so much more than seeing and believing.

"The pictures are obvious frauds," Appleton said. "And we will prove that beyond doubt—the jury will see it."

"Yes," Hinckley replied, "that's all well and good, but if Moody, or anyone else for that matter, can take a picture of a lady with her hand in a gentlemen's hair—a hand that one can just as easily adjust to surround the same gentleman's waist—then how can we ever trust the accuracy of a photograph again?"

"We can't," Bolles said.

"Precisely," Hinckley said. "But we *must*. We must be able to trust the *science* of photography. This is what is at stake here, Bolles—and I've been trying to tell you this all along. Before this spiritual nonsense began, it was nature—*and nature only*—that could be 'took' by the photographer's camera. But now, where are people to turn, when I can give you Lincoln hectoring a gang of negroes in a cotton field, or the parson in the arms of a whore? Gentlemen, we have treasured photographs in believing that, like figures, they cannot lie. But they are now being made to lie with a most deceiving exactness, and that is what our efforts must make clear—and punish!"

Did the photograph tell a lie? That was the ultimate question for Montgomery Bolles. After the arrest, Bolles had taken the negative from Edward

Moody's coat pocket himself. He had set the case down on the table between them, and there it sat during their interview, unopened.

"You know what is in that case," Moody had said.

And the inspector had returned a grave nod.

"And you know what it means, and who it was for . . . and what it could possibly do."

"We have apprehended you," Bolles replied, "at a great cost to the people of Boston. You and this negative have come back to us at a great cost. Do you have any idea what you've done?"

"I have done many things," Moody had replied, "but none of that matters to me any longer. I know what you are going to do with me—"

And he paused, grimacing.

"But what will you do with—*that?*"

XLI

THE JOURNEY INTO the swamp had not been without its consequences, and even now, many days later, Joseph could not stop replaying
what had happened there. He had returned to Mrs. Lovejoy's rooms after
stealing Vivi away from the scene on Washington Street. And yet the memories of what he had seen and done down south refused to let him go. He had
swum back to the crossroads, because his business there had not been finished. It would have been easier to have escaped with Moody and Vivi . . . to
have left it all behind, in the swamp.

He swam. The alligators and cottonmouths had disappeared. His movements were silent in the water.

He reached the crossroads with no plan. What was it that he was going
to do? He had the familiar sense of forward motion . . . of frantic energy, and
drive. It was the same sense that had saved him, time and time again. And yet
it was a sense that he had hoped to forget—someday.

But he would always be running. That is, until he stamped out whatever
he was running from.

The crossroads were quiet. Yellow Henry's bucket lay empty on the
ground, and the bow of her boat was still pressed into the mud. How big was
this piece of land? This strange island, this crossroads? How deep into the
brush had she gone?

The brush was entirely motionless—saw palmetto framed by other,
softer plants. There were amorphous limbs of moss-draped trees that bent
toward and away from one another. Yellow Henry—and Wilcox—were somewhere deep in that brush. There was darkness in the spot where they had both
disappeared.

He entered.

There was noise—a small animal scurrying away. The brush was
thick and yet a rough path opened before him. The earth was dry and hard
packed in some spots, wetter in others. There was no telling where the
land might end.

Then, not too far away, he saw the light, and heard the voices.

"You think it is the way it is supposed to be, and it is not. You think you know, and that there is only one way. But there is not. Now you are blinded, at least for some time. I wonder . . . will you finally see?"

Henriette held a lantern in one hand and her pistol in the other. The pistol was aimed directly at Wilcox.

Wilcox. The demon that had chased him for years. Even after the war, Joseph knew he'd never be safe, for everything that his pursuer represented would follow him, and shame him, and deny him whatever small successes he might achieve. There was no success—only escape. And running. He had dared to ask Isabelle for the one thing she would not do. He had asked Isabelle to run away with him.

Joseph wanted to run, even now, still unobserved. He could run. There had been no logical reason for why he should have come back.

Wilcox remained silent. He sat fixed upon a stump. There was a perfect stillness about him—he could have been part of the swamp itself.

"You think that I want to kill you, eh?" Henriette continued. "But no, no, *mon petit diable*, that is the last thing I want to do. There is too much that I want you to see, and there is too much that you can show others."

So—she was playing games with him. What did she have in mind? Would she lock the monster in a cage, and exhibit him to others as a magnificent demonstration of her power? Or, once the man had regained his sight, would she conjure up visions, and force him to watch things that would destroy him?

"No, no, *mon petit,*" she said. "My men will be here soon, and we will have some fun together."

Joseph pressed forward. Henriette was being careless. It surprised him how careless she was being, her ignorance of the danger she was in. Did she not understand the ferocity of this animal? After everything she had seen, and heard, and done . . . to draw it out . . . to take risks . . .

And like a curse, his thoughts at that moment leapt out of him. Wilcox opened his eyes. There they were—the eyes. The familiar pits of blackness.

"Ah, so—" Henriette said.

But she was not fast enough—or at least it seemed that way—for the old woman did not pull the trigger.

It was wrong . . . there was no time.

Joseph jumped out of the brush.

"Ah!" Henriette exclaimed.

But Joseph was too late: both guns had fired their shots.

Now he was on the ground. Wrestling with Wilcox on the muddy ground. Wilcox had been reaching for his own gun when Joseph burst forth and tackled him. There was no Henriette, no Isabelle, no swamp. There was just Joseph and his hunter, struggling on the dampened earth. Twigs broke and leaves tore in this place that was so used to violence. Maybe it was a panther that screamed from somewhere—the sound was angry, almost human.

It was hard to remember—a sight one never sees again. The demise of one's pursuer. Perhaps for good reason, there would be no memory of that. Just a body—belly up, putrid as a dead gator—with its own knife stuck into its heart.

Joseph breathed, then cried. Then he himself awakened.

"He'll be good food for the swamp," Henriette whispered. "You be sure to leave him there. He's taken enough from here already."

She was herself on the ground, propped against an old cypress knee, like a toy, sunk deep into the moss. Her clothes were drenched in blood—a pool of black seeping from the wound in her breast.

She touched the bracelet on his wrist.

"You have her now—you take her," she said.

Take her . . . as if he could. She could never have been taken. She had never belonged to him. She had never belonged to anyone.

He reached for Henriette's hand but the hand pulled back. Henriette was looking somewhere beyond him.

"*Mes amis . . .*" she said. "*Nous l'emporterons—*"

And with that she released a heavy breath and closed her eyes.

BACK IN BOSTON, he had gone immediately to Mrs. Lovejoy's store, knowing that Moody would have taken Vivi there. Moody of course assumed that Vivi needed to be protected, but it was he who would need the protection. *Did he know?* Joseph wondered. Did Moody have the power to see it? Or was Moody's devotion to Isabelle so strong that such thoughts had no hope of entering?

It was there, plain as day—to whom the girl belonged.

You had to look for it, and you had to have an eye—a trained eye. One that was accustomed to looking for such things. Joseph had always been able to sniff those matters out, even when the matter wasn't obvious. But Vivi was obvious—she was entirely Isabelle, and yet she wasn't. And so all of it made sense now . . . the danger she presented. The house of cards that, with the simple and gentle purity of her face, she had the power to strike down.

They would know. All of them would know.

But did Moody know? Of course he did! Why else would he have brought Isabelle's daughter back to Boston? They had discussed it—escaping. Joseph wanted to escape. During one of those lingering moments, Joseph had put forth his vision: San Francisco . . . the West . . . a photography studio. They would take Vivi far away, where she would finally be safe from her past.

Moody had not quite responded. He had merely nodded in his mysterious way. At Yellow Henry's, even after he had awakened, he had remained in a kind of stupor. It was hard to tell what Moody was seeing and hearing as he hatched his own plans in his head.

They had parted, in the swamp. And now the secret had come back.

"Vivi," Joseph said, "you do understand what is happening?"

She nodded.

"You understand that Edward is now in greater danger than he has ever been before?"

Again, she moved her head.

"I tried to stop him," Mrs. Lovejoy said. "I tried to stop him from going out those doors—with the girl. But he was resolute. There was no standing in his way. I have never seen Mr. Moody so . . . determined."

But Joseph had seen it, and Joseph thought he understood.

"What drove him out the door?" he asked.

"We were upstairs, in the gallery," Mrs. Lovejoy said, "which was, we thought, perhaps the safest place for the time being. They hadn't been here very long. I expected them to stop and rest. But Mr. Moody was pacing, and he looked out the window, and—"

Joseph waited.

"It was as if he saw something," Mrs. Lovejoy concluded.

"Or someone," Joseph said.

"Perhaps."

That was it then. Moody did know. Moody had seen everything.

Joseph turned to Vivi.

"You were here," he said. "You saw what he saw?"

Vivi nodded, and in that moment, she was the very picture of her mother. All traces of anything else in her had vanished, and now, here she was again—Isabelle.

Vivi held Joseph's gaze. But something else lingered . . . a sound from the depth of her enormous eyes that almost screamed, and demanded to be heard. What it said was not a word, or a group of words, or anything else like language. It was instead a cry that reached back through time, and returned to tell Joseph that she would save him.

XLII

Boston Daily Journal

Boston, Massachusetts

Thursday, August 18, 1870

SPIRITUALISM IN COURT—GHOSTLY DEVELOPMENTS

YESTERDAY THERE WAS reached another step in the interesting case of the People against Edward Moody, the alleged "Spiritual" photographer, charged with obtaining money by "trick and device." At a much earlier hour than that fixed for the hearing, the Suffolk County Court was overcrowded. Persons of all classes, professions, and shades of opinion were present: journalists, lawyers mighty in criminal proceedings, authors, physicians, artists, and sculptors . . . all deeply interested in a question that can only be answered by one of two alternatives— "A fraud" or "A miracle." And patiently during four or five hours, the audience, one of the most intelligent that ever assembled in Boston, sat watching each point made by the pleaders and testified to by the witnesses . . .

"PLEASE TELL US," Eldridge Appleton said, "who you are and what is your business."

The witness at the front of the courtroom wore an elegant black suit and a distinguished white beard.

"My name is Abraham Bogardus," the man said, "and I have been a photographer for nearly twenty-three years. I am connected with the Photographic Section of the American Institute, which was formed to protect honest people in the trade from false patents, and from any other kind of humbug we could discover."

"And is the defendant, Mr. Moody, a member of that institute?" Appleton asked.

Bogardus looked over at Moody, frowned, and looked back at the prosecutor.

"Not that I am aware of," Bogardus replied.

"Tell us, Mr. Bogardus, if you will," Appleton went on, "how many processes do you believe there are for taking these so-called spirit photographs?"

"I cannot say—we might count them by scores, as the science is still developing, so to speak. But I can take a photograph of a man with an angel over his head, or with a pair of horns on his head—just as I wish."

A noise murmured throughout the crowd in the gallery. The Spiritualists did not like such implications.

Appleton, who was pacing, returned to his table and picked up a photograph.

"Can you tell me . . ." he said, approaching the witness box. "Can you tell me, and all those assembled here, what exactly this is?"

Bogardus took the photograph, quickly glanced at it, and answered.

"This is a picture I took at the Institute in an effort to duplicate Mr. Moody's methods."

"Ah," Appleton said, "so this 'spirit photograph' is one you yourself produced?"

"That is correct."

"Let this stand on record as exhibit eighteen. Tell us, Mr. Bogardus, how did you take it?"

Bogardus frowned again.

"As I said, there are a number of ways to achieve this effect, but this particular photograph was done by taking a plate and coating it in the usual manner, and then taking a picture of the 'ghost' for later use. You can return the prepared plate back into the coating bath, and leave it there as long as you like. When the sitter came in, I simply used the same plate, and the first impression appeared alongside the sitter."

"So there were no 'spiritual' influences upon this photograph?"

"None whatsoever."

"And this is easily done?"

"This is very easily done."

Again the Spiritualists in the audience made their unsettled noises, while Edward Moody remained still. Moody's attorneys were scribbling and whispering. This witness was an expert—and a problem.

"I would like to submit two more exhibits—nineteen and twenty—for The People," Appleton said. "Now these are very strange ones, Mr. Bogardus. Please explain to us what these are, if you will."

"Happily. These photographs are the result of more experimentation. The first, as you can see, depicts the hand of the shadowy figure as placed in the hair of the sitter. This was not the effect that I ultimately desired, so I re-shot this ghost, and then re-shot the sitter. The effect, as you can see in the next exhibit, is that the arm is encircling the sitter's waist."

"And this was done by . . . ?"

"As I said, I re-shot the spirit—who was of course no more spirit than I am—and did a little maneuvering of the glass to position the hand and arm somewhat lower."

"Was this a complicated exercise?"

"It was not complicated at all."

"And the 'ghostly' effect," Appleton asked. "How were you able to achieve this?"

"We first take a dim impression from figures prepared for our purpose," Bogardus replied. "Sometimes this is a lady dressed in white and veiled over, sometimes a draped infant, and so on. I can take the figure less distinct by not having a proper focus, as the more out of focus the figure is, the more indistinct the picture. I might also focus the picture more properly if I want the figure to be more perfect—with distinct eyebrows, lips, etcetera. In the end, the recognition of the spirit likenesses depends upon the imagination of the sitter."

"Objection, your honor," one of Moody's lawyers called out. "The 'recognition' of spirit likenesses by individuals has nothing to do with the questions that Mr. Bogardus has been qualified to answer."

Judge Downing looked at Appleton.

"I would argue differently," Appleton said. "Through his experimentation with these fraudulent spirit photographs, Mr. Bogardus has come into contact with a number of gullible persons who have given him insight into the life of this crime beyond the taking of the actual photograph."

"I will overrule the objection," Judge Downing said.

"Mr. Bogardus, please tell us," Appleton went on, "what you have seen in terms of people's response to your 'spirit photographs.'"

"Frankly, Mr. Appleton, during our investigation, I have seen everything, and it disgusts me."

Moody's main counsel leapt up.

"Objection, your honor."

"Overruled."

"Please, proceed—" Appleton said.

"It disgusts me," Bogardus repeated. "I have seen perfect pictures of figures taken, with perfectly recognizable 'spirits,' and heard four or five relatives of that figure standing by saying that there was no likeness whatsoever. By the same token, I have also known persons to have demanded the purchase of portraits of children, believing the children to be their own, when I have known them to be someone else's. So I do stand by my conviction that the recognition of the spirit likenesses depends entirely upon the imagination— and a fanciful imagination at that."

It was nothing that the papers hadn't said many times before—that Moody could put anything before a grieving mother, and she would see her child in that instant. But there had also been those examples—undeniable examples—that seemed to have confirmed Moody's "gift." Still, the prosecution proceeded with the introduction of yet more exhibits, including numerous photographs of sitters who had been visited by the "spirit" of President Grant.

"Lastly, Mr. Bogardus," Appleton said, "would you describe this exhibit for us—exhibit thirty-two."

Bogardus looked at the picture and almost smiled.

"That is a picture of Mr. Barnum, which I—"

"Excuse me," the prosecutor interrupted, "you said Mr. Barnum. Do you mean Phineas T. Barnum—the great showman and impresario?"

"The very same," Bogardus said. "Mr. Barnum, as many know, has made a great career of exhibiting humbugs, but at the same time he has a severe distaste for those who adamantly declare their humbugs real."

"Meaning?"

"Meaning he has no patience for those criminals who take advantage of others' grief."

"I see. Briefly describe for us how you came to take this picture."

"Well, after Mr. Moody's arrest, Mr. Barnum approached some of us at the Institute, and offered to pose for a spirit photograph to demonstrate the absurdity of this whole business."

"And you took the photograph?"

"We took the photograph. And as you can see, we summoned an extraordinary spirit."

Gasps escaped the mouths of the onlookers. It was the spirit of President Lincoln.

"You summoned him?" Appleton said.

"Of course not," Bogardus answered. "We placed him there, using one of the previously described methods—at Mr. Barnum's request."

These final questions concluded Eldridge Appleton's presentation for the day . . . the Barnum photograph being something that he knew would excite great passion amongst the audience. But J. T. Townsend, Edward Moody's chief counsel, had a passion of his own to express.

"You say that the photographing of spirits is impossible," Townsend said, "and that anyone who claims to be able to do this is a fraud and a liar?"

"As a photographer," Bogardus replied, "I cannot produce the likeness of a person after death, unless it is from a copy. Neither can any other mortal."

"So, as a photographer and a man of science, you do not believe in the spiritual life at all then?"

"I did not say that."

"Well then, Mr. Bogardus—what do you believe in?"

"I believe in the Bible."

"Ah, how convenient!" Townsend said. "I happen to have a Bible right here with me."

Townsend walked over to his table, picked up the bible, and opened the book to a marked page.

"Now Samuel was dead," he began reading, "and all Israel had lamented him and buried him in Ramah, his own city . . .

> . . . and Saul had removed from the land those who were mediums and spiritists. So the Philistines gathered together and came and camped in Shunem; and Saul gathered all Israel together and they camped in Gilboa. When Saul saw the camp of the Philistines, he was afraid and his heart trembled greatly. When Saul inquired of the Lord, the Lord did not answer him, either by dreams or by Urim or by prophets. Then Saul said to his servants, "Seek for me a woman who is a medium, that I may go to her and inquire of her." And his servants said to him—

"Objection, your honor," Appleton said, standing. "This theological detour is being put forward to confound the witness."

"Your honor, I assure you," Townsend replied, "there is a point to this departure. The witness has stated that he does not believe the photographing of spirits is possible by any known means. But he has not stated whether or not he believes in spirits."

"It is immaterial," Appleton said.

"I will allow it for now," Judge Downing said.

Mr. Townsend went on:

> . . . and his servants said to him, "Behold, there is a woman who is a medium at En-dor." Then Saul disguised himself by putting on other clothes, and went, he and two men with him, and they came to the woman by night; and he said, "Conjure up for me, please, and bring up for me whom I shall name to you." But the woman said to him, "Behold, you know what Saul has done, how he has cut off those who are mediums and spiritists from the land. Why are you then laying a snare for my life to bring about my death?" Saul vowed to her by the Lord, saying, "As the Lord lives, no punishment shall come upon you for this thing." Then the woman said, "Whom shall I bring up for you?" And he said, "Bring up Samuel for me." When the woman saw Samuel, she cried out with a loud voice; and the woman spoke to Saul, saying, "Why have you deceived me? For you are Saul." The king said to her, "Do not be afraid; but what do you see?" And the woman said to Saul, "I see a divine being coming up out of the earth." He said to her, "What is his form?" And she said, "An old man is coming up, and he is wrapped with a robe." And Saul knew that it was Samuel, and he bowed with his face to the ground and did homage.

"Now, Mr. Bogardus," Townsend said, "you have stated that you believe in that good book known as the Bible. And I have just read to you an interesting passage from that very book. So I ask you, do you believe the spirit alluded to in this passage possessed a form of its own?"

The witness, somewhat baffled, glanced in the direction of the prosecutor.

"Objection," Appleton said. "This has nothing to do with the witness's expertise as a photographer."

"Oh," Townsend said, "it most certainly does."

"I'll allow it," the judge said.

"I repeat, Mr. Bogardus . . . do you believe the spirit alluded to in this passage—*this passage from the Bible*—possessed a form of its own?"

"I suppose that it must have."

"So then, from the reading of this chapter—again, from a book that you believe in—it seems clear that the spirit alluded to here appeared in form. Would you then consider it possible for that form to have been photographed, provided that photography had then existed?"

A look of confusion spread over the face of the witness, as the audience remained hushed in silence.

"Mr. Bogardus," Townsend repeated, "would it have been possible to have photographed *that* form back then, had photography then existed?"

"Perhaps," Bogardus said, "but—"

"Thank you, Mr. Bogardus," Townsend said. "That is all I wanted to know."

XLIII

INSPECTOR BOLLES AMBLED through the streets of Beacon Hill that day, even though walking directly up Pinckney or Mt. Vernon would have provided a more direct route to the square. The senator had been recovering for close to two weeks now, and Jenny had sent word—at Bolles's request—that Garrett was finally out of bed. What had it been? None of the doctors could say exactly. But the senator's episode on Washington Street was something that had been troubling Bolles since Moody's return.

What had the senator seen, and what did he now know?

The trial had progressed with no mention of the senator's name—which was precisely, Bolles knew, how Senator and Mrs. Garrett wanted it to be. The apprehension around the negative was still at the forefront of Bolles's mind, as was the fixation of all concerned on finding and punishing Edward Moody. Mr. Dovehouse had been strangely absent since Moody's arrest—an odd thing given his relentlessness during the investigation. And for Marshall Hinckley's part . . . he cared little about Garrett. Hinckley's main objective was to make an example of the Spiritualists.

The negative, mysteriously, had not made its way into evidence. The negative had refused to go anywhere except for that one final place.

As he walked, Bolles clasped his hand over his coat pocket, unsure of what he was about to do. Something was telling him to hurry, and yet the streets continually interrupted him: Spruce Street and Walnut, Willow and Chestnut. He re-traversed his own steps without realizing what he was doing.

At last he came to the great house on Louisburg Square. In all those years of visiting those houses, he had failed to notice the aggression that characterized them—how, in the tranquility of the manicured square, their rounded bellies pressed away from them, like blisters. It was beautiful, this square, that he had known since he was a boy—and yet something was now making it unsightly.

Jenny answered the door with downcast eyes, and nodded.

"Mrs. Garrett," Bolles said. "She is not home then?"

"No," Jenny said. "She won't be back for some time."

Bolles ascended the steps to Senator Garrett's room, for the senator, Jenny informed him, was still too weak to receive visitors in his study. The staircase creaked before Bolles stepped onto the second landing. The hallway was unlit, save for the cracked door toward the end.

Bolles knocked, but there was no answer.

"Senator?" the inspector said.

Again—no answer. Perhaps the old man had fallen asleep.

Bolles pressed the door forward, slowly, as to avoid making any noise, but preventing that kind of thing was impossible in a house such as this. Bolles at once saw the senator—in a chair by the window. A dull gray light was coating Senator Garrett with a soft and luminous glow.

"Senator?" Bolles repeated.

Garrett opened his eyes, and shifted.

"Ah, Montgomery," he said.

And he breathed heavily, and turned toward the window.

There was a chair near the senator, and Inspector Bolles sat down in it. The attack had ravaged Garrett—it had aged him many years.

"Senator," Bolles said, "it is good to see you recovering. I understand from Jenny that you are growing stronger by the day?"

"Stronger . . ." Garrett whispered. "Yes . . . stronger."

"Senator, I—"

But that quickly the weakened Garrett held up one of his hands. Even in this pathetic state, he could still command that old power.

"I know why you have come, Montgomery," he said.

"You do, sir?"

"I do. You have come to arrest me . . . and it is just as well. This old man has evaded his punishment for far too long."

"Senator!" Bolles exclaimed. "What nonsense are you speaking? I have come to do nothing of the kind."

Senator Garrett stared at Inspector Bolles with the glazed eyes of a man who wasn't there. Then he turned his head again, and cast his eyes out onto the square.

"It was you," Garrett said. "It was always you."

"I don't know what you mean, sir."

"The one who would do—right."

"Sir?"

"Not us," Garrett said. "It could never be any of us. We were all too weak. I was too weak, but you . . ."

And he stopped, for his breath was beginning to catch in his throat.

"Senator," Bolles said, "I have come to give you this."

The glass panes in the old window frame shivered in the wind. The gray light made the rest of the room inanimate and colorless.

Garrett moved his eyes to look at what rested in Bolles's hands. There it was. At last, by god—there it was.

The inspector did not move . . . and the senator could not move. For a long time Senator Garrett sat looking at the leather case. It was rough—almost crude. It was an ugly thing to carry.

Finally Bolles addressed him.

"You do know what this is, sir?"

"I do," the senator replied.

"I have taken great—"

"You have taken a great risk," the senator interrupted. "Your career, Montgomery . . . the risk you have taken. I cannot say that I—"

"That is not what I was going to say, sir," Bolles interjected. "I have taken great *pains* to see that no one knows about this."

"No one knows?" Garrett said. "What exactly do you mean?"

"I took it from Moody myself," Bolles replied. "No one else knows that I have it."

The senator's eyes had by this time filled with tears. But of course, there was no chance that he would cry.

"Montgomery, I—"

"Say nothing else, Senator. I do not need to know."

Garrett made to protest, but Bolles held up his own hand this time. Garrett retreated back into the chair, for at that moment, he had become the child.

Bolles handed the case to Garrett.

"For you, sir," he said. "To do with as you will."

Garrett took the stiff object from the young man. How Montgomery had grown from the little boy he had once known. He had changed, this boy. He would be such a fine citizen in this world. Montgomery was the promise of the nation.

"You have . . ." Garrett said, "You have . . . brought her back to me."

He sighed, and lifted one hand to his lips.

"And . . . you have not judged."

"Sir?" Bolles said.

And it was only then that Garrett realized that the inspector knew, but did not know.

"Judged," Garrett repeated.

The case was warm in his hands.

"Senator—" Bolles said, "you should know that nothing else will ever come of this. We are nearing a conviction of the spirit photographer, and all of this will soon be buried."

"Yes . . . buried . . ." Garrett intoned.

But he had already gone far, far away.

Boston Daily Journal
Boston, Massachusetts
Friday, August 19, 1870

THE MOODY EXAMINATION CONTINUED— P. T. BARNUM, ESQ., ON THE STAND

Mr. Appleton—*How long have you been acquainted with Mr. Moody by reputation in connection with the production of these spirit photographs?*

Witness—*I think it is five or six years since I first heard of Mr. Moody as the original spirit photographer.*

Mr. Appleton—*Did you have any correspondence with Mr. Moody on the subject of spirit photographs?*

Witness—*There was correspondence between us, but I think the letters were burnt in the fire at the Museum.*

Mr. Appleton—*State the evidence of their contents.*

Witness—*I was about to write a book representing the humbugs of the world, and I wrote Mr. Moody that I was going to expose the humbug of spirit photographs, and that I wished to purchase specimens of his so-called spirit photographs for the Museum; I bought a number, giving $2 a piece for them, and they were hung on the walls of the Museum for over a year; among them were the so-called spiritual appearances of Napoleon Bonaparte and Henry Clay, and the positions of the figures were exactly like the well-known engravings of these personages.*

Mr. Appleton—*Have you yourself ever had a spirit photograph taken?*

Witness—*I went some days ago to Mr. Bogardus's gallery and asked him if he could take a spirit photograph, telling him that I did not want any humbug about it; he said he could do it; I examined the glass and discovered nothing in it; I saw the process of pouring over the first liquid, and afterward the pouring over of nitrate of silver,* *and then saw it placed in the camera; when done it had my likeness and the shadow of Abraham Lincoln; I saw the ghost of Lincoln as soon as it was developed in the dark room; I was unconscious of any spiritual presence.*

Cross-examined: *I have never been in any humbug business, where I did not give value for the money; these spirit photographs were clearly labeled "humbug" on the walls of my Museum.*

Q: *So your "wooly horse" then, Mr. Barnum . . . was not a fraud before the public?*

A: *The wooly horse was a remarkable curiosity; it was exactly what I represented it to be, having a peculiar form and curled hair; it was exactly a wooly horse; it was not a horse "wooled over."*

Q: *And Joice Heth, whom you claim to have been the nurse of George Washington . . . a woman of 161 years in age, and owned by the general's father. Did you believe she was the person you represent her to be?*

A: *I have no belief about it. I bought her as such, as the bill of sale has never been disproved. I bought her and paid $1,000 for her, but before she got through to me I might have had some little doubt upon the subject. (Laughter.)*

Q: *Was this doubt ever suggested to the public?*

A: *I never put myself out of the way about it. (Laughter.)*

XLIV

IT WAS NOT funny. None of it was funny. And yet people were finding the space to laugh. Elizabeth sat upright, the large pages of the paper spread before her. She did not want to see any of this, and yet she could not look away.

They had been trying him for the criminal he was—rightly so. But little did they know what the real crime had been. He had dared to resurrect what should have been dead: in that offense lay the crime.

Elizabeth stood. She was tired of the testimonies, tired of the trial, tired of everything. She wanted it to go away . . . for Edward Moody to go away. She hoped that they would sentence him, and that all of it would disappear.

Upstairs, the hallway was quiet—too quiet. For the last few days her husband had been regaining more of his strength. He was "recovering"—a word the doctors liked to use repeatedly, but one that she knew was not quite appropriate. Her husband would never recover from what had happened. She seemed to be the only one who understood that.

Quiet. It was never a good sign when the house had that much quiet. The house had taught her to be wary of it—to fear it even.

Then the creak . . . and a door. Jenny emerged from Garrett's room.

What had Jenny done? Jenny stared back at Elizabeth. The woman of the house in Elizabeth could never comprehend why Jenny despised her so much. But there were those deeper relationships whose meanings Elizabeth intimately understood—relationships that time could never change. Jenny hated Elizabeth, and there was nothing Elizabeth could ever do about it. The natural order of things—that's simply how it was.

"Ma'am," Jenny said.

Her look was firm—and cold.

But there was something else there, and Elizabeth could see it. Jenny wasn't so smart after all.

"Jenny, you've been crying. What's the matter?"

"Thank you ma'am, it's nothing."

"Jenny—"

"The senator."

And with that Jenny bowed her head and disappeared from the second floor.

She had been in there. That impudent thing had been in there. What could she possibly have been doing?

Elizabeth approached Garrett's door, for she had abandoned the room since the incident. That infernal spirit photographer, and everything he had drummed up, would soon be banished—sent away.

"James," Elizabeth said.

He was staring out the window, not moving.

"James?" she repeated.

But still, he did not look at her.

"Elizabeth," he said. "Come here. Come sit with me."

Gentle—he was gentle. The way he once was—before the war. The voice was almost unrecognizable. She had not heard it in a very long time.

She sat before him. The light from the window had waxed his weary expression. Or maybe something else had altered it. There had been so much. Everything was gray—the sky, the air, the dull light that bathed him. He was awash in gray . . . but also in something else. What was it, she wondered. Could his sorrow be everywhere now?

He looked at her, and she glanced down to see what was in his hand. And all at once the air was stifling.

"Where did you get that?" she asked him.

Garrett did not reply.

Then her chest tightened, and she demanded:

"How exactly did you get that?"

"It does not matter how I got it," Garrett replied. "There is little that matters anymore."

So this is what it had come down to. Jenny's impudence . . . Jenny's maliciousness. Jenny had given him William's rattle. For years, Jenny had been set on torturing her.

"These negroes," Elizabeth whispered.

"It is not the negroes!" Garrett fumed. "It's you!"

The rattle gleamed as he held it—a silver coin in the mud of his hand. It was out of place, this rattle, in the dullness of Garrett's room.

The child had loved Isabelle. Her husband had loved Isabelle. She could never forgive Isabelle for that crime.

Or him—

"You brought this upon all of us," she said. "That's what you've never been able to see."

And at last the severity fell from Garrett's face, as he tried to choke back his own feeling.

"I have seen that, Elizabeth. I have seen it, better than anyone."

"You've tried to deny it," Elizabeth said, "just as I have tried. But there is no denying this any longer. I am sorry, James. Truthfully, I am sorry. I didn't know what else to do."

"Do?" Garrett said.

"Yes, James—do!" Elizabeth said. "I had to do something. You were young. Your career. I know how these women think! Something had to be done before it was too late. And so I . . ."

Elizabeth paused. She had never even thought the words.

"And so I got rid of her."

"Elizabeth!" Garrett exclaimed.

"I got rid of her, James. For you . . . for us! And I lost him, James. I lost my child—our child. It was the punishment for what I did."

She reached her hand out toward him—toward the rattle in his hand. But then, through her tears . . .

The rattle was no longer there.

The rattle was a teaspoon.

A teaspoon—William's teaspoon! How the boy had loved to use it. Stewed apples or porridge or warm milk mixed with cornmeal. His delicate little fingers still there, around the handle. How proud he had been of using it, before he had lost his will to eat.

"I see you have it," Elizabeth said.

Garrett did not reply. He was looking down at something now. Nothing made a difference anymore.

"Yes, James," Elizabeth said. "I paid the vile creature—with our silver. I paid him to take her away. I gave him everything—but that."

Garrett was turning the spoon over in his hands. It was so bright that he needed to look away from it.

"The girl—" Garrett said.

"I don't know," Elizabeth said. "I don't know. But what does it matter? I tried, and I failed. And now everyone will see."

"I don't know that I ever tried . . ." Garrett said.

"You didn't have to. I did it for you."

The spoon remained quiet, and the light upon it remained a thing of beauty. She would not tell him of the other times—the many other times over the years—when she had done things for him, and kept them from him.

This was the end then. There was no place left to go.

"I still miss him," Elizabeth said. "It never stops."

Garrett looked at his wife. How beautiful she still was. The ugliness of her actions had not diminished her physical beauty. The lines around her eyes now—even those were beautiful. What had gone so wrong between the two of them, that he had lost sight of who she was?

"Elizabeth—" he said, his body bent forward.

"Say nothing, James," she said. "Say nothing."

JENNY SAT IN her room on the top floor of the great house. She felt no guilt over what she had just done. Senator Garrett was a wonderful man—he had saved her! And he deserved to know. For nearly twenty years she had held on to the secret—not out of spite, or even malice, but out of respect for what the house had given her. These matters were always tricky . . . what to tell, and what not to. And of course, when to tell what needed to be told.

She had had no intentions of doing it that day, but the time had come, and the house would absolve her. There was guilt over not just what she knew, but what she herself had done so many years ago. She felt justified then, because she had been so jealous of Isabelle, though that emotion was also something that she rarely owned up to.

The missus had dropped the spoon in her haste to collect the silver. Jenny had found it hiding on the floor, beneath one of the shelves at the back of the pantry. She had picked it up and looked at it—it was still mysterious to her in that moment. And then she returned it to the place where it had been, because she knew that Mrs. Garrett would come back for it.

It was confusing at first, but the spoon was what eventually told Jenny everything.

For what reason Mrs. Garrett had to use the silver, Jenny did not understand, because Mrs. Garrett could have easily acquired the money to pay for the horrible thing herself. It was that most malicious part of Mrs. Garrett that likely drove her to use the silver—an added "detail" that would give Isabelle's disappearance the air of something everyone expected.

"She took the silver when she left," Mrs. Garrett had said to her husband. "That ungrateful negress took the silver."

And that's when Jenny knew. That is when the whole crime flashed before her.

It was convenient—to blame the negroes. It was a trick that always worked.

For years Mrs. Garrett had carried around that spoon—like a baby. Hiding it in places . . . talking to it. The spoon had been the boy's spoon, and there was certainly something to its escaping. The spoon hadn't wanted to go, Jenny thought. It had been determined to stay in the house.

The spoon had cursed Mrs. Garrett, and Jenny could see that. Sometimes the spoon was so poorly concealed that Jenny thought it had come out on its own.

"They are one thing before the whites," Mrs. Garrett had once said to a small audience, "and another before their own color. It is a habit—a long established custom that descends from generation to generation."

Of course that had been ages ago, and Mrs. Garrett hadn't said such things in years. But Jenny had never forgotten, and those words rang in her ears like songs. Mrs. Garrett had the makings of the cruelest plantation mistress. Dressing her up in Boston finery did not change the tiger's stripes.

And then there was the spoon, which might never have fallen, or found its own way to the floor rather, if Jenny hadn't said anything in the first place. Yes, Jenny had been the one to call Mrs. Garrett's attention to Isabelle's condition, though in the end Mrs. Garrett would likely have seen it on her own. But in those days, there was something cruel that lived within Jenny, too—something that screamed out for justice, something that wanted to make Isabelle suffer. And so Jenny had offered this business about Isabelle eating "enough for more than herself." It might cause some trouble—speed things along a little—but surely there was no harm in that.

The girl would leave on her own—that much was certain. But the spoon was the revelation that something else had happened.

How, through the years, had Jenny carried the weight of this indiscretion?

If she had spoken a day or two later, would Isabelle never have been sent away? Jenny's own confession was what needed to come to the surface. Because, after all, Isabelle had come back to claim it.

"Senator Garrett," Jenny had said. "I'm so sorry . . . I'm sorry for everything I've ever done."

She was crying now, her usual staunchness finally failing her.

"I would change it," she said. "If I could go back and change it all, I would."

Garrett, at his window, had received the story with alarming composure. His whole life had come down to this moment . . . welled in the reflection of a child's teaspoon.

"Ah, Jenny," he said, turning the spoon over in his hand, "you have been nothing but good to me these many years."

"But there is no excuse for what I done."

Garrett, again composed, as if readying to sing from a hymnal, breathed a sigh of acceptance for everything that had happened.

"We are the keepers of our own fates, Jenny," he said. "And while your meddling then may have been unkind, it was not responsible for the outcome. We all commit our crimes, Jenny . . . and in the end we must account for them."

XLV

THE FIRST WITNESS for the Defense was Jeremiah Gurney—the renowned photographer from New York whose visit to Boston in the early days had been so instrumental to the establishment of Moody's reputation. Once on the stand, Gurney described the visit, which had taken place on behalf of Charles Livermore, the New York financier.

"I witnessed the process of Mr. Livermore's photograph," Gurney testified, "but I did not discover any deception. I saw the process of preparing the plate for taking the photograph, and watched Mr. Moody develop the picture. I can say with certainty that I witnessed nothing out of the ordinary, and that upon the negative there emerged—a shadowy form."

Gurney was of course referencing the spirit of Arabella Livermore, the distinctness of whose face in that early picture had created thousands of believers overnight.

Townsend held up the picture, and the courtroom stirred audibly.

"And this is the picture to which you refer, is that correct?"

Gurney examined the picture.

"That is correct," he said.

"And in your opinion," Townsend said, "could this effect have been produced by *any* of the methods that the Prosecution has so eloquently laid before the court?"

"By having a person stand for a short time behind the sitter? I can tell you that wasn't the case here. Nor was it the case that a previously prepared glass was used, for I chose the glass plate for that photograph myself."

"And what of these other methods the Prosecution has set before us?" Townsend said. "Extra glasses or objects in the camera . . . reflectors . . . and things of that nature?"

"In all my experience," Gurney replied, "I have never known a picture to be taken by placing an object in the camera. It is not possible to take a photograph of an object unless it is outside of the instrument."

Appleton cross-examined Gurney, but Gurney's stature was so immense that even when his answers did not make sense, the people believed them to be true. Despite a week of damaging presentations by the Prosecution, Moody's trial, strangely, had become a place hostile to probing questions. The Spiritualists who dominated not just the galleries but also the steps and corridors outside, had somehow managed to infect the whole scene with the frenzy of their own beliefs.

More witnesses came forward for Moody. There was Charles Livermore from New York, who told the jury that he believed the likeness of his wife so pure and so genuine, that any doubt about its authenticity was a crime against "the larger mysteries that we are all called upon to believe." There was also William P. Slee, the well-known Spiritualist and photographer from Poughkeepsie, who had come on an investigation to Boston *with his own camera*, and who, upon witnessing Moody's entire operation, had been "unable to find any device or trickery" in the spirit photographer's process. And there was Andrew Jackson Davis himself, one of the fathers of the Spiritualist movement, who had sent numerous photographers of high reputation and authority to examine "the miracle" that was happening in Boston. "If these pictures be a swindle, or a sleight-of-hand deception," Davis said, "then Mr. Moody's ingenuity beats that of all the necromancers and prestidigitators of the present and the past . . . and frankly that is not something I am willing to give him credit for."

The stakes for Spiritualism had grown very high during Moody's trial, and so it went on like that, for days and days, almost to the point of monotony. Moody's lawyers went so far as to bring in an old woman from Delaware who told the story of a young man who had sat for his portrait with *another* spirit photographer there. When the portrait was developed, there appeared on the negative the spirit of an old man whom the sitter had apparently murdered for his money. The photograph, she said, had compelled the young man to confess the crime, and while she swore to having seen the photograph herself, she was not able to say for sure whether it still existed. The appearance of so undeniable a "truth," however, was enough, in her mind, to acquit spirit photography in general.

And then at last, nearly two weeks after Moody's trial had begun, Mr. Townsend stood from his chair at the front of the courtroom, and said:

"If your honor will indulge us one more line of questioning, the Defense would like to call . . . Miss Fanny Van Wyck."

The courtroom fell silent—the breath drawn out of it—and at the back the door opened, and the small woman appeared. She looked at no one as she held onto the arm of another Spiritualist, who accompanied her down the central aisle, through the parting and astonished crowd.

The medium crowned the witness stand like a rediscovered sculpture, the black gems of her eyes gazing out upon the audience.

Townsend approached her.

"Please state your name and occupation for the court," he said.

"My name is Fanny Van Wyck," she replied. "And I am a spiritual medium."

There was then a small wave of commotion in the courtroom, for there were many in the audience who had not heard Fanny's voice in years.

"Thank you, Miss Van Wyck," Townsend replied. "And what is it that you do—as a medium?"

Fanny did not move. She was the monument so many believed in.

"My object," she said, "is to give to those who believe, as well as those who do not, evidence of this new and beautiful phase of . . . *spiritual manifestations*."

"Spiritual manifestations," Townsend said. "And for how long have you been doing this?"

"It has been nearly twenty years since I commenced revealing the spiritual truth to those who have embraced it: scientific men, photographers, judges, lawyers, doctors, ministers . . . in fact, all grades of society. All of them now bear testimony to the beautiful truth that they have received through my mediumistic power."

"And Miss Van Wyck, can you—"

"What joy to the troubled heart!" Fanny went on. "What balm to the aching breast! What peace and comfort to the weary soul . . . to know that our friends who have passed away can return and give us unmistakable evidence of a life hereafter—that they are with us, and seize with avidity every opportunity to make themselves known!"

"Thank you, Miss Van Wyck," Townsend said, "but can I ask—"

"But alas, the enemies of truth want to close that old door of disbelief against them, and prevent them from once more entering the portals of their loved ones. But that old door is fast going to decay. It squeaks on its rusty and timeworn hinges . . . its panels penetrated by the wormholes of many ages . . ."

Appleton at that point leapt up from his chair.

"Your honor, I must object to this—"

Fanny shot him a glance.

"And through those penetrating holes," she demanded, "the bright and effulgent rays of the spiritual sun have begun to shine."

"Miss Van Wyck," Judge Downing said, "I'm afraid I must ask you to answer Mr. Townsend's questions as he asks them."

Fanny made no reply. She was gazing out upon the crowd.

"Miss Van Wyck," Townsend then proceeded, "are you acquainted with the defendant, Mr. Moody?"

Fanny's head turned, not toward her questioner, but toward Moody. There he was—the old, sad Moody. The same old picture of himself. But at that moment something strange happened . . . something noticeable enough for many in the audience to detect. A kind of shiver had run through Fanny, as if in looking at Moody she had been startled.

"Miss Van Wyck?" Townsend said.

"I am acquainted with the defendant," she said.

"Mr. Moody?"

"Yes, Mr. Moody," she said. "And to answer your next question, I am familiar with his spiritual photographs."

"And how long have you been acquainted with Mr. Moody and his photographs?"

"It does not matter," Fanny said.

Townsend looked surprised.

"Please answer the question," Judge Downing said.

"I have answered it—it does not matter."

Townsend hesitated.

"Miss Van Wyck . . . if you would please to tell the court: what your first experiences were with Mr. Moody's photographs?"

"My experiences were ones of horror," Fanny said.

"Excuse me?" Townsend said.

"Yes—of horror, because it was clear to me from the first what he was trying to do."

"But Miss Van Wyck . . ." Townsend stumbled, "you have described the 'beautiful truth' of spiritual manifestations. Why then would such a truth produce in you an effect of horror?"

"Because Moody's photographs are not the truth. They are nothing but a sham."

The courtroom gasped, and Judge Downing called for order.

"Excuse me?" Townsend said.

"Mr. Moody's photographs are nothing more than a sham, and he nothing more than a third-rate circus prankster."

Again the audience reacted, and Judge Downing banged his gavel. Appleton and his associates, while confused, were grinning broadly.

"Miss Van Wyck," Townsend said, "I must admit I am a bit shocked by your—"

"That is all there is to say on the matter," Fanny said. "Other than—"

Fanny was now looking over at Moody, who was staring back at her with a compassionate gaze. The two knew each other, and even though Fanny had just tarnished him, there was an understanding between them that no court of law could ever muddle. Moody smiled—the slightest, barely detectable smile. It crawled up one side of his bearded mouth, somewhat hidden, but it was there, and Fanny could see it. In that moment they were as close as two lovers who had shut out the world . . . two soldiers on the journey that no one else dared to take.

Then Fanny's eyes blinked, and she again became stone.

"I'm quite finished," she said.

Townsend sighed in disbelief.

"Thank you, Miss Van Wyck," he said. "I have no further questions."

LATER THAT EVENING, in the dankness of his cell, Moody read over the statement that the Spiritualists had prepared for him:

In 1865, in the city of Boston, while engaged in business as an engraver, I took a photograph of Mrs. Lovejoy, who is the proprietress at 258 Washington Street. The photograph was of Mrs. Lovejoy and of Mrs. Lovejoy alone, but it was in the process of developing the plate that I first discovered the appearance of a second form . . .

The statement was long—too long for Moody's comfort—and was even embellished in sections with information that Moody had never himself provided. It told the story of his rise to fame—his unlooked-for career as a photographer of spirits—and of the multitudes of believers whose lives had been transformed by the "beautiful truth." As he read, he realized how such elaborate words re-enlivened his treachery . . . how the statement prepared by the Spiritualists represented the greatest fraud he had ever been asked to commit. In the end, Moody was to assert that in the taking of his photographs, he had never availed himself of any deception: "These forms have appeared in each and every instance without my effort. They are forms captured by a power that is beyond the realm of human control."

Would he be able to read it? He had promised them he would. He had quietly agreed to speak whatever words they had prepared, because if he hadn't, they never would have allowed him to speak at all. It was not the certainty of prison that Moody feared at this point. It was the fate of dreadful silence that scared him most.

And as he thought this, the sound of the door's bolt tore through the silence. His cell was dark, his candle having shrunk to a mere stub. The door opened and closed—harsh sounds again—and the outside bolt echoed its first call.

Then, from the shadows, the small form stepped forward.

"Moody—" it said.

An odd feeling came over him. Then Fanny Van Wyck moved closer to the light. And for once Edward Moody was happy.

"I do understand," he said. "I understand why you condemned me."

"I would not say condemned," Fanny said. "Saved. I was trying to save you."

He looked down at the statement—the dull words of the Spiritualists.

"Ah," she said. "And what will you do now then?"

She was right, because Fanny had always been right. Since the moment he had met her, she had chastised him. There were powers in him, she had said, that he had criminally neglected. For Fanny, the crime had not been his fraudulent photographs—it had been his cowardice, and his failure to do what he had been called to do.

"I do not want to go to prison," he said. "But if that is my fate, perhaps it will be a start. The movement—"

"The movement!" Fanny exclaimed. "The drivers of that movement are no better than you! Or at least no better than how you have been. The movement will survive—they will see to that. And in my own ways, so will I. The question is, Moody . . . what do our friends have in store for you?"

"Our friends . . ." Moody repeated.

Could they be friends to him, even now?

"I see what you are thinking," Fanny said. "You believe there may be no forgiveness. You believe that the punishment *this* world has in store for you will not begin to repair the damage you have caused."

"No, Fanny," Moody said. "You are wrong this time. I know what I believe, and I do believe there is a way."

"Ah!" Fanny said, her eyebrows raising in surprise. "So you have come to something then, and believe what you should have believed all along . . ."

They looked at each other, as they had many times before. Something touched them, though they themselves had never touched.

"I see it," she said.

And then again:

"I see it."

The candle flickered.

"It was always what you were supposed to do," she said.

Moody eyed her—his face encouraging her to continue.

"You brought her back," Fanny said. "You placed her—"

And with those words her voice trailed off. The cell became a dark room for Moody—a record of all the things he had done, and hadn't done.

For years he had rejected the idea of bringing her back, so much so that he had forgotten that she had ever existed. He did not whisper her name. He did not look at her photograph. He did not read and re-read the letter she had written before she left. There had been no point. The loss of her had broken him. There was no point to bringing her back.

And yet—

How they do come back . . . how it is that we cannot control them. We cannot be the ones to tell them that they are not allowed to come back.

He placed her . . .

"You placed her just where she belonged," Fanny said.

"I?" Moody said, exhausted.

"Yes, Moody—you."

"I?" Moody repeated.

"You did it," Fanny said.

And her eyes narrowed.

"You . . . you summoned her back."

Moody's hand moved over his heart, as if the negative still somehow resided there.

"I am sorry," he said. "I am sorry for it all."

"There is nothing to be sorry for," Fanny said, as she moved back toward the door. The candle was almost extinguished now, and Moody could barely see her.

Fanny rapped her little hand on the door to call the guard.

"Edward Moody," she said. "It was perhaps the most honest thing you've ever done."

XLVI

O N THE LAST day of the Moody trial, Eldridge Appleton stood before the jury. "Now, the Law does not deal with the supernatural," he said in closing, "nor does it recognize the supernatural as an element when dealing with facts. And so in numerous reported cases, as where a man laboring under a hallucination hears voices ordering him to commit a murder—any defense based on the claim that those voices were real would be held untenable by the Law." The Law did not recognize the existence of any superior or spiritual influences to justify what it considered a felony. "If today Mr. Moody were to commit a murder," Appleton said, "and were to assert, as his defense, that spirits had urged him to commit it . . . *that*, my good gentlemen, would constitute no kind of defense at all. The Law does not excuse a murderous hand, whether guided by spirits or not."

For nearly two hours, Appleton rehearsed the "evidence," pacing back and forth before the jury, with all audience eyes upon him. Edward Moody's photographs had not simply been a crime against the Law—they had been a crime against his fellow men here on earth. "It is enough for the poor mother whose eyes are blinded with tears," Appleton said, "that she sees a print of drapery like an infant's dress, and a rounded something, like a foggy dumpling . . . and that all of it will stand for the face of her child, which she now accepts as a revelation from the world of the shadows." Those who went to see Moody were prepared to believe, and were prepared to believe anything on very slight proof. "The Defense has demonstrated nothing more than that," Appleton said. "The *existence of a belief* in Mr. Moody's photographs is not the same thing as *the truth* of those photographs."

But that, according to J. T. Townsend, was not the point of this trial. It was true that many of the exhibits entered into evidence depicted "indistinct and shadowy forms." But what of the forms whose faces were so distinct that all those who knew those souls in life swore to their legitimacy? And what sort of man must Edward Moody have been if the Prosecution's accusations were correct? "Such a man would require a gallery of *immense* proportions,"

Townsend said. "He would be compelled to have on hand the negatives of parents, aunts, uncles, cousins, and great-grandmothers of all the persons who called to get photographs. He would need to possess a dexterity surpassing that of the greatest magicians of the day. And he would need to be smarter than every photographer who had gone to inspect his method." For over five years, Moody had been engaged in the business of spirit photography, and had submitted his process to the investigation of scientific men. Not one of them had ever pronounced him a deceiver, because there was no proof whatsoever that he had ever deceived anybody.

"Because Marshall Hinckley and his men of science have encountered things that they cannot explain," Townsend said, "the Prosecution has hunted down this prisoner, and fixed upon him the brand of cheat and humbug. Suppose that when Mr. Morse was struggling to convince us that persons hundreds of miles apart might communicate with electricity, some skeptic should have requested a message sent from New York to Boston . . . that Mr. Morse, confident in the truth of his discovery, should attempt to send the message, but that, owing to some cause not clearly known to him, the attempt to transmit the message should fail. Would such a failure be counted a fraud by any court or jury in Christendom? And yet these so-called men of science who have testified for the Prosecution charge Mr. Moody with fraud because they believe him guilty of producing 'foggy dumplings.'"

Townsend paused and stared squarely at the jury.

"Men like these would have hung Galileo, had they lived in his day."

Far from the charlatan the Prosecution made him out to be, Moody was a revolutionary—a man ahead of his time.

But would the jury believe that, and how would they vote?

At last both counsels rested, and one final matter remained.

"Mr. Moody," Judge Downing said, "The People have pleaded their case against you, and your counsel has concluded with its defense. Before I send the jury away to deliberate upon your fate, is there anything you wish to say, relative to the charges that have been presented against you?"

Moody had been listening to the closing arguments with some attention, but none of what he had heard had changed his determination.

Moody stood.

"I would indeed like to make a statement," he said.

The courtroom was silent. Moody turned toward the jury, but also faced the gallery that was crowded with Spiritualists. Many of them, he knew, had had a hand in composing the statement. This was to be a great moment for Spiritualism.

Moody unfolded the paper.

"In 1865, in the city of Boston . . ." he began.

He read the first sentences about photographing Mrs. Lovejoy.

". . . but it was in the process of developing the plate that I first discovered the appearance of a second form . . ."

A second form. Was that what it had all been about then? The paper trembled in his hand. He owed the Spiritualists nothing. The Spiritualists had misguided him, and he would not sacrifice himself for them. And yet if he did not read it—

Moody let his arm fall, and released the sheet of paper.

"We are all," Moody said, "witnesses to those second forms, whether we have had spirit photographs taken or not."

Mr. Townsend leaned down toward the floor to retrieve the statement, but Moody stepped on the paper with the front of his boot.

"We are witnesses," Moody continued, "and it is all before our very eyes. We are in a great age of—"

His voice quivered somewhat.

"—*spiritual truth.*"

In the audience, those who were aware of his departure from the statement moved uneasily in their chairs.

"Yes . . ." Moody said. "We are in a great age of spiritual truth, and the signs are about us everywhere. I came to Spiritualism not as a believer, but as a skeptic. I was a broken man who believed in nothing but what his eye could see. And what my eye saw was horror—horror at what men could do to one another, and horror at our own denial of it."

Moody paused, and turned toward the audience.

"But it was nothing compared to the horror revealed to me in the great miracle of the spirit photograph."

All eyes were upon him now. Not a soul breathed or stirred.

"You there—all of you!" he exclaimed. "You have turned your eyes from the truth, as I did. And I do not speak merely of the spiritual truth . . . but the earthly truth as well, of which it is one and the same."

One and the same? More audience members shifted. What trick was Edward Moody up to now?

"I knew a woman once, who was wise enough to understand that photographs possessed a power like no other. She believed that photographs possessed the power to make permanent those things that we all lose. They are the record keepers of the things that we want to see once we've lost them . . . and they are also the keepers of those secrets we do not want to see."

He was wavering. What was wrong with him? Somebody needed to stop him.

"I did not want to see," Moody said. "I did not want to see what the photograph showed me. I did not want to see how much I had misguided others. But I was forced to see—forced to see what a criminal I had been. And now I cannot un-see it."

Moody could feel the room beginning to move, but any Spiritualist who might approach him now was of little consequence at this point. There had barely been anything left of her when he had taken that last glance at the negative. In the darkness of Yellow Henry's, one might have even said she was no longer there. He knew she was disappearing—that she would eventually disappear—and yet he had carried her back to Boston, as if she were as clear as the day she had come to him.

All emotion then fell from Moody's face, as if he had finally been granted resolution.

"I cannot un-see it," Moody repeated, "and like all of you—*all of you*—"

He paused. Would they ever forgive him?

"I am guilty."

The room erupted, and there was no way to distinguish the laughter of the men of science from the anguished cries of the believers. Judge Downing banged his gavel as the courtroom degenerated into chaos. The starvation was severe, and they fought with one another, because the truth was that they were all desperate to protect their own pieces of bread.

And in this madness, in the pandemonium of the courtroom, Moody saw her, standing with Joseph, tucked into the front of the crowd. Her palm was up, and her lips were behind it. She looked at Moody, puckered, and blew.

No one went blind this time—or at least it did not seem so—and Moody watched as both Vivi and Joseph disappeared. He would perhaps never see them again, for he would be going somewhere else now. And he knew that they too would be departing for another place.

Judge Downing was finally able to restore order in the courtroom, and Moody's attorneys, having given up on the matter, made no attempt to plead further. The extended deliberation that the Spiritualists had been hoping for was now a dead idea. The jury would return, and the decision would be read, and that would be an end to the question of Edward Moody.

And so the jury did return, and so the decision was read, but when the foreman announced the verdict, the room did not explode. There was a quiet—almost respectful—acceptance of the verdict that surprised even the staunchest of the nonbelievers.

XLVII

IT WAS NIGHT, and the old leather case lay in his lap. He hadn't opened it—had not been able to bring himself to open it—after Bolles had left him earlier that day. And now, as he stared down at the thing that held the spirit, he wondered if the inspector had ever discovered what was inside. Had Montgomery opened the case and seen the shame that the negative revealed? Garrett's shame . . . and his disgrace. These had been Elizabeth's words. But what shame could there have been in loving the one person he was not supposed to love?

Had he loved her? Had he ever been able to love her? Or did she just represent something he had wanted to possess?

He opened it.

The lip of the case was smooth, the surrounding leather cold. The edge of the glass shone like a blade. The glass sat comfortably within the stiff walls of its envelope . . . impatient. Did it want to come out?

He touched it. The glass was hard. He was surprised at its durability. The glass's edge pressed into his thumb as his other fingers settled along its sides.

But there was something else. In the case—a folded paper. It was a note of some kind—a message that was not supposed to be there.

Garrett pulled out the paper, unfolded it, and read:

> *You are a great man. You will do great things for people.*
> *You will open their eyes. You will teach them how to <u>see</u>.*
> *She is all that is left of me now. She is yours. Keep her,*
> *guard her. She needs you. Everyone needs you. I left so that*
> *everyone could have you.*
> *Please forgive me.*

No, it could not be. Her speaking to him—even now.

Her selflessness overcame him like a tide from which he could not escape. She had wanted to be gone so that *he* could be saved—so that his dishonest, ambitious self could be saved. Her child had been his, and the people would have punished him for it. Elizabeth was right—even after everything he had done in the name of progress, the people's eyes would see only one thing.

But there was the question that burned inside him hotter than anything he had ever felt:

Had she loved him?

Had she sacrificed herself, and her child—*for him?*

His career had been meaningless. His life, one grand absurdity.

He let the soiled note fall to the floor and removed the negative from its case . . . this odd piece of artistry, this mere bit of glass that had summoned a lifetime of memories. The night was dark, and the air outside was black. Garrett's window had become a mirror, and he looked at himself, ashamed.

He wanted to hold it up—to examine the negative—but he was afraid of what he would see. Would she be there? Would she scold him? Would his own face judge and scorn him? He did not want to behold the appalling things that he had turned his eyes away from for so many years.

And then, there she was—in the window.

His breath caught in his throat as he tried to cry out. She was not in front of the window, or beyond it, but in it somehow. Isabelle watched as he struggled to catch his breath, the soft folds of her hair at one with the rippled glass.

His whole body trembled. He wanted to speak, but couldn't. Then, finally—

"By my own life . . ." he whispered. "I never knew . . ."

But in speaking those words he faced his own dishonesty. There was something terrible that he had always known.

He felt his heart begin to pound. What more could he possibly say?

She was a dark shadow in the window. She was silver—black and white. Would that she would tell him what it was she wanted to hear.

"What is it?" he asked.

Isabelle made no sound.

"I will take care of her," he said.

But still she did not reply.

Senator Garrett's hand moved up toward his chest, for his heart was beating with such force that he could hear it. Garrett pressed his hand hard there, clutching at his nightclothes, until he felt the hot rush through every part of his body.

"Isabelle!" he exclaimed.

She appeared to smile, but her eyes were dark.

And as if the strength of his younger self had possessed him, he jumped out of his chair, and leapt toward her.

THE CRASH WAS a sound like no other the house had ever known. The night was hot, and the warm air swept in—the house was, strangely, not so determined to keep it out.

Jenny and Elizabeth emerged from their hiding places. The crash had come from Garrett's room, yet they both hesitated before entering. Elizabeth eyed Jenny, and Jenny eyed her mistress, and there the two women stood, glaring at each other outside the door.

But each face was pained. Only the worst could have happened.

Elizabeth pushed the door open—Garrett had not locked it—and the warm air opposed her, like a barricade. The room did not stifle because the room had been exposed . . . and yet something still kept Jenny and Elizabeth from the broken window.

The air had sucked the curtains out. Shattered glass lay on the floor.

Jenny ran to the window, but Elizabeth did not follow. Elizabeth did not want to see what her husband had ultimately come to.

"Oh, Senator!" Jenny shrieked.

And she began to utter unintelligible cries.

There was nothing that Elizabeth could have done to prevent this. She had given him everything. And he had been ungrateful.

Elizabeth leaned out the window, feeling as if she herself were falling. There on the ground lay her husband's shattered body, his blood seeping over the pavement like a slow, determined stain.

"Oh, ma'am . . . ma'am . . ." Jenny was going on.

But Elizabeth said nothing as she backed herself away.

Banner of Light

Boston, Massachusetts

Saturday, August 27, 1870

NO SUBJECT SINCE the days of the Rochester Knockings has stirred Boston, New York, and all of New England into so much discussion on the subject of Spiritualism as the late arrest of Mr. Edward Moody for pretending to take spirit photographs; and whatever is proved or disproved, and whatever Mr. Moody has done or not done, is all of little consequence in comparison to the vast amount of good results that must arise from getting such testimony as that of A. J. Davis, Mr. Livermore, Mr. Gurney (the oldest photographer in New York), and several others, into the daily papers, and bringing them under constant discussion. One thing is certain: The enemies of truth have learned a lesson that will be useful to them in the future, and probably will not again attempt to prosecute a subject until they know something about it—or at least have some credible authority to back themselves up, as they surely lacked both in this case. Whatever turn events take of late, every movement advances our cause and seems to be managed by our spirit-friends.

**Newsletter of the American Institute for
the Encouragement of Science and Invention**
New York, New York
Wednesday, August 31, 1870

THE PHOTOGRAPHIC SECTION of the American Institute held its regular meeting on Monday. Mr. Abraham Bogardus, the newly elected Vice-President, in the chair, introduced the following, which was adopted without a dissenting voice:

WHEREAS, recent investigations before the People of Boston, of so-called Spirit Photography, have failed to denounce the whole matter as trickery; therefore, be it

RESOLVED, That the Photographic Section of the American Institute take the earliest opportunity to condemn all such methods of working upon the credulous and uninitiated, and that they receive with wonder and amazement the decision of the jury; and be it further

RESOLVED, That to our worthy member, Mr. Marshall Hinckley, who initiated the complaint upon which the proceedings were based, we offer our thanks, for his praiseworthy though unsuccessful efforts in the cause of truth and common sense.

XLVIII

S O, THEY HAD acquitted him—absolved him of his crimes. And what was she to do with that now? What had she been left with in the wake of this verdict . . . a verdict that seemed designed to condemn her?

She placed the black thing on her head. Its ruffles boxed her in—like a picture frame.

"Ma'am," Jenny said, "the carriage is around front."

For the past three days Elizabeth had endured her own trial, though it had not been so sensationalized in the papers. There had been talk of sending Garrett's body down to Washington, to lie in state in the Capitol, but she had ultimately ruled against that. There had been arguments, and there were those in the Cabinet who thought her unreasonable, but she was not going to travel there—not after all of this. Governor Claflin had sided with her, proclaiming Garrett "a son of Massachusetts first," and so that had determined it. Garrett's body would remain in Boston.

They came from Washington, from New York, from Philadelphia, from Richmond. They came from Delaware and Ohio and Rhode Island and from the South. The Senate's Sergeant at Arms had taken charge of the body, attended by a committee of six of Garrett's colleagues. On day two the president arrived with his Cabinet. On day three, the Supreme Court, and most of the Senate and the House.

The crowds of public mourners numbered in the thousands. Elizabeth could not stand them, and wished that they would all be gone. She had spent over twenty years playing a role for Garrett, and yet this last role, she felt she could not play.

But she played it.

They had festooned Doric Hall with the most elaborate mourning garlands . . . beautiful and delicate strands of black crepe that hung like woven ivy from the hall's columns. An artisan had fashioned a chandelier of flowers, and from its center he had suspended a white dove carrying an olive branch. The chandelier and the dove were in the very middle of the hall, guiding the shapeless crowd toward the coffin that held the senator.

There were soldiers—colored soldiers—positioned around the catafalque. They competed with the wealth of flowers that every type of person in the country had sent along. In profusion—small bouquets from the freedmen and the poor, as well as large crosses made from hundreds of roses and carnations. At the foot of the coffin stood a magnificent design of tropical leaves and flowers—a gift from the Republic of Haiti.

"No other statesman," one of the papers would later write, "has been mourned with such sorrow—Abraham Lincoln excepted."

On the day of the burial, Governor Claflin said a few words before the funeral procession departed from the State House. Behind the governor hung two tattered flags, which Massachusetts soldiers had reclaimed from the battlefields. "These flags," Claflin said, "represent what this great son of Massachusetts achieved. Union—never to be divided. A land that is free."

The procession from the State House to King's Chapel seemed without end. All of Boston was draped in mourning. The bells tolled. The city's flags flew at half-mast. And Elizabeth followed the stream, like a dying fish caught in a current.

And then at last it came—the procession to Mount Auburn, where Senator Garrett would be interred, at the base of the little hill. A great mob of freedmen, headed by Frederick Douglass, followed the hearse past the Public Garden, and then over the bridge to Cambridge. The procession was mighty—a nation unto itself. An army of freedmen, and soldiers, and citizens . . . all passing through the college grounds where Garrett had found his voice.

At Mount Auburn, Longfellow stood by the grave, along with Whittier, and Emerson, and Holmes. The greatest literary men of the day had themselves looked upon Garrett as a kind of political prophet. Longfellow read a poem—an apostrophe addressed toward the river—as the sun disappeared behind the trees.

> River that stealeth with such silent pace
> Around the City of the Dead
> Linger and fold him in thy soft embrace
> And say good-night, for now the western skies
> Are red with sunset, and gray mists arise
> Like damps that gather on a dead man's face.

Good-night! Good-night! as we so oft have said
Beneath this roof at midnight, in the days
That are no more and shall no more return.
Thou has but taken thy lamp and gone to bed;
I stay a little longer, as one stays
To cover up the embers that still burn.

"Ma'am," Jenny said, "the carriage is around front."

It was all over now—it had been over for days. And yet Elizabeth insisted on going back. She would have one final look at that grim, spare monument. He had prohibited any tributes—simply his name, and the two stark dates.

She ordered the driver to take a different route. She did not want to retrace his procession.

The cemetery was empty and now she was alone. The trees were green with leaves. The late morning light found its way through the trees and dotted the stone monument with moving and carefree shapes. JAMES BLAINE GARRETT. There were two columns on either side of his name. The whole thing looked like some sort of altar, too strong ever to fall.

"Why did you do this?" she asked.

Though she did not speak the words aloud.

She was trying . . . even now in the quiet and the solitude, she was trying. But try as she did, she could not remember a time when she did not hate him.

"Hello, my dear," he said.

She turned around. It was Dovehouse.

"I startled you . . . I am sorry," he said.

She was wrong, for it had not ended.

Dovehouse stepped closer . . . toward her, and the grave. A bird whistled from somewhere in the trees.

"It was so good of the vice president to escort you through these days," he said. "And the colored soldiers. I would have offered my own arm many times, if I had thought—"

"Thank you, Mr. Dovehouse."

"There are no thanks due here," he said. "It is you who deserves to be thanked."

"I?" she said.

"Yes, you—for carrying James as far as you carried him."

"He carried himself."

"Now," Dovehouse said, "we both know that's not entirely true."

At the funeral, she had avoided him, and she was sure that he had felt it. And now he had followed her back to the cemetery, because Dovehouse was pernicious, and never gave up.

Together they stared at the embossed letters of Garrett's name.

"People will remember him with admiration," she said.

Dovehouse was silent for a moment, and then breathed.

"People will remember what they want to remember," he said.

He wasn't finished with her, and here was proof. He was baiting her. How heartless—to still be playing his games at a time like this.

"He didn't know when to stop," Dovehouse said. "It's one thing to give the negroes their own land and things like that, but moving them into their former masters' houses was a bit much, don't you think?"

She despised him.

"You benefitted—and you know it," Dovehouse said.

Elizabeth felt the searing eyes of his judgment, even though she could not look at him. She could not look at him or she would break. And he could not see her break.

"Yes," Dovehouse said, "that's right—"

Elizabeth put her hand to her mouth.

"He betrayed us all," Dovehouse said.

Elizabeth turned to him.

"He is gone," she said. "Just go away now and let him be."

"Let him be?" Dovehouse said. "Now isn't that a pretty sentiment. You confound me, woman. Your husband might still be alive today if you hadn't been such a fool."

The words stabbed into her. Dovehouse was right. It was her sentiment—the one sentiment she had retained at the expense of all others—that had resurrected everything, and set the whole hideous play in motion.

"He is gone now," she repeated.

Her weakness was amusing him.

"On the contrary, my dear," Dovehouse said. "The old boy lives on—"

And he smiled at her.

"—in others."

The man was despicable. He knew. But most of all, he wanted her to know that he knew . . . wanted her to know that he held the entirety of Garrett's legacy, as well as her future, in his hands. But it was silly to worry about it, because he had already played his cards. The looks from some of the wives at the funeral told her that some of it—if not all of it—had already gotten out.

"My condolences, Mrs. Garrett," Dovehouse said.

And he tipped his hat, and left her.

It would not take long—everyone would soon know—and the gossip about Garrett would spread through Boston like the smell of fire. That quickly, a forty-year career would be dismantled, and any righteousness he had maintained would be undone.

"You mean he—?" they would whisper.

"Garrett? Senator Garrett?"

"Did she know?" they would ask.

"Of course she did," they'd say.

And what's more, once people decided to start remembering, the girl's disappearance would become a thing of significance. They would speculate and conjecture as to what happened during that time, and some of them might even give nods to foul play. They would say horrible things, and they would say that Elizabeth had deserved it. There were so many women who had never liked her to begin with.

And so this was not the last time she would find herself alone, for loneliness would become her practice now, enforced by the fate she had created. Some people would call, and an invitation or two might follow, but eventually that would all come to an end. For Elizabeth Garrett, something beyond life had ended, while for everyone else, it was nothing more than the end of another August.

XXVII

"THIS GIRL HAS promise," Mrs. Lovejoy said. "Mr. Moody, did you see this rendering of the new engravings? She has captured the rosettes with incredible fidelity."

Moody took up the piece of paper, which Vivi had been drawing on with graphite. The paper showed the handles of forks and knives and spoons—all of which had been engraved with beautiful and elaborate patterns.

Moody studied the paper, looked at Vivi, then glanced back at the drawing.

"She has a gift," he said.

And he returned the sketch to Vivi.

The gallery was empty now, the spirits all gone, the dark room dismembered. On the walls that had once held the best examples of Moody's art, discolored shapes haloed the spots where the elaborate frames had hung.

The portraits were packed now—going off to a collector who had purchased them all in one swoop.

"Mr. Winter," Mrs. Lovejoy went on, "The girl has an extraordinary hand."

"I know her hand well," Joseph said. "As Edward says, it is a gift."

Vivi smiled—her mother's smile. It was such a strange thing to see her again in this room.

Trunks lay scattered about the floor, and the wagon would be arriving in a moment. The train tickets to California had already been purchased, and the train would take less than a week to travel from east to west. For Vivi, it would be only her second ride on a train. For Joseph and Moody, perhaps the last.

There was land there . . . lots of land. A small tract of it, somewhere in the headlands north of the great bay, had been given to a young senator from Boston. It had been ages ago, and the senator had all but forgotten it, until the time came when he needed to remember. There were very few who knew anything about that gift, but now Edward Moody was one of them.

"He left it to you—for the girl," the lawyer had said. "It was a last-minute change, and I didn't understand. But he said you'd know what to do with it."

There was a noise in the street. The wagon had arrived. Joseph Winter went downstairs to greet the drivers.

"Come along, my child," Mrs. Lovejoy said. "You do look so lovely in that new dress. How I wish I could be going with you!"

Then Mrs. Lovejoy and Vivi went downstairs too, and Edward Moody was alone.

It had started and it was ending here—in this space above the traffic. Moody looked about the room. They had been begging him to stay, but there was no going back to doing what they wanted him to do. Joseph had been talking of the need for more photographers—out west. There were many opportunities there, he said—lots of money to be made. But Moody had promised to leave photography behind. He would never take a photograph again.

Those empty walls were ghostly now . . . more ghostly than they had ever been. In their emptiness they glowed with the luminosity of a fading light. They were not chastising Edward Moody this time. Instead, they were embracing him.

Moody stood by the window, looking down upon the traffic, while the drivers emptied the rest of his belongings from the room.

"Mr. Moody, are you coming?" Mrs. Lovejoy called from downstairs.

"One moment," Moody replied.

For he was not quite ready.

He took one last turn around the empty gallery. He saw the Fanshaw portrait, and Arabella Livermore, and the hundreds of other faces that he had brought back from the dead. There had been a time when he hadn't believed in anything. Now there was very little that he didn't believe in.

He was standing in front of the panel—the panel that led to the passage. He pulled it, and it opened, and the thought of his journey confronted him.

There was nothing there—just darkness—leading down to a place that he could not see.

He stepped into the passage and touched the walls inside. They were rough with the cracks of broken plaster and exposed wood. The light from the open panel partially illuminated the passage. It may have been the first time that such free light had come into this space.

Ahead of him—the step that had somehow seized him. He remembered

Joseph, reaching up toward him. Unfreezing him from that spot.

He moved toward it.

Behind him now, the light washed his back. The last time it had been entirely dark, but this time he could see.

That top step was in front of him, a little ways down the corridor. It was sagging—a makeshift board that had been nailed to other pieces of wood, however many years ago. It had perhaps born the weight of hundreds. It had born his weight, and held him. And beyond it, stronger than any wood or mortar, was the darkness that led down to the tunnel.

Moody moved toward the step and stood upon it.

The step cracked.

From the darkness, a hundred voices echoed words he could not understand. There was no Joseph there this time to unfreeze him. But Moody had been empowered to move. He eased a few steps down the staircase, turned around, and examined the break. The step had collapsed upon what looked like something shiny—something dirty, but shiny. The thing inside was reflecting light.

He was almost afraid of it . . . the way it called out to him through the splinters. Something silver. Something buried there. Something that no one was ever supposed to find.

He touched the splinters. Then the board came up with no effort. Before him, in the step, there was a shining silver box. He did not need to open the box to know that it was hers.

But he did remove it from the step. He held it in his hands and opened it. There was nothing telling him not to. In fact, it was just the opposite.

Ah, so she had done it then. She had been doing it all along! At first what was in the box shocked him, and then—it came as no surprise.

He would give this box to Vivi, for there was only one explanation: that the box had survived for her. Vivi . . . Isabelle's Vivi. *His* Vivi. His last hope of bringing Isabelle back. There were many great things in store for this young woman, who had chronicled crimes that she never should have seen. Yes, Moody would see to it that Vivi realized her greatness. If such a thing were within his power.

But he imagined it in a way that she, and perhaps even Joseph, could not, for he knew the places to which true talent could lead her. The scene was clear before him as he sat in the tunnel's shadows. Vivi is an artist. She is illustrating catalogues. And she is drawing portraits for people, when the opportunities present themselves. She has money, and she has a sense of her own dignity, though the road for her will not be easy. Why, even when she passes a storefront window, and sees the picture frame with the somehow familiar glass inside of it, she wonders whether they will sell it to her, or if they will even let her in. She opens her purse. She has the money, and she enters. The woman in the store is kind to her. The woman reminds her of people and places she once knew.

Maybe the glass in the frame is an old glass—recycled, reused, its history erased. And maybe it isn't. Maybe the glass is brand new, like so much else in this new country.

Moody looked down into the box. The faces stared back at him. There were a hundred of them in there—maybe more. These were not negatives; these were photographs. Printed photographs. They were the faces of the unbroken—the faces of everyone who had traversed those steps.

Of course she had done it . . . but how had she done it? Had he really taught her so much? Had his trivial demonstrations invested her with the power to do *this*?

And so he went on again, the old selfish Moody, failing to realize that it had not been his demonstrations at all. His tutelage may have been part of it, but here was the evidence: Isabelle had truly possessed a gift.

He lifted the photographs out from their container. The faces—so many of them. Their eyes stared into his. There was something unshakeable in every expression—a defiance and an energy that no crime could subdue. They had been terrified in that tunnel . . . on their trains, and in their wagons. Those photographs recorded their fear—and their hope.

"Eventually all is lost," she had said to him that day in the meadow. "It's why the photographs are important. They help us see things. Keep things."

Isabelle had managed to capture something that his pictures never could have. She had captured the spirit of an entire people. To think that he had ever tried to put a price on what he photographed.

He thumbed through the pile—he was frozen there, once again. They were like playing cards—lives on playing cards. Their lives had been a gamble. He stopped at one. The face was familiar. It was a young man with a very different look in his eye. The sullenness was there, yes, and a bit of the terror too, but something else was there. What could it have been?

Moody held the photograph up to the light. There in the corner was the inscription in her hand: "Winter '52."

He already knew what Joseph's response would be.

"I did not remember, until recently."

Or—

"It was ours."

Or perhaps even—

"It was not my place to tell you."

No—it had never been Joseph's place to tell Moody anything. That had always been part of something else.

Moody closed the box and stood up. There were no voices in the tunnel. No cries from those in hiding, or soft moans from the distressed. But Moody heard them. The tunnel drew him, though he knew that he was leaving, and the eyes looked up from the darkness and watched him. There were countless eyes down there . . . countless faces, countless photographs. An endless flow of traffic that one could no longer hear. But he would not bury them. He would bring them out into the light. The box would go to Vivi and the box would remain open, and whatever had been behind it all might one day be understood.

And so he sees her again. She has purchased the frame, and the frame is just small enough to fit into her bag. She exits the store and there is traffic all around her. And people—many people—struggling for a place on the street. The world has been changing before her eyes. It is easier to disappear nowadays, for there are crowds in the great cities—everywhere. There is promise for her out there. There is promise, fear, and hope. And he watches: the moving girl is there until she isn't, until she's faded into the background of the righteous and the believing.

HISTORICAL NOTE

THOSE INTERESTED IN learning more about William Mumler and nineteenth-century spirit photography might wish to consult the following important works: Clément Chéroux et al.'s *The Perfect Medium: Photography and the Occult* (New Haven: Yale University Press, 2005); Martyn Jolly's *Faces of the Living Dead: The Belief in Spirit Photography* (New York: Mark Batty Publisher, 2006); Louis Kaplan's *The Strange Case of William Mumler, Spirit Photographer* (Minneapolis: University of Minnesota Press, 2008); and most recently Peter Manseau's *The Apparitionists: A Tale of Phantoms, Fraud, Photography, and the Man Who Captured Lincoln's Ghost* (Boston: Houghton Mifflin Harcourt, 2017).

The literature on Reconstruction in America is too vast and impressive to cover adequately in an author's note. The two main pillars that supported this book, however, were Eric Foner's monumental *Reconstruction: America's Unfinished Revolution, 1863–1877* (New York: Harper & Row, 1988); and David W. Blight's *Race and Reunion: The Civil War in American Memory* (Cambridge: Belknap Press, 2001).

The political events leading to Senator Garrett's moral crisis in Chapter 28 of this book have been simplified for the sake of storytelling. Far from a two-way bargaining effort around the Fugitive Slave Act and California's bill for statehood, the Compromise of 1850 involved additional debates around the establishment of the Utah and New Mexico Territories, the boundaries of the state of Texas, and the abolition of the slave trade in Washington, D.C. For a much fuller account of these debates than I have given, see David Potter's *The Impending Crisis, 1848–1861* (New York: Harper and Row, 1976), and Bruce Levine's *Half Slave and Half Free: The Roots of the Civil War* (New York: Hill and Wang, 2005).